**THE BLOOD LORD, CAOLIN,
SITS IN HIS FORTRESS
ON THE RED MOUNTAIN.**

The Blood Lord surveyed the line of hills between the Mountain and the Great Bay.

"There lies Misthall—" his voice grated. "The one they call Prince of Westria is riding there today with a party of young cubs from the city. To celebrate his birthday. . . ." For a moment thin lips tightened. "You will follow them, wearing the livery of a servant . . . apologise as if you had overslept, be eager to offer your master's gift. . . ."

**AND SO THE SAGA OF TREACHERY
IN WESTRIA CONTINUES**

Tor books by Diana L. Paxson

THE WESTRIA SERIES
Silverhair the Wanderer
The Earthstone
The Sea Star
The Wind Crystal

THE WIND CRYSTAL

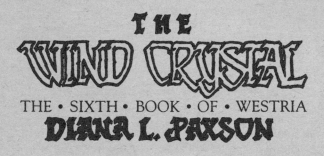

THE · SIXTH · BOOK · OF · WESTRIA

DIANA L. PAXSON

TOR
fantasy

A TOM DOHERTY ASSOCIATES BOOK
NEW YORK

THE WIND CRYSTAL

A Tor Book
Published by Tom Doherty Associates, Inc.
49 West 24th Street
New York, N. Y. 10010

Cover by Tom Canty

ISBN: 0-812-50040-7   Canadian ISBN: 0-812-50041-5

First edition: March 1990

Printed in the United States of America

0 9 8 7 6 5 4 3 2 1

To Robin—

In speech or in silence,
and in love,
always.
May the Wind Lord show you your song!

Relationships among the Ruling Families of Westria

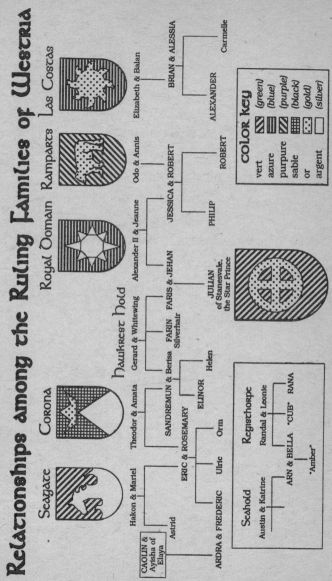

THE RAMPARTS

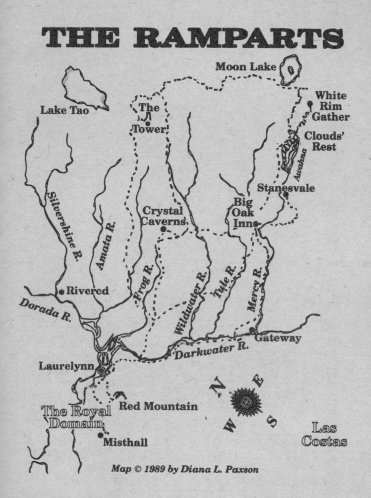

Map © 1989 by Diana L. Paxson

ONE: A Meeting at Misthall

The eagle soared across the great wind-scoured bowl of the sky. Clouds were puffing up on the western horizon, but above the hills the air had a painful clarity. The eagle's sight embraced field and fortress, wood and water, with equal precision. The land of Westria lay still in the precarious peace of early morning, balanced between winter and summer as the eagle balanced on widespread wings.

The man who watched from the tower on the Red Mountain saw the land almost as clearly. From the glimmer of white that flared over earth's curve northward as the first light of dawn touched the snows of the Father of Mountains, to the blur of hills in the south that led to Ravensgate and the sacred valley of Awhai, he surveyed the land. For a moment only, he faced the blue expanse of the western sea, wrinkled with wind, then turned quickly to the light that blazed behind the Ramparts as the sun rose.

He gazed upward, but the eagle was beyond his vision. The men who were beginning to emerge from their encampment on the lower slopes of the Mountain seemed as tiny as he was to the eagle, and as insignificant. The watcher moved slowly along the parapet, the hem of his red robe whispering over stone. The land was not yet his. But for almost two years he had held this high place despite the best efforts of those insects to dislodge him. And despite reverses, the mind behind those cold eyes still functioned with a crystalline clarity.

A silver bell tinkled faintly as he touched it, and presently an immaculate officer with a wolf's-head badge on the breast of his gambeson appeared at the top of the stairs.

"Captain Esteban," said the man in the red robe, "send Mañero to me."

"My Lord Sangrado!" The captain brought up one fist in salute.

The Blood Lord waited, controlling his impatience as automatically as he did all other human responses. Mañero had turned up at the gates of Blood Gard one morning, begging for food. He had already tricked two sergeants out of their breakfast when Caolin decided that anyone who could make these men laugh might prove useful.

A brush of grizzled hair showed first, with a roll of sticks and paper poking up beside it. Then a swift movement brought the man out onto the parapet.

"They are ready, then?"

"Oh, yes, lord!" Mañero bowed again. "My hands do not forget their skill."

"Show me," the Blood Lord's voice cut short the little man's explaining.

Mañero shot a swift look toward his master and grinned. Then agile fingers untied the cords, and rice paper crackled as the little man unrolled the first kite and lifted it.

"I cannot show you now, lord—no wind. But there will be—see how those clouds in the west move across the sky?" He lifted the kite, and a golden eagle stretched its wings suddenly against the sun.

"And you have prepared the strings?"

"With the ground glass," Mañero nodded. "Oh, yes. They will fight well." Rice paper crackled as a breath of wind touched the tower.

The Blood Lord surveyed the line of hills between the Mountain and the Great Bay.

"There lies Misthall . . . " his voice grated. "The one they call Prince of Westria is riding there today with a party of young cubs from the city. To celebrate his birthday. . . ." For a moment, thin lips tightened. "You will follow them, wearing the livery of a servant of Fredegar Sachs. Apologize as if you had overslept, be eager to offer your master's gift . . . and teach them kite fighting."

"That is all?" Mañero's bushy brows lifted.

"Make yourself agreeable. Keep your ears open and remember what you hear. If the conflict of the kites leads to quarreling, I will not be displeased."

"Ho! When grown men play a boy's game, then they fight all the same!" He gave a bark of laughter, saw that his master was not smiling, and turned it to a cough.

"Stay with them. If they like you, perhaps they will want to keep you on. Sachs will vouch for you."

The little man's nose seemed longer as he grinned. "You mean me to be your spy?"

The Blood Lord's head swiveled with vulpine swiftness. "I mean you to be my ears." His voice seemed to vibrate from the stones. "You hear me now, don't you?"

"Yes, lord." Mañero's tilted eyes had rounded, and the Blood Lord smiled.

"You will hear me again." The voice seemed to come from everywhere. "When you close your eyes to sleep, you will tell me everything that you have heard."

The Blood Lord studied the wary features of the man before him, and then for a moment he altered the shadows that usually veiled his ruined flesh into a mirror, laughing as the man before him tried to jerk back.

"Mañero, Mañero—who do you see?"

"Myself!" Mañero turned his face away.

"Yes," whispered the Blood Lord. "When you speak to yourself, you will tell all you know. And when I speak in your soul, you will obey. But you will tell no one—no one—that you have come from me. Do you understand?''

Mañero's swift nod was almost a shrug.

''And how will you serve me?''

''As I serve . . . myself . . . lord.'' The glint in the feral eyes found an odd echo in the Blood Lord's memory. Unexpectedly amused, he released the pressure of his will. The domination was not complete, but with this one, perhaps it was not necessary. Better to let Mañero's native wit and self-interest motivate him. He would be watched. By now, the Blood Lord had many servants in Laurelynn.

''Go then. You must be ready when they pass.''

Mañero shook himself, snatched up his toys and darted away.

When the little kite-maker had gone, the Blood Lord moved to the parapet again. The roof tiles of Laurelynn glowed red, surrounded by a dazzle of brilliance where sunlight struck the waters of the rivers that embraced its walls. Somewhere down there the Prince would be getting ready to ride—the Blood Lord's enemy—Julian. . . .

The season was nearing the crossroads of spring, when all powers were poised in equilibrium. Julian possessed the Earthstone and the Sea Star, but he had scarcely mastered them. Once, long ago, the Blood Lord himself had borne the Jewels, and he knew how the spirit could be shaken by pure elemental power. Without the balancing forces of the other two Jewels, the Prince was actually more vulnerable than he had been with none.

The Blood Lord and Julian faced each other now as declared enemies. From this moment, one of them must begin to increase, while the other began his decline. The battle between the man who had once been called Caolin and he who was the son of Jehan of Westria was barely begun. And Julian could not begin to imagine the Blood Lord's powers.

The wind blew pale hair back from Caolin's face as

he turned to go down into the fortress. Overhead, the eagle wheeled eastward and disappeared.

The unpredictable winds of March had begun to blow early, puffing wisps of cloud across an azure sky. But the blue mountains across the Bay glowed with luminous clarity. As the horsemen set their mounts up the road to Misthall, the breeze swept the grass on the eastern hills, rippling green and gold as the banner of Westria that fluttered above them. The wind gusted as they came around the bend, and the laurels bent to sweep the road.

"See . . . even the trees do you homage, Julian," laughed Robert.

The Prince shrugged muscular shoulders as he reined in, and his cousin edged his chestnut mare up beside the gray. Wind whipped stinging strands of mane around his hands.

"It's not the trees I'm worried about, it's the men."

The People of the Wood had given Julian their allegiance, and so had the People of the Sea, but the Guardians could not elect him King of Westria. He heard a burst of laughter as the others who had come out from Laurelynn to help him celebrate his birthday followed them. Court festivities still made him ill at ease, but perhaps it would be different at Misthall.

"They must learn to see you as a prince, my lord." Robert turned in the saddle with an easy grace that exasperated Julian even as he admired it. His cousin's jerkin and high boots were of tawny suede, the jerkin cut high to the neck and flared at the shoulder to display the orange silk of his sleeves. Until he saw it, Julian had thought his own dove-gray leather very fine. It was easy for Robert, trained from birth at his brother's court in Rivered, to play the princeling. But Julian had been raised in a stone quarry in the mountains.

"You must learn to speak to them as a prince," Silverhair added sharply.

Julian shook his head, trying to smile. "Uncle, if you could turn me into a bard with a blessing, I would be a

harper already. But it is too late to begin learning, even
if I had the time.''

"You had better make time, boy. Do you think the
Council will elect a king who can only stare at them like
a bump on a log?''

"That's not fair, sir!'' exclaimed Robert. "Julian can
be eloquent enough when the spirit moves him.''

"When the spirit moves him!'' Silverhair echoed.
"Oh, yes, and *I* am a Master of Music when the spirit
moves *me*! But if my music falters, the worst my audience can do is to laugh. A false word, a clumsy word,
or even *no* words from Julian could cost him Westria!''

"I will learn what I can,'' said Julian harshly. "But
not now!'' He could still sense Silverhair's disapproval.
Lately the harper's temper had grown more unpredictable
than ever. Perhaps Silverhair missed the freedom of the
road. Well, so did Julian!

A shadow slipped across the road ahead, and Julian
looked up to see a pair of turkey buzzards inscribing dark
circles on the clear blue of the sky.

If only I could just fly away!

And then they had rounded the last curve, and Julian
saw, lifting above the trees, the walls of the house they
had given him as a reward for defeating the reivers. The
hills rose swiftly behind it, but ahead the ground fell
away in gentle folds of wood and field to the bay.

Misthall . . . the dwelling of the king.

Twenty years of weather had silvered the beams of
Misthall, and neglect showed in missing shingles and
overgrown paths. Silverhair sighed. What had he expected? It would be even worse inside. Every shadow
would be a backdrop for ghostly images of Faris and
Jehan. It had been bad enough to return to Hawkrest
Hold, which held so many painful memories. But at Misthall he had been happy, until the king's long dying had
destroyed all joy.

No. He could not look at those empty rooms. To fill
them with life again must be Julian's task.

No child of my body will ever inherit Hawkrest, thought

Silverhair. *But at least the son of Faris and Jehan has come home to Misthall.*

From the garden, where they were setting out the food, he heard the sweet laughter of the boy Piper—who still did not speak, though he had learned to smile—and the merriment of the others, answering. He winced at the sound. But why should they be silent? For the sons and daughters of those who had shared Farin Silverhair's youth, Misthall was only a name out of story. He felt like his own ghost, standing here.

Silverhair shook himself, realizing that he had begun to wonder if those provisions included any wine, and he fled up the broad stairs into the hall. His feet still knew their way. A door swung open, and he stopped short as, silhouetted against the blaze of light, he saw the figure of a man with dark hair.

Silverhair must have made some sound, for the man turned, showing shoulders broader than Jehan's had ever been, and a quick lift of the head that the harper had come to know well.

It was not Jehan. Of course not.

Why am I dwelling on what is gone? Silverhair wondered as recognition sent a quick flare of warmth through him. Why did he find it so hard to admit that he cared for the son as much as ever he had cared for the father? *Perhaps because I loved Jehan as a boy worships his hero, who will right all wrongs*, he thought wryly. *And Jehan's story is ended—nothing will ever stain his memory. But Julian's tale is still being told. Will his story end in disaster, or victory?*

"They say that my father died in this room," said Julian.

"Yes," Silverhair answered gently. "I remember the day." He shut his awareness against the echo of memory, hearing the tremor in Julian's tone.

"He was greatly loved."

"Yes, it was a gift he had. . . ." What was troubling the boy?

"I wish *I* had it!" exclaimed Julian. "I would rather go out and fight a dozen battles—on land or on the sea—

than face the Council of Westria! Tomorrow they will debate my election to the throne. What am I going to do?''

Silverhair frowned. Julian was better loved than he knew, but it was true that he lacked the easy charm that had drawn men to Jehan's side.

"There are ways to sway them," he began carefully. "You call them bard's tricks, I know—" he held up a warning hand as the wary look came back into Julian's eyes—"but they are as necessary to a king as is skill with the sword. And I can teach you . . ." Silverhair let his hand fall. All of his efforts to coax speech from Piper had ended in failure. To whom *could* he pass on the many things he had learned with such pain, if not to this boy?

"Can you build a harp from a war bow? Uncle, all I know how to do is to bang on my shield or sound the battle horn. If the Council wants me, it will have to be satisfied with a plain warrior." Julian managed a bitter smile.

"You don't understand—" Silverhair began. Then a long horn call brought both heads around. As the echoes dwindled, they heard hoofbeats.

"You see?" Julian shook his head ruefully. "That's the Las Costas contingent. I had best go down. Alexander will feel slighted if I am not there to welcome him."

Silverhair remained where he was, trying to master his anger. "Lord of all Music," he whispered into the silence that followed, "my enemy still threatens, but it is not for myself that I ask Your help now, but for a child whose power of speech was stolen, and for a man who needs the poet's gift that he may claim a crown."

The silence seemed to grow deeper. The harper heard the rasp of his breath as he exhaled.

Why? He did not know if the question came from without or within.

Because I love him.

As Silverhair replied, he wondered how he expected the Prince to learn eloquence if he, who was accounted

a Master Bard, had never been able to turn to Julian and
say those words aloud.

"Julian!"
At the sound of that voice, Julian felt a giant hand
squeeze his chest. He turned swiftly and saw coming
toward him a girl whose copper hair blazed in the spring
sun. His focus narrowed. A glance showed him every
detail of the silver sea shells embroidered on the edge
of her grey-green riding tunic, slit so that her dark-
green breeches and gray boots flickered beneath it as
she ran.
Rana. . . . He forced himself to breathe. *She is
rounding out again, and her hair has darkened, but deep
ocean still glimmers in her eyes.*
It had been several months since he had seen her,
but his response was unchanged. Julian waited for her
to come to him, as he had forced himself to wait since
last summer, and would doubtless continue to wait until
her fear of men's lust had diminished enough for her to
listen to words of love. The men who had assaulted
her on the Far Alone Islands had not harmed her body,
but the wound to her spirit went deeper, perhaps, than
she herself knew. How long would it take for her to
heal?
Until the next Cataclysm, perhaps? Julian shook his
head, recognizing that he had worked himself into a bad
temper already. A fine way, he thought, to celebrate one's
twentieth birthday!
"The Las Costas barge pulled in just behind us, but
Cub and I came ahead while everyone was still arguing
about who should ride first. I sent my brother off to look
for Piper—he would tease if he heard me thanking you,"
Rana said swiftly. "The chalice you sent is beautiful, but
I do not understand why you gave—"
"No? You gave a thing of far greater worth to me."
The smiths in Laurelynn had crafted the piece exactly
as Julian instructed; a broad silver cup with nine moon-
stones set around the rim.

"The Sea Star belonged to you." Color rose beneath the freckles that dusted her fair skin.

"And to you," he said softly. "I told you that before. But *I* must wield it now. It seemed to me that you ought to have something in exchange."

She looked at him oddly. "I have a symbol of earth too. Did you know that? They gave me a basketry platter with the earth sigil on it in Awhai."

Julian took a careful breath. He had thought that he could give her this one thing without revealing his hope that one day she might be Mistress of the Jewels and his queen, but he could see the beginnings of knowledge glimmering in her changeable eyes.

Horns brayed close behind them. Rana turned to see, and the pent air eased out of Julian's chest in a long sigh. Banners fluttered above the hedge. As the riders appeared, Robert and the others who had been exploring the gardens came back to join Julian in the courtyard.

Alexander pulled up, his showy bay blowing and tossing its head after the climb. Julian felt Robert stiffen beside him and saw that Carmelle of Las Costas was with her brother. Her little mare was a dun, and while both she and Alexander wore the black of House Battle, the wind that tugged at her cloak showed a lining of amber silk that matched her hair, while his was red. Carmelle waved, smiling brilliantly, and Julian was suddenly sure that the effect had been intentional. He had started to bow in acknowledgment when he realized that the welcome was for his cousin. He straightened, suppressing a grin.

"So this is Misthall. I had thought it would be larger." Alexander looked around as if he were considering buying it. Julian, remembering how the unkempt garden and sagging shingles had shocked him when he arrived, understood, and yet he found himself bristling.

"It has not been lived in for twenty years. Would your own palace fare better if a son of yours should return to Sanjos after so long a time?"

Alexander looked startled. *Of course*, thought Julian, *he has been Lord Commander of Las Costas since he was seven years old*! Julian had always envied his cousin Robert his courtly upbringing, but Robert was a younger son. Clearly, nothing had ever been allowed to shake Alexander's complacency.

"May the Guardians preserve us!" exclaimed Carmelle. "You must not say such things, Prince, on a day of festival."

"Well, it is *his* festival, may the day be blessed," answered her brother with a grin. "And this is his hall."

Carmelle blushed, and Julian found himself returning Alexander's smile.

"What I should be saying is, 'Welcome'." He reached up to grasp Alexander's hand. "Your presence honors us. Dismount and let them tend your horses. There is food and drink in the arbor."

The table looked charmingly rustic. The breads and cheeses and fruit tarts made an appealing display against the green cloth, and the wine bottles were wreathed with wild flowers from the hill behind the hall. The wind that stirred the grasses scented the soft air.

"And how goes it on the Red Mountain?" Alexander gestured eastward with his goblet. "They tell me that the Blood Lord is back. I thought he drowned last fall."

"We hoped so, but the Master of the Junipers says he lives still." Julian grimaced.

"*Can* he be killed? My mother still lays the guilt for my father's death upon that man. She was in a fury when we learned that he had survived."

"He can be—he must be—killed!" answered Julian with more certainty than he felt. Killed, or burned out from within, he thought then, remembering the wreck that had once been the sorcerer Katiz, Caolin's master. "But while Eric is only Regent, he cannot marshal all of our strength against Caolin, and neither can I."

"And after the election?"

Julian shrugged uncomfortably. "At least I'll have the authority—"

"If they elect you."

Julian's eyes moved back to Alexander's blunt features, unreadable in the clear light. What was he saying?

Alexander continued. "The Estates are not accustomed to a master."

The Prince studied the Lord Commander, trying to decide if his strength was all in the long, heavily muscled body, or in his will also, and whether he was making a threat, or only testing.

"Is this a warning that you will oppose me?" asked Julian, and stopped abruptly. In sword play, he would have scorned such a sudden attack, but he was a novice at fencing with words.

Alexander opened his pale eyes. "I am saying only that we have been twenty years without a king. That is bound to affect the voting.

Silverhair was right about me, thought Julian, staring back at him. *Now what can I say?*

Carmelle's laugh trilled across the silence, startling them.

"But surely you will wish to live in Laurelynn now." She had laid her hand upon Robert's arm.

"My place is with the Prince, wherever he may be," Robert said stiffly.

"Of course," she said sweetly. "But still, you must have a home, and someone to rule it when you are away."

Julian waited for his cousin to laugh and mollify the girl with some bit of flattery. He had been a frequent observer of his cousin's easy flirting. He thought that the girls liked Robert because his beauty freed him from any doubts about his welcome. But Carmelle's attitude was subtly different. She had taken Robert's arm as he himself had never yet dared to touch Rana—with the certainty of possession.

"Hasn't he told you?" Alexander was watching them too. "My mother and the old lord arranged a marriage between him and my sister long ago."

Julian's lips pursed in a soundless whistle. Marriage! Now why hadn't Robert said something? He suppressed a grin, knowing he dared not tease his cousin over *his* secret for fear of what Robert might do when he discovered Julian's own.

"They make a fine couple, don't they?" said Alexander.

Julian nodded. Robert and Carmelle were a matched pair, polished like gemstones in the setting of their fine clothes, with all of the graces a courtly upbringing could bestow.

Rana and I will never look like that, he thought then. *That is, if she should ever come to me. But she shines like the sun on the water, and that will have to serve for both of us.* Instinctively his gaze sought her. She had drawn away to give him and Alexander privacy, and stood now at the far end of the table, licking her fingers and glaring at her brother, who had just tossed a sugar cake to Piper.

"You need have no doubt of my vote, in any case," Alexander said then. "If I upset my sister's plans, she will make my life insupportable!"

Julian bit his lip. Some supported him because they believed he had a right to the crown, or because the land needed a king, or out of that peculiar personal loyalty he seemed to inspire sometimes. But Alexander was offering his vote as one might give a sweet to a fretting child. Surely the sovereignty of Westria meant more than that?

But perhaps Alexander did not think so. . . . The Lord Commander of Las Costas was eating a piece of sugared orange peel with a meditative deliberation that suggested an unshakable confidence in his own security, whether or not a king sat on the throne.

Things had been simpler on the border, Julian thought. There his decisions had affected only one village. And yet the farming folk of Bear Valley were not so different from the lords of Laurelynn. Perhaps what was disconcerting him was Alexander's age; young men usually saw Julian as an ally, or as a rival whose strength must be tried. He had never encountered this serene arrogance in a man of his own years before.

The servers brought on hot sausages and biscuits from the ovens in the Misthall kitchen, and a compote of fruit and cream. Silverhair sat now in the overgrown wisteria arbor, tuning his harp.

"Sing for us," said Rana. "I've missed your music, Silverhair."

The harper smiled. "What would you like to hear? Something about spring?"

"It's too restless a day for that." She shook her head and the breeze toyed with her bright hair. "Play something about the wind."

"The wind. . . ." For a moment the harper's gaze grew distant with memory. "Do you think it can be captured in any human music?" Agile fingers stroked a ripple of sound from the harp's burnished strings.

"At the College of Bards, they said that you'd found a song for it," Julian answered him.

The others were moving toward the music now, chattering like birds, their bright sleeves and skirts fluttering in the breeze. Even Piper had left the food to listen, and Cub followed, still munching, to join the older boy at the harper's feet.

Silverhair shook his head. His voice harshened as he repeated, "No bard can capture the wind." Strong fingers plucked a dissonant fanfare.

> *With heat or with cold,*
> *The world I enfold—*
> *Yet the world holds not me.*
> *You see where I pass*
> *O'er tree and o'er grass—*
> *But you do not see me.*

Notes sparkled from the harpstrings like light from a crystal. Silverhair's voice soared above them with a bitter purity. Julian shifted uncomfortably.

> *I sing in your ear*
> *With each sound you hear—*
> *Yet you never hear me.*
> *Consumed by each breath,*
> *My absence is death—*
> *For you cannot keep me.*

Julian shivered, for a moment overwhelmingly aware of the vastness above him, as not so long ago he had learned to comprehend the depth of the sea. But *up* went on forever.

"I hadn't realized you had a jester, Julian. What is he carrying?"

Alexander's question jerked him back to earth. Turning, Julian saw a wiry little man with a seamed brown face surrounded by red-gray hair who grinned broadly at the murmur of surprise. He came to a halt in the midst of them, waving several brightly colored paper rolls.

The man's golden gaze held Julian's, and the Prince had the odd impression that in that one swift moment of contact, he was somehow being examined—judged, even. And then he was sure it must have been a fancy, for the fellow gave a little yip of laughter and presented his rolled papers.

"They look like scrolls. Is he going to read a poem?"

"Oh, no, lord!" White teeth flashed in the gray beard. "Mañero's poems are written in the sky. These are kites, mistresses. . . ." His quick glance invited Carmelle and the girls around her to come see. "Kites to dance among the clouds, and to battle there."

Julian felt the flicker of Mañero's amber eyes as if the man had touched him.

"See, I have glassed strings!" He held up a roll of cord that glistened in the morning light. "Will you try them, my ladies, my lords?"

"It sounds like good sport!" exclaimed Robert. "I used to fly kites off the Ramparts of Rivered when I was a child. I've heard of kite-fighting, but never seen it done."

"Oh, please, Julian, say yes!" Cub exclaimed. Piper's eyes were eloquent with interest. Bronze head and dove brown nodded in unison.

Perhaps if he's excited enough, he'll say something. Julian smiled.

"Why not? If everyone has finished eating. . . ." He looked around and saw answering grins. "Let's climb the hill behind the garden and play with the wind."

* * *

It began with laughter.

The two boys were only too eager to run the kites into the air, and when Cub, watching his kite instead of his footing, went head over heels down the hill, everyone laughed.

The wind was freshening. Soon it took only a few dancing steps to get Mañero's toys into the air. The glistening fins of Rana's flying fish fluttered exultantly.

"What about the glassed strings?" came Cub's cry. "We want to duel with the kites the way you promised, Master Mañero."

Capering, the little man attached coils of cord that looked as if they had been encrusted with sugar to two kites painted with feral eyes and fanged jaws.

"Careful now, lads, or they will cut you. See, you launch them like this—" Laughing, he cast first one, then the other kite into the sky.

"Let me have one of those," Robert said.

The young men were clamoring as loudly as the boys. Julian found a stick thrust into his hands, and instinctively leaned against the tug of the string. The eagle on the other end of his line spread its wings in golden splendor across the sky. Above him, paired kites were already dueling against the clouds.

"Hey, Julian, are you sleeping?"

Julian jerked around and saw Robert's laughing face, with Carmelle close behind him. Robert was reeling in cord intently, and Julian's eyes followed its arc upward just in time to see his cousin's bronze-antlered stag kite swoop toward his own eagle. He yanked on his line as the golden flier faltered in the sky.

"Pay attention, Prince, or your cousin will drag you down," said Alexander. The Lord of Las Costas was watching their struggles with a benign smile, as if he had been not seven but seventy years older than Julian.

But the man was right. A little breathless, Julian paid out line as he felt the lift of the wind beneath the eagle's wings. There—now he had some sky room. But his string was still vulnerable. Eyes slitted against the glare, he studied his position, wishing he knew more about the invisible currents in the sky. Was Robert's stag losing speed? Carefully Julian drew his kite toward it, but a sudden slack in Robert's string brought his own swooping past. Edges brushed, and now their lines were almost touching.

"Oh, Robert, you've got him now!" Carmelle grabbed Robert's arm.

Intent on the struggling shapes above, Robert shook her off. Carmelle snatched at his sleeve.

"It's all right, Robert . . . I can touch you. We're betrothed, after all." She tightened her grip and looked up at him with a dangerously sweet smile. A quick twist flicked Julian's kite out of danger. Then Robert saw what had happened and swore.

"Truce, Robert!" called Julian, sensing his cousin's confusion. Robert gave him a long look, then turned to the girl.

"Are we?" he muttered. Carmelle's smile slipped a little.

"Of course we are. Everyone knows it."

Her voice had sharpened too, and those nearest were turning. Cub and Piper were still locked in a duel of their own, but several kites already soared free. Robert's face grew hard. Very carefully, he began to reel his kite in.

"And for far too long. . . ." Carmelle's voice wavered, but she continued determinedly. "I've found the waiting hard too, dearest, but they said I was too young. I am eighteen now though." With a visible effort, Carmelle made her voice soften; her fingers caressed the fine orange silk of Robert's sleeve.

"They can't make us wait any longer, Robert! Let's marry at Beltane. We can live in the Las Costas palace in Laurelynn until we find a house of our own."

"*This* spring?" Robert sounded appalled, and Julian suppressed a grin. "How can you think of getting married now, with the Blood Lord still on the Red Mountain and war on all our borders?"

"All the more reason," said Carmelle tartly. "I've no

mind to wait until you men are tired of fighting before I have an establishment of my own.''

"But until the war is over, my place is with the Prince. You know that, Carmelle,'' Robert protested. "I can't live with you!'' The bronze stag tugged frantically as he hauled it in.

Carmelle stared, her fair face suffusing with angry color. Everyone was looking at them now.

"Can't or won't, Robert?'' she snapped at him. "Anyone would think that you didn't want to marry me!''

Robert shook his head, the stag kite hanging like a dead thing from his hand. This was no simple quarrel between lovers.

"Stop her!'' said Julian in a low voice, but Alexander shook his head.

"I gave up trying to control Carmelle years ago. Robert doesn't seem very happy, does he?''

"Please, Carmelle,'' Robert said. "We can talk about this later, when we're alone.'' He took a swift step back.

"Robert of the Ramparts, do you think that you can just walk away from me?'' she said furiously. Had she forgotten their audience, or had she ceased to care? "If you want to keep me, you will answer me now!''

Robert stopped short, and Carmelle's eyes brightened in triumph as, very slowly, he turned. His eyes were blazing too, and more than one of the young women caught her breath in admiration.

"Very well, my lady, since you request it, I will answer you,'' he said quietly. "It was our parents who planned this betrothal, not I! Have I ever led you to believe that I was in love with you?''

"But you must—'' Carmelle caught herself and glared at him in speechless fury.

And no wonder. She has been much courted, thought Julian, *for she is very beautiful. No one has ever said "no" to her before.*

"I will marry you if I must,'' said Robert, with a control that told Julian he was more angry than he appeared. "But you will never bind me. I serve the Prince, Carmelle, and he will always have my first loyalty.''

"And your love?" she hissed. Carmelle's glance raked the circle, and Julian flinched. "Do you think he will reward you? I have eyes, even if you cannot see. I've heard all about the voyage last summer. That Seahold girl has laid her plans very cleverly!"

She gestured across the circle, and suddenly they were all looking at Rana, who had gone stark white beneath her freckles. Julian took a step toward her.

"I've seen how your precious Prince looks at her," Carmelle babbled on. "She has caught him, and you'll be forgotten—"

"Woman, be silent!" Julian found his voice at last.

Robert looked as if he had taken an arrow in the gut, and Rana . . . softly Julian spoke her name. She had dropped her kite stick. It bumped across the grass, caught in a bush and held the kite tethered again. Two patches of red burned on her cheekbones, but she was not weeping. What he saw in Rana's face, Julian realized when at last she looked at him, was revulsion.

"My lord, I'm sorry," she said in a shaken voice. "I don't know how even a vicious mind like Carmelle's could . . ." the words trailed away as she met Julian's eyes.

His fist clenched on the cord of the kite he still held. He strove to school his features, but it was too late for that as well. In Rana's eyes Julian read his own self-betrayal and saw the deepening horror as she realized that what Carmelle had said was true. Did she see *him*, or the face of the man who had raped her?

He felt a tug on his line. The string of Rana's kite had tangled with his own. Instinctively he pulled on it, as if to hold her, but he had forgotten the glassed cord. Abruptly the pressure eased. He pulled again, but only his own kite answered. Wings fluttering, the flying fish lifted suddenly, and the wind whirled it away.

He heard a patter of running feet and knew that Rana had gone. The others were staring at him, their faces stiffening to hide curiosity, or incomprehension, or even satisfaction, as they met his gaze.

The highest heavens were hazed with a thin shimmer

of cloud. Below them, towering cumuli were moving in from the northwest, their white shapes shifting in a turmoil that matched his own. With a single movement, Julian slashed his line and let the eagle soar free. Wind whipped it upward. He blinked. For a moment it seemed to him that bright wings danced among those clouds. Then both fish and bird disappeared.

TWO: Welcomes

Lungs expanded to the rush of rain-sweet air as the windows swung open. The clouds that had followed them back from Misthall were driving up the river and spilling out into the Great Valley, fleeing the wind. Ducks clacked softly on the lake of Laurelynn. Then the boy's breath caught at the distant tremor of a drum, fading with the shift of the wind, then returning deeper than before.

"Piper, come *on*!"

He cupped one ear and touched Cub's arm. The other boy stilled, listening.

"It's like a heartbeat, isn't it?" Cub whispered. "The heartbeat of Laurelynn!"

Against the background of Cub's chatter, crockery was clattering as the palace awakened. A horse whinnied from the courtyard below.

"Cub, where have you—oh, there you are." Wind gusted through the sitting room as Rana came in. "Is Silverhair up yet? Oh, no, you're not going off without us!'' She caught her brother's arm. The inner door opened.

"There is no need to shout. I have been awake for some time.''

Piper reached for the teapot he had kept simmering over the brazier and poured a mug for Silverhair. Satisfaction amplified his memories of other mornings like this one as the harper lifted the cup to his lips.

"Do you want anything to eat before we go?'' asked Rana.

"Just let me finish my tea.'' Silverhair grimaced, and she laughed. The drums throbbed again, the wind brought a fragment of song. Cub was quivering like a leashed hound.

"Calm down. We'll reach the Rose Gate before the procession comes through. Lord Eric and Lady Rosemary were still waiting for their horses as I came in.''

"Don't tease me, Rana. Will you tell me who everyone is? Is Prince Julian going to be in the parade?''

Piper saw her laughter fade, sensed beneath her calm a pain like his own. He wanted to pat her arm, but Silverhair was already answering.

"Julian is not a member of the Council . . . yet. I suppose he is still in his chambers, jittering. The Master of the Junipers arrived last night with Frederic. Perhaps they can talk some sense into the lad.'' He flung the folds of his heavy gray-wool cloak across his shoulders and pushed through the door.

Piper covered the coals and followed the others outside.

Laurelynn shimmered like a city of crystal as sunlight refracted from wet tiles and cobblestone. Blinking, Piper splashed after Silverhair. Folk were exclaiming over sodden bunting, bustling to replace it with dry cloth and fresh flowers. Fabric flapped as someone hung out a tapestry of the Maiden emerging from the Underworld.

Someone was whistling—Piper felt the melody pulse within. His lips pursed, and a thread of sound followed him. From a window came the tune in a man's voice, and like an echo, the same song from many throats a few streets away. As Laurelynn awakened, it was finding its voice, and its song was the coming of spring.

The approach to the gate was already crowded. Someone made a place for Silverhair, but Cub grabbed the branch of a peach tree, the last pink blossoms still clinging, and pulled himself up. Piper looked at him with a pang that Cub did not recognize as envy. Then Cub reached, the tree trembled as Piper scrambled upward, and the two boys wriggled into place atop the wall behind it.

> Lady of the hills and streams,
> Shepherdess of love and dreams,
> Risen from the Winter's night,
> Welcome Spring, oh Maiden bright!

Below them, voices achieved a sudden unity. Piper opened his lips, but as always, there was only the ache in his throat. For a moment older memories clamored against the barrier: men's voices, hoarse with lust instead of sweet singing, and his mother's screams.

He fled back into the wordless present, fumbling for the familiar smoothness of his flute. Lips that could not form words closed with precision around the mouthpiece; a throat that would not carry sound expelled shaped air, and agile fingers transformed the flute into an extension of his flesh. Suddenly a new sound joined the singing.

> Winter white is past, Spring is green at last—
> Welcome, Maiden!
> Docile doe and fawn, see the Winter gone—
> Welcome. . . .

Voices held the last note, and the flute descanted above them in an exultation of released emotion. Piper met Silverhair's glance, saw the harper's thin fingers twitch invisible strings. The flutesong's variation built upon the original tune, and for a moment their smiles were the same.

Silverhair's fingers stilled while the flute developed the melody, as if Piper had heard the harmonies that sounded in the harper's soul. His awareness went inward, seeking the source of that music. He could still hear his own chords, but the flute was carrying the theme to realms he rarely dared ascend. Silverhair's whole being focused on his breathing. Air filled his lungs, released in a long, sweet tone. . . .

"The flute is the breath—"

A shout shocked him, shaking, into his body again. Rana looked at him with troubled eyes, and he forced a smile.

"They're coming! They're on the ramp now!"

The brick archway was set with pink sandstone carved with roses, and that frame was filling now with a moving mosaic of horses and riders, bright cloaks and colorful gowns. Silverhair took a deep breath. This was no time for mystical musings . . . but he had been so close! Such moments held the truth of his life, but they came at the will of the Spirit, not his own.

The singing surged triumphantly as the wood of the bridge rang beneath shod hooves. The heralds of Westria were entering the city on golden horses whose manes and tails shone silver, and their livery glowed like green flame in the morning sun. As the first rider reached the road, trumpets blared, as if the clarions worked in gold on the heralds' tabards were proclaiming their own entry.

"That's not the herald who was with us on Spear Island," said Rana.

The first rider, a solid woman with a wrist-thick braid of gleaming honey-brown hair, caught Silverhair's eye and smiled, and he bowed in reply. Her full cloak was lined in cloth of gold.

"Mistress Anne took over as Laurel Queen-at-Arms last year." He smiled ruefully. "It took her barely a quarter hour to extract all I knew about the heraldry of the lands I've roamed. But I also learned a few things from her. The heralds are panting to serve a king, any king—but I think their hearts are with Julian.''

"There are so many!" Rana shook her head as the cavalcade continued by, riders old and young, whose tabards were differenced in bewildering variety.

"Do you think they would miss such an occasion?" answered Silverhair. "There are few full-time heralds, but anyone with the knowledge can seek accreditation.''

"Just so they can ride into Laurelynn bedecked in green and gold?''

"Don't ask me what motivates heralds. They're even stranger than musicians!"

Rana gave him a startled look, then laughed. Silverhair grinned back at her. The morning air, or perhaps the music, had cleared his head. He was actually enjoying this. He took a deep breath, wondering how long it would last.

"The Seneschals don't appear to have done as well," Rana observed as the next group—a few men and women in faded red robes who sat their mounts like so many sacks of meal—came into view. "Doesn't lack of a king leave them more work to do?''

"Maybe the rest of them are working now," answered the harper. "But it's true, they had more pride in Caolin's day.''

The Constables came next, in blue, followed by white-robed Chirugeons. Then a new music set the crowd to murmuring.

"Will you look at that, now. Master Ras has truly outdone himself today!''

The bridge shook as two massive draft horses hauled a flat wagon bedecked with purple bunting and musicians up its curve. There were viols and recorders of every shape and size, two harps and a deep-toned drum—most of the City Consort of Laurelynn. A purple banner with the golden harp of the College of Bards swung behind them.

Master Ras of Santierra stood beside the banner, holding on to the pole. White teeth flashed in his dark face as he saw Silverhair. Then he leaned toward the viol section, gesturing. A golden head lifted and a bow waved in swift greeting.

"Aurel!" shouted Silverhair. "Master Aurel," he corrected, seeing the purple cloak the young man wore and began to grin. "We were friends when I was at the college," he said to Rana. "I have not seen him for . . . oh, nearly ten years now."

"Silverhair! You should be up here!" Master Ras had made his way to the edge of the wagon as the big horses slowed.

"Please come!" It was a woman's voice, tuned to the edge of laughter. Silverhair felt his smile still.

"Siaran. . . ."

"You can spell me at the harp . . . my fingers are getting tired," called the harp mistress. She beckoned with her right hand while the left sketched an arpeggio up and down the shining strings.

"I am hardly dressed for it—" be began, thinking of the purple cloak that lay still packed in its original wrappings in his rooms. How could he expect Julian to claim his full power when he himself had never been willing to put on that symbol of his own mastery?

"That doesn't matter." The wagon was passing them now.

Silverhair shook his head, knowing that for the first time, it did. "I must go to the Council. Where are you staying?"

"At the Guildhall," she called as the wagon lumbered on. Her words were lost as the choir of children who followed it launched into the next verse of song, but Silverhair waved vigorously until she turned away.

I will have to wear that cloak she sent to me now. . . . Curiously, the thought made him smile.

> *. . . . Risen from the Winter's night,*
> *Welcome Spring, Thou Maiden bright!*
> *Flowers frame Her hair, scent the morning air—*
> *Welcome, Maiden!*

Daughter of the Spring, in Her name we sing—
Welcome. . . .

Rana let her voice soar out with the others in welcome.
Now Eric and Rosemary were coming, riding white
horses whose heads tossed like those on the green banner
of Seagate that followed them. Rana waved as they
passed, wincing as the pitiless light glinted on the silver
that threaded Rosemary's fair hair and the lines carved
in Eric's brow by the years.

They're growing older. Reason wondered why she was
so surprised, but there was a whimpering child deep
within her who wanted them to stay powerful and strong.

In comparison, the face of Alexander of Las Costas
bore an almost brutal youthfulness. Rana looked at the
ruddy good health in his cheeks and the determined jut
of his jaw . . . and saw instead a woman's face, distorted
by disappointment.

Carmelle's accusation had been only a spoiled girl's
spite; reason told Rana that too. Lord Robert had shown
unexpected good sense when he rejected her. But even
now, the memory of Carmelle's words made Rana shiver,
or perhaps it was the moment when she had recognized
Julian's desire.

Run! cried that child inside her. But she had run from
Misthall. Not to talk to him . . . never to be alone with
him . . . that should be sufficient protection. Julian could
no longer be her friend, but he was still her king. Rana
forced herself to focus on the procession again.

Now Robert's brother Philip was crossing the bridge,
chatting easily with Sandremun of the Corona. They were
followed by Loysa Gilder of the Free Cities, glittering
like an advertisement for the goldsmiths. Behind her, the
speakers for the other Guilds were escorted by a gaggle
of apprentices staggering beneath the banners of their
crafts.

"What about the College of the Wise?" she asked
Silverhair.

"The College? I suppose that what's left of it is here.

The Mistress came down from the north by horse litter earlier this week.''

"She must have been Mistress of the College since the Jewel Wars!" This topic was safe enough. Rana allowed herself to relax.

"Not quite that long," said Silverhair, "but she must be in her eighties by now. They say she has become a hermit in the past few years. I suppose she will be waiting for the rest of them in the Council Hall."

The bridge was filling with clerks and attendants. Rana could hear Cub telling Piper about the delights of the fair in the great square of Laurelynn.

"I suppose we had better follow them, or we may have to stand," said Silverhair.

Rana bit her lip. Her parents would be saving a seat for her in the Council Hall. If she stayed away, they would wonder. *He won't see me. I'll just be another face in the crowd. Why am I so afraid?*

Voices lifted in the final verses of the hymn, mocking her fear.

> *Earth and sky and sea sing aloud to Thee—*
> *Welcome, Maiden!*
> *Hear Thy children's voice, as we now rejoice—*
> *Welcome. . . .*

"My lords and ladies of the Council, I bid you welcome!"

To Julian, Tanemun's voice sounded as if his throat had been chronically irritated by the dust of his files. The Seneschal touched flame to the kindling on the Council hearth and peered up at the eight wedge-shaped sections that the men and women of the Estates of Westria had filled to capacity with a multicolored, rustling crowd.

Julian wondered where they all came from, then stopped as he glimpsed one red head among the blacks and grays and browns, like the first poppy to bloom on a hill. *Rana. . . .*

"We are gathered this day to open the Spring Sessions, in the names of the Guardians and the Maker of All Things. May they bless our deliberations here.''

The hall rustled with pious agreement, and Robert leaned closer to Julian. As Lord of Misthall, the Prince could have sat with the men of the Royal Domain, but Eric had sworn that when Julian took his seat on that side of the hall, it should be upon the throne. And so Julian was back in the eastern sector, looking down at Philip of the Ramparts, who was his cousin and had once been his master. At least it allowed him Robert's company.

''I've just figured out Caolin's strategy—he's waiting for this old fool to bore us to death,'' Robert whispered.

Julian nodded. Whatever Caolin's sins, no one had ever accused him of being uninteresting, while Tanemun was a competent workhorse—no, a mule, thought Julian, considering him. He supposed that no one with originality would have been allowed the red robe after Caolin . . . which was one of the reasons why Westria was now in such political and economic disarray.

A fragrant trail of smoke curled upward from the hearth. Julian's gaze followed it toward the skylight, where a brave patch of blue proved that the wind had blown some of the clouds away. If only he could be out under that sky. . . . He realized that he had been dreaming when someone coughed behind him.

Tanemun had begun a summary report on the state of the country. Julian loosened the lacings at the neck of the embroidered green tunic they had insisted he wear today and looked around. Most of the audience was yawning, but the Councilors had begun to frown. He sighed. During the winter, he had forced himself to study the records, but it was depressing to have his suspicions confirmed.

Year by year, yields were decreasing, trade was diminishing, incidents of violence and judicial conflict becoming more frequent. It was a vicious cycle, for as the roads became increasingly dangerous, the traders were killed or went elsewhere, and with fewer outlets, folk grew or manufactured only those goods that could be used locally.

He tried to find a more comfortable position on the flat cushion, which had been compacted by years of compression until it was nearly as unyielding as the wood it covered, and rested a booted leg upon his other knee.

"You too?" whispered Robert. "But these benches are all that is keeping us from falling asleep. Don't complain!"

Julian realized that between Robert's jokes and sheer tedium, he was beginning to relax. *Whatever else is right or wrong,* he told himself, *at least I have good friends!*

He was profoundly grateful for Robert's supple strength beside him. The rivalry at the Initiation Retreat with which they had begun their relationship seemed not four years, but a lifetime ago. Even then, Robert had been elegant, and Julian, at least in his own eyes, misshapen and graceless. But by the time they had rescued themselves from the slavers who captured them on their vision quests, Robert's prickly condescension had become a loyalty that had never since wavered. It had mystified Julian then, and it was hardly more comprehensible now, when Robert could have been his rival for a crown.

But Robert, magnificent as usual in a short-sleeved tunic of blue silk with appliqués of brocade edging neck and sleeves and hem over an undertunic of fine garnet-colored wool, was watching him with the hint of wistfulness that always lay beneath his smile. Suddenly Julian wanted to grasp his hand, but what reason could he give for it, here, in the middle of the Council Hall?

His gaze fled to the adjoining section of the hall, where, beside the Master of the Junipers, Frederic sat on one of the upper benches, clad in the worn, undyed wool of a student at the College of the Wise. He looked thinner, but happy. Julian's lips twitched as he saw how faithfully Frederic's posture reflected that of the Master.

Does he miss Ardra? he wondered. *At least he knows that she will wait for him.* The Elayan princess was in Seagate, supervising the building of galleys of war, but until Julian's authority was confirmed, her appearance at this Council would have been unwise.

His gaze moved farther, and stopped, caught by an unexpected gleam of violet from the northern segment, where the black-and-white banner of the Corona hung against the wall.

Silverhair's wearing the cloak of a Master Bard! Julian realized in amazement. *I wonder what has happened to change his mind.*

And then the sound of his own name distracted him, and he realized that Tanemun had come to the real business of the Council at last.

At last! Caolin leaned forward abruptly, earning an angry look from the man crammed onto the bench beside him . . . and soothing that irritation with a mental touch so automatic he scarcely noticed it.

"However, the most important issue on our agenda is the claim of Sir Julian of the Stones to the throne of Westria." Tanemun took a small sip of water from the cup on the stand beside him. In any other man, the gesture would have been a deliberate move to heighten the tension. "To some of you, the background of this case is known in its entirety, for you were closely involved with the events in question."

Caolin permitted himself a small smile. These fools were not aware of just how many of the major actors in that ancient tragedy were here today. He had taken his place among the men of the Royal Domain, which, as Lord of the Red Mountain, was indeed his right. But he wore the face and form of a holder who had disappeared on his way to market some weeks ago. So far, none of his neighbors had questioned him.

"Yet even some of those who sat in this hall twenty years ago may feel the need to have their memories of the details reawakened. And so, by your leave, I shall attempt to recapitulate the sequence of events leading to the situation that faces us today.'' Tanemun cast a quick glance toward Eric, who sat hunched forward in the chair below the empty thrones, but the Regent did not stir.

Speak on, fool! thought Caolin. *Babble while you may. Soon enough the only truth anyone remembers will be my own!*

"On Midwinter Eve twenty years ago, King Jehan Starbairn died at Misthall. He left his queen, the Lady Faris, as Regent over Westria until their unborn child should be of age to be considered for the throne," said Tanemun.

Caolin took a sudden breath.

"And twenty years ago, at this same feast of spring's returning, the Lady Faris gave birth to a son."

Caolin stiffened as he caught the aromatic scent of the herbs that had been cast onto the fire. *Rosemary. At the Spring Sessions, it was always rosemary on the Council fire. . . .*

For a moment the years rolled backward, and it was Caolin's own hand that cast those herbs upon the pale flame. But there had been no Spring Council twenty years before, only the muted thunder of wings as Caolin's pigeons brought him news of the Elayan War. And while the armies battled, the queen had labored. Memory summoned up the musky scent of the birthing chamber, and then the clean wind that swept the peak of the Red Mountain, where he had understood how necessary Faris was to his own continued power.

But that was long ago; he forced those memories away. *I need no one now!*

"The child was named Star, and appeared strong and healthy, but the queen did not recover from her grief. On the first day of June, both she and the baby disappeared."

How bald a statement for an event that had shaken a kingdom! But even Tanemun had enough dramatic sense to wait for a moment before continuing the story. People were murmuring. Caolin blinked, abruptly aware that there were men and women in this hall who had been children then, or unborn, folk for whom the crisis that had nearly destroyed him was only a half-remembered tale.

"The search was long and exhaustive," said Tanemun, "but no trace of either mother or child was found. At the Midsummer Sessions of this Council, the Estates of Westria were called to elect another Regent. Caolin the Seneschal was defeated when it was learned that his treachery had led to the deaths of Lord Brian of Las Costas and many other good warriors in the Battle of the Dragon Waste."

Caolin's fingers caught like talons in the folds of his tunic. The man beside him turned a little, and then started in surprise. Automatically the sorcerer reached out to clasp his wrist. The fellow's mouth opened—

"Hush! You have seen nothing." Caolin's voice was pitched precisely to reach the farmer's ears; his cold gaze held the other man still. "You are bored here . . . you are dozing off. When you awaken, you will not remember me." He watched as the fellow's eyelids flickered, then closed, then let go of the man's hand.

Carefully the sorcerer reconstructed the image of the holder whose face he wore. No one else had noticed his lapse; they were intent on Tanemun's story. Coldly, Caolin noted the surprising flicker of emotion that had disturbed his control. He was safe enough even had he been recognized; those who reached the Council floor could claim sanctuary. But he had not believed that there would be so much power in old memories!

"After much debate, Lord Robert of the Ramparts was elected Regent, and Caolin was dismissed from the office of Seneschal."

For a moment Caolin saw Laurelynn burning in sunset flame. He quivered to an echo of old agony; then his disciplined will shunted the image away. Eric was sitting with his elbows on his knees, his face hidden in his hands. The face of the Master of the Junipers was a mask, and Farin Silverhair's eyes burned like coals.

Oh, yes, you remember. You remember, oh my enemies! thought Caolin, releasing his pain just enough to fuel the fury that had brought him here. *And I have not forgotten you!*

"In his will, King Jehan had specified that the queen should be Regent until her child was grown, and that if he did not become Master of the Jewels, the Council should choose another sovereign. Therefore, at the end of the Midsummer Sessions of the Council, the Estates voted that the term of the Regency should be for twenty years, at which time the Council should meet to choose a new ruler for Westria.

"Julian of the Stones has now reached his twentieth year, and has recovered two of the lost Jewels. Eric of Seagate, our Regent, had therefore proposed him as a candidate for the crown." Tanemun drank again from his cup, set it down, and gestured toward the narrow windows beneath the eaves. "The hour grows late, my ladies and lords. I propose that tomorrow morning's session be dedicated to debate regarding this candidacy."

A murmur of comment rose in the hall. Those faces that were not turned to the oblongs of golden light above them were focusing on the wedge of benches where the men of the Ramparts sat. People pointed to a solidly built young man with dark hair, and Caolin realized that it was Julian.

Why was he surprised? Had his hatred of old enemies blinded him to the presence of this new one? But Julian had been in armor the two times he had seen him before; he had been armed with the weapons of men and the power of the Jewels.

"Aye—" "We agree—" The responses from the Estates were coming in.

"Until tomorrow then, I declare the Spring Sessions closed." said Tanemun.

Julian had no glamor about him now, thought Caolin. Everyone was standing up, stretching muscles stiffened by long immobility. Julian rose to his feet as well, working his heavy shoulders back and forth as it to relieve tension. As his gaze moved past the folk of the Royal Domain, it stopped; for a moment Julian's eyes met

Caolin's. Automatically the sorcerer began to project his power, but the distance between them was too great for control. The boy blinked, frowned, then turned away to answer some question.

Caolin eased back on his bench, took a deep breath and let it go. *You do not know me, Julian . . . but I know you now. You do not hear me, but one day my voice is all that you will hear.*

"Julian!"

Julian turned at Robert's touch and forced an answering smile. "I'm sorry, I was distracted." There had been a sensation like the prickle of warning he sometimes felt while on patrol, but it was gone now. The hall was a mass of moving figures; there was no telling who had disturbed him.

"I said, let's get out of here," Robert repeated. "I have some Silverado wine in my rooms that would go down very easily right now."

Perhaps wine would relieve some of his tension. Julian followed Robert toward the aisle. And then, noticing a flicker of copper moving through the crowd on the floor of the hall below, he eased past his friend and pushed down the stairs.

"Rana!" Had she heard him? She was starting up the opposite aisle, toward the western door. He skipped steps to reach the floor and hurried across it. "Rana, wait," he called again, and this time she looked down at him.

Julian stopped in mid-stride. The dusting of freckles showed plainly against the sudden pallor of Rana's skin, but it was her eyes that halted him, as cold and gray as the winter sea—no, not cold, he realized—apprehensive, betrayed.

For a moment she looked at him, and the hand that Julian had lifted in entreaty sank slowly to his side. Then she disappeared. This time he did not try to follow. He had understood her silent rebuff only too well. She knew now that he, whom she had regarded

as protector and friend, wanted her much as did any
other man.

"This is not our week for women, is it?" There was
a hint of acid beneath Robert's light words. Julian turned
and sighed, realizing that his cousin had overtaken him
in time to understand the silent interchange. Then he saw
Alexander of Las Costas and his sister climbing the stairs
behind them, and understood the bitterness.

"My Lord of Las Costas, my Lady Carmelle. . . ."
The folds of Robert's tunic rustled as he bowed. Carmelle turned her back on him, her chin lifting in a gesture as eloquent as Rana's had been, though petulance
was its major message. But Alexander halted, frowning.

"I wonder that you venture to speak to my sister, Lord
Robert, after your words to her two days ago."

"I have no quarrel with Carmelle—" Robert began.

"Do you not?" her brother retorted. "To renounce
your betrothal before half the court seems insult enough
to me."

"Surely that is for Carmelle and me to decide."

"Not when you do it publicly. Then it involves the
honor of House Battle!" A muscle jumped in Alexander's jaw.

Is he really angry, wondered Julian, *or is he doing this
to still his sister's nagging tongue?* He moved to Robert's
side.

"That quarrel was the lady's choice, not mine,"
snapped Robert. "As the time and place of this one are
yours. My honor is unstained."

"He's right, Alexander," said Julian. "Such matters
should not be discussed here. Come to my rooms, and
perhaps we can—"

"There will be no negotiations until I have seen an
apology, in writing. If you are his master, then the responsibility for that lies with you."

"I'll give orders to no man in a matter of the heart,
my lord. And Robert is not my servant, but my friend!"
Julian heard his own voice deepen. He had stepped in

front of his cousin as he spoke, and his gaze held Alexander's until the other man's eyes fell.

"True," Alexander said softly. "Only a prince can have servants of such rank. Farewell. Perhaps when this Council is ended, we will speak again." Carmelle was already moving sideways through the benches, toward the southern exit, and her brother followed her.

"Phew!" exclaimed Robert when they had gone. "Was that a threat? Does he mean to make his vote his sister's dowry? Julian, I'll go after them. Words are cheap enough, and I can sweeten her up if I try." He started forward, but Julian grasped his arm.

"And after?" The Prince shook his head. "It's your whole life, Robert, and that's too high a price to pay." They reached the top of the stairs and passed through the double doors into the broad corridor that circled the hall. Julian saw Silverhair hurrying toward them and quickened his steps. The day had been wearing enough without his uncle's nagging.

Robert sighed. "I thought I could go through with the marriage, but Carmelle is a little bitch, isn't she? And who would want Alexander for a brother-in-law? Julian," he added softly, "thank you."

They wrapped the cloaks they had left on the hooks in the wall around their shoulders and came out onto the porch above the square. It was crammed now with booths. Crowds swirled among them, chattering and chaffering for wares. From beneath the awning of the clay-flute seller rose a discordant twittering. From the booth that sold the long, sugar-powdered *churros* came the rich smell of frying dough, and a spicier scent from the mulled-cider stall. Within a circle of lanterns, a storyteller was casting anxious glances at the sky and hurrying through the tale of how Coyote married a man.

A second storm front had followed the first. Westward, the deep yellow of the last sunlight streamed out between banks of cloud, washing the buildings of Laurelynn with gold. But the eastern sky was steel-blue; a rising wind was already flapping banners and fluttering the edges of the booth coverings, and as Julian and Rob-

ert passed down the broad stairs, they felt the first splat-
tering of rain.

Wind beat at the bricks of Laurelynn, howled angrily
around its towers, lashed the tiled roofs with flails of
rain. Piper sat on the broad ledge, windows open to the
murmurous darkness. He held his flute poised at his lips
and let out his breath in a sigh of sound.

There was no melody, only the pure essence of music.
The notes lifted and altered, and then he expelled the
rest of his breath with a squawk and set the flute down.
Why couldn't he capture the song the wind was singing?
He leaned out, filling his lungs with damp air. He could
swallow the wind, but never could he hold it; dizzied,
he released stale air and gulped again.

The world was filled with windsong. Everywhere the
air was a-rush and a-rustle; the newly fallen night
breathed in great gusts of excitement at the storm. When
it paused to draw breath, came the patter and plink of
water, and the deep roar of the rain-fed river below. The
wind shouted around him. The flute shrilled its exultation back again. For that moment, it did not matter
whether the musician matched it—he *was* the wind, tuned
to its song in a communion deeper than any communication with humankind.

"Piper, shut the window! You're drenched—look at
you!"

Piper. . . . The name dragged back his soaring soul.
Confused, he stared at the figure dripping in the doorway. A ripple of remembered music connected him, and
an uprush of anxiety set him moving. The harper was
shivering. Wincing, Piper closed the leaded pane, took
the cloak and found a blanket with which to rub the
harper dry.

"What were you doing? Do you want pneumonia on
top of everything?"

Piper heard the fatigue beneath the harsh tone. He
moved more quickly, turning up the oil lamp and setting
the flask to heat in the ring, shaking the spices into the
cider.

Outside, the wind was sighing. For a moment, Piper stilled, straining to hear its song. But the cider began to steam. He poured it into the stoneware mug and set the vessel between the harper's cold hands.

"Bless you, boy. How did you know what I needed? Springtime never used to be so cold! My bones ache in the morning, and they are worse when it rains. My fingers hurt all winter, even with Mara's gloves. . . ."

Silverhair's thin hands tightened on the mug and he took a deep breath of the fragrant steam. Piper sat down, his flute into his hand. As the harper drank, Piper's swift fingers released a ripple of music that resolved into the steady swing of a wandering song.

"But better a cold camp in the rain than the stuffy Council Hall!" Silverhair grimaced. "You and Cub were right . . . the fair was more interesting than the Council today. It's tomorrow that worries me. Julian is going to have to plead his cause, and Wind Lord alone knows what he will say! We were wrong to press for this election now, before we've recovered all four Jewels. I thought Julian would let me teach him some wordcraft, but he's sunk in the mud. If only we had the Wind Crystal now!"

He lifted his head suddenly, and Piper recoiled.

"I should have tried to find it. Julian *won't* learn, and you. . . . Wind Lord! *Why* are you still silent?" Thin fingers gripped Piper's chin, dark eyes stared. "Damn you, *say* something to me!"

The boy swallowed, and a strangled sound came from his throat. As he jerked away, the harper let go and stood with the heels of his hands pressed into his eyes.

"I'm sorry, Piper, I'm sorry. Talking to you is too much like talking to myself. I didn't mean. . . ."

Piper twitched. *Run!* said his nerves—*run, run!* Shadows fluttered around him, screaming his name. He clapped his hands over his ears. If he was very silent, perhaps they would not find him.

After a time, the pounding of his heart eased. The storm was still battering the darkness outside, but a soft ripple of notes nearby led him gently out of his fear . . .

harp music, a slow series of chords he had not heard before.

The chords repeated in sweet harmony, but the music was asking a question. Piper's lips curved. He took up the flute, and presently the descant of his song made a single music from the disciplined harmonies throbbing through the still air inside and the wild chorus of the wind.

THREE: Wordspells

Piper's music was still echoing in Silverhair's memory as he mounted the outer staircase to Julian's rooms the next day. The storm had passed, leaving a sky the color of Aztlan turquoise, veined by a few wisps of cloud. Unwillingly his mind moved back to those moments before the music had come to save them, as it had at other times when his temper failed him.

Wind Lord! I almost lost him! He shuddered, remembering hazel eyes gone round and staring like those of a trapped bird. It had been months since Piper had actually tried to run away, but the mind, as well as the body, could flee. *Why did I press him? Will I someday push him as far as Caolin's sorceries pushed Katiz?* The memory of the self-imprisoned wretch who had once been the greatest shaman in Awhai made him shudder again.

But the song had saved them this time. Humbled, Silverhair was stifling his pride and returning to Julian to try again to teach him some wordcraft. Anxiety hastened his pace, and suddenly he could not breathe.

Silverhair leaned against the rough brick of the wall,

waiting for the constriction in his chest to ease. Since his
embarrassing collapse after the battle with the otters the
summer before, such moments had come with increasing
frequency. Each time he knew the quick stab of fear, but
when he rested, the pain went away. Would a time come
when it did not? Still fixed on his inner landscape, the
harper's gaze passed over the courtyard below and the
jumble of wet red roofs to the gleam of the river and
the vibrant green sweep of the hills beyond.

*I know no songs to drive this threat away. I was angry
because I am afraid.*

If he complained to Rosemary she would cosset him
to death. If he sought the Master of the Junipers, Frederic would wonder why, and if he knew, so would Julian.
No. He would not add another anxiety to those that
clouded Julian's dark eyes.

The soft wind was scented with flowers. As it dried
the beads of perspiration on his forehead, Silverhair took
a cautious breath and began to relax again.

I will do well enough if I'm careful, he told himself.
Straightening, he started along the porch that led around
the building to the Prince's rooms. As he rounded the
corner, he was nearly upset by a wiry little man who was
hurrying the other way.

"Pardon, lord!" The fellow bowed with a flourish and
started to sidle by, but Silverhair grabbed him.

"You—you're the kite-flier, aren't you?"

"And you are the song-singer!" White teeth flashed
above the whiskers that flared to either side of the man's
face so that it seemed all nose.

Silverhair gave him a sharp look. There was a badge
on the man's shoulder. "You're in Sachs' household, I
see. What do they call you?"

"Mañero, master." Amber eyes gleamed. The tone
had been humble, too humble perhaps. Was the fellow
mocking him?

"You're the 'Fixer,' are you?" Silverhair translated,
grimacing. "What are you going to fix here?" The word
held a hint of slyness as well.

"Just bring a message—" The grizzled head bobbed.

"An errand for my master." A quick twist freed him from the harper's grasp.

Silverhair frowned, irritated for no reason that he could understand. But before he could object, Mañero was dancing down the stairs. Shaking his head, the harper continued toward Julian's chambers.

"My lord, you call me, and see how I come!"

Caolin turned from the man in the chair before him, frowning. How had Mañero gotten in? He had been expecting someone from Frederic Sachs to tell him that Loysa Gilder was here. Sachs had servants enough—it had been one reason for disguising Mañero as part of Sachs' household—and they had all been ordered to admit no one to the rooms set aside for the Blood Lord. No doubt they had thought the little man was on some rightful errand here.

"You said come—I am wrong? Sorry the servant whose master cannot make up his mind!" Mañero grinned.

"That has never been my problem," snapped Caolin. "I did call you. Is there a woman with Master Sachs in the hall?"

Mañero raised an eyebrow, and the sorcerer was aware of an impulse to blast him. But it would have been a pointless expenditure of energy.

The man nodded. "They said to tell you—"

"Very good." One mystery, at least, was explained. "Wait for me here."

Motioning to the other man in the chamber to stay still, he passed quickly through the corridor to the hall. As Caolin entered, Frederic Sachs pushed himself painfully to his feet, followed, after a moment, by Loysa Gilder. Her eyes widened as she looked from one man to the other.

"Is this who I think it is?"

"I am your master, Loysa." Caolin pitched his voice carefully, and as the vibrations reached her, she grew still. "Listen to me. The second session of the Council begins in an hour, and you must know what to do."

"You *are* the Blood Lord! By what right—" the woman began.

"Loysa, you don't understand!" said Sachs.

"Oh, yes I do!" she interrupted him. "The Council booted this man out of Laurelynn twenty years ago. What right has he to interfere now?"

"He made me what I am, Loysa," rumbled the older man. "As I made *you*. I still hold your notes-of-hand, woman, or had you forgotten? Even that gold chain you finger so proudly is mine!" He swayed, and Caolin gestured him back to his chair. For a moment, he surveyed the Guildmistress with disgust. He should have known that the high color meant stubbornness, as the carefully tinted blonde hair meant pride.

"He can take away your trade, Loysa Gilder. He knows your secrets—he knows everyone's secrets—he had that knowledge from *me*. Fear what he can do to your livelihood, but fear what I can do to your soul," the sorcerer said softly. Her gaze came back to him, and then could not break free.

"Yes . . . now you begin to understand. Today they will debate that boy's fitness for the throne, and this is what you must say." He moved closer and took her face between his hands like a lover, but it was not passion that made her twitch as he went on. She was pale beneath her paint when he finally let her go.

When Caolin returned to his chamber, he saw that Mañero had made himself comfortable in the leather chair. The Blood Lord frowned. He never used that chair himself, but there was something unsettling about the ease with which the little man had curled himself into the deep upholstery. He cast a quick glance at the other man in the room, who sat where he had left him, smiling happily as the flame on the hearth flickered in the draft from the door.

"Did you find out what I wished to know?" Caolin asked abruptly.

"Certainly." Mañero grinned up at him. "He will be wearing the white gown embroidered all around the edges with golden leaves. Very fine, like a maid at a fair!" The little man farted suddenly and looked away in embarrassment.

Caolin grunted with involuntary amusement. "And the harper?"

"He is with him. But they say that the Prince and his cousin sat late over their wine."

"Better still." Now the Blood Lord did laugh. "Perhaps tonight he will have reason to get drunk indeed. Come again to me tomorrow. You have done well."

A little reluctantly, Mañero uncurled himself from the chair. And then he was gone, and Caolin was alone— *alone*, he thought, turning to the man who still sat by the fire, *as a smith is at his forge, or a potter with his clay.*

And are you, he wondered then, *a vessel to be filled, or a weapon to be used against my foes?*

"Julian," he said aloud, "look at me."

The dark head lifted. Thickly muscled shoulders straightened, brown eyes dilated as they met the sorcerer's gaze. Once he had had another name, but it had been wiped from his memory months ago, and the sorcerer had never bothered to learn it anyway.

Caolin considered the young man critically, comparing his blunt features with those of the other, whose gaze he had touched in the Council Hall. Then he smiled. Now that the lad was well-dressed and well-fed, the resemblance between them was even greater than he had expected. When he picked this boy from the ranks of his men at Blood Gard, he had chosen better than he knew.

This face would never deceive anyone who knew the Prince well, but a little work with an actor's paint box— firming the line of the mouth, extending and darkening the black bar of the brows—would convince those who did not for as long as was required. A touch of makeup, oh yes, and even more delicate and sure, a touch of suggestion. But he needed more than this tranced obedience.

"In the name of Katiz, awaken!"

Stolid intelligence flooded into the face before him. The young man looked around.

"Where . . . where are we now?"

"Why, in your own city of Laurelynn, my Prince,"

said the sorcerer, hiding another smile. Caolin had needed a word by which to bind his captive that no other, even by chance, would use. Now the name of the old shaman of Awhai served him as the man himself had done long ago. The boy would become as mindless as Katiz when that name was spoken again, and between times, his will belonged to Caolin.

"I don't remember. . . ." The false prince sighed unhappily and rubbed his brow. "Why can't I remember? There's so much . . . I thought we were at Blood Gard."

"You have been sick, lord, you know that. Do not make yourself worse by fretting," Caolin said soothingly. The drugs that helped him to maintain control did have some side effects, but the worst of them took time to appear. "You will be better here."

"Have I been here before?" The words were cautious.

"In the winter a year ago, when you were knighted, and for a time last summer, before you fought the sea raiders, and off and on this spring."

"Yes, I remember . . . I think I remember. It is hazy though, like a story."

"It is sometimes like that after a sickness," Caolin said sympathetically. "But you must not let anyone suspect your confusion, or even know that you have been ill. The great lords you are going to meet will not help you to your crown if they think you a weakling."

"I don't want to meet them. I wouldn't know what to say."

Caolin could see a rim of white around widening eyes, and he stroked the trembling arm as he would a frightened horse. He had conquered the lad's resistance easily, but could he manage this fear?

For a moment he wondered if it might be easier to take Julian's form himself, just as he had stolen the semblances of so many others. He took a breath, began to focus on the image, and then twitched at the same odd discomfort that had stopped him when he had tried this before. It was almost like the feeling that prevented him from taking the form of Jehan; but he had loved the father, he hated the son. That was most likely the trouble:

too strong an emotion disturbed the detachment he needed in order to veil his own shape with another's form. And indeed, he could act much more freely if attention was focused elsewhere. He could act, and manipulate, and given the most unlikely of outcomes— abandon his puppet and flee.

"But *I* do," he said softly. His hand moved to the stiff fringe of beard. The boy jerked at his touch, but already the sorcerer's eyes held him captive. "Julian . . . Julian . . . these are the men you will meet, and these are the words you must say." In his own mind, the images began to form, and with all the force of his will, he projected them into the mind of the man before him.

There was no resistance. How should a blank page resist the words that are being written there? With calm precision, Caolin imprinted on that emptiness the eloquence with which he had once swayed the Council of Westria.

"Uncle, stop nagging! If the Council cannot hear the truth, what's the use of fine words? Everyone knows that I was brought up in a stone quarry." Julian's words came disjointed over his shoulder as he clattered down the stairs.

"I'm not asking you to deceive anyone, Julian," Silverhair replied as they reached the ground. "Only to hone your words with as much care as you do your sword!" He had not meant their discussion to become an argument, but Julian was as stubborn as one of his own stones.

"Just because you've finally admitted that *you* are a Master Bard, do you now think that everybody should be one?" Julian turned to wait for him, and Silverhair resettled the folds of his purple cloak self-consciously. That had been a sharp thrust . . . but no one disputed that the boy was a swordsman.

"What I think is that you should learn to be a king!" Silverhair glared at him. A clear spring sun had chased the clouds away, and Julian carried his cloak over his arm. In the gold-embroidered white tunic that Robert had persuaded him to wear, he certainly *looked* royal. As they moved toward the square, the warming air grew murmurous with the sounds of the fair.

"You are going to have to give a speech tomorrow," the harper went on. "Do you have any idea of what you will say? As you keep pointing out, there's no time to train you. So will you at least read the notes I've made?"

"The speech you have written for me, you mean," said Julian. Silverhair started to shake his head, but Julian went on. "You *do* mean it, and you may be right, but if I had to speak all those fine phrases, I would feel a fool!"

"Why do you persist in misunderstanding me? You were only raised in a quarry, not born there!"

"Uncle, be still! I am as I am, and I cannot change."

Julian had stopped, his shoulders hunched as if he were bracing himself against the wind, but there was only a playful breeze. They were almost to the square now. The plaintive harmonies of hawkers crying their wares came to them.

In Julian's voice there had been no laughter. There was power there though, strength like the roots of the mountains, like the springs of the sea. *You have changed, lad.* With a curious pain, Silverhair remembered the boy he had met on the road to Bongarde. *You could not have silenced me with a word two years ago!* The Prince had the force, but Julian could not—or would not—find the words to express his will.

The harper remained where he was as Julian flung his cloak over his shoulder and strode away.

Caolin adjusted the blue cloak to hang at a more graceful angle and stepped back to regard his work. The boy looked nervous; he supposed that was inevitable. The sorcerer's fingers dug into the thick muscle of the lad's upper arm, and his captive gasped; in that moment of focus, Caolin locked onto his will once more.

"Be still! You are the Prince of Westria!"

"Ye-es . . . of course . . . I am."

"That's better," Caolin said softly. At the other end

of the corridor he glimpsed a figure in black and red, and pointed. "And there's the man I've brought you to see. He's a great lord too—the Commander of Las Costas. You will remember what you must say to him."

The lower passages of the Council Hall were shadowed and Alexander did not know Julian well. For a first attempt, this should do very nicely. Caolin pushed the boy forward and replaced his own face with that of Mañero.

"My lord . . . Alexander. I think we need to talk."

The Lord of Las Costas stopped, noted the uncertainty in the stance of the man who faced him, and began to smile. "Certainly, Julian. I was wondering how long it would take you to realize that you needed me."

"*Smile*," thought Caolin at his pupil. "*Meet him half-way.*" He relaxed a little as the boy managed a weak grin.

"I believe you spoke of an apology?"

"I did," said Alexander, "but not from you. My sister's happiness means a great deal to me. Have you persuaded that stiff-necked cousin of yours to see reason?"

"He will—" a shrug—"if he wishes to remain my companion."

"You surprise me. Yesterday you gave the impression that you valued his friendship above your crown." Alexander moved closer, frowning, and Caolin projected certainty. "Then you will make sure he goes through with the marriage?"

"I have had a night to think on it. I will persuade him."

"*Good . . . good. You are doing well.*" Caolin blurred Mañero's semblance and stepped back a little. With luck, Alexander would not remember that anyone else had been present at all. This was what the Blood Lord had hoped for when he had kept the boy alive a year ago. He grew still as a spider who feels the betraying tremors in the carefully woven strands of his web. It was a feeling that had once been very familiar, in the days before he had an army, before he had wielded the dark knowledge of sorcery. He felt a tingle of pleasure in triumphing through wit and will.

"Do I have your word on that?" the Lord of Las Costas said then.

"*Agree—and quickly!*" thought the sorcerer, and saw the confirming nod.

"Upon my honor—"

"Then I will support your bid for the crown."

"It is no light thing to bestow a crown. This is is no bauble to be awarded for fame, or beauty, or even for sentiment's sake." Philip of the Ramparts paused for a moment, surveying the assembly. Julian's breath caught as Philip's gaze touched him.

I never thought it was! He forced himself to relax. *And the Guardians know I would refuse it—I think I would refuse it—if there were not such need.* He controlled his features, for others had followed Philip's glance, and the white tunic made him easy to identify. Robert gave him a quick, encouraging grin and settled back on the bench as Philip went on.

"We are considering the destiny of a nation here, for a land is judged by her leaders. Westria has been governed by House Starbairn since the Jewel Wars, and no one has ever wondered why. If King Jehan had not died untimely, his son would no doubt have inherited without question."

The drift of scented smoke from the hearth glowed in the pale sunlight that shafted down from the high windows of the hall. Julian's eyes followed its slow spiral toward the small circle of blue above, wondering once more if his father's death had been simple misfortune, or if there was some deeper necessity that justified the tests and obstacles that were delaying his own succession to the throne.

"Instead, we have had twenty years of Regency," Philip sighed. "I do not criticize those who have carried that burden. I saw it kill my father; I have seen Lord Eric grow grey. Now the time of waiting has ended, and may the Guardians be thanked for it, for we cannot go on this

way. Those of you who have seen war know how it is
when a commander is struck down. For a time, his second may hold the fighters together, but he must be confirmed in that authority or discipline and morale will fail.
I think that the same thing has been happening in Westria. . . ."

Once more Philip paused, and a little murmur of
agreement rippled among the benches. These were harsh
words, but everyone knew how constant war had been
along the borders this year. Philip had earned the right
to speak his mind.

"It cannot go on. One way or another, we must decide
how we are to be governed in the future, and by whom.
As I said before, let us look upon this as an opportunity
to examine the laws by which we live. Do we in truth
need a king? And if we do, who shall that ruler be?"

Philip gestured around the hall, inviting a response,
and Julian stared at the man who had been his master.

"What does my dear brother think he's doing?" muttered Robert.

Julian shrugged. For one wild moment he wondered
if this was his cousin's final ploy to escape the kingship
if the election did not go to Julian. But second thought
told him that Philip was right. And the Lord Commander
of the Ramparts was possibly the only man who could
have questioned the old ways without being accused of
self-interest.

Julian had doubted his own fitness to rule ever since
he met the Lady of Westria on the road to Bongarde. But
he had never questioned the need for a king. Silverhair's
tales of his wanderings made clear that other lands did
well enough, though governed in other ways. Why indeed was Westria a monarchy?

Philip sat down amid a rustle of commentary that
whispered through the hall like high wind through a
wood.

"Does . . . does anyone wish to respond to the comments of my Lord of the Ramparts?" asked Tanemun
anxiously.

Julian settled back on the bench as the noise in the hall grew louder. It was going to be a long day. . . .

"Tomorrow will see the end of it, then," said Alexander pleasantly. "With my support, I don't think you need to worry, Julian."

The crush of the crowds trying to leave the Council Hall had brought them together, blinking as they met the level rays of the sinking sun. Caolin moved out from behind the pillar where he had been waiting for them. He still wore Mañero's face, but the other Julian was safe at Fredegar Sachs'. He wondered what this Julian, the real one, would say.

"I thank you, my lord," the Prince answered slowly. "That is very generous, after yesterday—"

"After this morning—" Alexander corrected.

It was Julian's turn to look surprised, and Caolin suppressed a smile. He had never realized what an exquisite pleasure it could be to lead men astray. Long ago his subordinates had accused him of being incapable of laughter. But they had been wrong; he had only now identified the peculiar brand of humor that was his own.

"But I haven't seen you since—"

"Yes, since this morning. We met in the lower corridors of the hall." Alexander's voice had risen, and men were beginning to turn.

Good, thought the sorcerer. He grinned and pointed, mimicking Mañero's glee. *Come and listen*, said his gesture, *come and see*! For the meeting this morning he had needed privacy, but he wanted everyone to hear what was going to happen now.

"I don't understand," said Julian. "I came straight across the square with Silverhair."

"We met in the corridor." Alexander's chin began to jut dangerously. "You assured me that you would compel Lord Robert to fulfill his contract with my sister."

Julian had become very still. "That I would *compel*—"

"Not in those words perhaps, but you did agree to persuade him."

Julian stared, and once more Caolin bit back a smile.

You cannot escape the trap, lad—you lose either Alexander's support or Robert's friendship. Even before I learned sorcery, no one could beat me at this game! As if he had heard, Julian turned, but he saw only Mañero.

"Alexander, what I said yesterday holds. I will never interfere in the personal life of a man I call friend."

"I know who I saw! I know what I heard!" The voice of the Lord of Las Costas had become low, dangerous. "And *I* do not play foolish games. Julian of Stanesvale, you gave me your word!"

Caolin saw the glitter in Alexander's eye, the subtle shift in Julian's stance, and nodded. Better and better! Perhaps Alexander would kill him; it could destroy Julian's credibility if they even came to blows within the sanctum of the hall.

"I don't know what you think happened, but—" Julian took a step toward the other man, and Alexander's hand went to the hilt of his sword.

"Hold!" Eric thrust between them, leaving a swathe in the crowd behind him as if a tornado had blasted through.

"Twenty years ago the Master of the Junipers stopped me from fighting your father in the hall." He glared at Alexander until the younger man let his hand fall to his side. "We should have known better, and so should you!" He looked at Julian now.

"I have no wish to fight him." Julian turned away.

"No?" spat Alexander. "But you will, if not with swords here, then with words in the Council Hall. No man mocks me!"

Except for me, thought Caolin. *And I make fools of you all.*

"Deny what you will, that man was with you and heard it all!" Alexander pointed, and Caolin jerked back. But the Lord Commander was not pointing at him. The sorcerer heard a bark of laughter, looked where everyone else was looking, and saw, as if in a mirror, the grinning face of Mañero.

For a moment, control slipped, and Caolin wore no one's face at all. Then Mañero began to laugh. Eric reached out to grab him, and swore as the little man slipped through his grasp. Suddenly everyone was trying to stop the fugitive, and falling into each other as they failed.

Caolin reached the shelter of his pillar and leaned against it, waiting for sight and hearing to clear. His will shut down the reactions of panic, and he forced himself to recreate the face of the farmer he had worn the day before. Then slowly, silently, he moved away.

As he reached the far door, he could still hear Alexander promising revenge.

"Alexander is my first arrow, and he is speeding from my bow," said Caolin. "But will it be enough?"

The young man who was and was not Julian looked up inquiringly. Outside, it was dark, but the city was still celebrating. As the sorcerer closed the window, he could hear people singing, the barking of hysterical dogs, and one exultant howl.

"You are the perfect confidant," Caolin went on. "Better than the wolf who followed me long ago, for you hear and can respond. Better than Ordrey, who is a man, because you will never act on your own. Do you think I should do something more to ensure my victory? No, you don't think—but I do, and you will help me."

The sorcerer sighed. He did not *need* a companion; he no longer counted the years he had worked alone. But he did need tools, and talking to this one helped him to get his ideas clear—

—Including the realization that it was not enough to make Alexander of Las Costas dance to his tune. He must do something about Julian.

The sorcerer straightened and looked around. The small sounds of nightfall in the city came faintly through the thick walls. Fredegar Sachs' house was well built, and the chamber he had given to Caolin was a large room on the top floor, with heavy curtains to the windows and a stout door.

He had to be sure. . . .

Today he had done all that the powers of the mind

could compass to ensure Julian's failure—all that an ordinary mind might do. But in the challenge of returning
to this city, he had ignored his other powers. It was time
to make use of them now. His temple on the Red Mountain might be the setting for his greatest magics, but he
was not bound to it. Frowning faintly, Caolin set himself
to ready the room.

First, he must have utter cleanliness, both physical
and psychic. At his direction, the lad whose mind he
had enslaved swept and scrubbed. When he was finished, the sorcerer strode widdershins through the room,
scattering shining drops of salt-charged water with a
whisk of rosemary, and then, a second time around,
smudging the place with the pungent smoke of smol-
dering sage.

When the space vibrated with emptiness, Caolin began
to lay out his tools: a cloud-pale cloth of silk with which
to cover the cubed altar; more incense, an owl's feather
with which to fan it; a candle, a crystal, a bell, and
beside them, vellum and ink for the spell. He drew his
wand from its case and went to the east, inscribed the
sacred symbols upon the air and circled sunwise, doing
the same at each of the quarters. When he was finished,
the room seemed slightly blurred beyond his circle, like
distant mountains seen through the heat shimmer on a
scorching day. Now his privacy was ensured by something more effective than the lock on his door.

Lifting the wand, he turned east again,

> *East wind, eagle wing;*
> *Spellsong now I sing;*
> *Dawn light, cloud bright,*
> *Come to my summoning!*

Light flickered from the crystal set into the tip of the
wand. Air stirred behind it, a soft caress on Caolin's
hair. The sorcerer bowed and turned to his right.

> *South wind, hawk wing;*
> *Spellfire now I sing;*

> *Noon light, sun bright,*
> *Come to my summoning!*

The air grew warmer as he turned again.

> *West wind, gull wing,*
> *Spelltide now I sing;*
> *Sunset light, wave bright,*
> *Come to my summoning!*

Now there was a hint of moisture in the air that brushed his cheek. Nodding in satisfaction, he turned once more.

> *North wind, raven wing,*
> *Spellstone now I sing;*
> *Moonlight, midnight,*
> *Come to my summoning!*

Air swirled deasil, fluttering the altar cloth. On the altar, the candle flared madly. Upward he pointed the wand.

> *As I have called you, now I compel—*
> *Sylphs, be still, await my will!*

Through word and rhythm lay the way to master the Spirits of the Air. The winds he had summoned hushed, but he could feel their pressure. The air quivered as if it held a flock of invisible birds.

Caolin took a deep breath and let it out carefully, as though the spell were a feather balanced on his finger. Then he looked down at the young man who sat silently beside the altar, seeing not him, but that other, whose binding was the purpose of his ritual.

In one of his books of ancient legends he had read how the Guardians had bound the wolf that would have destroyed the world with a chain made of impossible things—the roots of a mountain, the sound made by a moving cat, the breath of a fish—that was yet stronger than any dwarf-forged iron. The Blood Lord's task was easier: to leash the tongue of one young man who had never been known for eloquence—only to leash it, for if Julian were suddenly struck dumb, they would know that it was by sorcery. No, Caolin's goal was to keep Julian from using words to win a crown.

He cast more incense upon the charcoal. From a vellum packet he took a thin coil of dark hair, then reached out suddenly and plucked a few hairs from the head of the boy before him. The sorcerer began to twine them all together.

> As two in one are twined, these spirits now I bind
> In joy and in sorrow, today and tomorrow!
> So shall it be!

Three times he passed the twisted strand through the scented smoke that eddied from the silver bowl, chanting the rhyme; then he laid the plait upon the altar.

Now he unfolded a dirty scrap of paper. It was only a note to Lord Eric, but Julian had written it, and Julian's sprawling handwriting would be another link in the chain. Mañero had brought him the paper, and the hair. For a moment the little man's long nose and bright eyes were vivid in memory. He was a strange servant, but a useful one, as the sorcerer had foreseen. He must remember to reward him.

On the altar was a box with a square of dried ink. Caolin took the young man's hand, jabbed his thumb suddenly with a thorn and held the finger there while dark blood dripped onto the ink block. Abruptly he let go, and the boy sat back, sucking his thumb and staring at his master. But Caolin's attention was on Julian's note.

"These are the sounds of creation, the ordering of all reality—" he whispered the alphabet that had been old when the Ancients came—"and in their disorder, the breaking of beauty." Frowning, he dipped a quill into the ink and began to inscribe the letters backward across the page.

"By the written word, I bind thee—that your words shall reverse your meaning. So shall it be!"

When he was done, he laid the twisted hair upon the paper and folded it. More incense went into the bowl. The fumes eddied in the still air, swirling along the curve of the barrier that confined them. Caolin lifted the folded paper and held it in the smoke, took a careful breath, and gathered all of his concentration for the final step in the binding.

"These words are Julian's, and their breaking . . . this spell for Julian, of my making. . . . His tongue shall be trammeled, his thought confused, his spirit weighted, his eloquence unused! The breath be bound, the words not found." His voice deepened, and he swayed to the rhythm of the spell.

> *Thy words shall be dust—*
> *May the wind blow them away—*
> *By earth be thou bound!*
> *Thy words shall sear thy lips like fire—*
> *May the wind fan it till you fear to speak—*
> *By fire be thou bound!*
> *Thy words shall be like water—*
> *May the wind dry them on thy tongue—*
> *By water be thou bound!*
> *Thy words shall be like the wind—*
> *And like wind, may they blow away—*
> *By air be thou bound!*
> *Nor earth nor fire nor sea inspire;*
> *Nor shall the air thy meaning bear!*
> *By all the winds of north and south*
> *And east and west, I stop thy mouth!*
> *So shall it be! So shall it be!*
> *As Above, so Below—so shall it be!*

He cast the paper onto the coals, and in a moment he smelled the scorching of wood fiber and the reek of burning hair. Smoke billowed chokingly around them.

"There, it is done!" Caolin sat back. "Do you think it will hold?"

The young man's mouth opened, but no words came. His eyes widened. Curious, the sorcerer watched the captive's lips move, the soundless straining of throat muscles, the flutter, like a broken bellows, of the lungs.

"Didn't I tell you? The spell has to hold *you* utterly if a part of it is to bind *him*, but don't be afraid. After tomorrow's Council, I will lift it, for I will have need of your tongue, and it won't matter what our precious princeling says then."

Wind swirled suddenly and the candle winked out. Ashes scattered across the white cloth, and the owl feather lifted of its own accord and settled gently to the floor.

The breeze off the river had strengthened. The words of the hymn folk sang on the eve of the last day of the festival sounded louder as the wind carried them through the streets of Laurelynn.

> *Now we wander in our sorrow,*
> *Balanced between hope and fear,*
> *Longing for a fairer morrow*
> *For the folk who gather here—*
> > *Where is the Maiden? Where is she hidden?*
> > *When will she bring the blessings of Spring?*

Silverhair, following the others toward the palace, remembered his mother's sweet voice lifting in that song long ago when he and his sisters were small. He remembered singing it himself at spring festivals at the Hold, when he and Faris were the ones who wandered through the gardens, hiding colored eggs for the household's children to find when they made the final search at dawn.

> *Night and day in fragile balance*
> *Wait the turning of the tide.*
> *Will the powers of light advance,*
> *Or will the powers of dark abide?*
> > *Where is the Maiden? Where is She hidden?*
> > *When will she bring the blessings of Spring?*

Every year they sang, and the hours of light began to
grow longer than the hours of darkness. But there was
always that moment when all things hung in the balance,
when one wondered whether the Maiden really would
return, or whether this would be the year when the world
slid backward into winter again. And so the people carried their colored lanterns through the streets of Laurel-
lynn, garlanded with flowers.

What ritual could bring light into the lives of men?
The town was buzzing with rumors. Julian's terse ac-
count of the encounter with the Lord of Las Costas was
bad enough. But what had actually happened might be
less important than what people believed. Those who
spoke for each Estate would do the voting, but their decisions must represent a consensus. The provincial commanders would be meeting with their landholders long
into the night, seeking agreement as earnestly as now
folk searched for the Lady of Spring.

> Everywhere the dark is falling,
> Lanterns glimmer in the night;
> As the Mother searches, calling,
> We are looking for the Light—
>   Where is the Maiden? Where is she hidden?
>   When will she bring the blessings of Spring?

Along the dark streets, mothers were calling indeed,
seeking children who had taken too great an advantage
of the evening's liberty. The gate to the palace gardens
creaked as Silverhair pushed through.

The others were already gathered around the little
shrine. They had hung their lanterns upon the overhanging branches of the plum trees, and a breath of wind sent
light glimmering across the grass—pale rose and blue,
amethyst, and gold and green. Gowns and cloaks blos-
somed with soft splendor as it touched them.

With eyes thus enchanted and ears seduced by the
beauty of the song, it was hard to believe in hatred. A
flute picked up the melody, descanting sweetly while the
little ones laid their flowers upon the empty altar. So

Piper *was* here; he saw him now—part of the ceremony, and yet alone with his song.

And there was one other who stood alone, untouched by the lanterns' unstable light. Silverhair moved softly through the trees until the same shadow wrapped them both.

"Julian," he said desperately, "all will be well."

The boy let out his breath in a long, shaking sigh.

"You want me to hope, uncle, after you've . . . nagged me so long? If I'd learned a speech—your speech— maybe, but it is too late now. Tomorrow morning the Maiden's statue will be back on her altar. The children will cheer. And I will be before the Council, but who . . . will cheer . . . for me?" he said with difficulty. "With Alexander, what happened? I don't understand. I'm wandering in the darkness like the Lady, but I can't find my way."

Shaken by this abrupt capitulation, Silverhair put out a hand to Julian's sleeve. He had wanted the boy to listen to him, but not this way!

"It isn't too late, Julian. Come up to my chambers and I will find phrases for you that will sway them, or what was all of my training for?"

"Uncle, my lips will . . . *mangle* your words," Julian replied with a shaky laugh. But he let the harper draw him out of the darkness and up the stairs.

Around the shrine, they were singing once more.

> *Lady, listen to the living.*
> *Let the winter's cold be gone!*
> *Life and love Thy gift—in giving*
> *These, we greet Thee with the dawn!*
> *Here is the Maiden! In the heart she is hidden!*
> *Soon she will bring the blessings of Spring!*

The lamps had burned low when Julian left and balled scraps of paper scribbled with bits of the speech Silverhair had prepared for him littered the floor. Would it serve? Julian had learned the words, but could he say them? It had been so hard for him. Surely it was only performance anxiety, but Silverhair's nerves twitched with apprehension.

Julian is different, he told himself. *If the Wind Lord ever speaks to him, it will not be in the same voice he uses to me.*

Piper lay curled in his blankets, his flute on the pillow beside him. Silverhair had not even noticed him come in. The child's face was closed now, like a sleeping flower, but his cheek still glistened with the moisture of spent tears. Had the music of the flute not been enough? Had Piper remembered festival eves when he sang with the others and searched for colored eggs among the flowers?

Silverhair sighed and pinched out the pallid flicker of flame. The last of the lanterns had burnt out in the orchard below, and the town lay still under starlight. Whatever had upset the child was past. He felt weariness dragging at his bones and knew that there was no more he could do for Piper, or for Julian.

But the memory of Piper's fluting was like a Spirit singing in the night, enticing him into a series of dreams that misted one into another without apparent beginning or end. He was looking for something, or someone. Was it Julian? He could not remember. He knew only an ache of loss and the distant, desolate weeping of a child.

FOUR: Speech and Silence

Grass and trees blurred by; wind sang in Piper's ears. The other children were strung out across the grass behind him, shrieking like jays. Piper dove through a tangle of greenery, the sharp scent of bay laurel filling his lungs; then broke through into a blaze of sunlight.

"Piper! Piper! Go, Piper!"

Faces were all around him, mouths open, shouting. He missed a step—

"It's all right, Piper. Go on, take the prize!"

A familiar voice, and a familiar gleam of copper hair. *All right . . . safe here . . .* Something glittered, and he flung himself forward; fingers closed on the gritty surface of the sugar egg, intricately patterned red and green and gold. His breath grew easier, he met the Maiden's enigmatic stone smile.

"A good race!" said the steward of the palace. "And the prize well won. So, lad, and what's your name?"

Piper stepped away from the man's grin; a frightened squawk was all that would come.

"His name's Piper. He doesn't talk." Cub, still pant-

ing, answered for him. "If someone else had to win it,
I'm glad it was you!"

Piper was not quite quick enough to avoid the other
boy's punch, but it didn't matter. He hugged the brightly
colored egg to his chest, grinning.

"He won! Look, Piper won the boys' race!" cried
Rana. "Hurrah for the Companions!"

"Hurrah indeed. Let us take it as an omen, Julian."

That was Silverhair's voice, a light baritone with a
resonance that Piper would always recognize. Some of
the tightness within eased at the harper's smile.

The Prince was smiling too, but the warmth did not
reach his eyes. "I hope so."

"You're nervous, that's all. It was years before I could
eat dinner on a night when I was going to sing." Piper
could hear the anxiety Silverhair was trying to hide. Shyly
he offered the harper his sugar egg.

"What? No, child—it's the Wind Crystal we need now.
Share the egg with your friends." The words were for
Piper, but Silverhair's eyes were still on Julian. Slowly,
Piper took back the egg. Some of the brightness had
gone out of the day.

"The Council Hall will be filling up by now." Silverhair turned to the Prince. "We should go."

"Yes," Julian sighed. His big hand brushed the boy's
shoulder. "You did well, Piper. Take care of your prize."

Piper watched them go. *If it had been the Jewel, Silverhair would have let me give it to him.* He looked down
at the egg, surprised to see an ovoid of colored sugar
instead of shining crystal.

"Aren't you going to eat it?" Cub eyed the egg wistfully. Silently, Piper placed it in his friend's hands.

"Into whose hands shall we deliver the Kingdom of
Westria?" Tanemun peered up at the rows of brightly
clad holders crowded into the Council Hall and sighed.
"For two days we have debated this decision. But it must
be made, and soon. I call upon all of you to seek within
your hearts for the wisdom to choose well."

"He makes it sound about as exciting as buying a new cow." Robert crossed his arms with a sigh.

"That may be a good thing," Frederic answered from Julian's other side. "These folk take care of their livestock."

"Well, he's a prime piece of beef." Robert punched Julian's arm. "They ought to be satisfied."

A smile forced its way past Julian's frozen lips. He could feel the warmth of his friends' bodies to either side. Without them, he would have been shivering, although the day was mild. He wanted to thank them, but he could not find the words.

"I'll speak then." Philip stood up and looked around. "And I'll try to be brief, for I think that I may have contributed to the confusion. It is simple enough. We need a leader who will put the good of the land before his own. We need someone whom folk will follow, and who will listen to what they say. Yet if necessary, he must be able to decide what to do . . . and have the energy to do it.

"A leader"—he paused with a half-smile—"no, a queen, or a king. The land might survive without someone to carry the staff, but would it still be Westria?"

"Thank the Guardians for that!" said Eric from the Regent's throne. "Lord Philip should know that this is no time to be pondering philosophies like a first-year student at the College of the Wise. Yesterday he called this an opportunity. I call it a crisis! And you don't meet a crisis by questioning the truths you've lived by. We need a strong leader to pull this country together, and we need him *now*. That's why we need a king. When that damned fortress is gone from the top of the Red Mountain, I'll be happy to discuss theories with Philip over a bottle of wine."

Laughter gusted through the chamber. Julian let out his breath again. They were both right, really. But was there ever a time of such security that the reasons for things could be debated at leisure, or were great events always the forge on which men must beat out their philosophies?

"Do not despise the students. They may be wiser in their innocence than men of greater years in their experience." A quiet voice brought immediate stillness to the hall. Heads turned as the Mistress of the College levered herself to her feet; astonished as if one of the beasts carven into the frieze below the ceiling had come down off the wall.

It was the first time she had spoken in this Council. Frederic said that even at the college she rarely emerged from her rooms. He must ask the Master of the Junipers what could be done when—if—he ever became king. If the College renounced its power, was it any wonder that Westria was faltering?

"Time spent seeking self-awareness is never wasted." Her dark gaze swept the chamber, and Julian was suddenly convinced that she knew exactly what stories were being told. "The way of Westria may not be the best form of government, but I can tell you why it was chosen for our land. . . . Do you remember the Cataclysm?" After that first movement, the Mistress had become still, as if her voice had absorbed all of her power.

"Perhaps you think that a silly question? Like all legends, it is easy to take for granted. Each of the lands born from the chaos of the Cataclysm has its own virtue, and the gift of Westria is to honor the other kindreds with whom we share the world. All men must maintain the balance, but not all know how to speak to the Guardians. The ruler of such a land must be a walker between the worlds, one who can master the elements. It is a lasting dedication, and easier if one is bred up to it. From parent to child the power is passed, until the pattern breaks or the line fails."

"But the pattern has been broken." Loysa Gilder stood up. "Julian of Stanesvale was not raised to be king."

"He is still the blood heir of House Starbairn, which has led us for five hundred years. He is descended from the priestess who made the four Jewels." From the heralds' bench, Mistress Anne answered her.

"We were talking about training—"

"Julian of the Stones is being trained and tested as no

king of Westria has been since Julian the Great battled
the sorcerers long ago!'' The voice of the Master of the
Junipers cut across her words.''The powers that were
given to his predecessors unasked, Julian must earn, and
learn how to use—''

"But will Westria survive his education?'' Loysa's
gesture of appeal was directed not to the commanders,
but to the landholders on the benches behind them. "How
many of you lost kindred while he was trying to master
the Sea Star last year? Guardians preserve us from the
inept enthusiasms of a power-mad boy!''

"Would you have had us lie down tamely while the
sea reivers picked our bones?'' exclaimed Lady Rosemary, who spoke for Seagate while Eric was confined to
the forced neutrality of the Regent's chair.

"There have always been raiders. Were these so different from those we have fought every other year? Julian
seems to have thought he was fighting a war. Did you
know he is commissioning warships as if he were king
already. What must Prince Ali think of that? If we give
Julian the crown, Elaya will be sure we mean war!''

"'Julian is young, and young men are always hot-
heads,'' Eric burst out. "Surely I should know. But with
experienced advisors—''

"You don't seem to have controlled him so far. Will
he take your advice once he is on the throne?'' Loysa
asked acidly, and a murmur of agreement answered her.

"Whew!'' said Robert softly. "You could file iron with
that tongue. Lord Eric can speak for himself, but anyone
who thinks you are a hothead clearly doesn't know you
very well.''

"No,'' Julian sighed. "That's the trouble. We should
have waited—'' he swallowed "until I had all four of the
Jewels.''

Especially the Wind Crystal, the unspoken thought
went on.

"Julian's actions in Seagate were necessary,'' rumbled
Eric, "and they had my approval. What did you know
about it, sitting safe in Laurelynn? Great Guardians, do

you think I would have let him play games with my own province?"

"I think you would have done anything to get your son back again," said Loysa.

Eric flushed dangerously. Julian started as Frederic jumped to his feet beside him. His voice cut through the babble in the hall.

"You have been misinformed. My father would not barter with outlaws, nor would I." Frederic sounded quite composed, but his face had gone as pale as his father's was dark with anger. "Ask the men of Seagate who were there, the men whom Julian's wisdom allowed to reach port safely, while the enemy was destroyed by the storm."

Julian winced, recalling only too vividly how he had felt when he thought his devotion to duty had condemned his friend.

"I begin to see why you love him," whispered Robert.

"Don't envy him," answered Julian. "I don't want ever . . . to have to worry like that about you."

"We could argue 'till the Dorada runs dry and get no further," said Eric suddenly. "It doesn't matter what *I* think . . . I'm not a candidate for the crown. If you question Julian's judgment, then question *him*! I think it is time we stopped discussing him like a steer at a fair."

"I told you it was a cattle show," whispered Robert. Julian swallowed, but his throat was dry, his tongue like leather in his mouth.

"I agree!" Loysa Gilder answered with edged sweetness. "Let Sir Julian speak on his own behalf."

I can't do it! Julian rubbed his sweating hands along the skirts of his tunic. *Give me a stone to shape, or a ship to sail.* Desperately he looked around, and Frederic, not understanding, smiled. *Give me an enemy I can slay with my sword!*

"What say you all?" asked Tanemun. "Is it your will that Julian of the Stones be called before you here?"

"Let him speak!" said Lord Philip. "I'll hear him gladly," said Sandremun. But their agreement was lost in a general babble. In the end, even Alexander of Las Costas nodded, and Julian groaned, for he had counted on his enemy to save him.

Lead-footed, Julian made his way down the stairs to the Council floor. He remembered enough to bow to the hearth, and saw that they were setting a bench for him in front of Tanemun. He tried to find strength in memory of the impossible things he had done already, but he had never felt such pressure at the roots of the Red Mountain, or such terror in the depths of the sea.

He took his place before the bench, seeking to steady his breathing as the hall grew quiet around him.

The Seneschal cleared his throat. "Julian of the Stones, you have been proposed as a candidate for the throne of Westria. Is this with your will?"

Julian forced sound past numb lips. "It is."

He had sworn himself to this service at his knighting, and there was no escape from it. He wondered if the Lady of Westria would let him fulfill his vow as a simple member of the border patrol.

"By what right do you claim eligibility for the crown?"

"By right . . . of descent from Julian the Great. By right of mastery of two of the Jewels." He breathed a little easier.

"Members of the Council—" Tanemun turned—"Sir Julian of the Stones stands before you. You have heard his answers to the first challenges. His health and wholeness you can see. The law of Westria confirms his eligibility for consideration. My lords and ladies, what other questions would you put to him now?"

Lord Philip rose in place. "As you have stated, your descent gives you a right to be considered for the crown. Do you think that because you are son to our last king, the crown *belongs* to you?"

Julian shook his head. He knew that Philip had meant the question as an opportunity. They had even talked about the answers. But where were the words?

"No more . . . than it belongs to *you*," he managed,

and waited out the murmur of laughter. "My birth only gives me a responsibility."

Philip grinned and sat down again.

"The reivers you fought this summer were mostly Elayan." Lady Rosemary speaking for Seagate, was standing now. "Should we take revenge upon Elaya?"

This too, had been discussed before.

"No." Julian searched for the rest of the answer. "When I was born, Elaya was . . . fighting us, because Westrian soldiers . . . had raided across the border. We said the men . . . should have been punished, not the nation, as I . . . as we . . . punished the reivers last year."

He had answered, but it had been like trying to walk against the wind, and these first three questions had been friendly!

"It's getting worse. Soon you won't be able to say anything." Words whispered inside his skull. *"You're a stonecutter, not a wordsmith . . . you'll fail."* He remembered saying something like that to Silverhair, not so long ago.

Julian licked dry lips as Loysa Gilder stood, cast a swift glance at Fredegar Sachs, who sat behind her, then favored him with a false smile.

"We have heard a great deal of debate regarding the relationship of king and kingdom. Let Sir Julian tell us how he defines it. What does it mean to be Westria's king?"

There was a little rustle along the benches as men settled themselves expectantly. *Getting ready to hear a nice piece of oratory,* thought Julian. Silverhair had predicted this. Snatches of the speech the harper had made him memorize rioted in Julian's head.

"The king is the center of the circled cross. He is the point of balance, he—" suddenly the rest of the phrase was gone. "He balances them—the elements," he finished lamely. What came next?

"The king is the head of the kingdom, but a head without a body—" His throat closed. Someone suppressed a laugh. Memory flailed desperately. A moment ago the rest had been on the tip of his tongue, but now thought and speech were severed. Severed. . . . "If the head's cut off, it's dead!"

I wish I were dead! thought Julian. Fear sent tiny tremors through his body. He clenched his fists in the skirts of his tunic, planted his feet more firmly and drew up support from the earth until his limbs were still. The strength of earth that was in him would not let him give way. *I have already been buried,* he remembered. *Why am I so afraid?*

"The king lives for his land . . . and dies for it!" The tracery of scars at his temple where the sorcerer had once struck him tingled. "He *is* the—" Fear closed around him like a thick, white web; he fought for breath. Panicking, he cast his awareness into the dark currents of the sea and let them carry him away.

". . . carried on its rhythms, bound to its seasons," he heard himself say. But with awareness, the paralysis returned. He tried to moisten his lips, but they were burning.

"Thy words sear thy lips; the wind dries them on thy tongue," said that whisper within. *"Thy words are dust— the wind blows them away."*

He had heard that whisper before . . . in his nightmares? *This* was a nightmare from which he could not awaken! His gaze sought the Master of the Junipers; for a moment, doubled vision saw him hunched on his bench, yet standing like a tower in the midst of the people while walls of light rose around them. *That voice! I know. . . .* Julian tried to raise his own barriers, but the enemy was already within.

"Is that all you wish to say?" Tanemun's voice seemed to come from a great distance. How long had Julian's silence gone on?

I offer my service to all of you, and through you, to the land of Westria . . . until the Lady of Westria releases me or my life ends; this I swear in the name of the Guardian of Men! That vow came from the depths of his spirit. Had he spoken it aloud?

His senses expanded. He could not find his own words,

but suddenly he was hearing the inner dialogue of everyone in the hall: a confusion of fatigue, disapproval, disappointment and, more clearly, Robert's indignation, Rana's pain, Silverhair's frustrated fury . . . and from someone, a sudden flare of pure malevolent glee.

"Are you finished?" There was kindness in Tanemun's voice. Julian turned to him in mute appeal, and remembered suddenly how only that morning, Piper had offered them his prize.

This is how Piper feels, always.

"You may be seated, my lord," said the Seneschal. Julian nodded. His tongue was bound, but he could still master his body. Stiffly he climbed the steps. Frederic reached out to help him sit down. Robert squeezed his arm.

"What happened?" he whispered. Julian shook his head.

"My lords, my ladies—" Alexander's voice cut through the babble of comment—"we should thank Sir Julian for a most . . . helpful . . . statement. After that, what is left to say?" Irony sharpened to something harder as he went on. "If Julian wants to serve Westria, well, he has proved that he can swing a sword. But not the staff! A king must be more than a brawling bully. What kind of a sovereign stands tongue-tied before his Council? No, my friends. This man has made his incompetence clear. Let him use his sword in whatever army he chooses, but we must find someone else to sit upon the throne!"

There were several minutes when the tumult in the Council Hall was louder than the roaring in Julian's ears. Then a clarion blast split sound from silence. In the startled stillness, a woman's voice came clear. Green cloak gleaming, Mistress Anne stepped onto the floor.

"I am not a member of this Council, but I beg your indulgence. For twenty years Westria has survived under a Regency. Can we not endure a few months more? Despite the debate, Julian has been our only real candidate. If he is rejected, it will take time to choose again. At the turning of autumn, let us meet and make the decision then.''

Alexander looked thunderous, but everywhere men were acclaiming the compromise.

"May the Lady be praised!" said Frederic, sinking back with a sigh.

But the voice Julian heard came from elsewhere.

"Do you think that six months will save you? Your words are blowing away on the wind!"

That voice had taunted him before, on Spear Island. He tried to speak, but no words would come. Shaking, Julian at last understood what had been done to him.

"I can't ask him if he wants to see you," Robert said. "Julian hasn't spoken since we came back from the Council Hall."

Rana stared at him, the hood sliding back from her windblown hair. "Not to you? Not even to Frederic?"

Robert stood silhouetted in the doorway to Julian's chambers. For a moment, he stiffened. Then he shook his head.

"Frederic has gone to fetch the Master of the Junipers. Maybe *he* can get Julian to see that this is not total disaster."

Rana sighed. "You're right. There's something strange here." She followed Robert into the comfortable disorder of the outer chamber, draping her cloak across the others on the chair by the door. "Julian has never let setbacks stop him before, and when you think of some of the dangers. . . ." She fell silent, remembering, and saw from Robert's face that he had his own memories.

"I'm sorry I shouted at you." She lifted a battered bow case from a camp stool and sat down. Someone's uneaten supper was still on the table, next to a pile of books and a half bottle of wine. "I was worried."

That did not begin to express the turmoil she had battled in deciding to come here. Today words seemed to have deserted them all. "Let me see him, Robert. Maybe he will respond to me."

As the lamplight fell full on Robert's handsome features, she glimpsed in his eyes the pain.

"Do you love him?" His voice was harsh.

A month ago she would have said "of course" and never guessed that those words might have a different meaning for Julian. But what had happened at Misthall had given a new and terrifying meaning to the word "love." Robert must have known all along; only she—in her innocence—had assumed that Julian was unlike other men.

"Never mind—" Robert continued while she was still searching for a reply. "He would be furious if he knew I had asked you that question. It doesn't matter anyway, if you can help him."

But it does matter, she thought as she stood up. Robert was gazing at the shut door with the same look in his eyes that she had seen in Julian's, and she realized suddenly that he had a secret too.

The draft as she pulled the door open set the candle aflutter, but the dark shape on the bed never moved. Julian's room had the same stark neatness she remembered from their days on the road, when his pack had always been the most securely wrapped and quickly stowed. Outside, the wind was rising; somewhere a branch tapped fitfully.

There was no peace in this room, despite the stillness. Julian's breathing was too carefully controlled.

"Julian," she said aloud. "You haven't lost all hope of the crown. In six months—" But he must know that; it was the first thing Robert and the others would have said to him. "Julian, don't punish yourself like this. Don't punish *us*! I can see that you are hurting. Won't you tell me—"

Julian's breathing grew suddenly ragged and she stopped, appalled by her own stupidity. He must think she was mocking him.

"Julian, say something," she whispered. "Curse me if you have to, only . . ." She touched his shoulder.

He moved with sudden violence, curling away from her, knees drawn up, head down. Her throat aching with pity, Rana retreated. Julian had not needed to speak, after all. She could read in his bent back the denial for which he would not, or could not, find words.

"The word is mightier than the sword, but you are mightier still, for you command silence!" Ordrey lifted his goblet and grinned at his master.

Caolin smiled slightly. The occasion did seem to call for celebration, and Fredegar Sachs' cellars were famous. The goldsmith had sent up several bottles of dry white wine from Las Costas, but no wine ever pressed could match the intoxication of pure power.

"Here's to th' Blood Lord!" Mañero stuck his long nose into his cup and gulped his drink down.

Ordrey grimaced. He had just returned from a journey to Elaya; his round face and bald crown were red from sun and wind. But Caolin knew that his habitual pink plumpness would be restored by a few days' rest. He noted with amusement that his old servant did not seem to approve of his new one. It did not matter, so long as they both obeyed.

Ordrey poured more wine, and his frown faded. Only the man who was and was not Julian stared unhappily, and that made Caolin smile once more. He had done his work well.

Suddenly, Mañero belched, then broke into song, splashing wine onto the floor.

> *Have you heard of the Blood Lord?*
> *He has no need to swing a sword—*
> *He is as mighty with a word!*

On the Red Mountain, such conviviality would have been bad for discipline, but this was Laurelynn. Caolin's foot caressed the Elayan rug that cushioned the floor. It had been a long time since he had lived in such luxury.

> *The Blood Lord knows the many ways*
> *To wield his weapons to amaze—*
> *To catch a thought and—*

Mañero laughed and shook his head. "Can't think of an ending!" One bright eye glinted over the edge of the cup at Caolin.

"—and turn a phrase," added the sorcerer indulgently. Ordrey looked up in surprise.

"You are merry, my lord!"

"Merry?" Caolin raised an eyebrow. That was a response for men who did not share his disciplines. But surely he could permit himself some small satisfaction. "My long exile is ending at last, and my enemy is in my power."

"Through the magic of the word?" asked Ordrey.

"My words. Don't you yet understand? I am Master of the Powers of Air." Caolin rose and moved to the window, his robe whispering across the thick rug. In the garden below, rustling branches shared secrets in the dark.

"I am the wand that writes the fates, I am the sword that separates potential from possibility. From my throat comes the vibration that unmakes the world." The sorcerer turned suddenly, and his mute captive shrank back.

"Who am I?" he half-sang, and suddenly the other three were trapped; the mental bond thrummed like a cord.

"You are the master . . ." came the reply from two voices as the third man choked, his throat muscles working helplessly.

"Let him go," whispered Mañero. "We will all sing like birds together. Set him free."

Caolin put his hands on either side of his captive's head, holding his gaze, and allowed the hum he heard with his inner senses to vibrate the cords of his own throat. At this moment he had no need of candles and talismans; the sound was the spell.

"As Katiz was bound, I bound you—in speech and act, in dream and fact," he chanted. "In Katiz' name, I loose you—in word and deed—to serve my need!" He could feel the fellow trembling between his hands.

"Julian, listen, your voice is returning; the words of

men once more you're learning. But as you speak, remember still, your speech or silence awaits my will!"

The sorcerer stroked gently along the exposed throat with his fingertips, bent, pressed his lips to the other man's, then drew away.

"It is done," he said softly. "Julian, speak to me."

"Master. . . ." The boy swallowed, then sighed. "I was afraid—"

"There is nothing to fear, so long as you obey," answered Caolin. "So long as you remember that the words belong to me."

There was a short silence.

"Good enough!" said Mañero, picking up the bottle and belching again. "So long as this wine belongs to me!"

Piper held out a mug of tea, but Silverhair reached past him to the jug of wine. Dark drops splashed like blood across the table as he poured again. Piper clasped cold fingers around the warmth of the mug. He had seen the harper this way only a few times before, but he remembered the flush across the cheekbones, the beginning of a slur in the harper's words. Was Silverhair going to turn into that person he did not know?

"No kin of mine," mumbled Silverhair. "A short piece—you'd think he could have learned it—but there's no poetry in the man, no music in him at all." He drank, and Piper, feeling the mug growing cooler between his hands, sipped at the tea himself. "No child of my own, ever, only Julian—but he's not mine, blood or spirit! How could he fall apart this way?"

Piper heard the pain, set down the tea and brought the harp from its bench beside the bed. Silverhair looked up at him with a grimace that was meant for a smile. But instinctively he cradled the harp against himself. Thin fingers tested the strings.

"Swangold has never let me down. Never, through all our years together!" He adjusted a peg until the note rang true.

"Stubborn! Stubborn and dumb. Julian will never let

me teach him!'' His fingers drew from the strings a minor melody with the clarity of barren mountains against
the stars. Piper took up his flute and echoed it.

''Perhaps I should go back to the desert. At least it
was warm. I could go to Willasfell—'' He gave a bark
of laughter as Piper's music shifted to one of his own
melodies. ''You remember that song?''

Piper nodded.

''I wonder what happened to that child. I thought I did
the right thing. I couldn't take her with me, but I should
have gone back to see her. She was the Willa, Piper . . .
more powerful than a queen. But she wanted to come
with me.'' He grimaced. ''*She* valued my skills! *She*
talked to me!''

The music the harper was drawing from Swangold's
strings grew ragged. He played one-handed, holding his
cup with the other, and as he drank, the music disintegrated until Piper could no longer follow it. He shook
the flute to get rid of the spittle and slipped it back into
its case at his belt.

''Wasted,'' whispered Silverhair. ''My whole life's
wasted, and why? Eighteen years of searching for someone who was dead before my journey began. I was looking for a child's dream.'' He set the harp on the table,
pulled the jug to his chest. ''Two years following a farm-
bred lout who will never make a king . . . even if that
could justify the rest. I'm growing old. And there is no
meaning in my life at all!''

Piper began to shiver. The harper had refused the food
he brought, and now the harp. Feelings for which he had
no names ached in his throat. Music was the only language they shared. Desperate, he pushed the harp toward
Silverhair again.

''Oh, no. You'll not catch me in that snare!'' Swangold fell over, and strings hummed in muted protest as
the harper's hands closed on the boy's skinny shoulder.

Whimpering, Piper was jerked around. Harsh breath,
a sour reek of wine, and the cruel hands holding him
sent awareness fleeing in a confusion of past and present
realities.

"Speak to me, you little idiot! You're trying to cheat me, you and Julian, so I'll die without—"

Sounds without meaning, shaking that made his teeth clatter in his skull. A scream strained Piper's throat, but memory supplied the feel of a reiver's hard hand across his mouth. Mind fluttered frantically. Trapped, awareness whirled away, until there was only a small, struggling animal.

"You *can* speak, damn it!"

Terror twisted free. There was the crash of a larger body falling, but the point of panic that was Piper huddled, whimpering, as the room grew still.

Run . . . get away! His galloping pulse steadied and vision returned. Silverhair was lying on the floor, his breathing harsh and slow. *Run . . . he'll wake!* Piper got to his feet, wrapped his cloak around himself. Carefully he set Swangold upright.

The harper never moved as Piper tiptoed to the door and scrambled down the stairs into the windy darkness. Every tapping branch was a pursuing footstep, every fluttering shadow an enemy. Only flight could save him. But where?

A memory from the morning echoed: *"It's the Wind Crystal we need now . . ."* If he could have given Silverhair the Crystal, the harper would have been happy. *The wind knows where it is. Find it, and everything will be all right again. Faster, faster!* Piper began to run once more, chasing the wind.

FIVE: A Bird on the Wing

"I've lost him." Silverhair's head was throbbing, but
he welcomed the pain. It distracted him from memory.
Morning light gleamed painfully from the burnished
metal and ceramic glaze of the palace breakfast room.
He closed his eyes.

"You don't know—" began Rosemary, but the harper
shook his head.

"I know enough! I was angry . . . not at Piper, but
he might have thought so. When I woke this morning,
he was gone."

"Had you been drinking?" Frederic's voice was very
quiet.

"Frederic, that hardly matters—" the Regent began,
but Silverhair stopped him.

"It does matter," he said with difficulty. The Queen
of Normontaine had told him so, and others had said it
as well. He remembered the disgust in Julian's eyes when
he had sought to numb the sorrow after his harp had been
destroyed. He had avoided wine after that . . . for a
while.

"When I drink . . . I say things." How hard *these* words were to say!

"You were upset about the Council. We all were," said Eric.

"Don't try to excuse me!" cried Silverhair. "Don't you see, I've excused myself too many times. A little relaxation—a way to ease the pain—I know all the excuses there are. And maybe they are valid, for other men. But not for me anymore!"

He took a deep breath and fought nausea as the reek of cooking food caught in his throat. Rosemary put a mug of strong tea in his hand.

"That poor child," she murmured. "That poor, wounded child."

"Yes," he answered her. "And wounded again by the one he trusted most. I might even have struck him—I can't remember! Where could he go?" Silverhair clasped the cup, trying to draw some of its warmth into his cold hands. Even Julian's failure in the Council meant little now; the Prince was still alive, there would be another day. But for Piper, what hope was there, speechless and alone?

"I'll set the city guard to searching," said Eric. "And send messengers along the main roads."

Silverhair looked up at him, and the Regent's face told him that he too remembered another search, long ago. Faris had run from the Blood Lord as Piper had run from him. How, then, was he different from Caolin? The city guards had found no trace of Faris and her baby twenty years before. Would they do better at locating one skinny child?

"And what about you?" asked Frederic then.

"Leave him alone, boy—he has enough to bear. Is that the kind of courtesy they're teaching you at the College of the Wise?" Eric growled.

Frederic continued to watch the harper. At the moment, he looked uncomfortably like the Master of the Junipers.

Not courtesy, but priestcraft, Silverhair thought then.

"Don't scold him, Eric. He's right. I have spent most of my life running away from things."

But even now, he could not face Eric's concern, Rosemary's affection, the implacable compassion in Frederic's eyes. He turned away. Through the window he saw a skein of waterfowl unraveling across the sky.

"I can't drink. That escape is closed to me now." His voice grated in his ears, and even with his head throbbing and his throat aching with loss, he wanted the first fiery jolt of the wine and the numbing insulation that came after.

"I want you to witness this." he shivered again. "I take oath now, in the name of the Guardian of Men and the Lady of Westria. I swear this by the Wind Lord, and . . ." he whispered . . . "and by that music which is life to me. I will touch no wine, no spirits, from this day forward. May the power of song be stricken from me if I fail!"

Never again . . . never again, lamented the thirst within him. But Rosemary had put her arms around him, a small protection against the pain.

"Don't condemn yourself," said Frederic softly. "If you fail, you will start over, and be healed by your song. But we will help you, and you will not fail."

They loved him. Even knowing what he was, what he had done. Silverhair's throat ached with words he did not yet know how to say.

Wind Lord, forgive me, he prayed, *and let us find the child!*

The wind blew south and east, ruffling the slow-moving surface of the Darkwater and rustling in the tall oak trees. Piper crouched in an elder thicket as the barge on which he had stowed away in Laurelynn slid away down the green tunnel of the stream.

He had hidden here since just before dawn, afraid that movement would give him away, waiting until the bargemen cooked their breakfast and packed their bedrolls, watching them work the poles back out of the mud and, cursing, get the unwieldy craft moving against the sluggish current again. As the barge dwindled in the distance, the deep-voiced chant of the polemen blew back upon the breeze.

Piper bit into the apple in his hand, its skin a little wrinkled from storage, but its flesh firm and good. His nose wrinkled at the sweet scent—for over a week he had smelled nothing but apples, *he* smelled of apples—but his stomach welcomed the food. Like an echo, the incessant gnawing of the beavers resumed. There was a burst of exasperated chittering as they discovered where the bargemen had pulled the poles that blocked the channel away.

The river was growing shallow here; shadowy fish shapes danced across the glitter of fool's gold on the bottom, and Piper eyed them hungrily. Nearby, a blue heron poised, waiting for its prey.

The bargemen would unload their cargo at the Gateway landing. Piper imagined sunlight glaring into his hiding place, rough hands holding him, harsh voices asking questions. Once again fear clamped his throat, but the only sound was the squeaky *kong-ka-ree, kong-ka-ree* of a redwinged blackbird in the willow tree. The trees made a green wall behind him, laced with driftwood from the spring floods. He would hear any intruders long before they could come upon him here.

He pursed his lips and echoed the blackbird's song. After a moment of surprised silence, the bird answered, and he smiled. With a last call, the blackbird swooped low over the water, scooping up insects from the hovering cloud.

It had been time for Piper to leave the barge anyway, for the wind that guided him was blowing eastward now, toward the white peaks that floated above the valley's haze.

His stomach growled. The air was heavy with the moist smell of greenery, but he couldn't eat leaves, and it was too early for blackberries. Before he fought his way out to the grasslands, he needed food.

Piper slipped off his boots. Then he waded through

the tules into the cool water and imitated the heron, waiting for a fish to swim between his open hands.

"As well search for a single fish in the sea as one boy upon the roads of Westria!" said Robert. A last plum blossom drifted down, and he dashed it away.

"There has been no word of him?"

The Master of the Junipers spoke gently, but Julian could hear the overtones of anxiety through the whisper of the wind among the new leaves. Since words had failed him in the Council Hall, he had learned to listen more carefully to others, and not just to what they *said*. . . .

"There's no trace of him here in the city, and the riders we sent along the main roads found nothing. It has been over a week . . . he could be anywhere."

Julian tried to force sound through his lips and coughed. The Master turned quickly, and clinging to the adept's deep gaze, Julian felt a little of the tension ease. He drew breath again.

"How . . . is . . . Silverhair?"

"He wanted to run off to search for the child—" the priest's gaze went inward—"as he did once before. But we made him see it is useless with no idea where to go. I am not sure that was wise. It is very hard for him to do nothing but wait for news."

Julian nodded. Frederic had told his friend of that odd, wrenching scene in Lady Rosemary's rooms on the morning after Piper disappeared.

"He . . . has not come to me," whispered Julian. He *could* speak if he forced his body to obey his will. Whatever binding the Blood Lord had laid upon him was gone—now his own fear was silencing him.

"He feels that he failed you, and combined with his guilt over Piper. . . ." The Master shook his head.

"Tell—" Julian began. *Tell him* . . . No more would come. And what good would such secondhand comfort be? Perhaps tomorrow he would nerve himself to leave his chambers and go to his uncle.

Even if I can only listen to his pain. Julian remembered how he had once prided himself on being a man

of deeds, not of words. *I chose silence.* He understood
that now. Had Piper chosen to be silent too?

Julian gazed across the grass that glimmered as the
afternoon light filtered through the shifting leaves. Another man sat there, his face upturned to the sunlight, a
man who had been known as Malin Scar in the days
when he was the Blood Lord's servant and his task was
to hunt Silverhair down.

"What about him?" Strangely, that question came
easily.

Curiosity stirred in the adept's dark eyes. Then a kind
of brightening for a moment revealed the beauty that lay
within that rather ugly face and bent body; Julian had
seen it once or twice before. The Master smiled as if he
understood the question better than Julian himself.

"Even for him, there is hope of healing. After his
attack on me, he saw too much too quickly for the mind
to comprehend. Too much light can blind the senses as
well as too much darkness. But he can speak now, though
he rarely has much to say."

Malin Scar looked around then, and his eyes met Julian's—eyes darker than the Master's—but no longer light-
less. There was a secret behind them, but now it was
Julian who was afraid to understand.

The Master was finishing—"He has certainly become
quite adept at taking care of me."

Wryly, he tapped the staff that was more to him now
than a magician's tool. He had never really recovered
from the stroke that felled him at the beginning of the
search for the Earthstone, but one forgot that; the Master
of the Junipers' own silences hid his pain.

Is that true for everyone? wondered Julian. The trees
rustled in answer, but he could not understand them.
Malin Scar serves the Master as Piper served Silverhair,
he told himself then, *but who will accept such silent service from me?*

Piper picked up the sticks that had fallen from the
armload the farmer was carrying and pushed through the
massed lilac flowers of the ceanothus to follow him. Be-

fore him, the foothills rolled away in folds of red purple. The air hummed with the ecstatic song of hurrying bees. This was a country of red earth and gold and purple flowers, of scrub oaks and scattered pines. It was pinewood they carried, fuel for the holding below. Then the man turned. Piper tensed, ready to drop the wood and flee.

"What're ye doing there? I told ye to be off, didn't I?"

Piper stood his ground, shaking his head, until the farmer sighed.

"Ye want work, is that it? Well, *say* something, lad!"

Once more Piper shook his head, opening his mouth helplessly. He wanted to wing upward into the great mountains that hung like a luminous mirage above the forests' dark clouds. But before he could go on, he needed rest and food.

"What is it? Ye can't speak? Reivers' work, I'll warrant. I've seen it before. Well, ye seem honest . . . come on, then!" the farmer added suddenly. "The Guardians know there's work enough in garden and stable for a lad at this time of year, and it won't strain our storeroom to feed one mouth more."

The man strode off as if ashamed of his generosity, but Piper, following, began to whistle a tune that held the warmth of the spring sun, the ripple of birdsong, the color of all of the flowers of a Westrian spring, and the resinous fragrance of the pine branches in his arms.

Rana took a deep breath of pine-scented steam and slowly let it out, feeling as if she had inhaled all of the woods in Westria. The walls of the stillroom disappeared, and for a moment she was back on the road to Ravensgate. She could almost feel the sun on her back and hear the hush of the waves on the rocks far below. Then the scent faded, and with it, the memory. Her eyes were stinging, and Rana could not tell if it were from the sharpness of the fragrance or from longing for a time when she had known neither love nor pain.

She blinked at Lady Rosemary. "What is it for?"

"Chest troubles, and worry." The older woman settled the glass top back over the mesh where the pine needles lay, and added fuel to the flames that were keeping the water in the vat below it boiling merrily. Rana drew the bracing scent carefully into her lungs, feeling their expansion. A tingle spread through her limbs.

"For Julian?" Rana asked. Rosemary nodded, her eyes on the glass tube that ran through the trough of cold water that was being pumped up from the river. Where the water drained away, the pipe continued on into a glass jar.

"The oils hold the spirit of the plant as well as its physical essence, and so they work both on both the body and the spirit of man."

"Just breathing it should plant the idea of opening up in his mind!" Rana wondered if the scent would make Julian remember the coast road too, if he would remember how strong and steady he had been at the beginning of their quest for the Jewels.

"It's not ideas we want, but something deeper. Scent sends messages to a part of the mind that cannot be reached by words. If rational argument did any good, Julian would be singing like a mockingbird. His conscious mind knows that there's no reason why he can't speak freely," said Rosemary.

"But something stronger is holding him back?" Rana frowned. "Julian has always seemed so . . . controlled . . . even when *Sea Brother* nearly went under. Even when he . . ." Her voice faltered. Julian's expression had not been controlled at Misthall. But he had kept himself from speaking. He had learned emotion from the sea, and it was *her* fault that he dared not give way to it. Maybe the habit of denial had grown too strong; was that why Julian was speechless now?

Rosemary gave her a quick glance and then pointed to the jar. "See, the vapor is condensing already." Rana got a grip on herself and peered obediently into the jar.

"It looks like water."

"Yes, but with a little time, most of the oil will rise to the top where it can be skimmed off. The liquid that remains will make a good astringent for clearing the skin or washing wounds.'' Rosemary poured more warm water into the boiler.

"Will you teach me?'' Rana asked suddenly. "I don't want to go home while things are still so unsettled, but I must have something useful to do, and this—'' perhaps the scent had begun to heal her too, for she felt more at peace than she had since she came to Laurelynn—"if it's allowed. . . .''

"I learned the basic procedures at the College of the Wise,'' said Rosemary. "But since then, I've been experimenting, and this knowledge is mine to share.'' The older woman smiled. "Distilling works best with the aromatic herbs. The essences can be used in medicines, heated for inhaling, or mixed with neutral oils for absorption through the skin through massage. Other herbs must be treated in other ways . . . dried and powdered, or made into tinctures or infusions.

"They are all here—'' Lady Rosemary gestured proudly toward the shelves crammed with bottles and bags and packets of herbs. As the scent of pine faded, Rana smelled a dizzying variety of other fragrances, as if every odor in the world had been collected in that small room.

She recognized some of them; her mother used to give her madrone bark tea for stomachaches, and mugwort for cramps. There were mullein leaves, which made a good tea for coughs, and next to them she saw a flask of oil.

"What is this for?''

"Oil made from the mullein flowers . . . it's good for earache and external infections,'' said Rosemary. "Are you serious about wanting to study with me? I'll work you hard, you know!''

"Good,'' said Rana. "I'm tired of being the only one who doesn't know anything.'' She continued to move along the shelves. "You have sage as an oil too. I've only seen it used as a spice, and of course for smudging.'' Even a whiff of that scent made her think of ritual fires and the touch of air as the prayer fan sent the harsh, purifying smoke swirling.

"When the heated oil is diffused through the air, its effect is even more stimulating, without the harshness. Some people find smoke difficult to breathe." For a moment she watched Rana in silence; then she nodded.

"Very well. Frederic used to work with me sometimes, but now he's at the College of the Wise, and neither of my younger boys is interested. It will be like having a daughter, without the strain that often grows between mothers and daughters. And perhaps you can teach me also," Rosemary went on. "I know very little of the plants that grow in the ocean."

Rana stared at her. "Neither do I." Her throat closed, for even at the thought, she could smell once more the briny salt tang of the sea.

"You have the means to learn . . . isn't that true?" asked Rosemary.

Mute, Rana nodded. She could still call on the People of the Sea. The healing herbs of Water grew on the seashore, and those of Earth and Air were here in this room. Those powers would be hers. Only Fire was left. . . . Suddenly the scents were making her dizzy. Coughing, she turned away.

"Your friend Eva taught me some useful things," said Rosemary conversationally. "She knew about southern herbs that I had never—"

"Has anyone written to her?" Rana asked abruptly, thrust back into awareness of the world. "She's Piper's grandmother. Has anyone sent word to her that he has disappeared?"

Rosemary pushed gray-gold hair back from her brow with a sigh. "I did, in the last pouch of messages to Bongarde. I told her not to come here, that the searchers were sure to find the boy soon."

"Do you believe that?" Rana's voice was harsher than she intended. "Nearly a month has passed."

"It will do Piper no good if his grandmother kills herself hurrying to get here," said Rosemary tartly. "And perhaps I do believe it. My son came back to me alive when all hope was gone. I think that Eva can bear the waiting. I am more worried about Silverhair.''

Rana nodded. She remembered her disgust when she had seen the harper drunk for the first time. But once he had his harp back, he had not seemed to need the wine. It could not have happened often, but this time it must have been bad, for Piper to have run so fast and so far.

But I ran from Julian, she thought then, *and with far less cause.* She could not love him, but she could not seem to leave him either. *Something still binds us, or why do I ache with his pain?*

The guitarist was playing rather badly, but the melody was one of Silverhair's songs. Piper snuffled and wiped his nose with his sleeve. The Big Oak Inn was full to-night, for the men of the pack train with which Piper had been traveling wanted to relax before the last push over the crest of the mountains and down into the Barren Lands. From here the trail ran very close to the fastness that hid Awahna, and rumor called it perilous. And so they laughed and called for more drinks, and the musician played on.

Piper remembered Silverhair's stories. He could almost feel the harper near him, but that made him start crying again. In all these weeks of wandering, the fear had faded, but Piper's goal grew ever more clear.

He must find the Wind Crystal. Silverhair wanted it. The Crystal would make the harper smile once more. When Piper closed his eyes, he could see it, like a great translucent egg shining in the sun. But where? He didn't want to go to the Barren Lands.

The music finished. The coyotes were holding their own celebration in the hills. The mule drivers called for more beer. The inn was stout and sturdy, built of big, rough-barked logs. For generations it had watched over the crossroads, and its famous beer went to men's heads quickly in the mountain air.

"East of here, there's trees like towers," said one of the men, gesturing broadly. "Drive the whole pack train 'round one and th' head would never meet up with th' tail!''

"That's nothin'," exclaimed one of the mule drivers. "Ever'body knows that. *I've* seen them trees."

"Oh, you've seen everything! See the tree girls come out to dance for ye, I'll wager, if ye drink enough of this beer."

"Only when th' moon's full," the muleteer nodded wisely. "Only when 'tis full."

"There's a whole forest turned to rock in the Barren Lands," said the woman who ran the pack train. "Met a man once in Rivered who showed me a piece of it, with the rings and the grain of the wood clear as anything, but all pure, hard stone."

Others had heard of this one. The tales got wilder as the beer went around. Piper sat by the hearth, chewing his fingernails and wondering what to do.

"South aways I seen a fortress, or maybe it's a temple, growin' out o' the stone. Heard it was the temple o' the Guardians, but we didn't see 'em. A terrible, fierce place, it was. Nobody wanted to meet whatever lived there!"

"There's a city in the Barren Lands whose queen rules the whirlwind," said one of the younger men. "No one dares try to break their hold on the trade routes for fear of her. They're as rich as the Ancients in that town, and the roof of *their* temple is covered in gold!"

"I'd like to go there," his friend grinned. "Make love to the lady and steal some o' that gold!"

"No you wouldn't. They'd kill you. No one sees the Willa, they say, except when she goes on procession through the town. And she never grows old."

Piper smiled to himself, remembering Silverhair's stories of Willasfell. He knew that *this* tall tale, at least, was true.

"*I've* heard that on the edge o' the Barren Lands there's a village of folk that fly like birds." The old man's voice seemed loud in a chance moment of silence.

"By magic?" There was a babble of comment, and Piper edged closer.

"Not from what I heard . . . not wholly anyhow. Call

themselves Wind Riders, an' they strap big kites on their backs and soar.''

"Come on. Ye think ye're Coyote, t'fool us with such a tale?''

"Well now, I wonder,'' said the leader. "I saw somethin' once myself, when a rock slide took out the road and we was lookin' for another way. There was somethin' hanging in the sky like a big bird. Thought it was an eagle then. Size and distance is hard to judge in the high country sometimes. But it was too big for an eagle. Yes, I wonder now.''

Piper pressed close, wanting to know more, but the talk veered away to other things. He could almost see them, dark specks against the clear blue. And who would know how to find the Wind Crystal better than people who lived by the wind?

He leaned back against the hearth and slid his flute from its case. Fingers slipped into position, lips and throat together made the precise adjustment to shape breath into song. In came the air, and Piper was filled with the energy of creation. Out it flowed, soft as a sigh, whispering through the conversation so that people started listening before they even knew there was a sound.

It grew louder, and other voices stilled, for the flute-song transformed the inebriation of altitude and small beer into something purer, lifting spirits as the Wind Riders were lifted by the wind. Piper portrayed the flying people in sound as the old man had portrayed them in words, and playing, envisioned them ever more clearly, until he knew them, and knew where to go.

Then the flute warbled and trilled in pure merriment. The mule drivers got up to dance, falling into the benches and each other, and laughed as they picked themselves up again.

Master Ras was laughing—a deep, rolling laughter that filled the Guildhall.

"If you play it that way, they'll dance the ribbons into

such a tangle they'll never unwind them. The poor lad
will be bound to the Maypole forever!''

Thirty young faces, flushed with embarrassment,
watched him. Thirty instruments clutched in sweating
hands vibrated in response to the Master Musician's res-
onant tones.

''DA, da, da . . . da. DA, da, da . . . da! That is how
it should go. Come now ladies, gentlemen. Let us try
this again!''

Silverhair sighed. He was beginning to see what he
had been spared, as well as what he had missed, by
working alone all these years.

Master Ras lifted his baton. More steadily this time,
the drums took up the beat, and flutes and shawms, harps
and dulcimers and viols joined in.

''They're getting a little better, don't you think?''
asked Mistress Siaran.

Silverhair hitched his Master's cloak more securely
across his shoulders. Its new violet had an intensity that
was almost violent next to the richly faded plum color of
hers. He felt conspicuous, but he supposed that he would
have been uncomfortable no matter what he wore. They
all knew who he was . . . or thought they did. Right now
the contrast between truth and legend was more painful
than usual.

''Maybe, but they're going to have to sound a *lot* better
by Beltane. We were easier to listen to in my first year
at the College of Bards,'' he said sourly,

''Well, at the college, the consort included students of
all years, and we could afford to be more selective. These
poor children have been gathered from all over Westria.
We'll keep an eye on the ones who have promise. It's the
best we can do until the college is open again.''

''And when will that be? The masters and students
who weren't killed by the reivers are scattered, and they
say that the redwoods are growing through the burned
shells where the buildings used to be.''

Master Ras's baton hit the music stand with a sharp
rap, and Silverhair stopped short, fighting for control.

''And none of that would have happened, except for

me. Caolin attacked the college out of pure malice, to hurt me. Queen Mara tried to protect me in Normontaine and nearly got killed. I failed Julian and I drove Piper away. Get clear of me, Siaran, while you can!''

''Oh, my dear, we've shared too much for me to disown you now,'' she said. ''You are as bad as your nephew, you ridiculous man. Next you'll be blaming yourself for the Blood Lord's sins!''

Oh, I do, I do, Silverhair said silently. *Caolin might never have returned to Westria if I had not betrayed his identity seven years ago. I have been fleeing his justice ever since then, but one day he will claim his price from me.*

''And what about the Cataclysm?'' Siaran went on. ''Was that your fault too?''

Silverhair shook his head with an unwilling smile.

''I'm glad to know there are some limits to your responsibility.'' She seated herself on a bench by the wall and motioned to him to join her. After a moment, he obeyed.

She would not understand; how *could* she? Perhaps she was right, and his self-judgment was too harsh, but all he could do was to try to bear it without doing any more harm. There was wine on the side table; he was shocked by how badly he wanted it, but there was no more escape for him that way. He could run away again— *like Piper*—but he had no idea of where to go. Perhaps death would free him finally.

Master Ras was having the strings play separately. Silverhair winced at the tinny sound of viols that were not quite in tune. The master stopped them, and the air trembled to an even greater dissonance as unsure hands attempted to tune a half-dozen viols to each other once more.

''Wind Lord help them when they get to the harps!'' muttered Silverhair.

''Wind Lord help *us*!'' corrected Mistress Siaran. ''I don't think they can hear just how awful they sound.''

''Is this meant to be my penance?'' He drew the harp case that he had set on the bench earlier a little closer,

as if to protect Swangold from the sound. "Very well."
The humor left him suddenly. "What does it matter?
Everything I have tried to do has failed."

"Except your music."

"It will die with me. . . ."

"The college could preserve it—" she began, and
when he started to shake his head, she gripped his arm.
"Listen to me, *Master* Silverhair! Did you learn nothing
from your time with us? The College of Bards is made
of music, not of wood and stone. It is here! We have
come to you. Teach your music to us, now!"

"Neither you nor Master Ras has the time—" he began, but a new voice interrupted him.

"But *I* do!"

Silverhair looked up and saw Aurel, still looking far
too young for the Master's cloak he wore. Grinning, he
pulled up a chair.

"They make me ashamed to be a string player," he
said, nodding toward the consort. "May I take refuge
with you here?" Unwillingly, Silverhair responded to his
smile. "I learned some of your music when you were at
the college, and some from that book you put together
for Master Sebastian. But the book is gone. . . ." *Burned
with Master Sebastian*, they all thought silently. "Teach
me the rest, all of it!" Aurel went on. "You must have
made more songs in the years since then."

Silverhair stared at him, remembering those songs, and
those years. "Is that enough?" he asked slowly. "Is that
enough to justify all of the pain?"

"For me it is. The only thing that matters is that in
other times, people who never heard of your deeds will
sing your songs just because they are beautiful."

"It may not justify the pain," said Siaran softly, "but
perhaps it balances it. Swangold is the one thing you
have never betrayed."

Silverhair looked from one to the other, a thousand
heard and unheard melodies echoing in his memory.
He did not notice when Master Ras threw up his hands
in mock despair and sent his poor students outside to

relax in the spring sun and mutter about his heartlessness.

"Silverhair, my old friend! Play me a tune to take that dreadful noise out of my ears."

Only then did the harper realize that the Guildhall had emptied and the consort's master was looking down at him, his dark face illuminated by the brilliance of his smile.

"A new song?" asked Aurel eagerly.

"I don't know . . ." he began, but already his fingers were busy at the straps of the harp case. He drew Swangold out and cradled her against his shoulder, letting his fingers wander up and down the strings. The high A was flat, as usual, but otherwise the harp seemed to be in tune.

"You see?" said Siaran softly.

Perhaps she was right, he thought as the first wisps of melody began to emerge from beneath his exploring fingers. A time might come when his body would refuse to respond to a woman, but he could not imagine not wanting to waken Swangold's music. Testing chords turned into a progression that in turn sparked memory of a melody.

> *Bird of my heart, tell me, what is the song you are singing?*
> *Where have you come from, and why are you singing to me?*
> *All that I know is that suddenly my soul is winging*
> *Into the sunlight, and something is setting me free!*
>   *Are you the eagle, who looks on the sun in his splendor,*
> *Glimpsed in the distance, a speck on the breast of the blue?*
> *All-seeing eye, can you see such a personal wonder—*
> *This brightness within me—Oh, Skymaster, can it be you?*

"He can sing it, why can't he believe it?" came Aurel's voice from somewhere in the other world outside the music, but that did not matter now.

> Are you the swan, floating white as a cloud on the river,
> Reflecting its beauty below on the mirror-bright stream?
> This gift is too lively a thing for so stately a giver.
> It's making my heart beat too quickly to be just a dream!
> Maybe the dove, who at dawning so softly is calling,
> Sends me this song—but her music is too full of pain—
> I hear her sweet voice when the shadows of evening are falling;
> It brings back the memory of all my sorrows again.

Silverhair's fingers had warmed to their work. For a little while he let the harp take over the music, fragmenting the tune like a flock of birds taking flight from a tree, then drawing them together into a new harmony as the same birds will form a new pattern against the sky.

> Are you the meadowlark, arrowing upward, rejoicing?
> Bravest of spirits—if anyone, it should be you!
> But I am still earthbound, it is not my song you are voicing.
> Yet something within me knows all that you're singing is true.
> It is the song, not the singer, that spirit inspiring,
> Transcending the bonds of the body, can learn how to soar,

*And bear me to realms where the beauty that I've
been desiring
Is mine without fear, nor shall I be alone
anymore!*

Though all else be lost, this much remained to him—
the power of song that was lifting him now to the realm
of the Wind Lord, where all is harmony.

SIX: Riding the Wind

Julian ran through the mists of morning, head down, arms pumping, pushing his body until the breath sobbed in his chest. But he could not outrun fear. It was early; invisible birds hailed the rising of a sun that he could not yet see. At this hour the lake of Laurelynn was a gray shield scored with tiny ripples. Sometimes he would meet a servant coming down to draw water, but his speed gave him an excuse not to reply.

He had grown soft, living in palaces. Speech was still difficult, but at least his body could move freely. Julian ran, propelled by the bellows of his lungs. Wind whipped his hair and numbed his skin, but no matter how fast he went his thoughts paced him still.

One morning he heard feet on the path behind him. He went faster, but the other was coming swiftly. Julian slowed, looking back over his shoulder, and in a single moment of recognition knew the balance and grace of the other man's body. He continued to jog as the runner drew up beside him, summoning up a smile to answer Robert's grin.

"Out of condition!" Robert gasped between strides. "Not like . . . we were . . . on the borders!" A lock of brown hair fell over his forehead, sheened with perspiration already, but his blue eyes shone.

Julian glanced at him from beneath bent brows. He had raced Robert once long ago when they were rivals, before they took their names. Robert had won that one, and they had never rematched.

He drew breath suddenly and leaped forward. He heard a startled gasp behind him, then the sound of feet pounding and a steady rasp of breath as Robert came after him. The world blurred. The patch of path just ahead was all he could see, the roar of wind in his ears all he could hear; all he knew was the jar of impact as his feet hit dirt, and the clench and stretch of muscles bearing him on.

Then a stone rolled beneath him. Julian staggered, and in the next stride found that the life had left his legs. A few more steps and he came to a halt, muscles quivering. Vision cleared as he sucked in air. Neither of them had won this time, but that didn't matter anymore.

Robert clung to a tree beside the path, shaking his head. "Need to do this . . . more often . . . but not now." He pushed off from the tree and stumbled forward. "Don't stand still . . . muscles will stiffen."

Julian nodded and staggered after him. For a few moments, it had been all right. He had been flying, he had been free. And he was not alone.

Piper toiled up the path out of the canyon, a single moving speck against an immensity of tumbled granite spiked with lodgepole pines. In the valley, they must be gathering the last of the flowers for Beltane. Here, the sheltered hollows still held snow, but among the rocks, the first purple bells of the cassiope were beginning to ring. A chill wind whispered over stone, twitched playfully at Piper's cloak, and rushed away. Where it passed, it left a silence so profound, it rang in his ears.

The path he followed through the canyon was well cared for once, but this winter's washouts had not been repaired. How long had it been since two-footed creatures walked this way? The mule driver had believed that the village of the flying men lay eastward, but it was not on the caravan roads. Did the emptiness around him hold its secret, or would he wander until he too became a ghost upon the wind?

He sipped from his water bottle and trudged on. Lakelets flashed like spangles in the sunlight; eastward he glimpsed the purple haze of the Barren Lands. He was not exactly afraid. In the high country, even death seemed irrelevant. But the music of his flute would have been an intrusion on the stillness. Even the tiny dun sparrows that had cheered him earlier were silent. For hours nothing had moved but the treetops that tossed in the wind; the only sounds had been the gurgle of falling water or the sharp clatter of a sun-loosened stone. He felt very much alone.

When the sun was overhead, Piper took shelter among a tumble of boulders where tufts of dwarf phlox and cress and close-growing bryanthus cushioned the stony ground. He had only a heel of bread and a fragment of hard cheese, but the sun on his shoulders was comforting. He curled up for a nap, pulling his faded cloak over him so that he blended into the weathered stone. . . .

Cool shadow moved over him. The change in temperature was enough to wake him; he was already stirring when a whistle, clear and piercing, jerked him upright, staring. The shadow passed; Piper saw the sweep of mighty wings against the pure sky—no, not wings, but a thing like a great purple kite, with a man strapped to its breast. As he blinked, the whistle came again, and was answered.

There was a second shape in the sky. As it slid between him and the sun, stretched silk glowed a brilliant gold, with darker circles like the eyes on a butterfly's wing. Warbled notes passed back and forth between the gold wing and the purple; then the gold flier tugged on the crossbar and the nose dipped slightly, gained speed, and began to rise.

As the purple followed the gold, Piper got his breath

back. Need ached in his chest, but his flute was already at his lips. The air he had sucked in burst out in a shrill, inquiring trill. Bright wings spilled air; purple and gold kites slid into a tight spiral above the rocks as the flute called with frantic sweetness, *"Come back, come back; I am here, here, here!"*

Another exchange of whistles and the gold wing rose, hovering like a hawk on the wind. But the purple flier swung away in a generous circle and then came down in a long, low-angled glide, alighting neatly on a round boss of stone. He squatted there, crouching like a perching bird, with one knee on the crossbar that formed the bottom of a triangle beneath the purple silk, and the wind slipped by beneath the great kite's wing.

"Who're ya? Are ya' lost? What ya' doin' here?"

The flier wore tight-laced, padded leather, dyed a dull purple to match the silk of his wing. A quiver of arrows was bound to his back, beneath his broad belt a bow. Piper stared. Even had he been able to speak, words would be beyond him now.

"Lost 'n' starvin', Olin. Look 't 'is bones!" a clear voice called from the gold glider as it swept low and then lifted again. Piper saw a woman's bright face, framed by a leather cap edged with downy feathers that fluttered in the wind.

"Y'r 'lone?" snapped the man.

Piper nodded vigorously. He played the four ascending notes once more. The man shook his head.

"Best take ya then. Don' weigh mor'n a deer. Come." From around his waist he unwound a coil of line. "D'ya want t'be fed? Then come on." Pale eyes flickered in a weathered face. Brows, lips, mustache slanted as he frowned.

"Don' fear, boy," the woman called. "Olin won't let ya fall."

Piper was afraid, but longing lifted him to his feet and sent him scrambling upward.

"Put y'r arms around m'neck, boy, 'n' hook y'r legs round m' waist."

Close, Piper saw lines of laughter as well as the impatience in that brown face. Two gold badges and a silver one were sewn to his cap, and from its crown dangled an eagle plume. Piper jammed his flute back into its case and wrapped his cloak around himself. Then, heart pounding, he clasped the smooth leather of the flying jacket while Olin roped them together and made a quick, automatic check of his straps and lines.

"Hol' tight, rabbit." Suddenly the flier laughed. "If ya don' die o' fright, ya'll see a wonder!"

Piper shut his eyes as Olin reached up to grab the two down-bars of his wing and stood. A few running steps, Piper felt muscles contract against him and was pulled horizontal when the flier's body straightened. Then suddenly they were rising. Piper gasped, his arms and legs vising around the man's torso. Olin grunted. The wind buffeted them, and there was a sound like laundry flapping on a clothesline.

"Ya can open y'r eyes now," came the voice in his ear.

Piper blinked rapidly as gray slopes blurred past. Above him, the glowing silk wing stretched drum-tight as it caught the wind. The sky spun crazily, then steadied. The high country was falling away below them in a monochrome confusion of burnished granite and dark foliage and white mottlings of late snow. The chill of the upper air bit into his bones, but Piper didn't care.

As they lifted higher, he got some perspective, and his spirit stilled with wonder to see the stone spine of Westria displayed below. To north and south stretched the massed peaks of the Ramparts. To the west, forested foothills faded into the gray mists that veiled the Great Valley. But they were wheeling eastward, where the mountains fell steeply to the shimmering purple heat-haze of the Barren Lands.

Perhaps he made a sound without knowing it, for the flier laughed.

"Na, that country's not f'r Wind Riders. Too hot, too still. Our gather's closer—look down."

As the spiral continued, Piper saw a green valley carved into the mountains, with two tiny lakes glittering among the trees, and set into the ledge above them, doll-sized buildings of gray stone. Banners on tall poles fluttered from the sheltering ridge. Olin's shrill whistle jarred his eardrums; responses, sweet with distance, trembled in the air. Suddenly the sky was full of fliers, their angled wings glowing russet, pale yellow, silver, and soft green.

They seemed to descend in a slow swirl of butterflies. Then the ground rushed up to meet them. Olin's legs swung forward. With both arms he reached and pushed firmly on the down-bars to lift the nose of the wing. There was a sudden stillness, then a thump as the flier's feet touched the ground. Piper clung as Olin sank to his knees, grabbed the cords at the front, and pulled the nose down to the ground.

"White Rim Gather—here y'be."

The wing flapped lightly in the wind, but they were sheltered behind it. Now the wind that had lifted them aloft held the craft down. Piper caught his breath. As Olin untied him, he saw people hurrying toward them, whistling greetings and chattering like birds.

Rana was whistling as she came down through the orchard to the archery range that lay along the shore. The same light wind that was chasing the puffy clouds across the sky ruffled the waters of the lake. A stray gust blew bright hair across her face, and she retied her scarf to keep the strands out of her eyes.

She heard the thrum of a bowstring before she saw the archer, the thunk as the arrow drove home, the sounds almost immediately repeated again and again in deliberate rhythm. Strange, how the sounds themselves defined the man who made them. Only one archer she knew shot with such dogged regularity. For a moment Rana hesitated, then she shrugged and went on.

When she emerged from among the trees, Julian was plucking his arrows from the straw target. All of them had hit near the center; he must have been practicing a lot lately. When he turned, he saw her and stopped short, but Rana was stringing her own bow with ostentatious concentration. Slowly he came back to his own stand.

Rana thrust four arrows through her belt, adjusted her wristguard and lifted the bow. She took a deep breath, then another, centering down, balancing, trying for the perfect poise in which she and the bow would be one. She could feel her arm trembling; she relaxed it just a little, then snatched an arrow from her belt, nocked it, and drew.

She fumbled the release—she could feel it as the string snapped against her fingers. The arrow wavered a little as it lofted; then the wind that kissed the surface of the lake carried it to the left of the target. A moment later Julian's arrow pierced the third circle of his target. He plucked another arrow from his quiver and prepared to draw again.

Allowing for the wind this time, Rana aimed, but the sound of Julian's arrow hitting home distracted her, and her missile struck the edge of the straw.

Maybe I had better leave the combat shooting until I've regained some accuracy! She put the other two arrows back in her quiver. All of Julian's first four arrows had hit his target. But they were nearer the edge this time.

Think of the Huntress! she told herself. The Maiden had many faces, and one of them was that of the Lady who watched over the wild kindreds, to save or to slay. For a moment the image came clearly: fierce, uncompromising, totally committed to the task. Rana drew and released and *knew*, even as the arrow left her fingers, that it would fly true.

As her arrow struck, she heard the twang of a mishandled bowstring. Julian's missile rattled through the grass, coming to rest at the foot of the high wall beyond the targets. He was scowling, and Rana suppressed a smile.

After that, Rana shot better, although she did not make another bull's-eye. Julian's score sank steadily. They emptied their quivers at almost the same time. Julian was still gathering his arrows when Rana approached to retrieve hers.

"This wind makes for chancy shooting," she said brightly. There was no reply. "Not a good day for practice, really," she went on. "But you can't count on still weather for battle. This is better than shooting from shipboard anyway. At least the land stands still!"

Julian stared at her, and suddenly Rana *remembered* the last time she had used a bow in war. The image of a ship's deck red with the blood of men and sea otters replaced that of the archery range, and her stomach churned. She swallowed sickly. In Julian's eyes she saw the same memory of horror. She took a step toward him, wanting the comfort he had given her after that battle. Then she stopped again, with a shiver. In the anguish of that moment, she had accepted Julian's embrace as that of a brother, but she knew that it would not be a brother's touch now.

In a moment she had controlled her reaction, but he had seen, and too quick to understand where she was concerned, he had known why she was afraid. He turned his back on her then, but she could hear his breathing, swift and uneven as if he had been running.

"This is ridiculous!" She strove to soften her voice, knowing that the anger was for herself, not for him. "We can't avoid each other forever, Julian. I just need time. I need your help. Won't you at least talk to me?"

His knuckles whitened as he gripped his arrows.

"Rana. . . ."

She had to strain to hear.

"Please . . . go away."

"Leave us!" The edge in Caolin's voice brought the bathhouse attendant up short, staring. His eyes went from the man whom he believed to be Prince Julian to the other, whose dark-red robe would seem to place him in the Seneschal's office, though he had not given a name. The sorcerer fought the compulsion to cough on the steamy air, and held the man's gaze.

"My lord wishes to bathe in privacy . . . do you understand?" Caolin waited until he saw the widening in the eyes, the change in breathing, and knew that the unease he was projecting was getting through. "You will keep the others from disturbing him. When he is ready for his meal, I will inform you.''

Good, thought Caolin as the fellow made an awkward obeisance, then turned and scurried for the door, the two girls who had brought towels following him. Elk Creek was only a tiny village on a minor tributary of the Dorada, all aquiver now at the honor of a visit from the Prince of Westria. That was why Caolin had chosen it for their first resting place. Within moments this interchange would be all over the village. And how long would it take for news of what happened in the village to spread up and down the valley? The sorcerer took a deep breath of the cool clean air that flowed in as the man opened the door. Then it shut, and steam billowed around him, damp and choking.

Water lapped softly as the man in the pool stretched out tired limbs. Caolin saw the dark hair sleeked close to his head, and blinked. For a moment, it could have been Jehan. He reached for the scented oils. He knew what to do. He had performed this service often, long ago, when he served the king.

''Why'd you do that?'' The rough voice shocked him back to the present. ''That one kitten with the towels had tits like melons. I'd rather have one of them bathe me than you.''

''You are not king, not yet,'' hissed the sorcerer.

Jehan might have asked for a woman, but not in that way. The village had already honored its royal guest by bringing out the wine, and before Caolin could stop him, the false prince had taken full advantage of it. Caolin heard a soft giggle from the pool and frowned. Ordinarily the lad would never have been so bold. He must be taught to fear his master, drunk or sober, at ease or in extremity. And this business with women. . . .

Softly, and out of tune, the boy began to whistle a bawdy song. Caolin bit back a reproof, thinking. Perhaps it would be better to let him go after them; there was no surer way to antagonize men than by threatening their womenfolk.

''Water's nice an' hot anyway,'' the slurred voice went

on. "From Laurelynn to here in one day's a long ride. Bet you're sore too. Come on in. Like you said, I'm not king yet!" The young man laughed and his arms moved.

Caolin flinched as the water splashed toward him. Mist swirled aside; he saw the dark gleam of the pool. His ears rang, and he fought for breath as the wet darkness rose above him and sucked him down, down, down. . . .

Rap, rap! From the depths that had engulfed him, Caolin recognized the sound of someone knocking. He lurched toward it as if it were a lifeline and wrenched open the door. The taste of brine still rasped his throat; he coughed as if seawater still filled his lungs. Then the fresh air blew away nightmares he thought he had set behind him months ago, and framed in the doorway he saw Ordrey.

"You have messages?" Caolin knew that his voice was a croak, but the sound of it helped him to reclaim reality. The devouring sea was far away. The evil ocean had not been able to kill him, but all of his horror of drowning had been reawakened by the sight of that pool. He took a deep breath, grateful that only Ordrey was here to see him trembling, drew in another, and felt his control return.

"A report, my lord." Ordrey looked at him curiously. "I have been into Seagate, as you ordered," he went on. "Eric has given the girl a shipyard, and she's building galleys—ships of war—for Julian. She's not well guarded, lord. It would be easy to arrange—"

Caolin's lifted hand cut him short.

Ardra. . . . The name Ordrey had diplomatically left unspoken resonated in the sorcerer's awareness, and as he thought of his daughter, the waters she loved once more threatened to overwhelm him.

"Not now!" he whispered. "Afterward . . . there will be time to dispose of her." There was a stone bench just outside the bathhouse, hard, cold, dry. He sat down. "Now I have work for you. That lout in there wants a woman. Find him one."

"Let him do his own wooing!" Ordrey leaned against

the weathered boards of the wall. "I've had a long, hard day."

"It will be better," Caolin said in the same harsh whisper, "if you find one who is unwilling . . . a girl with a father, brothers, by whom she is beloved. Take the guard, and when you bring her to him, make sure that the villagers know."

Ordrey's lips pursed in a silent whistle, and then he grinned. "As you say, my lord! And when he's done with her?"

The sorcerer shrugged. The first stars were pricking holes in the indigo of the evening sky. A clear sky—and tomorrow would be dry. His dizziness was passing. There had been only a moment of weakness, and it was over now.

"Whatever you will, but be quick about it, for in the morning we must be gone. . . ."

It seemed to Piper that he had always lived with the Wind Riders, had always awakened to see the peaks shimmering like golden islands in a sea of shadow in the dawning, and flaming like roses as the blue shadows of evening crept across the snows. But for him, the beauty of White Rim Gather was not its chief wonder; it was the fact that here he had found a home. His rescuer, Olin, lived with the other unmarried men in their own lodge, but the girl in the gold glider, Tania, was the eldest of a large and active family that found no difficulty in making room for one more.

Even communication was no problem. Piper quickly understood the clipped way of speaking of the gather-folk, and when they realized that he could not speak, they taught him the whistle code they used for communicating in the air. They thought that he must be the shocked survivor of a party wiped out by raiders, and he did not try to correct them. Soon it was his life in Laurelynn that became hard to remember, except that sometimes he heard Silverhair's music in his dreams.

They wintered in a sheltered canyon at the edge of the Barren Lands, but as soon as the passes cleared, they moved back to the gather at White Rim, in the high country. The sparse granite soil of their valley grew some corn and vegetables, but mostly they were hunters, shooting deer from the air and setting traps in places that could be reached only by those with wings.

Piper watched wistfully each morning as the fliers launched themselves from the ledge on the mountainside above the village. They were mostly young men and women, though their elders went out sometimes to maintain their skill. Coloring differed, but all of them looked like members of the same family—small and wiry, but muscular. The strength was necessary. On the ground, the great kites were mule-stubborn to move. But in the air, they became wings.

The boy watched the gatherfolk dance with the wind and forgot to breathe. There was no freedom like this freedom, where the slightest shift in balance could send one soaring across the sky. Piper watched, and forgot who he was and why he had come.

But when the sudden storms of early summer in the mountains thundered on the pine-shingled roofs of the lodges and drove the Wind Riders indoors with the others, he would take out his flute, and they were glad to listen to his piping.

For most of the morning it had been raining. Deprived of their daily run, Robert and Julian had taken refuge in the armory, an old building as big as a barn, and as drafty. Crates along one wall held shields whose leather was cracked with age, spearheads and sword blanks filmed with orange rust, arrows with motheaten fletching that looked as if they had lain there since the war with Elaya.

It was a good place in which to work out when it rained, and Robert had brought in mats and weights, wooden swords, and even staves with which to practice the fighting form taught at the College of the Wise. The Master of the Junipers had begun to train Julian when he was recovering after finding the Earthstone. Perhaps it was some instinct for self-healing that drew Julian to staff work now. As rain hissed upon the shingles, he repeated the intricate step and shift in balance that brought the staff whistling up and around and down again and again. Rain echoed his movements, drumming on the roof, then slapping the sides of the armory in a succession of percussive harmonies.

Balance—that was everything. When he got it right, the staff would leap in his hands like a startled bird. He moved his grip a little higher, leaned into the swing and felt the smooth wood vibrate like a live thing. Up, stretching the shoulders, then the quick twist that switched ends and brought the staff hurtling down. He eased back, and the tip grazed the floor, then settled gently to the packed earth.

"Very neat," said Robert. Turning, Julian saw that his cousin had finished with the weights and was sitting on one of the boxes, watching him. He nodded and leaned on the staff while he caught his breath. Rain lashed suddenly against the side of the building, then diminished into a drizzle with the shift of the wind.

"Leave that for now and come wrestle with me," Robert said, getting to his feet. He was already stripped to undertunic and clout; now he pulled off his upper garment as well.

Julian considered him, struck as always by his cousin's physical beauty. Robert struck a wrestler's pose, mocking his own consciousness of his appearance. He was a little taller than Julian, his muscles beautifully defined and so evenly developed that folk tended not to notice them, except at times like this, when he was being appraised with an opponent's eye. But Julian knew that the strength was there, as well as the agility. He had seen it too many times in battle, and felt it when they had practised together before.

But it had been some time since they had wrestled. Last summer Julian had learned a trick or two from the crew of the *Sea Brother* that might give his friend a surprise. He was already nodding agreement when he realized that once more, Robert had asked his question in a way that would let Julian respond without using words.

Julian found it hard to believe that once he had thought
Robert inferior to Frederic in sensitivity. He still loved
them both, but in these days Frederic's attention was focused on the world of the spirit and his love for Ardra.
Since the Council's end, there had been times when Robert was the only one whose company he could bear, the
only one who laid upon him no burdens of hope or disappointment, or fear. For a moment then, he thought of
Rana, but he thrust the memory away. He could not face
her—especially not her—not now, when he was not
whole.

He leaned the staff against the wall and pulled off his
tunic and breeches. He bent his knees a few times, swung
his arms to release the tension in the heavy muscles of
his shoulders. A boyhood spent chopping trees and chip-
ping stone had left him with a physique that he had always considered distorted, but his overdeveloped arms
and shoulders would be very useful now. He gave his left
leg a last shake and stepped onto the mat.

Robert had already moved to the corner of the mat.
Julian faced him, and both men bowed. They had
scarcely straightened when Robert darted forward, arms
flicking out to grapple. Julian jerked away ungracefully
and leaped aside to get more room for maneuvering. Legs
flexed, he swayed, letting his arms swing outward, his
strong hands open and ready. His first attack having
failed, Robert came in again more cautiously, muscles
sliding beneath his smooth skin. His blue eyes were
dancing with anticipation, and Julian found his own lips
curving.

Robert's hands blurred forward; Julian began to turn,
knew with an instinct too swift for thought that this was
a feint, and twisted, his hands swinging up so that only
a swift swerve kept Robert free. Julian moved a little
forward, widened his stance and stood as if rooted while
the other man danced lightly around him. Now Julian
saw the sheen of sweat on Robert's skin.

Another feint. Julian saw it coming a fraction late and
rocked as the other man's hands closed on his arm. But
his swing dislodged a grip that was not yet solid, and

Robert leaped out of reach again. He was turning, re-turning. Julian launched himself forward, grasped his cousin's upper arm and pulled, started to pivot, his right foot sliding outside Robert's, and lost his balance as Robert's other hand slammed into the back of his head. Julian brought his opponent down with him, bodies slamming hard, muscle against muscle sliding beneath sweat-slick skin. But he hit the mat first and lay gasping as Robert rolled away, crowing.

"First fall to me!"

Julian grunted, then came up in a swift rush, hooking Robert around the waist in a sudden, violent embrace, grabbing his buttocks and swinging him upward, hoisted on one hip and spinning. For a moment he saw Robert's arms flung outward, blue eyes wide with surprise. Then Julian thrust outward and dropped his cousin neatly onto his back.

There was a long whoosh of breath, then Robert lay blinking while Julian stood over him, trying to get his own breathing under control.

"Second . . . to me." The words came easily, as if the exercise had also warmed up his tongue.

"Damn you," Robert responded when he could speak again. "That was supposed to be *my* throw!"

Julian grinned. After a moment, Robert rolled upright and sprang to his feet again.

"All right, if that's how you want it!"

No time for thought now. Robert gripped, wrenched; only Julian's greater weight kept him upright. He got a hold, but the other man was too close for leverage. Julian caught the tang of Robert's body, mixed with the muskier smell of his own. Their breathing grew harsh in each other's ears as they swayed, their feet shifting like dancers' as each man tried to hook the other's leg from under him.

Julian was sharply aware of Robert's muscles shifting under his hands, the weight and poise of his body. Consciousness telescoped to the single desire of each to bring the other down. Breath rasping, they grappled, their balance swinging ever more violently as new reserves of strength were summoned. And this time they went down gradually, almost deliberately, and as they hit the mat, their bodies were already flexing, rolling over and over in an attempt to force a formal fall.

Strength strove with suppleness; a lock would be lost in a wriggle in which opponents changed places, then shifted again. Legs hooked and hands groped frantically. There were no messages but those of the flesh, a kinesthetic communion that prescribed its own responses. In Julian, the will to domination rose like a tide; strength called forth by the strength that strove against him, filling him with an energy that willed to defeat its opponent by *becoming* him—every bone, every muscle, every inch of skin.

Slowly Robert was borne backward. His eyes were unfocused, fixed on something deep within. Julian pressed him down—as if seeking to follow him into that inwardness—until the other lay stretched beneath him. They breathed in unison.

And then Robert gave a little sigh, and the resistance went out of him. But tension still held Julian rigid. His fingers dug into Robert's shoulders, and he saw awareness leap suddenly into the blue eyes. He could feel the hard core of Robert's manhood through the thin, sweat-soaked cloth of his clout, the tension in his own. And then, very deliberately, Robert ground his hips upward, back and forth, and back. . . .

Julian gasped, feeling all the tension within him focus suddenly in his groin, and understood finally what was happening between them, and was unable to deny it, could not even want to deny it now. Rain thundered suddenly overhead, swallowing all other sounds.

Julian forced the vise-grip of his fingers to loosen, and he saw Robert's eyes widen in wonder, and then on his face a smile of such piercing sweetness that even if Julian's body had not compelled him, pity would have prevented him from pulling away. Freed, Robert's hand lifted, stroked back Julian's hair.

Julian sighed then, and let his head drop to his friend's shoulder, trembling as Robert's hand traveled down the

taut muscles of his back. He lay still, only his breathing
growing more ragged as the other's hands moved elsewhere, until all sensation distilled into a swirling joy that
swept outward as if a whirlwind had carried him away.

Rain was pattering gently upon the shingles. Julian
became aware that he was lying on his back, every muscle spent and strengthless as if he had ridden the whirlwind indeed. *Who am I?* he wondered. *What have I
become?* He felt at once strange to himself and confirmed
in his own identity, as if he had looked into a magic
mirror that reflected parts of his body that he had never
before seen.

After a time he realized that Robert lay propped up on
one elbow, watching him, a faint frown clouding the blue
of his eyes.

"I think . . ." said Julian, staring at the sonorous ceiling. "I do believe that fall belongs to you."

Robert blinked, then crossed his arms and dropped his
head upon them and began to laugh. Julian waited peace-
fully until he finished. What were these storms of the
flesh, after all? He had time. All the tensions that had
bound him had been blown away.

"By all the Guardians, Julian," Robert gasped finally,
"that's the last thing I expected you to say. I was afraid—"
He began again, "For so long, I have dreamed. . . ."

He couldn't finish that sentence either, but Julian nodded. "How long have you known?"

"That I love you?" Robert laughed. "Since I stopped
hating you, I suppose. When we were sixteen. That I
love you in this way? For a year or two maybe, since I
met someone who showed me why no woman has ever
meant anything to me."

Julian considered that. For him, it had always been
women, until now. And Rana. . . . He bit his lip, realizing that the thought of her still had the power to move
him. Perhaps she could stop being afraid of him now.

Robert sat up suddenly. "Julian! I don't know what
you think happened just now. It meant more to me than

I suppose you can imagine, but you don't have to do it again. You don't have to change—''

"I already have." Julian turned his head and smiled. "Don't you have ears? I can talk again! Listen to me!" Suddenly a whirlwind of words pulsed in his awareness, and the wonder of it soared like a song. "Do you think I would try to deny it—'' he went on—"that I would throw your gift back in your face that way?"

"Some men would," said Robert soberly. "There are men who would hate themselves for having allowed it, and transfer that hatred to me."

"I don't know where we go from here, Robert—'' Julian pulled himself upright as well—"but I won't deny what I have done. I responded. Therefore the ability to love you must be a part of me. I won't break faith with you."

"Julian, don't say any more. You make me afraid." Robert hid his face against his drawn-up knees.

Julian reached out and very gently stroked the other man's hair. He had never dared to do that before. Robert was the one who had offered his love, but Julian realized abruptly that *he* was the one who had been set free.

SEVEN: Wind and Fire

The sky shone like a crystal bowl, brimming with golden light. As the sun descended, range upon range of peaks sprang into splendor, faceted slopes returning the radiance of the longest day. Stillness beat against Piper's hearing as if the whole world were waiting for the festival. He had to concentrate to hear a low murmur from the drummers, the soft rasp of wood being dragged across the packed-earth platform to build the fire. He wished that he could ask what they were getting ready for.

He wandered past the shed where they stored the baled furs they would be taking to trade in the valley, and the fine quartz crystals and little leather bags of gold. At least Piper understood *this*. For the past week everyone had been calculating their value in trade for spirits and spices and tools, and above all, for the lengths of tough, tightly woven silk from which they sewed the wings of their gliders . . . and the springy poles of giant bamboo, which they strengthened with glue and sinew for making their frames. Piper had listened carefully to those discussions, fearful that the Wind Riders would send him back to the lowlands with the pack train.

A whistle from above drew his gaze to the heights. The cliffs above the gather were sprouting the bright silk of wings like spring flowers. But the dark masses of the stunted pines behind them were still. Even so high, there was no wind, yet the fliers crouched as patiently as a row of tethered hawks in their mews. What were they waiting for?

A deep drum boomed, shocking as thunder. Suddenly all the confusion resolved into pattern. The folk of the gather were forming a circle around the piled logs. Old Tam, the headman, grasped Piper's hand and pulled him into the line, and he realized that Olin and Tania were not here. He remembered the fliers on the cliff, and gave the trill of notes that was Olin's name in the skies. Tam shook his head and smiled.

"He has another part . . . y'll see. 'Twould have been me up there not s' long ago. Ah, I could climb th' skies 'n' steal the lightnin' when I was young. But winters pass. 'Tis th' turn of younger wings now."

The eagle plumes tied to the old man's topknot trembled, and Piper remembered the black-tipped feather on Olin's flying helm. Many of the others wore feathers from breast or wing, but most of those who had earned the white tail feathers were up on the heights. Piper felt a flutter of excitement. What was Olin going to do for the festival?

The great drum beat again, steadying as other drums joined in. Piper's breathing deepened, quickened in time to the drumbeat. As one being, the circle began to move.

But they were dancing widdershins! Westrian rituals never began that way. His grandmother used to tell tales of evil folk who danced the wrong way 'round. Scraps of stories half-remembered buzzed in Piper's brain. He stumbled, but the dancers pulled him along. The faces around him were joyful. Could he trust them? He remembered the terror and the glory of his own journey through the skies. Surely, if these folk were evil, they would not so blithely dare the mercy of the wind!

Piper ceased to hold back, and the rhythm quickened. A single voice soared, and suddenly everyone was singing.

> *Dry the day, and still and fair,*
> *Thirsty earth call powers of air,*
> *Call cloud beings, rain folk come—*
> *Datta, da datta, da datta, da dum!*

The verse was punctuated by a rumble of drums; voices triumphed the chorus.

> *West wind, wet wind, wild wind, come—*
> *Datta, da datta, da datta, da dum!*

Around the people circled, and around again. The dust puffed up at each footfall and hung in the still air.

> *Out of sea mist, clouds are born.*
> *Thunder being, sound your horn.*
> *Windherds make cloud creatures come—*
> *Datta, da datta, da datta, da dum!*

The chanting grew deeper. Piper felt it vibrate through him. His lips parted. At the chorus, the breath rushed out of him in a harsh sob. But no one was listening. Heads tilted back, eyes fixing on the western horizon, where clouds were billowing above the jagged line of the ranges as if to engulf the setting sun. This was no simple noonday storm. Throats quivered with sound; his own throat muscles vibrated in sympathy.

> *Beat the air with mighty wings.*
> *Now the Bird of Thunder brings*
> *The storm—Skyfather, hear and come—*
> *Datta, da datta, da datta, da dum!*

The dancers whirled around and around as a sudden chill gust bore the dust away. Clouds built rapidly, fortifying the sky, small cauliflower cloud forms heaping one upon another, darkening bases bulging into towers of light. Cold wind swept the circle. Lights twinkled on the clifftop; another gust blasted the valley, swirling up its slopes in a sudden draft. "Never fly in a thunderstorm," the Wind Riders told their children, but now lanterns swung wildly from bright wing tips as the fliers launched themselves into the wind. Voices shrieked out the chorus. From Piper's lips came a screech of pure sound.

The western horizon was walled by glowing ramparts and towers edged with flame. Bats fluttered across the sky like shattered shadows, keening at the edge of sound. The luminous blue veil of early evening deepened to display the first stars, against which the wings of the fliers swung twinned points of light in graceful circles to join their stately round.

Below, the dance was slowing. The drums beat out a softer rhythm. Wordless, the people gazed while invisible wings bore their beacons in precise spirals up the slopes of the sky. Up and around, circles within circles, intersecting circles, circles wide and narrow, the figures flowed one into another as the dance went on.

From time to time, lights staggered; the erratic pressure of wind on Piper's cheek told him that the heavens were not as serene as they seemed. What must it be like up there in the windy darkness? His fingers tightened on Tam's gnarled hand and he whistled the trill for questions of danger.

"Risky? Yes 'tis," the old man replied. "In general, wind's formed by what it flows over. The other side o' the ridge that shelters our lodges lifts the wind we need in order to fly . . . generally. The banners show which way 'tis flowin', but now our fliers can't see 'em. That's why night flyin's forbidden. An' even if they could see, there's no thermals in darkness, an' th' great storms don't follow rules . . . they'll suck ye up or cast ye down for th' fun o' it, even weigh ye down with hailstones, as happened to me one time. And 'tis a great one we're callin' now!"

"*Why?*" Piper's whistle asked then.

"*Because* o' the danger!" Tam answered harshly. 'Tis a pride in men to ride th' skies. Since before th' Cataclysm we've done it, when the Ancients ruled the air by machines and magic. They're all gone now. But our folk still seek th' skies with only skill to protect 'em. Skill and love," he added with a sigh. Above, the Wind Riders danced with the stars.

He did this when he was young, thought Piper. *For love . . .* His throat ached with longing to be part of that perfect pattern in the skies.

"We gotta remember we're in Wind Lord's hand. Every year we call th' storm t' clear the air before the traders go down t' th' valley, and every year our best fliers go up to make th' offering. 'N' sometimes Skyfather takes one. . . ."

Piper realized that he was standing on his toes, stretching as if he could will the wind to whirl his slight body into the skies. *Silly! Wishing won't get you up there.* Embarrassed, he forced his heels down.

"*Up!*" he whistled. "*I want!*"

The headman laughed. "That don't surprise me. 'Tis few that Wind Lord lets find us . . . maybe He called you here. But that's His choice. Even our own kids gotta pass His test before we let 'em learn."

A sharp gust blew the hair into Piper's eyes, then lifted it away. Overhead, the stars had disappeared. Some of the lanterns had gone out; the precise circles were wavering.

"*I want,*" Piper repeated. "*Please!*" If he could speak the language of the winds, it would not matter if he could talk to men.

"Couple weeks, our kids'll be goin'. Y' could join 'em. If th' Lord o' th' Sky People accepts ye, I'll train ye like one o' our own." The old man's arm went around him in a quick hug.

Piper felt the pressure of muscles hardened by a lifetime of lifting the heavy wing. But if once he could slip the bonds of earth, all weight would be gone. Piper quivered like a jessed hawk, wanting to be free.

And in that moment of pure desire, distant lightning

reached for heaven. The drums awoke, but their rumble was lost in the first sharp crack of thunder.

> *Lightning, lightning, strike the sky!*
> *Land below and power on high.*
> *Link to let life's waters come—*
> *Datta, da datta, da datta, da dum!*

The first flier swooped in a low arc above the valley. Something bright hurtled earthward to strike the wood heaped there. Fire spilled from a wooden lantern, licked hopefully at the logs and was blown out by the wind. The Wind Rider's spiral carried him down to a landing, but a second was following. Again a wooden lantern blazed down. Wind gusted, and the flier came down in a tangle. Folk ran to free him as more fire flared from Wind Riders' hands.

> *West wind, wet wind, wild wind, come!*
> *Datta, da datta, da datta, da dum!*

Every hair on Piper's body lifted in anticipation. The wind grabbed him, and Tam's hand was torn from his grasp. He cried out in excitement intensified to ecstasy. And light and sound responded in a single explosion that answered all questioning.

When Piper could see again, he was flat on his back in the dust beside a roaring fire, his mouth open to the first drops of rain. He drew a painful breath and his nostrils flared at the odd, acrid tang in the air. Above there was only wet darkness, but around the fire the gatherfolk were dancing wildly, arms outstretched, faces upturned. Water hissed at the edges of the bonfire, rain mingling with thin flurries of snow, but the flames devoured the oil-soaked logs. Shouting, the Wind Riders plunged torches into the flames and carried them back to rekindle their household fires. Still gasping, Piper got to his feet.

Lightning flared again eastward; he glimpsed the angular shapes of folded wings being borne down the hill.

After a moment came the thunder, and the valley was swept by wings of rain.

Wind Lord. The words were clear in his head, though even now his throat would not lend them sound. *Wind Lord, give me my heart's wish! Let the Guardian of the Sky People grant my desire!*

At least one of my wishes has been granted! Standing on the balcony outside the Prince's room, Silverhair listened to the music in Julian's voice as he joked with his cousin, still surprised that the boy's state of mind should matter so. But that last storm seemed to have cleared more than the air. The valley lay drying now beneath an immensity of cloudless blue, and Julian was laughing as he and Robert finished breakfast.

The harper filled his lungs with clean air, and let it go. Pale swirls of vapor rose from the puddles in the yard below. A woman came out with a wicker basket of wet clothes and began to hang them from a line. In the plum orchard, the sparrows were greeting the day with a chorus of clear whistles and buzzing trills, and every polished leaf flashed back the light.

Into this familiar scene stepped a new figure. He paused, looking around, and the harper tried to see beneath the broad hat that shaded his face. Then the man's arm lifted and blue-gray wings opened as the bird he was carrying balanced and ran up to his shoulder. The bird's back was a rich russet, and its white throat gleamed in the sunlight as it looked about. A kestrel, then. And suddenly the movement of the kestrel, and the turn of the man's head as he spoke to it, resonated with something Silverhair had seen long ago, and he knew who the man was.

"Bird!" Surprise made his first try a croak. Silverhair swallowed and called again. The other stopped, peering upward, and the harper saw the slick skin of old burns on his face, that you forgot as soon as you saw the brightness of his eyes. "Bird . . . up the stairs. Here I am!"

He waited as the other climbed up to him. Except for the lines that come from peering into a bright sky, and a few threads of gray in the dark hair, this might have been the same boy whom Silverhair had left at Hawkrest Hold when he set off to seek his sister twenty years ago.

"Were you looking for me?"

Bird nodded and smiled, his dark eyes darting past the harper as the door opened and Julian came out to see who Silverhair was talking to. Robert was at his shoulder, as he always seemed to be these days.

"This is her child?"

Julian looked a little startled, and Silverhair smiled.

"Yes, this is Julian." He laid his hand on Bird's arm, and the kestrel moved aside with a soft chirk of inquiry. "And this—" he turned to the Prince—"is Bird, who grew up with me and your mother, and who has forgotten more about hawks than you or I will ever learn. . . . But I thought you were keeping the mews for Sandremun. What are you doing here?"

"When I heard that you had found *her* son, I began to train my successor," said Bird. His eyes fixed on Julian, piercing as those of the bird he bore. "I have come south to serve you, my lord. I will train birds for you that can hunt the wind!"

Julian looked a little taken aback; then a brightness came into his face, and he gave a nod.

"You must understand, I have no household. I do not know—"

"Nonsense, Julian," said Robert. "The palace mews are empty. Eric won't mind, and I'll pay for the hawk-meat myself if need be."

"I don't like to take your money . . ." the Prince began.

"What other use do I have for it?" said Robert, punching Julian's arm with rough affection. "You can pay me back when you come to your crown!"

Silverhair looked from one to the other. Bard-trained ears caught overtones in their voices that had not been there before, and he began to understand what had put such joy in Robert's face and such peace in Julian's eyes.

The Prince's attention came back to Bird. "Then I am

grateful, but I still don't understand why you have come."

"You see my face." He held up a hand to stop Julian's reply. "It doesn't matter . . . these scars are something any man can see. But perhaps you don't know that your mother's arm was scarred the same. She was still a child herself when she pulled me from the fire. She gave me my life . . . and so I offer my skill to her son."

Julian looked at him. "Hawk Master, you give me hope again. I've been hiding in my corner like . . . like a broody bird!" Suddenly he smiled. "Caolin is not going to sit still and do nothing, and anyway, I'll have to face the Council again next fall."

"It's past midsummer, Julian," said Robert. "That's not a lot of time."

"You need the Wind Crystal," added Silverhair. Until now, he had feared to mention it. "The records of the College of Bards might have held information—"

"If Caolin had thought of that, I don't suppose he would have burned the place," observed Robert, "but that doesn't help us now."

"No . . . but both Master Ras and Mistress Siaran are here in Laurelynn, and they might know. They were at the college far longer than I," Silverhair said.

"Go to them, uncle," said Julian. "The two Jewels we have were found in the keeping of their elements. The intuition of a musician should help us second-guess the Powers of Air. Or of a Hawk Master—" he turned back to Bird—"or even of this gentleman," he held out his hand to the kestrel, who considered it for a moment, then sidled quickly down Bird's arm and hopped onto Julian's wrist, "if he will talk to me!"

My dear boy, thought Silverhair, *who would not answer your questions if you ask them with that smile?*

"At least he has his smile back," said Rana brightly. "I don't care what the gossips say." She handed another bag from her basket to the Master of the Junipers. His study in the palace reminded her of his cottage on the Lady Mountain, with its piles of books, the inevitable teapot, and the smell of the air, as if incense had recently been burned in the room.

"Here's more willowbark for your stores, and bearberry leaves for bronchitis." She set two of the packets before him and began to turn over the others. "Lady Rosemary says she'll send over some more peppermint as soon as it's properly dried." Even the wrappings seemed to carry with them the pungent aromas of the stillroom. Rana took a deep breath and blinked, wondering why there were tears in her eyes.

"What *do* the gossips say?" asked the Master. Some of the chamomile she had brought him was already steeping in a pot on the hearth. He lifted the lid and peered in to check its progress, then set it back again.

Rana gave him a quick glance, but his face showed nothing. Was it really possible that he had not heard? "They say that Julian spends too much time with his cousin," she said carefully.

"Rana, your voice is like an overstressed harp string. Is that all they say?" The Master's voice was still the same—like brown bread and honey, harsh and smooth together. She looked up at him with a sigh.

"They whisper that he and Robert are lovers," she said flatly. "The maids at the palace are saying they share a bed."

"Would it be so terrible if it were true?"

Rana sat up, staring. The Master was setting out cups now, limping a little as he moved from cupboard to table. Had she feared to shock him? Or had she hoped to?

All of the arguments of idle tongues bubbled into memory: this relationship would give the Ramparts too much influence in the affairs of Westria; if Julian did not marry and beget an heir, the next generation would have to go through the turmoil of king-making again. They even whispered that Robert had put the Prince under a spell.

Then she met the Master's clear gaze, and none of those reasons made sense anymore. "I don't know."

"But it upsets you to think about it." He lifted the teapot with a steady hand and poured.

Rana turned over the remaining packets of herbs: blossoms of red clover to purify the blood, and vervain to calm the troubled mind. *I should ask him to put some of that in my tea*, she thought ruefully.

"Yes, I suppose it does, and I don't know why. Two of my father's men were bonded, and they lived together more happily than many married couples I've seen. But for a king it's bound to make things more difficult, and I can't help thinking that maybe it's because of me—" She stopped herself.

He did not ask her why she thought to claim responsibility . . . he never asked questions. She remembered the time she had left the door to the cellar unlatched and her little brother had tried to climb down the ladder and fallen and broken his arm. The Master had splinted the bone, and once Cub was sleeping, sat with her until she stopped crying and was ready to admit what she had done.

She was weeping now without sound. "Julian knows . . . why I won't ever marry . . . not him, not any man," she whispered finally. "When I realized that he wanted me, I felt so sick that I ran away, but I can't forget the way he looked at me!"

She rested her face against her crossed arms, shaking, and felt, after a time, the warm weight of a shawl across her shoulders, and a clean handkerchief pressed into her hand. The scent of incense grew stronger.

"Was it rape?"

Rana drew a long, shuddering sigh and looked up at him, but his face showed nothing, and she nodded.

"It was reivers, on the Far Alone islands. They did me no lasting harm. You don't have to tell me that no decent man would care. Julian doesn't care. But I do. And I let him see that. He looked like a man with a gut wound that day, and that *is* my fault!" Her tea was lukewarm, but she gulped it down and held out her cup for more.

"Do you love him?"

Robert had asked her that question, not so long ago. She had not known the answer then. To love—to care so

much about someone that it was like a physical pain—
she understood that now. Was that why this news had
shaken her so? Julian had not been able to help desiring
her, as she could not help her horror of desire. But because he loved her, he had tried to hide awareness of his
body's needs. Could she do less for him?

"It is justice," she answered painfully, staring at the
wisp of steam. "Robert loves him, and Robert is doing
for him what I cannot do. And if I love Julian—" she
shook her head, knowing that she could no longer deny
her spirit's hunger—"*because* I love him—I must wish
them joy."

The Master nodded. "There is the love that possesses,
and the love that puts the good of the beloved above its
own. The first may give you joy, but the second will
bring you peace, if you persevere."

Something in his voice told her that he had known
both ways of loving. In his presence, Rana could glimpse
the peace he had found. But she was still in the midst of
pain. How long would it be, she wondered, before she
could join the Master of the Junipers on the other side?

"Ye'll be goin' a long ways away now," said Tam.
"So ye must think well. Not ever'one's meant t'be a
flier, an' no shame to any that stays home!" He glanced
upward, where the wind flags on the ridge were flapping
merrily. It was a fine, bright, summer day; heat already
shimmered from the stones.

"What's he doin', tryin' t'scare us?" muttered Lis,
the girl next to Piper in the line. "Any who feared 'd be
hidin', not here. An' it never happens, my Ma says, not
now. We're bred t' the skies on both sides, all o' us."
She darted Piper a swift glance. " 'Cept you. Maybe
that's who he's tryin' t'scare. Ye sure ye wanna stay?"

Piper nodded. If he became a flier, maybe they would
accept him. But Tam's speech scared him. He was not
afraid to leave the gather, but at moments like this, the
whirlwind of his awareness cleared and he knew how his
silence disenfranchised him. What if it prevented him

from flying as well? He wiped perspiration from his brow.

"D' ye have yer bags, then? Don't want t' go hungry cause ye left somethin' behind!" Tam chuckled, and parents who were trying not to look as if they were hovering hid smiles.

"Let's *go*!" Lis exclaimed, twitching her knapsack into place.

Something like a laugh burst unexpectedly from Piper's throat. *Oh, yes, let's be going. I want to be free!*

He danced a little. Tam lifted a grizzled eyebrow, gestured with his staff, and stepped forward. Swiftly or lagging, the five boys and three girls who were going for this year's testing fell into place and followed him.

"What are you doing here?" Caolin looked from the garden, where the false Prince Julian and his men were sampling the local wine, back to Mañero. Every village they had visited had its vineyard, and the boy had developed a fondness for the stuff that was proving useful.

Mañero tipped his head to one side and laughed, and Caolin started to turn away. The little man ceased to be amusing when he presumed.

"The Guildmaster send me, of course. Master Fredegar send me with messages, like always. Messages and talk. So the news goes up and down, always talking in that town!"

"What talk?" Caolin turned again. Ordrey was with the drinkers, after all, and he could be depended upon to make sure the party followed the course they had planned. From Elk Creek they had moved on to Los Cerros, and from there to this place, which was called Jade's Crossing, not that it mattered. They were all the same. But word about the "royal" progress was spreading nicely, and the parties became more drunken with each hamlet to which they came.

Mañero grinned. "Talk about the Prince—the real Prince—about Julian."

The Blood Lord stared at him, waiting, and after a

moment a pink tongue flicked out as if the man's mouth had gone dry.

"They say that Lord Robert has seduced him, master. Robert the Fair, with the beautiful blue eyes." Singing, Mañero began to caper about the yard.

> *See the pretty boys, with their pretty toys.*
> *How they play, how they play!*
> *Does Peter pecker Paul, or do they do it all,*
> *Every day, every day!*

Mañero yipped as Caolin's fist grazed his ear. "Don't you think it's funny? No, he doesn't," he answered to himself, rubbing his ear. "The man doesn't think that is funny at all. But he did notice—"

Caolin's ears roared, but with an effort that surprised him, he kept his features still. The drinkers beneath the arbor were gone. Instead of their sour singing, he heard the music of a gitarra, and his fingers twitched as if once more they plucked sweet strings. He saw eyes like blue jewels, glinting with laughter . . . the eyes of Jehan, the King.

But Jehan's body is corruption, and the trees of the Sacred Wood are rooted in his skull. Jehan would never return to weaken Caolin with the illusion of love. For at the end of all things was . . . nothing. He who has lifted those masks the world calls spirit, or soul, or individuality, knows that, and can move men as he wills until they know it as well, and there is only dust and darkness, and peace. . . .

Caolin willed the memories back to the depths and after a time became aware that the rays of the sun still beat upon his head and that Mañero was still muttering.

Had Julian finally grown tired of trying to seduce the redheaded girl? The sorcerer was already aware that Robert was a lover of men, but he had not expected that Julian. . . . Caolin blinked again. This was better. The Prince would be more vulnerable this way—if what Mañero had told him were true.

He felt the breeze that stirred his hair, and the heat of

the sun. "Ordrey!" His voice was not loud, but it carried. In a moment the portly figure appeared. The pink skin atop his head looked polished, and there was a rosy flush in his nose and cheeks. But Ordrey had not survived so long in Caolin's service without being able to carry his wine.

"M'lord!" His grin soured as he recognized Mañero.

"I'm returning to Laurelynn. Take over here. You know the itinerary. I will send word if I cannot return soon."

Ordrey laughed happily. He had not been allowed to exercise his particular talents for a long time. The villages of the Dorada would not forget the "Prince's" visit soon.

"And what about him?" Ordrey pointed to Mañero, who lifted a bushy eyebrow in mockery.

"He goes back with me to Laurelynn." Caolin's voice sharpened. "What happens to him after that will depend on the truth of what he has said today!"

"I thought that whom I made love to was my own affair," snapped Julian.

The Master of the Junipers turned from the bookshelf with a smile. Dust motes danced through the long window beside it, open now, for the weather was growing warmer as they moved into the month of June.

"Of course people are interested. You are the Prince of Westria. Their lives may depend on whom you marry, or if you marry at all."

"Philip has several children," Julian answered harshly. "If it comes to that, I suppose I could nominate one of them as my heir. But it's a little early to speak of bestowing a throne I have yet to earn." Suddenly he understood why his uncle had spent so much of his life wandering: all of the poking and peering into his private life had made him long for the freedom of the road.

"Very likely," the Master answered peaceably. He set a book on the table in front of Julian. "This is a history of the Jewel Wars from the College of the Wise. I suppose that years ago Caolin carried off everything in the palace relating to the Four Jewels of Westria. This was the only book on the subject at the College. The Jewels were always the business of the kings.''

''Maybe the Blood Lord went through the College library as well.'' Julian opened the book, turned several pages, and let it close again. ''Do you think this thing with Robert will really turn people against me? I won't hurt him by rejecting him now!''

''Have you no better reason than that for going on?'' the Master asked.

Julian thought of Robert's physical beauty, which he had always envied . . . his now for the asking. Nor had he now any cause for envy, for with Robert he had rediscovered his own body, made perfect in his lover's eyes. But was that love? Robert cared for him with a single-minded intensity he had never known, healing wounds made by an orphaned childhood and by Rana's rejection. Julian's throat ached with astonished gratitude, and he responded with fierce loyalty. But was that love?

''I don't yet love him as much as he loves me—or as much as he deserves from me—but I will.'' As the words left his lips, another voice seemed to speak within him: *And yet before you turn from him, his passion for you will tire. . . .* He glimpsed a silent battlefield beneath a bloody sky, and Robert, sobbing as he looked down at a body lying there.

The Master of the Junipers nodded. ''Until he met your mother, your father was known as a great lover . . . of women, and also of men.''

''I've heard some of the stories,'' Julian said dryly.

''That's not quite what I had in mind. What would people have said had he loved just one man?''

''But he did,'' said the Master. ''I thought you knew. For many years, Jehan's lover was Caolin.''

Someone was singing in the street below; the sound came so clearly through the open window. . . . *How can they still make music*, thought Julian, *when I can hardly breathe?* He tried to imagine his handsome father lying down with the taunting demon he himself had faced at

Spear Island, and swallowed bile, as if everything he and Robert had done together had become unclean.

". . . but of course you never knew him," the Master was saying. It came to Julian that the priest had been speaking for some time. "Caolin was flawed, but he was not evil then. His love for Jehan nearly saved him . . . perhaps it could have if the king had known how to love Caolin and others at the same time. Caolin was sinned against as well as sinning. Your mother accepted that, and tried to atone for it."

"Are you telling me that Caolin loved my father? I'll believe in lust, maybe—lust for power!" Julian spat out the words. He had heard the Blood Lord boast of having caused the death of both king and queen. Who, if not their son, would avenge them?

"It was perhaps the only selfless emotion that Caolin ever knew," the Master said into the silence. The light had deepened; suddenly his thinning hair seemed aureoled in gold. "You must remember in dealing with him that once he was capable of love. If that memory can be awakened, he may be vulnerable."

"You sound as if love were a flaw!"

"To a man who has no emotions left but pride and the desire for mastery, it is. You have seen Katiz, Julian. He fell into darkness and was drowned, but to Caolin, those depths are a refuge. For such as he, even hatred is a weakness, for to hate, you must feel."

Julian shook his head. His ears were ringing. A surge of vision like the one that had troubled him a moment ago showed him a face thrust close to his, its ruined features contorted with passion, but whether it was in love or in hatred he could not tell. He knew only his own fear.

"All this talk of love and hate is confusing me, and there's nothing I can do about the Blood Lord right now!" he exclaimed. "My job is to find the Wind Crystal. Does that book of yours have *any*thing useful to say?"

"In Westria, the east is the quarter of the Powers of Air," answered the Master . . . as calmly, thought Julian, as if they had only been discussing the weather. "And since it is also the direction of the Ramparts, it seems reasonable to look for the Wind Crystal there."

Julian laughed suddenly. "Old friend, that's a lot of mountains. Do you suggest I climb them one by one, or will you be my guide?"

"I will not set foot in those mountains until I seek Awahna once more," the Master said softly. "But the Guardians have helped you before. Perhaps the Great Eagle knows where the Crystal is, or perhaps you can persuade Him to search His mountains. Look for the Lord of the Feathered Kindreds. If the Jewel is in the Ramparts, I think it must be in the open air."

"The Ramparts!" exclaimed Julian. "Well, at least that's my own country. I would not mind seeing the mountains again."

The high country of Westria lay open to the immensity of the empty sky. Day after day the pilgrims toiled beneath it, tiny specks of life in a wilderness of forest and stone. Single file, the children who with this ordeal were beginning their training as Wind Riders followed their guide through the wilderness, and sometimes only the knowledge that all of their elders had made this journey kept them from sitting down beside the trail and sobbing with exhaustion, or even with fear.

They had scampered like the mountain goats they hunted over every slope within five miles of the gather, but now they were in a country whose shape was strange. As they wound up and down, more than one wondered if Old Tam was leading them in circles. Only Piper was neither impatient nor afraid. He traveled with as little care for where the path might take him as a puff of milkweed on the wind. He had lived in an endless present ever since his mother stopped screaming two years ago.

The days of July lengthened toward the Feast of the First People. Piper wore out one pair of boots and was given another. Every day they marched a little farther, stopping in the early afternoon to make camp and to listen to Tam's teaching. The other children complained because they must make this journey afoot, like animals, but perhaps Piper's journey from the lowlands had toughened him, or perhaps, although at fourteen he was still no larger than the others, an extra year or two of age helped him to endure.

He whistled as he walked, listening to the others chatter. Each child was apprenticed to one of the fliers, who in exchange for service would train him and help him to build his own wing. Then came the demonstration, and for those who mastered their element, the first eagle plume. All of the children had seen that testing. But none of their elders had ever revealed what happened at the end of this journey, and the whispers the children exchanged around the fire at night rivaled any of Silverhair's tales.

Piper lay snug in his blanket, listening to the soft music of the stream. He rested on the fine sod of a tiny mountain meadow set like a jewel within the forest. If he turned his head just a little, he saw the tightly closed heads of fairy daisies; it seemed strange to lie like one of the Guardians upon a bed of flowers.

"But she *did*—don't ye believe me?" For a moment Lis' voice grew loud, and Piper turned to hear.

"Arla lost her little brother, that's what my gran' told me. She left him playin' by the stream-side while she went t' gather berries, an' she came back just in time to see a big eagle carry 'im away!" There was a respectful silence.

"Did th' eagle eat 'im?" asked one of the boys at last.

"Dunno," Lis replied. Her voice lowered again. "But a long time later, Arla fell 'n' broke 'er arm when she went t' check a trap. She couldn' manage her wing, 'n' there was no trail down from there. She would o' starved, but every morning when she woke, she found game—a squirrel, or a ground-chuck sometimes, or even a fawn. An' th' last day, when she was ready t' fly home, she woke real early and saw a naked man settin' down a quail beside th' fire. . . . But when she moved, he turned into an eagle 'n' flew away!"

There was a murmur of wonder, and Tam growled at

them to be still. Piper sank back into his blanket, dizzy with visions of a flight whose freedom disdained even a glider. The jagged silhouettes of the pine trees were a dark barrier against the mysteries around them. But his thoughts spiraled beyond the meadow, past the forest and the soaring masses of chiseled stone, until sleep overwhelmed awareness with a sweep of its dark wing.

But in his dreams, it was Piper whom the eagle carried off, Piper who was transformed into a creature winged in light and soaring through a sky that blazed like a bowl full of stars.

EIGHT: A Feather on the Wind

The sign of the Dancing Owl tavern swung drunkenly in the windy darkness, first staring at the prospective customer upright, then flipping upside down to survey him with a jaundiced glare.

"Gotta broken hinge, huh? 'S not my fault, old bird!" Robert came to a halt, saluting grandly. The owl came rightside up, and he cheered. Julian slipped a hand beneath his elbow, and his cousin's blue eyes glinted with mischief. "Not drunk, Jul—just happy!" The three other young men who had come with them reeled around the corner, singing.

"Then we don't need to go in there, do we?" said Julian. Robert still seemed steady, but they had visited four taverns already, and Julian's own head was buzzing.

"You came for information. Learned anything useful yet?" When Julian shook his head, Robert grinned triumphantly and reached for the latchstring. "Then we gotta go inside!"

The others were piling up behind them; Julian released Robert's arm and let them propel him through the door.

A wave of overheated air closed over him as he entered, heavy with the smells of wood smoke and unwashed bodies and spilled beer. In a few moments he found himself at a creaking wooden table, and a girl whose scarred cheek set one side of her face at odds with the other was bringing them ale.

"Refugee—" Robert gestured as the girl wove among the tables for another round. "Raiders got her family last year, nearly got her. The woman who owns this place is from Rivered, and it's mostly Ramparts folk who come here."

Julian nodded. "I think you brought me here once when we were still on the border patrol."

"I remember," said Will, who had been one of Julian's men in the mountains and was newly come to serve him again. He was not the first. This summer the raiders who had plagued their borders seemed to be giving them a respite. Several men from the old patrol had turned up when word got around that Julian was settled in Laurelynn. Soon, he supposed, he would have to find them something to do.

"We were on escort duty for Lord Philip," Will continued, "and wasn't he half-pissed when he found out where we had been!"

"He said that if we were so thirsty, we could carry water!" Robert clapped his hand to the small of his back dramatically. "I still ache when I think of it, but the steps of the Council Hall have never been so clean."

Even Julian grinned, remembering. They had been raw seventeen-year-olds, eager to prove that they could drink like men. But they had only succeeded in getting as sick as dogs. No wonder his memories of this place were hazy. Three years—sweet Lady—it seemed a long time ago.

"Ah, a game!" Robert pointed, and Julian realized the intermittent "thunk" he had been hearing was the sound of darts hitting the board. "Wonder if my eye's still in. Come on, lads, and we'll see if the locals can outthrow real mountain men!" He got to his feet and winked at Julian, who realized that his friend was giving him a cue.

"Not until I've had another round of ale. You go on— I'll be along soon." For a moment their hands clasped, then Julian let go.

More eyes than Julian's followed Robert as he led the others across the room. They had all of them worn old clothing, but Robert the Fair would have been remarkable in rags. Especially now, when his face shone with joy.

Have I the power to make another human being so happy? wondered Julian. *If I had known that, I would have become his lover long ago.*

Boasting good-naturedly, Robert inserted himself into the game. Julian turned to survey the rest of the company. He should have known them for mountain folk without the telling. The deliberate speech—vowels drawn out, terminations dropped with a twang—was the speech of his home. And though some wore the bright garments of the city, others were still in leather and homespun, with long untrimmed beards or tightly braided hair.

He drank his ale slowly, listening. One group by the wall seemed subtly different from the rest. It was not a family; their similarities were more in build and style than in feature—beards clipped close, boots tightly laced at the ankles, and short jackets rather than the rough coats most mountain people wore. And the women were dressed like the men.

He leaned toward a woman at the next table. "Who're they?"

"Back-country visitors," came the answer, "though I never found out from where. They come in every year 'bout this time, tradin' furs and quartz crystals . . . and gold."

The tavern girl came through with a pitcher, and Julian had her refill the old woman's mug as well as his own.

"They come in for supplies, then?" asked Julian.

"Sugar and tea, all the usual things," she answered. "But that's not what the gold's for. . . ." She let the silence lengthen, and he raised an inquiring eyebrow.

"Silk!" she whispered. "Rolls and rolls of heavy silk, wove as tight and dyed as bright as the weavers of Laurelynn can make 'em. My youngest girl married a silk-weaving man, and I know. Silk, 'n' heavy bamboo poles, that's what they buy. And then they're off, the Guardians know where, and we don't see 'em again fer another year."

Julian sat back, thinking. Crystal and gold and furs meant the high country, so they might be worth talking to, but there was something else—something having to do with silks like the wings of butterflies.

When a place emptied at the table beside the strangers, Julian picked up his mug, made his way over, and sat down.

"Buy you a round?" he asked when the girl came their way again. They looked startled, but he had never met a mountain man who would refuse a free drink, and these were no exception.

"I'm plannin' a trip into the mountains," he said then. "Need a guide. Know anyone who's free?"

"Depends 'n where," one of the men said guardedly. He was darkly tanned, with his purple tunic tucked neatly into gray breeches and his mustaches curled. "Man c'n get lost twenty mile from home." The others, seeing that one of their own was taking care of the conversation, continued to talk in soft tones.

"That's why I want a guide," said Julian, thinking that their accent was unlike any he had encountered before. "I'm a mountain man myself, but I want to go . . . southward," he hazarded. Even to the rulers of the Ramparts, the land beyond Awahna was something of a mystery.

"I'm lookin' for someone—" he added suddenly—"a boy who ran off from here almost three months ago." He waited, wondering why he had said that. They still had no idea of which way Piper had gone, but all of the probable places had been searched long ago.

The man in purple exchanged a quick glance with the pretty blond woman beside him. Julian grew still, senses for which he had no name focusing suddenly.

"The boy can't talk," he said then. "Raiders took out his family two years ago. Only a grandmother left. We're worried—"

"Thought so!" exclaimed the girl.

Julian saw the look of warning the man gave her, but his ears were buzzing with mingled relief and wonder. They knew something! Was some power helping him at last?

"Did he come to your village? Please, I have to know."

"Found a boy wanderin'," the man said finally. "Took 'im in. Might be th' same, maybe no. Can't tell ye where." Steady gray eyes lifted and held Julian's gaze. Eyes used to long distances, thought the Prince, and with the double awareness that came to him sometimes, he was hearing a line from an old song. Softly he chanted:

> Rare is the realm where the eagles, ascending,
> embrace empty skies,
> Soaring the skyways in freedom unending,
> the Wind Rider flies. . . .

"Is it true then?" he went on quickly, seeing the man's hand move toward his knife. "I don't need to know where your village is, only that the boy is safe . . . and that the legend is true."

"Lotta information t' give a stranger," the dark man said slowly. But his hand was back on the table, and Julian relaxed again.

"I am Julian of Stanesvale. I used to be on the border patrol."

"An' now y' guard Westria." The girl grinned. "Both ways, we've heard o' you. He's Olin, 'n' my name's Tania."

Julian felt himself flushing. His rank had not seemed relevant here.

"Piper—the boy—is like family to me. And also—" now it was he who held the Wind Rider's gaze—"I think that the Wind Crystal may be among the peaks somewhere."

"Mmn," said Olin. "Sworn not t' tell where th' gather is, but th' boy's not there anyhow. Wants t' join us. Gone t' th' Eagle with th' others t' be tested now."

Julian stared at him. "The Eagle," he said flatly. "You mean the Guardian of the Kindreds of the Air?"

Olin grinned. "Got more 'n' one secret up there!"

"You go t' Cloud's Rest, ask ol' Eagle 'bout the Crystal 'n' the boy," Tania added eagerly.

"You'll tell me how to get there?"

She nodded. "Y' got the right, y'r Master o' th' Jewels."

"But none else, mind," said her companion. "Th' way's for the Jewel Lord!"

"I understand," Julian said slowly, thinking of Robert's reaction were he to say that he was going off alone . . . and Silverhair's. "I will find a way."

"There must be ways to deal with the Powers of Air," said Silverhair. He gestured outward. Half of the upper story of the Guildhouse was an open porch from which one could see most of the valley when the sky was clear. The high winds of the past week had scoured the heavens to a clear, bright blue. "Didn't the archives at the College of Bards have anything to say?"

Mistress Siaran turned, still leaning on the rail. "There are old stories, like that of the adept Prospero, who bound a Spirit of the Air to his service for a time. One hears of folk who can speak the language of the birds, and there are many tales of weather-workers here in Westria, but that skill we still practice, so there's no mystery."

Silverhair nodded. "Yes, there are still adepts like the sorceress of Willasfell, who could call the whirlwind."

"We know the ways of land and sea, but the air is a mystery," Siaran sighed. "Legends say the Ancients knew where every drop of rain would fall; they were on first-name terms with all of the storms."

There was no storm today, only an invisible hand that stroked across the grasslands and wrinkled the green surface of the river, tugged playfully at Siaran's bronze hair and stirred the fringes of her shawl.

"Such knowledge . . . such power," Silverhair sighed. "I remember Caolin regretting its loss, long ago. But if we are to believe the old stories, the Ancients poisoned the air until it turned against them. Is knowledge always evil, then? Caolin uses what he knows for ill, and now we are seeking the knowledge with which to defeat him. Must we choose between sharing his evil or being conquered by it?" He turned toward the southwest, where the Red Mountain bulked against the pale sky—immense and brooding when seen from this direction as from no other, its shadow weighting the land.

"We need Wisdom," said Siaran.

"What?" It took the harper a moment to understand the word.

"Wisdom and Understanding," she went on. "Isn't that what balances Knowledge? That's what they teach at the College of the Wise."

"They teach it," he agreed, "but do they *understand* it?" He drew out the word ironically. "Sometimes I think that our knowledge has become as impoverished as the learning of the Ancients. I would trust my soul to the Master of the Junipers, and Rosemary's boy, Frederic, shows promise, but what about the rest of them? How many priests do you know, or priestesses, who are truly of the *Wicce* now?" He used an ancient word that encompassed a universe of magic.

"Those who know the songs and spells have power," whispered the harp mistress. "There is magic in our craft too, Silverhair, as *you* know. What really happened when Caolin captured us at Santibar?"

Silverhair frowned. There had been good reasons for Caolin's anger. For the first time in years, he forced himself to think backward, to picture the scene, to open himself to memory. . . .

Once more he was kneeling in a dusty road, Swangold in his arms. He touched her strings in desperate appeal— a prayer more for Siaran and the others than for his own safety—and again the answer came to him. He quivered like one of his own harp stings, resonating in sympathy

with the harmony that ruled creation. For a moment there
was no reality but that sound.

"Farin . . . what happened? Are you all right? Farin,
I'm sorry!"

Gradually he became aware of his body again. Siaran
was holding him. He clung to her friendly warmth as if
to root himself to earth once more.

"How could I have forgotten?" Was it really that easy
to make the contact, or had he changed? Had he truly
only to look within?

"There's no need for forgiveness," he said harshly.
"I needed to be reminded. I have heard the Wind Lord—
heard Him, and tried to forget it even while I wanted that
music as a dying man gasps for air!"

"But why?"

"Because then I would have had to live by it," he
breathed.

There was no pain in his body, but as in that moment
outside Julian's rooms, when the invisible fist had
squeezed the air from his lungs, he was afraid. After
each moment of extremity in which the doors between
the worlds of flesh and spirit swung open for him, he had
always shut them again.

"Oh, Siaran, you spoke more truly than you knew!"
He groaned, hiding his face against the sweet-scented
coils of her hair. "For all my great oaths, I have done
no more for Julian than any bard could do. Even at the
Council, I failed him. Yes, I do have the magic, but what
will I become if I use it? That's what makes me afraid."

"But isn't that what Julian has had to face each time
he mastered one of the Jewels?" she asked softly. Silverhair nodded.

"I was never really willing to understand." He could
still hear the music. Now that he had recognized it, would
it ever go away? "He *must* have the Wind Crystal! Surely
Wind Lord can teach me how to find it, if I can learn
how to hear."

"I shouldn't have spoken," said Siaran. "I love you
the way you are, Farin Silverhair. Don't go away from
me."

But already it was too late for that. Though her warm arms held his body, he could feel his spirit fluttering like a banner. His inner music soared triumphantly, and high against the blue blaze of the sky, a red-tailed hawk danced with the wind.

The wind from the river was heavy with the dank smell of decaying vegetation, spiced now and again by a whiff of dead fish. Caolin's nostrils flared as he walked toward Laurelynn's great central square, but it would not have suited the character of the smallholder whose face he was wearing to use a bandana to filter out the smell.

It got better as he moved toward the center of the island. Caolin drew in a great breath, his eyes closing as he filled his lungs with clean air. Then the sorcerer brushed against someone's arm and sprang backward, with an effort deflecting into a stream of curses the power that would have blasted the fellow.

The man he had bumped into clutched the packages he was carrying and started to reply in kind, and with a surge of new anger, Caolin recognized the purple cloak and silver hair.

"But o' course ye wouldn't look where ye'r going!" he drawled viciously. "I know ye now—think y' own the town, hangin' about the palace with that perverted prince o' yours!"

As the sorcerer spoke, Silverhair stilled, his head tilted as if listening. "And as soon as you speak, I know *you*, Caolin, whatever face you may wear," he said softly. There was a short silence.

"Do you?" Caolin asked in his own voice. "Well, you *are* a musician. Perhaps your magic has taught you to hear better than most."

Silverhair shrugged. "What are you doing here?" His voice was strained, and Caolin smiled. He had almost forgotten how much he hated this man.

"Oh, I go up and down . . . up and down. I have my interests to watch over."

"You'll be going nowhere if I call the guard—" the harper began.

"Do you really think that those brick-coated bumblers could capture *me*? You are the one who is in danger now."

"Perhaps." The harper's gaze had gone inward, as if he were listening. "But if you couldn't destroy me on Wizards' Island, I don't think you can harm me in the middle of Laurelynn."

"Nonetheless, the time will come when I will destroy you, Farin Silverhair. I have sworn it, and I have never yet failed to keep my word."

Silverhair took a deep breath. "When the time comes, I am willing to answer for my sins against you," he said quietly. "Are you as ready to take responsibility for what you have done to Westria?"

For a moment Caolin felt as if the wind had suddenly turned cold. This assurance was something new. What secret had Farin found? Caolin met the harper's steady gaze, and his eyes narrowed.

"There is no sin, there is only power."

"You believe that, don't you?" the other man said curiously.

"I have reason." The sorcerer's good humor was returning. "Who is there to punish me?"

"Julian."

Caolin shook his head. "When I am ready, he too will fall into my hands."

"No! My life stands between you and Julian!"

Interesting . . . this threat had stirred Silverhair, where his own danger left him unmoved.

"I will brush you aside like a feather in the wind," said the sorcerer. He surveyed the harper scornfully. Clearly, the man's talents had won him neither wealth nor power if he had to carry his own packages through the streets of Laurelynn.

For the first time, Caolin looked at the parcels closely. Journey bread, dried fruit, and jerky. In the days when he used to victual armies, he had learned to know those merchants' marks well.

"Are you planning to protect him by spiriting him away?"

Silverhair started to cover the bags with his cloak and then controlled the movement. *Now why should he try to hide plans for a journey?* wondered the sorcerer. *Unless I've guessed right, and Julian is leaving Laurelynn.* He suppressed his laughter.

"I'm going away," the harper said quickly. "I've spent too much time on the road to be comfortable in cities."

Caolin smiled, and saw once more in Silverhair's eyes that betraying flicker of fear. "I'm in no hurry for my revenge. I may even miss you once you're gone." He could no longer contain his laughter. Bowing, he stepped aside, and the harper moved swiftly.

Farin never did know how to lie, thought the sorcerer as the purple cloak disappeared. *But why should he be so afraid to have me find out that they're going away? Surely if the Prince leaves town, all the city will know.*

It would be easier to persuade people that the fool whom Ordrey was bear-leading was the real prince if Julian were known to be away from Laurelynn. But he must contact the woodsrats in the north, and the Arena slavers who waited for his word, and tell them to raid elsewhere this year. The last thing he needed just now was for Julian to win more reknown fighting reivers!

But what if the thing he wanted to conceal from me was not the fact that they're going? But where— The sorcerer stopped suddenly. *Or why. . . .*

Abruptly Caolin knew what they were going for . . . the Wind Crystal! Julian had taken him by surprise when he had found the first two Jewels, but it would not happen again.

Caolin began to hurry, his mind awhirl with plans.

"We have tales o' fliers who rode th' whirlwind," said Old Tam, "but 'tis not a thing that anyone would do of a purpose. A little dust-devil maybe, but not one o' the great ones." He shook his head, gave a final twist and tied off the silk that held his feathers to the prayer stick he had been making. In this sheltered hollow, there was no wind to blow them away. The children held up their own sticks and grinned.

"Get ye goin' now. Ye'll need th' time t' get up an' place them an' be back before th' light fails." Tam slipped the unused feathers back into his pouch and levered himself upright. Some of the children were already scampering down the slope, heading for the pinnacles where they intended to make their prayers.

Piper picked his way along the ridge of stone. Lis was ahead of him, but soon she disappeared around the shoulder of the peak. Storm-twisted pines reached up from its hollowed flanks, and late flowers glowed like scattered amethysts where a pocket in the granite had collected a few inches of granular soil. But his attention was on the buttress of gray stone that rose above.

It stayed his goal for so long that he was startled to find it suddenly before him. Eagerly he pulled himself upward. The hollow where they made the prayer sticks looked like a cup-sized pock in the stone below. Westward, the clouds were building luminous bastions where rising warmth met a moist layer of air.

Piper slid his prayer stick from under his belt and reached out as if to embrace the sky. The crisp wind tingled through his every vein. A little more air and his solid flesh would float on the breeze. He leaned into the wind.

"Help!"

Drunk on infinity, it took a moment for Piper to understand.

"I'm . . . stuck. Please, help me!" The voice belonged to Lis.

She didn't know that Piper was there. And she had never been friendly. . . . Piper turned.

"Oh, turds!"

He heard rock fall, and a little gasp of pain. Stone pricked his palm; he licked away the bright drop of blood.

My blood . . . and hers. . . . The thought came clearly. *They're the same.*

Down the other side of the pinnacle he glimpsed bright hair. His questioning whistle pierced the air.

"Stranger, 's that you?" she called.

He whistled affirmation and the head moved; he saw her face and one arm.

"Rock broke," Lis said. 'Can't go up or down!"

There was no handhold within her grasp, but a foot or two above it, a fracture line angled across the stone. Once more he whistled, then began to inch his way forward. A moment ago he could have launched himself upon the wind, but now he was acutely aware of the gulf below.

"What're ye doin'? Fool, I still can't reach ye."

Then he was above her, knees flexing as he eased one foot from the path and let it dangle down.

"Crazy," Lis said more softly. "If that rock's rotten too, we'll both fall."

Piper shook his head. He had tried each handhold carefully. If he was wrong . . . then for a few moments, both of them were going to fly.

"Come!" his whistle summoned. *"Quickly, come!"*

Her hard fingers closed around his ankle. He winced as his leg took her weight and clutched desperately at the stone. Somehow he pulled his leg up. The fabric of his breeches started to tear as she shifted her grip; for a moment the weight was unendurable, then one of her hands groped for the crack. He jerked her other hand toward a stone knob, gripped the cloth of her tunic as she heaved herself upward.

And then they were both clinging to the crack, gasping in the thin air.

When they reached the ledge, he dropped to his knees, staring at the prayer stick still lying there.

"Think maybe this is high enough to leave 'em," Lis said at last. "Nearly made ourselves into 'n offering!" She wedged the feathered stick from her belt into a crack in the stone. He nodded, and jammed his own down beside it. The blue feathers looked rather tattered. Would the Spirits understand?

For just a moment, the roaring of the wind in his ears was replaced by a chiming of sweet bells.

"Come on . . . Crazy!" Lis called to him. But now there was affection in her tone.

Grinning, Piper followed, finding it easier as the strengthening wind pressed him against the stone. He did not see it pluck one of the feathers from his prayer stick, nor did he notice as it bore the bit of blue spiraling into the azure immensity of the sky.

> *By power of soaring sky and rolling sea,*
> *By mighty earth and fire, be bound to me!*

Caolin lifted his cupped palm, and twin points of light danced in his other hand. With the breath of his nostrils and spit from his mouth, with a smear of dirt from beneath his nails and a drop of his blood, the sorcerer anointed the connected crystals, imprinting them with his identity. Fredegar Sachs had ordered his household to bed hours earlier. No other voice, no other consciousness, troubled the sorcerer's concentration.

> *Thy emptiness with energy I fill,*
> *That thou mayst be obedient to my will!*

With a smooth crystal rod, he stroked down the axis of each twin crystal again and again, letting his energy flow through his palm, feeling it amplified as it spiraled down the rod.

> *First Vibration, amplified in sound,*
> *To bear my words, to do my will, be bound!*
> *And when I will, they quality shall be*
> *To carry words of others back to me . . .*

He let his breath flow out in a whisper of tone that grew until it resonated with the word that was the seed of the sorcerer's power. *Nada . . . Nada.* As he chanted it, the clear quartz began to cloud. The crystal continued to buzz faintly even after Caolin fell silent.

> *As Two are one, conjoined naturally,*
> *Let One be two, linked by my sorcery!*

He laid the crystal on the marble slab, with swift precision positioned the straight blade, then struck with the hammer. Steel clanged, and at the same moment came a sharp sound like a squeal of pain.

When Caolin's ears stopped ringing, he nodded in satisfaction, for both of the murky crystals on the slab were whole and perfect, separate physically, but with their energy field the same.

"Where you go, I shall go with you!" whispered the sorcerer as he lifted the larger of the two. "We'll find someone to carry you, and when I speak to your twin, you will answer. Ah, yes, my small servant, then you will answer me!"

"I don't want to go off without a word," said Julian. "But I do have to go alone." Outside, the wind was shaking the sycamores as if to dislodge all of their secrets. He forced himself to sit still. "This is the time to do it. Eric doesn't need me here, and the Sea Star will be safe in the care of the sprite who lives in the lake of Laurelynn."

The Master of the Junipers shook his head. "You're more like your uncle than you imagine," he said, handing Julian a packet of tea. "But at least you have some sense of responsibility. You know that I will not be able to stop him from following you."

Julian slid the tea into his pack and shrugged. "I was bred up in those hills. If I can get a good head start, it will take more than Silverhair's trailcraft to find me." With the supplies the Master was giving him, he could eat well enough at this smiling time of year. His horse was tethered out of sight below, with the rest of his gear tied up in the bedroll behind the saddle. Hard traveling perhaps, but he had fared rougher on campaign.

"Why hurt him this way?" The flickering lamplight made it hard to tell whether or not the old man was frowning, but the Master's face had always kept his secrets well.

"The Wind Riders told me that I must come alone, that's one reason. And Caolin likely has men watching

Silverhair, for another. My uncle told you that he met the Blood Lord, didn't he?'' Julian picked up a bag of salt and stowed it, and another that held shaved willow-bark for fever tea.

''And the third reason?''

Julian sighed. ''I'd rather hurt Silverhair's feelings than see him dead because I dragged him through the mountains. He says that he's in good health, but I don't like the way he looks sometimes. If I get well away, he will have to come back here. I'm not taking anyone with me—not Robert—not anyone.'' He banished a picture of Rana riding before him, the sunlight bright on her hair. Why was he remembering that now?

''Robert won't like being left behind any better than will Silverhair,'' observed the Master.

''That's true,'' Julian grimaced. ''But there's been enough gossip about us already.'' It was not lack of love that compelled the Prince to go without him—Robert had become like another self to him. Perhaps it was too much love.

Last night he had dreamed. He was scaling a mountain. Above him blazed the blinding expanse of the sky. At the top was something he needed as a drowning man needs air. But as he glimpsed the summit, someone screamed. He looked down, saw Robert clinging to a knob of stone. Slowly, relinquishing the radiance that had almost been within his grasp, Julian went back down. Then, the dream had fragmented into impressions of Robert grabbing him, begging . . . . He had wakened as Robert touched him, not in panic, but in need, and after that, his own body had answered all questioning.

But he could think again now, and the dream frightened him.

''Folk have to see that I can still act independently. Maybe *I* have to find out if I can bear to be alone.'' He closed his pack and strapped it tightly. ''Will you give me your blessing?''

For a moment the old man's hands rested lightly on Julian's hair. There was a murmur of invocation and Julian felt, rather than heard, the presence of the powers on which the Master had called: the deep stability of earth, the powerful tug of the sea, and the two others that he did not yet know, teasing at his awareness.

"Let the Wind Crystal itself call you," the priest said then. "Listen with your spirit, not with your ears."

Julian was still wondering how he was supposed to do that as he crossed the bridge out of Laurelynn. The wind was whispering an answer to the reeds, but he could not understand it. As he reined his mount onto the road, an owl blurred by on silent wings.

NINE: Jewel Song

Piper stood laughing, his face uplifted to the clouds of opalescent spray. As the young sun lifted above the heights, a first ray struck like an adept's wand, transforming each invisible droplet to a point of jeweled fire. The stream, full-fed by last night's rain, launched itself over the precipices with abandon, rebounding from rock to rock in bursts of spray.

In the forest behind him, the others were groggily wrestling with soggy blankets. But Piper's discomfort had given way to wonder. It was worth a wetting to find these falls. And gradually the music of falling water crystallized into a bird's sweet song.

Carefully he stepped forward. There was a whir among the ripples, and the bird came to rest upon an outcrop that divided two skeins of rushing water, bobbing and bowing like an old courtier garbed in a neat suit of gray.

Holding his breath, Piper eased down upon a stone. The dipper began again, continuing to sing even as it winged upward through the spray. Suddenly the voices of the bird, and of the waters, unlocked the music within him. Piper reached for his flute and let out all his longing in a pure breath of sound.

The dipper's bright eye fixed him in astonishment. Swift fingers molded a trill like the bird's own melody. The dipper skimmed downward and began to glean among the shallows, pausing every few moments to answer the flute's sweet music with another warble of its own.

Since Piper left Laurelynn, he had known no such communion. He was one with wind and water and bird, and awareness soared away on the song. . . .

Startled, the bird flitted upward, poised for a moment beside a hummock of woven mosses, and disappeared. Piper blinked, music fading in mid-phrase.

"Sorry . . . made it fly away. Only wanted t' hear!" Lis shook her head. Her cheeks were wet with tears. The others were there too, beginning to stir with the waning of the spell. Piper smiled to reassure her. Their presence was the one thing that had been missing here.

"Tam sent me," she said then. "Time t' move on."

As they reached the top of the bank, the sun lifted suddenly above the trees. Piper's eyes widened as the dazzle of light on mist refracted into a rainbow that curved into the clouds that swathed the higher slopes of the mountainside.

"That's where we're goin'," said Lis. "Cloud's Rest . . . end o' th' journey. We're almost there!"

Ground fog hung heavy in the Great Valley. The damp air caught in Silverhair's lungs as he climbed the stairs to his chambers. He suppressed a cough as he saw his door already open and someone waiting for him inside.

"What's wrong?"

It was Lord Robert, sitting on the edge of the only chair that was not piled with supplies for their journey. Silverhair dropped the saddlecloth he had brought in to mend and took the sheet of paper that the younger man held out to him. He recognized Julian's strong, sloping writing and blinked, trying to bring it into focus.

"Julian has left Laurelynn without us!" Robert's voice

wavered, but Silverhair's attention was fixed on the paper in his hand. No matter how he looked at it, the sense stayed the same.

I didn't even leave a note when I ran away, he thought. He was hurt, and angry . . . and amused, he realized suddenly, because he knew, perhaps better than Julian himself, why the Prince had gone alone. But it was going to be hard to make Robert understand. He handed the letter back and reached down to pick up the saddlecloth.

"When did this come to you?"

"This morning," said Robert. "Last night was my brother's birthday. Julian left the celebration early and made me promise to sleep at Philip's if it got too late and we were drinking. When I did get home, Julian was gone, and then a tavern girl came with this message. She said that a young border rider had told her to deliver it to me this morning."

Silverhair observed him sympathetically. If Robert was suffering from a hangover as well as from his outrage, he must be feeling fragile indeed. The bard knew how that felt too.

"Damn him, *damn* him! Has he gone mad? How could he just—"

"Oh, easily!" Silverhair lifted a pile of sheet music off the bench and sat down. "Did you never work alone when you both were on the border patrol?"

"It's not the same thing—" Robert began, but his voice lacked conviction. "If he'd gone off this way last year, I could understand, but now. . . . We planned the journey together. Why couldn't he just tell me they made him promise to go alone?"

"For the same reason he couldn't tell *me*. We would have argued him out of it," answered Silverhair soothingly.

"What a cowardly thing—"

"Of course it is," the harper interrupted him. "He couldn't face you—he loves you. He could have predicted every word you were going to say."

Robert reddened. "And what about you? You're his uncle. Aren't you furious with him too?"

Silverhair sighed. "Furious? No. In a long and misspent life, I've left too many people behind me to resent being left in my turn."

"You're grinning! Are you mocking me?"

"Robert . . . Robert, remember, I love him too," Silverhair said softly. "We are not going to let him get away with this!"

The door banged open. For a moment they saw only a cloaked silhouette, and hoped. Then the figure came into the light and they recognized Rana. She pushed back the hood from her bright hair, scanning the room.

"Were you looking for me?" asked Silverhair gently. Her gaze came back to his face, and she read there the answer to her question.

"It's true then," she said tightly. "Julian has gone. How soon can we start after him?"

Robert looked taken aback, then his eyes narrowed. "We? What makes you think you're going to go? Haven't you already caused him enough pain?"

Rana recoiled, but her voice was steady as she answered him.

"Yes. I have. That's why I mean to go."

"What do you mean?" Robert scowled.

"Have you forgotten what Julian is looking for? Frederic is away at the college, and the Master cannot travel so far. Perhaps it will not matter, but if Julian does need help with the Jewels, who is there who knows anything about them but me?" Her hand went to her breast in a gesture that had once been habitual, and Silverhair remembered abruptly how she had come to them like one of the Guardians of the Sea, with the sacred stone blazing between her breasts like a blue star.

"I owe him that much. But you needn't worry, Robert. I won't come between you. Do you want me to tell you why I'm not a threat to you?" she cried out suddenly, and the harper recognized, without understanding, the note of pain. "Julian knows!"

"No! Rana." Robert shook his head. "I didn't mean—"

"Children, be still!" Silverhair's command shocked them to silence. "This isn't your decision, Robert, or mine. I couldn't keep her from going with us two years ago, when she was only a girl, and you won't do it now. For the Guardians' sake, let us stick together. I don't want to know what Julian is going to say if he hears that we let her follow us alone!"

I sound like a grandfather. I'll spoil my reputation for misanthrophy, he thought wryly. Rana was looking at him in wonder. But he no longer cared what people said of him, and Rana was a useful hand on the trail.

By the time Robert and Rana left him, they seemed resigned to their prospective companionship. Silverhair slid Swangold from her case and sat down in the empty chair with the harp cradled in his arms. His agile fingers strolled lightly along the strings, finding the instrument for once completely in tune.

His pack was still next to the door, ready for the departure they had planned for the next day. The note he had been writing to Eric to tell him about the meeting with Caolin lay folded on his table. They would need to get off quickly. It was all very well for him to assure Robert that they would find his missing lover, but Silverhair had enough respect for Julian's woodcraft to know that the Prince would not have left an easy trail. He had searched the Ramparts long ago, after his sister Faris had taken the infant Julian and run away. There were a lot of places in those mountains where a man could get lost.

I didn't find Julian then, he thought ruefully. *What makes me so sure I will have better luck this time?* He struck a familiar chord, modulated, and with the other hand filled in a snatch of melody. *Wind Lord, you see everything from the skies . . . can You see Julian? Can You show me where he is now?* He felt the familiar rush of sensation as the world fell away.

He tried to form the noble chords of the Wind Lord's song, but his fingers persisted in plucking out another melody. It was only a ballad, but it seemed faintly familiar, as if it were something he had sung a very long time ago.

High in the sky when the wind is upwelling,
Freely I roam—
The breast of the storm is my refuge and
dwelling,
The clouds are my home!
  Launch on the lift, sister,
  Hear the lines sing;
  Ride the ridge wind, brother,
  Steady your wing!

He closed his eyes, thinking back nearly twenty years to the time when he had toured the mountains with a band of players called "Los Pajaritos." They had been somewhere near Awahna in a village like any other, except for one group that didn't dress like the others and that had appeared suddenly out of the night. And after the performance, when they all settled down to some serious drinking, one of the girls had sung that song. And it seemed to Silverhair—but he had been very young then, and very drunk as well—that he had seen the strangers leap like birds into the air and soar homeward in the dawn.

"I believe that Piper has been staying with the Wind Riders," Julian's note had said, "and there I may find news of the Crystal as well."

Who, if not Wind Riders, could those flying folk have been? Silverhair remembered where he had met them, and there were not so many roads in the high country that a man could pass unnoticed once you knew the direction he had gone.

"Oh, Julian," he said aloud. "Did you think I could be duped so easily? I lost you once—I will not lose you again!"

"Oh, he trick you, master. He trick you fine and got clean away!" Mañero danced into the room.

Caolin's glance transfixed him, and the little man was suddenly still. Deliberately the sorcerer folded the letter from Ordrey. Mañero had not moved, but his eyes danced. Caolin frowned. This servant was growing in-

creasingly unmannerly. He folded his hands, waiting until Mañero began to twitch before he spoke again.

"Well?"

"Prince Julian's left Laurelynn!" Mañero began
laughing. "Joke on everyone, no?"

No, not when he had been watching so carefully and
waiting so long!

"Cur!" The sorcerer was on his feet, his scarlet robes
billowing around him. A chill wind swept the room.
"Garbage-eating, cowardly shit-licker!" The words
ended in a snap, and Mañero whimpered. "Were you
guzzling? Stuff pitch in your bung hole, or you'll lose
your dinner too." Caolin's voice thinned and held in a
long note that sent Mañero curling into the corner. "You
were paid to watch the harper, fool. . . ." The cold
deepened as the word lengthened into a low hum.

Mañero clapped his hands over his ears and howled.
The sound pierced Caolin's concentration. He drew
breath.

"Was *watching* the harper," Mañero gasped. "Lad
tricked his uncle too." The little man gave Caolin a quick
glance, and when the sorcerer did not move, sat up again.
"*And* his lover!" He caught his breath on a laugh.

"He didn't tell them where he was going?" Caolin
asked coldly, trying to still the leaping of his pulse.

Mañero shook his head. "But the harper, he think he
knows where. They be following tomorrow, him and
Lord Robert and the girl."

"Where?" The sorcerer stooped, taloned fingers closing on the man's shoulder. "Where are they going?" He
could feel the warm flesh quivering beneath his hand.

"South," Mañero sighed gustily. "Silverhair think he
head for Stanesvale, then maybe Awahna, who knows?"

Caolin let go of him and stepped back, wiping his
hands mechanically on the folds of his robe.

It can't be in the Valley, he was thinking swiftly. *If
one Jewel was there, they would all have been.* He tried
to imagine it and felt his balance waver, reached out
for the arm of his chair and guided himself down. The
Sacred Valley. . . . Even in thought, he could not form

its name. He would destroy it one day, when the rest of the land was safely in his grasp. But he could not follow Julian there.

Nor should he. The pounding Caolin's ears faded as he realized how foolish it would be for him to undertake such a journey himself. He would send someone— already an idea was coming to him—after Silverhair. With Julian finally out of the city, the sorcerer had plots to hatch here in Laurelynn. *Silverhair is not the only one who understands what stories can do. Julian may be surprised by the welcome he receives when he comes home again!*

"Good, eh, master? Not Mañero's fault. And funny— all of us left swearing the same?" The man gave him a sly grin.

"No," said the sorcerer. "And if you were not such a feckless fool, you would understand why there is no reason for amusement. When my enemies are at my mercy, *then* I will laugh. What we must do now is to follow them."

"Follow? I can go *with* them!"

It took Caolin a moment to realize what Mañero was saying.

"What makes you think they would let you?"

"I follow like a shadow, then trick them so they take me. I fool them, oh yes!"

"And delay them?" asked Caolin. "I'll be sending an armed party in pursuit. Can you mark the trail?"

"Can do, oh, many things. You see!" Mañero sank back onto his haunches, panting. With relief probably, thought Caolin as he took up pen and paper again.

"Oh, I will see," he said gently. "And if you fail me, you will see more than a little wind." The pen scratched across the rough paper for a few seconds more; then the sorcerer dusted sand across the surface to dry it and rummaged in his pouch for a seal he had not used in twenty years.

Caolin's hand trembled as he lifted it away and saw the crossed keys of the Seneschal in relief in the red wax once more. He did not think they would have changed the seal, or that even if they had, the man to whom it was going would notice any difference. But it would intrigue him.

"Very well. I will give you the chance. Do everything you said and more! Get your gear together. And leave this letter for Alexander of Las Costas on your way." Caolin pushed the sealed and folded message across the desk, then pulled out a small suede sack that clinked softly as he hefted it, watching the sudden glitter in Mañero's eyes.

"And every evening," the sorcerer added softly, "*every* night, at the hour after midnight when all is still, you will go apart and open your mind to me."

He tossed the bag suddenly. Grinning, Mañero snatched it from the air and edged swiftly through the door. But as he scampered down the corridor, it seemed to the sorcerer that he heard the words, *"But master, you should have laughed."*

Caolin stood frowning after him. Whether from fear or from greed, he thought that Mañero would be faithful. But what if he and Silverhair were mistaken about the way Julian had gone?

Julian reined in, shading his eyes to peer into the valley that was set like a cup in the hills before him. Misleading pursuit by going east instead of south toward Awahna had seemed like a good idea when he left Laurelynn, but he was beginning to wonder. Perhaps he should have headed straight for Stanesvale; he suspected that his foster mother knew things about these mountains that she had never told. Surely she must have heard of Cloud's Rest. Did this road go anywhere?

Since morning he had been winding through a parkland of scattered oaks and pine trees, varied by patches of chapparal. As the sun strengthened, heat began to shimmer from the southern slopes in visible waves of rising air. Most of the birds were already hiding in the shade, but a turkey buzzard floated above the ridges, riding the tides of warm air.

Julian had seen deer in the dawning, and once a brown

bear rearing suddenly from a quivering tangle of manzanita, but no human life for many hours. He told himself that he needed to buy bread, that his horse could use rest and water. But the truth was that he had lived on game before now, and the bay mare was plodding along contentedly. Yet the single set of hoofbeats only made the road seem more silent. He kept listening for the sound of Silverhair's harp, for Piper's cheerful whistle, or Rana's laughter. And when he saw something that amused or astonished, he found himself turning to tell Robert.

In a few weeks have I become so dependent? he wondered then. Since he had met the Lady of Westria on his way to Bongarde, he had become enmeshed in a web of relationships that linked him to Robert and Silverhair and Frederic, to Rana, and to Westria.

I am no longer Julian of Stanesvale. I may never be Julian of Westria. Who am I? Awareness followed the question inward until meaning disappeared.

I'm Julian. . . . "I'm Julian!" he said aloud.

"And this is Cave Hollow. Have ye come t' see the caverns?" a girl's voice answered him.

Julian jerked in the saddle, staring. The mare came to a halt before a small steading set around with oak trees. A barefoot girl with flaxen braids was standing by the gate, smiling up at him.

"What kind of caverns?" he asked, still getting his bearings.

"A magic kind," she grinned.

"What do you mean?"

She shrugged. "Stone growin' like flowers, stone flowin' like water, all hard, with crystals inside. My family takes care of it. I c'n guide ye in t' see." She jerked her head in the direction of the house, and Julian saw the offering basket on its tree stump. This holding looked more prosperous than most he had seen; fences were mended, and behind the house he could see a thriving garden. Likely they made part of their living by showing travelers the caves.

"An' some folk say the stone sings t' them," the girl went on.

Julian felt his pulse leap suddenly. Singing stones with crystals inside? Surely this quest could not end so easily! And yet, even if the Wind Crystal had not come to rest here, he might learn something that would help him to understand it.

"All right." He tossed a silver piece into the basket. "Let's see these magic caverns of yours!"

It was cold underground, a steady, damp chill that deepened as Julian followed the girl through the jagged gash in the side of the hill and into the cave. Each swing of the lantern showed him new strangeness: shelves and canopies of limestone where the flat clay floor had fallen away, surfaces scarred before the Cataclysm with a scribbling of men's names, a ceiling pocked and rippled like a frozen rain cloud, and everywhere the infinitely varied ornamentation of melted stone.

It was marble; touch told him that much, for Julian knew rock. But this marble had been liquified and re-formed into icicles of solid stone. Light glittered from a drop of water at the tip of one protrusion, and the girl held up the lantern so that he could see.

"Water brings th' stone down an' builds it up again—from th' top like this an' from the floor—" The moving light showed him a column like a guttered candle growing from the clay. "But th' warm air from outside makes these all brown. Come on, 'tis prettier deeper in."

She darted ahead, at home in these passages as he had been in the trackless forests around Stanesvale when he was a boy. Her light shone through a drapery of creamy stone, as translucent as bacon rind. They went up and around and down again, slipping where the ground was muddy. Then darkness enclosed him as the lantern disappeared.

"Wait . . ." her voice came hollowly from the next chamber. Julian stood still, and in a moment she returned. "Not that way, there's a lake there—see? 'Tis low now, but it rises twenty feet come wintertime."

Julian stared down into water so clear that one could see where the bottom fell away to darkness, so still that it mirrored the cavern above. *This is the domain of earth and water*, he thought then. *What can I learn about the Powers of Air in here?* He felt a tug at his sleeve.

"I've got it all ready ahead. Come on!"

Julian climbed around a corner and stopped short, gazing. The entire chamber was encrusted with what looked like a butter icing, in every shade from apricot to cream.

"Pretty, huh? Next one's even better. Wait here." Once more she disappeared. A glitter caught Julian's eye. Some of the points were broken, and now he understood why the formations were translucent: the surfaces might be opaque, but he could see the crystalline structure of the calcite within. Carefully he tapped one of the stalactites and heard a shimmer of sound. *Stones that sing. . . .* Understanding tugged at his awareness, but already the girl was calling him.

Julian felt his way through another passage and came up into wonder.

The child was grinning, and indeed she had not lied. At every glance the eye found something new to study, but his guide, having shown him her treasure, was beginning to shift from foot to foot impatiently.

"Let me stay here alone," he said suddenly.

She shook her head. "No one does that."

"Has anyone ever asked?" Julian said then. "Just overnight. If I'm not out by this time tomorrow, come fetch me."

She took a great deal of convincing. Surely he would be afraid of the dark; he must not try to go farther, for no one knew how far the cave system ran. Julian did not tell her that the knowledge that had come to him with the Earthstone was beating in his blood, and that he knew already just how far below the surface they stood, and how the strata of rock lay between them and the air.

"Not our fault if th' dark 'n' the silence strike ye mad!" she said finally. Julian laughed. " 'Tisn't funny, but that's nothin' to what my Da will do if ye harm any of the stones!"

Still shaking her head, she skipped down the passage, and he was left alone.

Earth and water made this place, Julian thought as he gazed around. *Are making it*, he corrected. *And drop by drop, the crystals grow.* He could sense that there were fissures of quartz running through the limestone nearby. Even the Wind Crystal must once have grown this way. . . .

Julian made his way slowly around the chamber. The walls and ceiling were fringed with delicate hanging straws, or draped with the curtain swags of heavier stone. And there were forms even stranger: twisted spirals and fragile, curling growths like lichens, but all stone. Luminous in the light of the candles, each one was a masterwork, and as the knowledge of Earth and Water woke once more within him, he saluted the elementals who had wrought them so well.

One of the candles flickered out. Julian picked his way around the cave and blew out the rest of them. He had other senses, and it was time he used them. Steadying his breathing, he pulled his cloak under him and sat down cross-legged on a flat section of clay floor.

No night beneath the stars could ever match this darkness. For a time, the muscles of his eyes twitched vainly. It had been the same in the mines. And though Julian did not hold the Earthstone, he had mastered its lessons. He disciplined his will to seek another kind of vision now.

And presently he began to perceive the trigonal patterns of radiance that were the structure of the stone. Senses for which he had no names told him when one kind of mineral mixed with another, showed him shape and mass, stratification and faulting, told him where stone was solid and where water seeped downward to fill the secret springs.

He understood exactly where he was. He could have returned to the surface unguided, or crept through the bowels of the earth to the utmost cave. But that was not the kind of knowledge for which he had come.

Julian had never known a place to be so still. Even the

occasional drip of water only emphasized the silence. Here were no human voices, no movement of bird or beast. No breath of air whispered through these passageways. No music played. Lack of stimulation made his ears ring.

Can I learn about sound through silence? Can these stones sing?

He tapped a stalactite with the hilt of his dagger and heard a long, pure vibration like a bell. Another stalactite, shorter, gave him a higher tone. Carefully he experimented. Each stone chimed clearly in the stillness. As he struck one, others began to resonate; harmonics built until, he could no longer distinguish one from another. Then he let the long echoes die away.

Sound is made by moving air, but it is also true that sound can make air move, he thought then, for he could see the crystals vibrating as treetops bow when the wind passes by. *And when the breath stirs the cords of the throat, what then?*

Carefully he exhaled. The sound was swallowed by stillness. Drawing in more air, he let it out in a long, wordless tone. Playing with the sounds he could produce here, Julian forgot friend and lover, forgot that he had ever been speechless, forgot time. He knew only that he was the Jewel Lord, and for this he had been born.

Loudly and softly he sang, tuning and toning his voice until the stalactites resonated as the harmonics in a harp ring when one strikes the dominant. He sang to the stones, and they gave back the song. Was this how the first Mistress of the Jewels had learned to wield their power?

He had no sense of the hard floor beneath him, or of the chill damp of the air. From audible sound he passed to awareness of subliminal levels of vibration, and thence he followed the song of the crystals into a silence that encompassed all sound. . . .

To the soft chime of bells and the whisper of rattles, the children of the Wind Riders were dancing. Mist veiled the forests below them, cloud wreathed the luminous granite heights above.

Piper moved with the others, tranced by the rhythm till past and future faded. Where the slide of loose rock ended, an arena of bare granite made a dancing floor. The expanse of pale stone was flecked with glinting quartz, sheared smooth by the earth powers long ago and worn smoother by the feet of the generations of dancers who had come here for initiation upon the eve of the festival that honors the animal powers.

The rock had been chill to bare feet when they began their dancing, but now they felt no cold. Step-together-step, a small step and another, the movement carried them inward in a slow, sinuous spiral, and then outward again. Unified by repetition, a dozen voices soared.

"I circle the earth, I circle the sky."

"Skymaster, hear us!" Old Tam's voice rose beneath the chanting. "The children are here, ready for yer callin'."

"My body's unbound, my spirit can fly."

The song had become a part of Piper, of all of them, as they were a part of each other. There was only the song and the sky, only the earth and the dance. From time to time one of the children let go as the circle wound past the cliff face and began to climb. Piper smiled encouragement as Lis started upward. Then the dance went on.

"Inward I seek, and outward I spin."

"Spirit of the east wind, Guardian, guide them! Wind Rider, welcome them—welcome thy children," Tam cried.

Piper heard a warbling whistle, glanced upward and thought their dancing had set the sky in motion, for where the sun had burned through the clouds, the air was aswirl with specks of deeper blue.

"Finding the way to freedom within!"

Piper let the dance carry him, understanding gradually that he was looking at a flock of mountain bluebirds spiraling in reflection of the dance below. Awareness spun outward. His spirit soared with the birds.

"*Piper. . . .*" Slowly his name floated into consciousness. "*Piper, it is time. Listen now.*" Focus returned. The cliff face was in front of him. The other children had disappeared.

But that didn't matter. His whole body heard the calling.

"*Piper, come up, come to me.*"

Of course. A lightness within drew him upward, and he felt with his foot for a place to stand. Hold by hold he crept up the cliff, and the world fell away below. He was aware of an immensity of air all around him but did not fear, for the higher he climbed, the stronger came the calling, until he could almost float upward on the strength of the summons alone.

Until, suddenly, groping hands closed on rough bark. Piper pulled himself up on gnarled branches, and over the edge of the world.

It was a nest, larger than any bird's nest ever seen. Still, the brush inside was softened with a thatching of downy feathers. It opened into a dark cleft in the mountainside.

Piper blinked and looked around. The only sound was the sighing of the wind. A few peaks lifted like islands from a sea of clouds, but he could see nothing familiar. The wind was cold. How did he get here?

He looked back down, but the world had disappeared. He drew back, whimpering. They had tricked him, trapped him here to starve! He was alone as never before. Alone . . . and afraid.

What am I doing here? He felt his existence with a frightening clarity. And then, *who am I?* He was awakening from a tangled dream that thrust him into a new nightmare. His fingers sought the only familiar thing left to him—the flute case hanging from his belt—and he pulled the instrument free.

At the first note, the wind stilled. At the second, Piper's terror left him. At the third note, he saw a faint pathway leading into the dark. Flute still in hand, he followed it.

Still dazzled by daylight, he had only his feet to guide him. Something rustled, then he was struck to stillness by a harsh cry.

"You're from no nest of the Wind Riders, and no valley rat either!"

Piper stared wildly, and adjusting eyes showed him a humped shape to go with the sounds he heard.

"Well, outlander, what are you doing here?"

It was an echo of his own question. Automatically Piper tried to reply, and then remembered. Throat muscles strained, but all that emerged was an echo of that first cry. He caught his breath on a sob.

"Why do they send these stupid children?" The voice scraped with exasperation. "Did they teach you nothing down there? You can think, can't you? Don't you know you don't need a voice when you talk to me?"

Piper dared to look up again. He expected to see a bird, but it seemed to be a man, with long, brown-gold hair. His broad-shouldered body was cloaked in shimmering brown as well, but what held the boy's gaze was the dark face with its fierce beak of a nose and luminous golden eyes.

This is not a man . . . Piper saw that in the fierce gaze of his eyes. One bare foot gripped the stone like an eagle's claw.

"My lord. . . ."

"That's better. Now you tell me what you're doing here."

"I want to fly," Piper's thought began. But that wasn't all. He was thinking so clearly here. He remembered how he came into the mountains, and why, and the story spilled from his mind into that of the Guardian.

"Wind Rider chicks get one boon if they make it this far," came the Eagle's reply. "You've earned that much, I suppose. What do you want? I can give you your speech back, and then the Wind Riders will train you. But that's not what you wanted before. . . ."

Piper remembered how the other children had listened

to his music by the waterfall. He belonged to them now! Everything in him was clamoring to take the gift the Guardian offered, and with it, the freedom of the skies. But here he could remember his grandmother's smile and Silverhair's music with equal clarity.

"Could you give me the Wind Crystal if that's what I asked you for?"

"The Wind Crystal is not mine to bestow. Nor yours either, boy. But I could give you a song that will lead you to it . . . if that's the gift you ask."

There was a silence. Piper knew that this was a test like the one he had passed on the ledge outside, but agonizingly harder, for this time he knew the price as well as the prize. His throat ached so that he could not have replied even if he had words.

If he accepted speech, he would lose the eternal present that had shielded him from memory. But if he remembered, the task undone and the love of those he left would weigh too heavily for him to fly.

"Give me the song. . . ."

Displaced air blasted through the cavern, and he rocked back on his heels. The Guardian's human shape was gone; he glimpsed a form neither man nor avian limned in lines of light; the air shuddered as great wings spread wide. The cry of the Eagle tore time from space, and the eternity between them rang with echoes that grew into a mighty music that remade the world.

When Piper could think again, he was standing on the other side of the mountain. Mist still cloaked the ranges, and there was no trace of the way he had come. For a moment he feared, but his ears still rang with music. Wondering, he lifted his flute to his lips, and the pure notes of the melody he was hearing floated free.

He heard an echo. From the north it came to him, as clear as . . . crystal.

His speech was still bound, but his wandering spirit had at last come home. Piper understood who he was, and where, and why, and that was a gift he had not even known enough to desire. The wind blew more strongly.

He glanced down to his left, and for a moment he glimpsed the impossible beauty of a valley where waterfalls cascaded like crystal ribbons over walls of white stone. But the trail that wound down the slope before him led northward, toward the song.

Piper slipped the flute back into its case and started walking, and the cool wind dried his tears.

TEN: The Breath of Awahna

"Why you take so long?"

Julian reined in sharply. Smoke was curling from the chimney of the rambling log house in which he had spent his boyhood, but the yard of Stanesvale seemed empty.

"We get here two days ago . . . been waiting for you."

Julian looked up and saw Mañero straddling the roof of the barn, whittling. The towheaded boy who sat beside him waved and grinned.

"Get down from there!" The order was an automatic reaction. Julian wondered which one of his foster brothers the child belonged to. In the years since he'd been home, they had grown.

"It's all right, Julian. We got a rope to swing on—see?" He crawled to the projecting eave and launched himself into space. The mare plunged and snorted as the boy swung outward. Mañero grinned as Julian wrestled her down.

"You must be one of Gil's brats. What do they call you?"

"I'm the youngest." The boy looked up at him with a broad grin. "Name's Stone, like yours."

Julian found himself smiling back. The milk name by which Megan had called him was traditional in the family, but it touched him to realize that the boy was proud of it because it had been Julian's.

"And what about *him*?" He gestured upward.

"Oh, he came in two days ago with th' others . . . you know, with Lord Robert 'n' the girl 'n' Silverhair."

Julian's face must have shown his reaction, for both the boy and Mañero were laughing. Stone made a dash for the house, shouting that Uncle Julian was home, and Mañero put his knife away and slid down the rope to the ground.

"My master don't want me in Laurelynn," said the man mournfully. "Headin' home, found harper and all stopped by a fallen tree on th' trail, guided them 'round. Mañero knows all the trails—useful, huh? Help you too, maybe."

"I doubt it," answered Julian, dismounting.

His eyes were on the porch, which was filling now with people. He glimpsed Robert's lithe grace with a tremor of the flesh that surprised him, and gave an involuntary smile as he recognized the swing of the bard's purple cloak. There was a third figure in the shadows. Someone moved, and he glimpsed copper hair. Julian swallowed as he realized that Rana had come too. Was it possible to love both Robert and Rana at the same time? He took a deep breath, fighting vertigo as if he were poised on a ridge between two watersheds, knowing that survival depended on maintaining a precarious balance between.

Suddenly Julian understood why he had wanted to go off alone. But Robert and Rana and Silverhair were here, and he knew now that sooner or later he would have to find the words to master the complex of emotions they stirred in him. Then his foster mother was pushing past the others toward him, and if he had meant to be angry, the moment for it was past. At least his feelings for her were clear. He dropped the reins and held out his arms.

* * *

"Won't your friends be needing you?" Still talking, Megan quartered a potato and tossed it into the pot. Julian, who had followed her into the kitchen, shrugged.

"They seem to have made themselves welcome here without any help from me."

She raised an eyebrow, handed him a scrub brush, and pointed to the tub and the pile of potatoes that was waiting there.

"Now I know I'm home." He grinned at her. Through the kitchen window he could see the familiar folds of the blue ridges and the bald rock face that had always reminded him of an old woman huddled into her shawl.

"Well, if you really want to stay here, you may as well make yourself useful. But they're bound to be wondering. . . ."

"Let 'em!" Julian scrubbed viciously at a potato. "They'll expect me to yell at them for coming after I told them to stay home." he explained. "By now, their imaginations must be accusing them far more effectively than anything I could say."

Megan laughed. "I was surprised to see any of you. It's been, what—over three years since you were home? Yes, for I remember that Barris' second girl had just been born."

"Where are they?"

"Gil and Barris? Working down at the Sweetwater quarry—not likely they'll be home while you're here. Lorena went with them, and Kari is helping her sister with a new baby, which is why I have the children." She dropped the potatoes into the stew pot and began to disjoint the chicken while she waited for Julian to wash some more.

He nodded. The third brother, Jord, had married into a valley holding and become a farmer.

"It's hard to believe that it's been so long," he said finally. Certainly Megan looked as she always had, though there might be a few more lines around her calm hazel eyes, and her dark hair held a strand or two more of gray. "Nothing has changed here."

"Only you, my son," she said, smiling. "Three years ago you were still my baby. Now you have another family."

Family. Farin Silverhair, his uncle, whom he'd loved and hated in turn; Rana, whom he had thought the only woman in the world for him a year ago; Robert, his cousin, who had believed in him before he believed in himself, who was his lover now.

"You mean *them*?" Julian nodded toward the hall. He could hear a murmur of voices and an occasional chord as Silverhair tuned.

"I mean Westria."

"Do you really believe that?" Julian shivered.

Megan finished wiping her hands, then pulled out one of the bricks in the side of the kitchen hearth. From the cavity behind it she drew out a lump wrapped tightly in strips of silk gone brown with age and laid it in his palm.

"For twenty years I have kept this. It was on a chain that hung around your mother's neck. The Master of the Junipers told me to hold it until you were grown."

Julian worried at the bindings with his knife. From the shape, it had to be a ring. Suddenly one end came free.

"I meant to send it when I heard you'd found your family," Megan went on. "But I had no safe messenger."

The last of the bindings came away, and gold gleamed in his hand. Julian turned the ring and saw a clear jade stone with the laurel wreath and circled cross of Westria incised on the smooth surface so that it could be used as a seal ring.

"The king's signet . . . my father's ring," Julian said softly. "Did you know?" He looked up at Megan. "Did you suspect who my mother was?"

She stood with arms folded across her breasts, her eyes fixed on the hills. "I knew she was a lady. Remember, I served for five years in Laurelynn and saw all the great ones."

Julian nodded. Laurelynn was where his foster mother

had lost her mountain twang. She had met her husband
there.

"Perhaps my heart knew," she said softly. "I tried to
bury her like a queen."

Julian watched her, wondering. If she had been certain
that he was the heir of Westria, would she have protected
him better from her sons' casual brutality? Could he have
grown as strong in any softer school? These hills bred
endurance. Julian realized that the face of the old woman
he had always seen in the mountain was her own.

He tried the ring. "It will need to be bigger before I
can wear it." He met her eyes and managed a smile.
"And I will need to be bigger before I have the right to
put it on. Do you have a piece of thong?"

She nodded, kissed him suddenly, and turned to her
stew pot again.

"Tell young Stone to bring me some onions from the
storeroom, will you? And then I think it is time you saw
to your family!"

This is where Julian grew up, thought Silverhair, gazing around the cluttered, comfortable room with its great
stone hearth and the dressed skins and woven hangings
covering the log walls. *Until three years ago, this was
his family.* He looked down the long table at Julian's
foster mother, who was dishing out more stew for her
grandchildren, and thought that perhaps the Master of
the Junipers had done well to leave the boy with her after
all.

He sighed, full of sausage and cheese, garden salad,
roast venison and savory chicken stew, brown bread and
freshly churned butter. The others were still working
away at second helpings, especially Mañero, who had
not stopped eating since he sat down.

Mistress Megan was a fine cook, and talking to her
had certainly improved Julian's mood. Or something
had—he possessed a kind of hard-edged, purposeful
quality that the harper had not seen in him before. Had
something happened to him on his journey? If this for-
bearance lasted, he would ask.

He passed the salad bowl to Rana, who handed it on down the table to the children. Julian and Robert were together on the other side, sitting with legs touching though there was plenty of room. Robert had been very quiet, as if still unsure of his welcome, but his movements were tuned to Julian's in a way that would have betrayed their secret had anyone been watching them.

Rana appeared to be giving her entire attention to the food, and Silverhair sighed. Robert had been afraid that her presence would disturb Julian, but it seemed to the harper that it was likely to be the other way around, and there was nothing he could think of to do.

"The Wind Riders?" Megan turned to Julian. "Yes, I have heard of them. The tales say their village is on the far slopes of these mountains, facing the Barren Lands."

"First I must find the boy," said Julian. "They said he was on the way to some kind of initiation at Cloud's Rest." He looked at Megan, who was frowning. "Do you know where that is?"

There was a long silence. "Perhaps. It is not much spoken of, even here. Most of our folk stay close to their holdings, but my father was a great wanderer when he was young. He even tried to find a way down into Awahna . . . but he would never tell me what he saw."

"And Cloud's Rest?"

"I'm not sure. You'll need to go back to the Big Oak Inn. That's where you strike the Moon Lake road, which leads across the mountains. When you pass the lake they call Tenaia, you'll be close to it, but I don't know if the way will be open to you."

Silverhair was trying to remember the road to the village where he had heard the Wind Rider's song. Was it north or south of Moon Lake?

"That gives us a starting point anyway," said Julian. "If I must seek the village of the Wind Riders, I'll leave you at the lake and go alone. But perhaps Wind Lord will hear our prayer. Will you play for us, uncle? I think it is music that must show us the way."

Certainly something has happened to the boy! Silverhair could only nod his agreement, for the thought of playing brought the music itself, sounding so loud in his spirit that he was sure the others must hear. How, in one moment of peace, had he made so simple and sweet a surrender after having struggled against it for so long? Even a thought could send his spirit soaring, even now. . . .

Silverhair fought to retain his hold on ordinary reality. *Someday*, he thought as the harmonies faded, *that music will carry me so far I cannot return*. He reached blindly for the nearest food to bind him to earth again.

"I will play for you, but not tonight, please," he told Julian. After the moment that had just passed, he did not dare.

"Tell us a story, then," said Rana.

"Tell us a story about Coyote!" cried Stone.

"He's always asking for Coyote tales," said Megan, "and he's memorized all the ones that I know. They tell me that you've traveled to many lands. What stories do you know?"

Silverhair thought for a moment. "What about Coyote and the bluebirds? That is a tale I learned in Aztlan."

Robert shook his head indulgently and took another drink of beer, but Julian was grinning. Mañero cut himself a slice of the apple pie and began to gobble it down.

"Tell us, tell us!" the youngest grandchild cried.

"Well, it was like this," said Silverhair. "Coyote is friends with everyone, when it suits him, and one day he asked the bluebirds to teach him to grind corn."

"Bluebirds try to eat the corn, not grind it," objected Stone.

"Do they?" asked the harper. "Well, maybe it's different in Aztlan. Anyway, that's what happened, and they worked until the sun was high and everyone was thirsty. The birds wanted to fly up to the top of a mesa, which is a kind of flat-topped mountain they have down there, and get a drink from the spring, but Coyote, of course, couldn't fly."

"Why not?" asked the little girl.

"He didn't have feathers, silly," whispered her brother.

"That's true," said Silverhair, "and so the bluebirds had to give him some. When he was fixed up, they all started flying, but the bluebirds, being used to it, went much faster. And they started gossiping about what a messy eater Coyote was, and how he'd dirty their water—"

Mañero, at this point, belched loudly, and everyone laughed. Silverhair waited until there was quiet again.

—"and so they decided to play a trick on him. When they reached the spring, they drank quickly, and when Coyote got there and took off his feathers so that he could drink too, the bluebirds grabbed them and flew away."

"But what happened?" asked Stone.

Silverhair shrugged. "Well, Coyote was stuck on the top of that mesa, and for all I know, he's sitting there still!" The adults laughed, but the boy was looking disappointed, and Silverhair began to wish he had chosen a different tale.

"Not the way I heard," said a hoarse voice beside him. Mañero set down his cup and looked around with a grin. "What I hear is Coyote got so mad, he jump off the edge."

Stone stared at him with round eyes. "He died?"

"What d' you think?" asked Mañero, cracking a nut from the basket on the table. "Bluebirds think so. They 'fraid his spirit be angry and get 'em."

"So what did they do?" asked Julian finally.

"Bring him back to life. They always do that when Coyote's killed."

Mañero calmly continued to eat nuts, but everyone else was laughing.

"All right, all right," said Megan to the children. "If you're done, you may set the leftovers out for the animals."

"That's right, it is the eve of the Feast of the First People," said Julian. "I had forgotten. Come on, I'll help you. Is there grain in the barn to give the deer? We always used to feed them when I was a boy."

"Nothing has changed," Megan answered. "You go on then, all you children!" She smiled, for Rana and Robert had risen along with Julian.

Silverhair stayed where he was. "I need all of my energy for digestion."

"I go for a walk," said Mañero. He passed wind with a sharp report that made the children giggle. "That'll settle me!" He pushed back his bench, and weaving slightly, headed for the door.

Silverhair eased down before the fire. Megan was moving back and forth, putting the rest of the food away. From the meadow behind the house they could hear the laughter of her grandchildren, and the deeper merriment of those whose childhood had ended too soon.

"Take care of him," Megan said suddenly, pausing beside the harper's chair. "My part is done."

"Done well. His mother was my sister, and I loved her . . . like the other half of my soul. Faris had courage like the flare of lightning in an empty sky. But she did not have the strength that endures." He could hear his voice shaking, and strove to control it. "Julian has that, mistress, and I think he has learned it from you. You have done well."

Megan was weeping silently, holding on to the stones of the hearth. Above the whisper of the fire and the children's laughter, they heard the sweet discordance of coyotes singing on the hill.

"Is that Julian singing?" Rana reined in. It was not a great voice, and the song was one of those endless, pointless ballads that soldiers sing while on patrol, but it was a pleasant bass, and she had never heard it before.

"Yes, and he didn't learn it from me!" the harper said ruefully. He kicked his mount forward until they were riding side by side.

The road here was almost level, passing through a mixed forest of sugar and yellow pines and spicy cedars, their needles strewn so thickly that the hooves of the horses made hardly a sound. The strengthening sun drew out a balsamy fragrance from the needles that smelled like Rosemary's stillroom.

So far, this expedition had been like a holiday, for the terrain on the western side of the Ramparts rose gradu-

ally, with only the occasional gash of a canyon to slow
them, or a bare sweep of granite and a view of the folded
blue ranges to show them how far they had come. The
Westrian side of the mountains welcomed the traveler; it
was only on the east that the peaks rose in a stony wall
to discourage entry from the Barren Lands.

Julian finished his song and Robert laughed, flinging
his arm across his lover's shoulders in a quick embrace.
Rana's fingers clenched on her reins.

"Perhaps we could take the lead for a while," said
Silverhair.

"No." She drew breath carefully. "I would still know.
This is *my* punishment for coming along. Robert is giving Julian what I cannot, and I have no right to complain."

"But it still hurts, doesn't it? The heart does not
reason very well, I know."

Rana gave him a quick glance, saw his weather-
browned face as thin as always, but the lines of pain that
had sharpened it were somehow smoothed away. There
was peace in his face, and that had never been a quality
that one associated with Silverhair. Once she had dis-
liked him. Now talking to him was almost like talking to
the Master of the Junipers.

A breath of coolness soothed her burning cheeks. She
looked up and saw that a puff of cloud had appeared in
the clear sky above. As she watched, it expanded, built
by the invisible spirits of the air into a castle of pearl and
purple, as sharp and solid to the sight as the polished
granite domes of the hills.

"Do you think we will have rain?"

"Very likely." The bard's voice held amusement,
though his features were unmoved. "It has rained every
day at this time since we left the inn."

Her lips twitched. He smiled back and began to hum
a simple tune.

"What are you singing?"

"*A fu le le a dio, a fu le le.* . . ." He repeated the
words. "It's a chant they sing in Elaya to honor the

Lightning Lady. *'A storm wind is a-coming, a strong wind. . . .'* I think we are going to see her soon!''

"They speak of the storm as a woman?" asked Rana.

"Some of them do. They call her Oya, sudden as that storm. She rides the whirlwind and sweeps the land clean. Oya kills the monster and is the monster; she makes things happen. Oya goes between the worlds.''

Rana looked back. The storm cloud was still swelling. Her skin prickled with the energy in the air.

"Storm comin'.'' Mañero appeared from among the trees ahead of them. He had stuck with them despite Julian's attempts to discourage him, proving that in this kind of country, two legs could go as quickly, and for longer, than four. "Better hurry. Trees are thicker up here.''

Yes, hurry! Rana's spirit cried. A gust of cold wind whirled a shower of pine needles down from the trees. *Strike hard, strike now!*

She no longer hated all men simply because one of them had hurt her; she had thought that she could live without desire. But knowledge of Julian's feelings had awakened an ache like a hungry animal within her, even while she feared it, and sometimes she hated Julian because she could not love him—especially now, when he no longer wanted her.

The storm wind was coming, coming. . . . Rana lashed her mount forward, leaving Silverhair standing, and bucketed past Robert and Julian before they could call. The trees were swaying around her; branches rattled in a rising wind. The horse came to a plunging halt in the midst of them. The voice of the storm grew louder. The metal clasps of her jerkin buzzed, she sucked in the charged air in great gasps.

Strike me, Lightning Lady! Strike now!

Suddenly the rest were surrounding her. Julian grabbed her rein. Rana struck out at him, and then, destroying sight and sound together, came the storm. In that moment's fierce glare, Rana saw Julian's face white as he shouted soundlessly against the detonation of the thunder. Then all was darkness and a sudden roar of rain.

Presently the senses began to recover. Rana's throat was raw. The horses were huddled together, the riders' cloaked shapes dimly seen through veils of water. A cloak, not her own, half-covered her as well. She felt Julian beside her and let out pent breath in a long sigh.

The air was heavy with the scent of water and ozone's sharp tang. All of her tension seemed to have disappeared. *Thank you, Lady*, she said silently, for Julian's arm around her was like a brother's embrace.

"Air and water mingle too. I had forgotten that," Julian said softly.

Rana nodded, remembering the storm they had survived upon the sea. Air and water, she thought, and fire. . . . There was a meaning here that hovered just beyond her understanding, but for the moment it was enough to be at peace.

Piper clung to a niche in the slabbed slate of Bloody Canyon, watching the cataract boil past where there had been a path a half hour ago. The storm clouds, having spent their fury, were already dissipating into wisps of fluff that the summer sun would soon mist away. He wiped spray from his forehead with a sigh. At least the storm had not swept him with it down the mountainside.

The most precipitous part of the descent was already behind him, but this had not been a good spot to get caught in. Still, he was alive. Soon the shouting of the waters would become a musical tinkling as the last of the cloudburst trickled down to the dancing stream.

Sunlight glittered blindingly from wet surfaces; the needles of the dwarf pines shone like clustered crystals, every branch tip bore its own teardrop of flashing light. Piper's eyes watered. Was the Wind Crystal itself as lovely as this jeweled world?

A soft wind brushed his cheek, a last sparkling spray showered earthward, but the gleaming sheet of water thinned above the path until there remained only water-slick rock and mud, starting to steam in the summer sun.

Piper could see the heat-shimmer on the drylands below him, the flat glare of Moon Lake, and the pale line of road that led north through the purple distances. By nightfall he could be out of this canyon, and then he could go faster. He had to go faster, for the song that the Eagle had given him drew him on.

"If it wasn't Piper, somebody his size certainly slept here." Robert drew back an overhanging pine branch, and Julian saw the soft grass crushed into a nest beside the scattered ashes of a small fire. "He's about two days ahead of us, whoever he was."

He let the branch fall. Sunset gilded the grass of the meadow in long rays. Light rippled across the dark blue of the lake as the soft wind stirred it, and an early owl was calling through the pines. Peace lay on this place, as palpable as the sunlight. One would sleep well here, and have only fair dreams.

"Two days, or maybe three," answered Julian. "The rain won't have disturbed it. But was that before or after he was at Cloud's Rest? We'll camp here anyway, until we know which direction he's taken."

This is Tenaia, he thought, looking around. *Do those clear waters flow into Awahna?* He had grown up near the road to the Sacred Valley, but he had never before been so near. He could feel it, like a tone just too low for his hearing, a fragrance too faint for recognition, a movement too swift to be seen. Perhaps when they had eaten, he would climb the slope and look around. Surely that much would be allowed.

The stillness deepened. The setting sun shone through the clouds that edged the western horizon; more clouds lay across the folded ranges like strands of saffron wool. Rana and Silverhair were already gathering wood, but Robert was waiting with a kind of patient attention that made Julian wince. He held out his hand, and Robert put his arms around him with a smile that seemed to gather the last brilliance of the day.

"I've missed you!" whispered Robert. Julian nodded, finding that the human contact helped him to bear the beauty around him.

They moved apart as Mañero trotted past, then stood,

strong arms still linked, to watch the sky. Its color was
changing from crimson to a shadowed purple now. Julian
found himself almost afraid to breathe. Slowly he turned,
and saw rising above the rosy peaks the great golden orb
of the moon.

In the moonlight, Swangold's strings were silver. The
harper tuned carefully, then played a few arpeggios for
the pure pleasure of seeing the light shimmer beneath
his hands. The mountains lay like sleeping beasts
around them. Silverhair could hear no sound but the
restless lapping of the lake, see no movement but the
stately progress of the moon-bright clouds across the midnight sky. Their little campfire was only a spark in this
immensity.

He was glad he had found this rock by the lake's shore.

> *When day has faded from the sky,*
> *How still the shadowed byways lie.*
> *Now others may seek home and bed,*
> *But I will try the night instead!*
> *   In their windows candles glow.*
> *Safe within, they little know*
> *What silent feet go by their gates,*
> *Where the friendly darkness waits—*
> *   So softly go and softly sing.*
> *   Darkness is a quiet thing. . . .*

It was an old walking song, but it suited his mood. A
night bird swooped low across the water, calling softly,
then sped toward the other shore.

> *I am not lonely though alone.*
> *Knowing much, I pass unknown,*
> *And hidden whispers tell me where*
> *Invisible companions fare,*
> *   Where the field mouse scuttles by,*
> *Where the cheerful crickets lie.*
> *I hear the hunting owl lament,*

Go my way and am content—
So softly go and softly sing. . . .

The harper sensed someone moving behind him and turned, still singing, to see who it was. The fluid walk could have been Rana's, but the breadth of shoulder marked the figure as Julian. He moved slowly along the shoreline. Then the path led up the bank, and Julian went on across the moonlit meadow and disappeared among the shadows beneath the pines.

Silverhair continued to sing, letting the night itself provide the words.

The moon walks in the fields of night.
Treetops net her silver light,
Until upon the path is laid
A shining net of dappled shade.
Walking under such a sky,
On such a path, it seems that I
Could walk the silent night away,
Nor rest till darkness yields to day—
So softly go and softly sing.
Darkness is a quiet thing. . . .

Julian walked softly through the darkness beneath the trees. Silverhair's song had ended, but now the harp was building a shimmering web of music, as if the night itself had found a way to sing. The mountains seemed to have lent Silverhair's music some of their own strangeness. Perhaps it was the distortion of distance, but as he began to climb, Julian could no longer be sure that the harmonies he heard were coming from the harp at all.

Snow-clad peaks floated above the ranges, shining in the moonlight with an impossible purity. In the folds between the ridges, mist grew luminous, and what had seemed so solid by daylight now appeared less substantial than the clouds. The campfire where he had left the others sleeping was only a pinprick of light from here. How far had they come from the lands of men! Uncanny, the drovers had called this road. They pushed hard when

they had to take it, for fear they would be changed before they reached the other side.

I have been changed already! thought Julian. *How
could I ever have left my mountains?* He breathed in
brisk air and felt a tingling along every nerve, as if his
stolid lowland flesh were being replaced by some finer
fiber. The path was growing steeper, but he sprang from
rock to rock with ease.

And then he was on the height. Logic told him that
the path ought to continue, but he could not see another
way down. Perhaps the contrast between moonlight and
the darkness beneath the trees was affecting his night
vision; perhaps the path ended here . . . or it might be
that there was a way but it was closed to him. If this was
the barrier, he had no choice but to accept it. He stood
still, holding his cloak closed against the wind.

Northwest and southeast, the moon limned the outlines of the long ranges. The Great Valley was lost in a
luminous haze, and the western faces of the peaks that
protected Westria from the Barren Lands blazed in the
moonlight. But the mountains that cupped the glittering
lake below him were exquisitely clear—except to the
south, where the contours of the land were masked by
low-lying clouds. Nothing to see in that direction . . .
but strangely, Julian found that he was still staring. He
stood on one edge of a watershed that must drain that
way. If these were the headwaters of the Mercy River,
then beyond those clouds lay Stanesvale.

And beneath them?

Julian drew a careful breath. There was a ringing in
his ears . . . no, it was Silverhair's music, but how could
he hear the harp all the way up here? Softly it sounded,
as if the stars were singing, a sweet chiming that thinned
to the edge of silence and then repeated in a different
harmony. Thus the stones had sung to him in the crystal
caverns, but this was a greater music. He struggled to
understand.

And as he listened, his gaze was still fixed on the
luminous clouds that veiled the Sacred Valley. Could such
a glow come only from the moonlight? Julian blinked,

for his eyes were watering, but it had seemed to him that
he had seen a hint of color there.

Wind Lord, send thy servants to lift the veil! his spirit
cried. *I know I am not yet called to seek it, but the way
that I must go is long and I am weary. Lord of all wisdom, let me glimpse it with my mortal eyes!*

"*Be still then—*" Was that his own hope or Another
speaking? Julian let out his breath in a long sigh.

*Vision blurs. Hearing trembles to a shimmer of sound.
The shining swirl of cloud grows brighter. He sees cliffs
like soaring towers; the smooth cleft face of a granite
dome. Distant waters stream like skeins of crystal toward
the radiance that hazes the valley floor.*

Awahna. . . .

A gentle wind caressed Julian's hair. A warm wind—
why was he shaking so? He was still standing on the hill
above Tenaia. Nothing had changed. But he felt a wet-
ness on his cheeks and knew that he was weeping, and
his throat ached with longing to shout, or to sing.

He understood now the note that rang in the Master's
voice whenever he spoke of the Sacred Valley. And he
knew that like everyone else who had even glimpsed that
vision, until his life's end he would carry a sense of having been exiled from his true home.

*Caolin wanders in a dream of darkness, lost among the
tangled trees. He is young once more, still wearing the
coarse, undyed robe of a student at the College of the Wise,
but the chill of the mountain night bites through the thin
garment. He has lost his cloak—he cannot remember
where—he has stumbled through this wilderness for far too
long. He must be close to the Valley. Soon the golden gate
will swing open and reveal all of the knowledge that the
masters at the College denied him. They cannot refuse him
the reward after he has struggled for so long!*

*He plunges forward, but the path that was so clear a
moment since has disappeared. He flails out, forcing a
way among the twisted trees. But there is only mist
around him, and then a sudden sense of space that brings
him up short. He makes a frantic grab for a branch as a*

*swirl of cloud shows emptiness before him, an infinitude
of darkness . . . darkness.*

"*But you have chosen darkness,*" *his own voice speaks
across the years.*

*And his fingers lose their grip upon the pine tree, and
he falls. . . .*

Caolin woke up shouting. His lamp was flickering
wildly, but the rest of the house was still. He took a deep
breath, waiting for his pulse to slow. It had been nothing
but the reflexive twitchings of the imagination. But he
had believed that particular dream banished years ago.

He thrust drenched sheets aside, shivering, stripped
off the tunic he had slept in and pulled a chamber robe
around himself, willing the demands of his body to cease.
The world lay in the hushed stillness of the hour before
dawn. He would have awakened soon in any case; he had
always found it easiest to work at this time, when other
men were still the prey of dreams.

His desk was covered with the letters he was preparing
for his agents among the woodsrats of the north, the
raiders from the Barren Lands, sea reivers who had not
been caught in Ardra's disaster, and desperate men Elaya
was glad to let him woo away. Caolin's army—the force
that still held the fortress on the Red Mountain—was a
pittance compared to the army he was building, but it
must have patience, it must do nothing now. If the people of Westria felt secure, he could make them believe
that they had no need for a king. Once they had agreed
to his rule, he would show them his power.

But now he thrust those papers aside and pulled out
the map of the Ramparts, on which he had marked the
route Mañero's communications described.

The last report had put them in Stanesvale, planning
to move east, following the Moon Lake road. The sorcerer's finger traced the way they must be going. He saw
the empty area that no map of the mountains showed,
and began to shiver once more.

But he kept his hand on the paper. *Mañero,* he said
silently. *Mañero, even in your sleep you must hear me!
Tell me . . . where are you now?* He thrust consciousness

inward, as he had done so many times before. *Mañero, answer me!* Awareness winged southward, seeking his servant's spirit.

It had always been easy . . . until now.

But this time there was only a haze that defeated vision, a buzz that absorbed his attempts to call his servant's name. After a time, the sorcerer pulled himself back into his body. He was cold.

"Three days ago he come here," said Mañero, pointing to the mark in the sand beside the road. "Young, maybe ninety pound, maybe five feet 'n' a few inch tall."

Julian looked back at the cool white peaks of the mountains with a sigh. He supposed they were lucky to have got their horses down Bloody Canyon with only a little scraped skin. The humans in the party were in one piece as well, and there had been no sign at all of raiders. But sweat was already trickling between his shoulder blades, and every step would take them farther from Awahna.

"He headin' north 'n' hurryin'. You better go fast too!" Mañero stood up, grinning. Julian grimaced, but he had learned to trust the little man's trailcraft.

"But why would Piper come this way?" Rana squinted across the broken lands that sloped toward Moon Lake.

"He has a reason," said Silverhair. "If the Wind Riders spoke truth, Piper took almost two months to find his way to them, but since we picked up his trail at Tenaia, he has been moving as quickly as he can. He knows where he's going now. Isn't it possible that he learned something in that initiation, that his search is the same as our own?"

"Wishful thinking! Of course you want to find him," said Robert, "but finding Piper won't help Julian get the Jewel."

"We're going north," said Julian. "Unless you have a better plan?"

Robert flushed and fell silent. Since they had left the lake, these questions had been worn smooth by argument. Julian had been so sure that when he found Piper, he would find some news of the Wind Crystal, but the only place with enough magic to hold it was Awahna, and that way was closed to him. To their right, the Barren Lands shimmered in waves of heat. To the left, the Ramparts rose in a stony wall. Even if he was wrong, he had no choice but to follow the child.

A whistle pierced the heated air. A shadow flowed across the road, and Julian squinted upward. A dark shape slipped between him and the sun; he blinked, saw the glowing purple silk of the glider, and the darker shape of the man it bore. A second glider, golden, circled above.

"Ho, Jewel Lord!" came the call.

"Is that you, Olin?" Julian replied. "I tried to reach Cloud's Rest alone, but Piper's trail seems to lead this way. What happened?"

"Don' know. Skymaster tells us th' boy got somethin' t' do. Tam sent us t' tell ye." The purple wing swooped dangerously low, crossed above a tumble of white rock, and lifted suddenly into the air.

"But did the boy go this way?" Julian cried.

Now it was Tania's golden glider that approached him. "Eagle says he go north. You find 'im, take care of 'im! Tell 'im he c'n come back when job's done."

"That is all we want to do, in Wind Lord's name!" Silverhair said harshly, and Julian nodded.

"Skymaster help ye then, an' good huntin'!" The voices grew faint as the gliders lifted again.

"What price for wishful thinking now?" muttered Silverhair. "He has to be looking for the Jewel!"

But Julian stood watching as the Wind Riders slid away down the wind, caught another thermal upward, and when they had the height, dove forward, again and again, until they were only tiny specks in the sky.

"Launch on the lift, sister; hear the lines sing, ride the ridge wind, brother; steady your wing!" Memory replayed the chorus of their song.

"This mornin' you complain 'cause the road too steep," said Mañero into the silence. "Nice 'n' flat now. What you waitin' for?"

Julian shook himself, suddenly conscious of the solid flesh that held him to the ground. Had the Wind Riders offered Piper the freedom of the skies? And if they had, why had the boy refused it?''

"Go ahead and laugh," muttered Robert. "You'll eat our dust, old man!''

"Maybe." Mañero's yellow eyes glinted. "Maybe I be there, find boy, before you! You want to bet, huh?''

"Why don't all of you save your breath for the road?'' Julian dug his heels into the bay mare's sides, and after a startled moment, the others followed him. If somebody didn't wring Mañero's neck soon, it was going to seem like a long journey indeed.

ELEVEN: Windsong

The Puerta del Agua Inn leaned against the city wall at the end of one of the twistiest streets in Laurelynn. It was an unlikely setting in which to find the man who sat on the other side of the scarred table, but then, thought the sorcerer, his guest would have thought it an equally unexpected place to find Caolin.

"I must admit that I found your letter . . . intriguing—" Alexander of Las Costas' tone was measured—"though highly irregular. If there is some illegality in the process by which the Estates of Westria are proposing to choose a new sovereign, it is my duty to investigate, which is why I am willing to give you five minutes to show me why I should not report you to Master Tanemun. Your name is familiar, but I have not, I think, met you before?"

"I think not." Caolin smiled slightly. Mañero had been wrong to accuse him of having no sense of humor. The name he had signed to the letter, and the face he was wearing now, belonged to a man called Ercul Ashe. It would almost have been worth letting Alexander report him to see Tanemun's face when he heard the name of a man who had died twenty years ago.

"But that does not matter. The future of Westria is at stake, and you may be the only man who can save her."

"From what?"

"From the clumsy hands of a backwoods fool."

Alexander sat back in his chair. "I begin to understand you now." Caolin poured wine into two goblets and set them on the table. The vintage matched neither the battered pewter goblets nor the dingy atmosphere. Alexander's eyebrows lifted a little as he recognized its quality.

"Is Fredegar Sachs in this?" he asked abruptly. Caolin shrugged, and Alexander sipped his wine. "He must be. That woman who's running the Guilds now does whatever he says, and at the last Council she made her feelings pretty clear."

The sorcerer watched Alexander's eyes. Were they beginning to dilate already? The drug with which he had painted the inside of the Lord Commander's cup should begin to work soon. The noise from the common room below grew louder as someone opened a door. Then it was closed again, and the upper floor was once more still.

"Your father was a great man," Caolin began. "He saw that it is impossible for one man to rule a kingdom of this size effectively."

"No one else seemed to think so!" Surely Alexander's face was a little pinker than it had been.

"That's because the king's Seneschal was a man of supreme efficiency," Caolin replied.

Alexander's face flushed suddenly. "His Seneschal! Caolin! He hounded my father to his grave!"

"And so the Council of Westria hounded *him*," the Blood Lord answered very quietly. "And what is Westria today?"

"A damn mess," mumbled Alexander. "Not m' own province, but the rest of it."

"And do you think that Julian of Stanesvale is the man to put things right?" The auburn head shook slowly, and Caolin continued, "Jehan ruled well because he was well served, and he was trained from birth in the arts of sovereignty. Who will run the country when this stone cutter's fosterling has you under his heel?''

''My father was right!'' Alexander took a deep breath, fighting a lassitude that he undoubtedly attributed to the wine. ''The province ought to have the right to self-rule.''

Caolin sat back, suppressing a relieved sigh. He knew that Lady Alessia would have filled her son's head with hatred for her husband's enemy. He had hoped that she would also have bred the boy on Brian's dreams. Those dreams had made Brian vulnerable to the Seneschal's snares, and now perhaps they would deliver his son into the Blood Lord's hands. How he would enjoy watching Lady Alessia's despair when she learned of how her son had helped Caolin to that power which she and the others had denied him so many years ago.

''Your father was a brilliant man,'' whispered Caolin. ''Only, he was ahead of his time. No one could have unseated King Jehan, but the situation is very different now.''

''Yes. Julian may be . . . descended from kings, but he was raised in a sty. Did you know that he has already insulted me?''

Caolin nodded, suppressing the satisfaction that his own face would have shown, as he remembered how he had arranged that. When this was finished, he must tell Ordrey to bring his puppet back to the city. Rumors of his outrages in the provinces were already drifting back to Laurelynn; it was time to add substance to the stories with which he had seeded the taverns and inns.

''Alexander, listen to me.''

The eyes that lifted to his were almost black. Caolin stared into those dilated pupils and tuned his voice to a croon.

''Julian is your enemy . . . and Westria's enemy.''

Alexander nodded.

''You have to stop him. I can help you, if you will listen to me.''

"Jumped-up upstart! He won't rule me!" Alexander's dark gaze refocused on the candle flame.

"Look at me—look at me—" The sorcerer recaptured the southern lord's attention. Alexander was proving more resistant than he had expected. "Yes, that's right. You see only my face, you hear only my words . . . you can prevent Julian from being king if you listen to me."

"Damn right," mumbled the young man. "He *insulted* me!"

It was sheer stubbornness that was protecting him, thought Caolin. Alexander's father had also been a singularly stubborn man. Had the son inherited his personal integrity as well, or only his father's colossal pride? Then Caolin smiled—Brian could not be led, but he had been driven easily.

"If Julian gains the other two Jewels of Power, no one will be able to deny him the throne," the sorcerer said softly.

"Well, *I* don't want 'em! Westria's done well enough without magic, *I* say."

That's just as well, for they would destroy you, thought Caolin.

"Julian is on his way to find the Wind Crystal now," he said. "There are those who would like to see your father's plan become the law of Westria. A man like you would have great influence if that came to pass. We could help it to happen . . . if you are willing to help stop Julian."

Alexander straightened a little, blinking. "Where's he gone?"

"Into the mountains," said the sorcerer. Mañero's last report had them well past Moon Lake on the road to Lake Tao. If Alexander took the road that followed the Wildwater, he should cross their trail.

"We've planted a spy who will mark the trail for you. But you don't want to let Julian know that you're following until he has found the Jewel."

"How'll I know?"

The sorcerer drew out two little leather bags on thongs. "Open this—" He pushed one of them toward Alexander, who clumsily loosened the cord and spilled out the silk-wrapped crystal inside. As he touched it, Caolin dropped its sister into his own palm.

"*Alexander* . . ." Caolin projected his will on both the inner and outer planes. The crystal rattled across the table as the young man jumped and clapped his hands over his ears.

"What is it? I *heard* that—inside! But I never had any gift for mind speech—they tested me."

"They don't know everything at the College of the Wise," Caolin laughed. "With these crystals, I'll be able to speak to you even though you're miles away. Go somewhere quiet at midnight and hold the crystal in your hand. Put it back in its bag now—that's right, it won't bite you. It's only a tool."

Alexander gave him a quick glance and then reclaimed the stone. His movements were regaining their coordination. The drug must be wearing off, but the young man was still too shaken to be puzzled by the change.

"How long will it take you to gather your men? You won't need many, Julian's party is small. But they should be warriors."

"My guard came with me," said Alexander, still fingering the crystal. "They're all good men. A day to organize mounts and supplies, and I'll have to send instructions back to Sanjos. We could leave the day after, if all goes well."

"If all goes well, you will be Protector of Westria, so do not delay," said the sorcerer as Alexander of Las Costas turned the cloudy crystal back and forth to catch the candlelight, and smiled.

"Look at the stars," Rana breathed. "They're like a trail of crystals across the sky!" She had thought the stars bright above the desert, but as the road curved back up into the mountains, visibility seemed to increase with every step. Now the bright pathway blazed above them. "If we could follow that road, I wonder what we'd find?" she asked Julian, and he laughed.

Since the thunderstorm, there had been no strain be-

tween them. It was like being with her brother—better than
that, for they did not quarrel. But the flesh made no demands. Perhaps the stress of the journey was altering all
their energies, for Rana could not help knowing that at
night, when Julian lay cocooned with Robert, their bodies'
warmth was the only comfort the two men shared.

"Hey, Mañero, where are those hot springs you promised us?" came Robert's voice from ahead.

"Soon stream gets warm, no alarm! Hot springs near,
have no fear."

Rana stubbed her toe on a root and felt Julian's strong
hand beneath her elbow. "Sorry. I was stargazing. It's
hard to believe that even the Wind Crystal could be as
beautiful as the jewels up there."

"Yes," Julian said softly, and then, "Rana, thank you.
I get so worried about finding the stone that I forget what
it's for. But we're all part of the same beauty—the Crystal, and the stars, and you and me. . . ."

"I'd best go on before Robert does the little man some
mischief," he added hurriedly. "I still don't like Mañero, but he has his uses. *I* wouldn't have known that
there were hot springs up here, and I'm going to enjoy
getting clean."

For a moment Rana stood still, peering after him. She
had done something to help him, but she was not sure
what, or how. Then there was a splash, and she began
to hurry. Julian was right. After the sweat and dust of
the Barren Lands, a hot bath was all that mattered. She
would wash her tunic and breeches too, even if she had
to put them on damp in the morning.

The steam that was rising from the water blurred the
stars. Rana made out the dim outlines of ancient cement
work, saw Robert folding his clothes carefully and setting them aside, and Julian, already stripped, poised at
the edge of the pool.

"Just how hot is it?" he asked.

"Not bad! Plenty deep. You jump right in, like me,"
came a voice from the mist. A water-sleeked head floated
into view.

Julian leaped forward. Water fountained around him;

then there was a yell that echoed from the mountaintops, and he appeared to levitate back out of the pool.

"Not bad?" Julian scrambled over the edge, his body steaming. "It's boiling! You treacherous dog. I'll drown you!" The mist swirled as Mañero laughed.

"Gotta come in th' pool t' drown me. Get soft, living in Laurelynn, ho, ho! Prince better be a tough ol' dog, like me."

Julian spluttered, and then suddenly he was laughing as well. "I'll get you for that, Mañero, oh I will!" He put one foot back into the water, winced, then resolutely continued on in. "Guardians! How do you stand it?"

For a moment the steam cleared, and Rana saw starlight glitter on the choppy water around Mañero and on the little man's wet hair.

"Come in, I teach you. Hot or cold all the same to me!" A sweep of his arm sent a wave of steam swirling toward Julian.

As the air blurred between them, Julian's figure wavered. Rana took a step forward, feeling her body coarse and clumsy. Through the thick air, she could only glimpse his transformation. She reached out toward him . . . and clutched mist.

"You cannot hold him," Robert said softly behind her. "Even in the night, when my arms are tight around him, I can feel his spirit striving to break free. Julian gives me his body's love, but that's not what I wanted—not all I wanted, anyway. We caught up with him, but Julian is still getting away." He moved past her and carefully began to ease into the pool.

Rana stood with her hands empty at her sides. Robert was right, they could not try to keep Julian earthbound. If she wanted to follow him, then she must change too.

She tugged off the clumsy boots that weighted her feet, stripped off her stiff jerkin, soiled tunic and breeches, everything, until she stood naked, stretching out her arms to embrace the wind.

Julian lay in the gray hour before dawn and listened to the wind. The weather had changed while they slept; the wind was already blowing vigorously. It was probably the fall of a yellow pine that had awakened him; those were the trees most likely to go down. But the College of Bards had never fielded such an orchestra as he was now hearing, from the bass boom as the wind thrummed past the pines' thick branches, to the shrill hiss of the needles, or the hushed murmur as it fell. Even here in the valley, every narrow leaf of willow was whispering, each green-gold alder leaf clicked metallically.

Wind whirled down a shower of twigs. Banked ashes swirled, and a glimmer of light woke in the fire pit. Julian eased carefully away from Robert, tucking the blanket well in behind him, and looked for the water can. Steam hissed angrily as he doused the remaining coals, and Rana turned over, murmuring his name.

"Go back to sleep," said the Prince softly. "I've put out the fire. I'm going for a walk now."

He had to brace himself against the gusts as he made his way across the meadow. A light glimmered in the window of the tiny cabin whose owners had offered them this campsite, and faint beneath the crying of the wind he heard a baby's waking wail. The folk here lived by trapping, gathering the fruits of the forest, tending a small garden . . . and hunting crystals. Julian sensed that they had knowledge he needed, but could he persuade them to put it into words?

In the east, a colorless radiance suffused a sky swept clean by the wind. Where the forest plunged down to the edge of the flat, Julian put out his hand to the nearest tree trunk and felt long tremors, like the vibration in the sound box of Silverhair's harp when he played. Filled with sudden anticipation, he began to scramble up the mountainside.

From the ridge he saw a dim, swirling mass of foliage that reminded him of the storm-tossed sea. Torn pine tassels flicked past him; his face was stung by bits of flying bracken. Nearby, a yellow pine bowed and straightened like a worshiper at a festival, its long branches tossing in a frenzy of adoration. But standing alone, it was too vulnerable for climbing. Julian eyed the stand of spruce trees above him speculatively. They seemed to be deep-rooted, and they protected each other from the wind's worst fury. There was a lesson in that too, but he had no time to consider it.

"Brother, will you bear me?" The branching silver scars at his brow tingled, and senses that the Earthstone had awakened perceived the tree's agreement. He set his arms about the trembling trunk and pulled himself upward.

Clinging to the spruce tree, Julian gave himself over to the dizzying swing and return, until his head rang like a bell. His stomach leaped with every swoop and recovery, but in the east, the sky was glowing. He fixed his eyes on the horizon, and as the first bright gold edged the mountains, he found his equilibrium. Was this how it felt when the eagle rode the wind?

He used earth wisdom to link his awareness to that of the spruce tree, secure in its connection with the soil. Now he was certain of his center, no matter how wildly he swung. He *was* the center, poised between earth and heaven. *Poised between male and female also*, he thought, remembering Robert and Rana asleep in the camp below.

And the sun came up in splendor, and suddenly Julian could see the wind. It stroked a mighty hand across the forest, and every upturned leaf and needle blazed back white light. Air ebbed and flowed up the slopes and down into the valleys in pulses of radiance that swirled and broke against the ridges like sea foam on the strand.

The air is a sea also! he thought exultantly. *Now I understand. . . .*

The friction of wind on leaf, on stone, on itself, was creating energy. Julian felt it building around him and within him, recharging the life force of the land. If this storm had brought rain, it would have eased the thirst of the body. But the tingling that flared through him was feeding some subtler appetite.

He stared at his arms, surprised that they were not

glowing. He threw back his head and shouted, joining his cry to the mighty music of the wind. The wind plucked at his garments; he felt his grip loosen and flung one arm outward.

I am free! I am free! I am riding the wind! Julian's other arm was slipping, but what did it matter? He leaned back, waiting for the gust that would carry him—

—"Julian! Julian!"

That was Siverhair's voice, but he should not have been able to hear it. Slowly Julian realized that the wind was sinking and that he was still perched in the tree.

His voice cracked . . . "I'm up here!"

"Are you crazy?" came the harper's call from somewhere below.

Julian shifted his grip, gasping as locked muscles moved. Crazy? Perhaps, but he had learned something, if only he could put it into words. The forest shimmered with the last breath of the windstorm, but already the stillness of the high country was returning. The faceted peaks gleamed like crystal in the light of the newborn sun.

"Crystal? This whole country's made o' crystal, don't ye know?" The miner gestured expansively at the glittering rocks above them.

Silverhair blew steam from his tea to cool it and drank thankfully. The miner's wife had it waiting for them when he and Julian came down from the mountain, and the harper needed it. It had been a shock to him to find Julian in that tree.

"But if we were looking for it especially," said the Prince, "where would we go?" He fidgeted as though his body could barely contain his energy.

The woman pointed to the ridge. "That's what we're after today. Folk pay for 'em on both sides o' the mountains, enough t' keep us goin' anyhow."

"Can we go with you?" asked Julian. The others were finishing breakfast. It looked like the day would be clear and bright. "The boy can't be more than a day ahead of us," he went on, "and I think I might learn something useful there."

None of the others would have gainsaid him, and the miners' children were excited at the prospect of company. They chattered continuously as they rode up to the place where they had to leave the horses, and their voices rang as they climbed the steep path to the ridge top, though only Mañero had breath to reply.

The harp case bumped against Siverhair's back as he pulled himself upward with the staff that Julian had cut for him, wondering why he had insisted on bringing the instrument along. The woman seemed to find it no hardship to hike with her baby strapped to her back, but she was younger than he. The shortness of breath that had troubled the harper in Laurelynn had not returned, but with every step his back and legs protested the strain. Still, after so many years, it would have been equal torment to have left Swangold behind.

She's a part of me, he thought wryly. *They'll have to bury me with her still in my arms.*

"Look—" said Julian softly.

The harper straightened with a groan and saw that they had reached a ridge whose gravelly slope was studded with giant boulders and edged with twisted dwarf pines. The whole world lay spread out around them.

"From here you can see the structure of the mountains." Julian pointed, and for a moment Silverhair saw edge and cleavage as if he were gazing into a crystal. Then the glare of sunlight on granite made him blink, and it was only rock and trees once more.

"You've already learned something, lad, if you can make even me see!"

"I had better," Julian answered with sudden intensity. "When we find the Wind Crystal—if we find it—there won't be much time to study its ways."

Robert was sitting on a fallen log, panting, and Rana leaned against a rock like a castle buttress, but the miners were already beginning to search the stony surface like hunting dogs seeking the scent of game.

"Uncle, how was the Wind Crystal made?"

"Made? As far as I know, it grew in perfection. But if you want to know how it was tuned to serve the Powers of Air," said Silverhair, "The first Mistress of the Jewels accomplished that with song."

"I thought so." Julian turned to watch the miners, and the wind blew the dark hair back from his brow. "I spent a night in a cave on my way here, and the stones sang to me."

The boy had certainly learned something, thought the harper. Julian had come down the mountainside this morning as if his feet had wings.

"Take out your harp, Silverhair, and play!"

The harper had his breath back now, and that had never been a request that he had to think twice about answering. He plucked the octaves and saw Julian's eyes closed, as if he were listening.

"Play a chord, then go over there and play it again."

"What are you trying to do?" Silverhair struck the notes Julian had asked.

"I'm trying to hear. . . ."

Silverhair quartered the area where the miners had been hunting as the miner and his family watched with ill-disguised amusement, and Rana and Robert in amazement. But the harper was beginning to understand what Julian wanted now.

And this is not something I've taught him, he thought, fascinated. *Wind Lord has taken him in hand at last, and thanks be to the Maker of All that I am here to see!*

"Did you hear it?" Julian asked suddenly. "Stand here, uncle, and play those three notes again."

Silverhair repeated them, and it seemed to him that he did hear something. Julian stood opposite him, and in a voice that none of them had ever heard from him before, he echoed the tones. Then he stopped. In the sudden silence, they heard a faint, sweet chime. The harper repeated his notes, but Julian sang a third higher, and suddenly the echo rang out triumphantly.

The miner darted forward and began a careful excavation of the gravel. "Stop!" he shouted suddenly. "I've got it—I can feel it tremblin'."

Silverhair clasped the harp against his chest. The man's
wiry curls quivered as he worried at the soil. Then he
dropped his pick and plucked a piece of pitted, brownish
rock from the ground, shook sand free as he turned it,
and whooped in triumph as the chunk of crystal matrix
flared in the sun. From the great boulder that overlooked
the slope, Mañero howled.

"Oh, what a beauty! What a beauty!" The children
leaped around their parents, but Silverhair stared at Julian.

"How did you know?"

"I didn't." He shrugged self-consciously. "But I
wondered."

"C'n you teach us that song?" The miner held out the
crystal for them to admire.

"I think that each crystal has its own song," answered
Julian. "But you might try singing at each other in the
way the harper and I were doing just now."

"That tune's a bit like th' one th' flute boy would
play," said the woman.

"Piper!" exclaimed Rana. "Was he a boy about fourteen with brown hair, and the flute was wooden, and he
didn't talk at all?"

The miners nodded. "Stayed a night an' played for
us, seemed glad o' a hot meal, then went on. That was
gettin' on two days ago."

"He's singing to it," breathed Julian. "Piper has
learned its song somehow, and that's what drew him
here."

"The Wind Crystal?" asked Robert.

Julian nodded. His voice shook. "We must be very
close to it now!"

Silverhair bowed his head. *I didn't really believe that
we would find it . . . after all I've seen, and heard. The
quest has always been enough for me. But Julian will be
my teacher now!*

"Listen!" said Julian. "Is there any place in this area
that's special—a place that draws the eye but where you've
never dared to go?"

"I don't know—" began the miner, but his wife

grabbed his arm and began to whisper. "Well, there's one place. We call it th' Throne. Might that be what yer lookin' for?"

" 'Tisn't far," the woman added shyly. "Maybe ten mile from here. Sticks up on the edge o' a cliff like a tower o' stone."

Caolin let his focus sink into the heart of the cloudy crystal he held in his hand. The light of his candle refracted along internal fissures like the walls of a tiny tower and caught the inclusions in sparks of light as the snow-dappled peaks of the mountains toward which he was directing his will glittered in the light of the waning moon. Fredegar Sachs and his household were long abed. The building creaked in the darkness; a shutter rattled lightly as the night wind caught it, then was still.

"Alexander—" The sorcerer spoke with both his voice and his will, and the crystal quivered in his hand. "Alexander of Las Costas, answer me!" His voice sang with command.

He waited, his gaze unfocusing. The glimmering terrain within the crystal blurred. Within its shadows he glimpsed a clearing beside a road, a long ridge black against a scattering of stars.

"Alexander . . . " In the room, the call was no longer audible, but the Blood Lord's spirit was perceiving the campsite clearly through the senses of the man he called.

"I hear you . . . " Alexander's response was slow with sleep, and Caolin suppressed annoyance. The young fool had been ordered to await his communication at this hour.

"Where are you?" the sorcerer asked.

"How should I know?" came the answer, as rueful as angry. "This isn't my kind of country." Caolin increased the pressure of the demand he was projecting, and in a moment felt Alexander's uncertain laugh. "The guide says we're about halfway across these mountains, at a place called Bear Valley."

"Another day of travel should get you over the pass,

and you'll strike the border road on the day following,''
sent Caolin.

"And what about the others?''

*"When you reach the border road, they will be about
two days ahead of you, so you'll need to push hard. Road
runes will guide you—watch for them.''*

*"But where are they going? They seem to be making
a circle through the mountains. Are we being made a
game of somehow?''*

"No—'' Caolin forced his thoughts to become soothing, remembering Alexander's pride. *"They have a reason. Be glad you did not have to follow them all the way
to Stanesvale.''*

Alexander was not the only one who found Julian's
route inexplicable, but the sorcerer was not about to give
him the satisfaction of telling him so. Mañero said they
were following that idiot boy they had picked up on the
coast two years before, but that seemed unlikely. Could
Alexander be right? Caolin rejected the idea with a mental shake. It was nearing mid-August. If Julian wanted
to master the Wind Crystal before the next meeting of
the Council, he would have to find the Jewel soon. He
had no time left for games—if it had been a game and
not sheer ineptitude.

*"Is there anything more? I'm sleepy—it's been a hard
day.''*

Once more Caolin controlled exasperation. *"Sleep—you
have done well.''* He made it a command. *"Tomorrow night
you will report to me again.''* Something suspiciously like
a snore was the only reply.

The Blood Lord dipped a pen in the blue ink and traced
Alexander's route an inch or so farther on his map of the
Ramparts. It was drawing ever closer to the red line
drawn from the reports he had been getting from Mañero. For all his complaints, Alexander was making good
time. The two lines would meet . . . soon.

The great clock on the tower of the Council Hall beat
out the last strokes of midnight. Presently it would be
time to contact Mañero. But though Alexander might be
exhausted, the Blood Lord was still wakeful. He rarely

slept more than three or four hours a night, and he had always preferred to work during the hours of darkness that other men wasted on dreams.

Caolin pulled out a fresh sheet of paper and dipped his pen in black ink. *"The Prince of Frogs lies in the mire. . . ."* He considered the line with a faint smile. The broken-down bard who had been spreading songs for him was doing a good job. He had already overheard some of his verses in the taverns. It was time to provide more.

> *And fills his gullet with a fly!*
> *The Prince of Stones looks rather higher—*
> *He takes his pleasures in the sty!*

The sorcerer drew the last exclamation point and frowned. It was scurrilous, but not damaging. He needed something that would build on the reputation his puppet had been making for Julian in the villages. Something . . . obscene. He began to cast about for a rhyme for "rape."

The knock on the great door below boomed like thunder. Absorbed in his versifying, for a moment Caolin thought it *was* thunder. Then it came again.

"—patience! Why can't. . . ." the voice of one of Sachs' servants came faintly from below. The sorcerer blew out his candle, stepped to the window, and eased open the shutters. Shadows shifted in the street below.

"Who's making such a racket at an hour when decent folk are in their beds?" He could hear the steward clearly now, as clearly as he heard the reply

"Open in the name of the Regent of Westria!"

Caolin recoiled from the window. *Eric's* men! How had the Regent found out that the Blood Lord was here? Suddenly he remembered that conversation with Silverhair in the streets of Laurelynn. That had been a self-indulgence for which he reproached himself. Still, he had not told the harper enough for anyone to trace him. If Eric had been *sure*, he would have acted before now. It must be sheer dogged persistence which was one of the

Regent's few admirable qualities—that had finally brought him to the Guildmaster's door.

For a moment Caolin stood unmoving; then he swept the papers on his desk into a satchel. What else could betray him? Quickly he bundled the books and folders of reports into a cupboard and locked it, then added a spell of concealment that should distract any casual searcher. The noise below was growing louder. He wrapped his cloak around himself and stood for a moment, considering whose face he would wear. Not Ercul Ashe—Eric would remember those features, even after twenty years. But Mañero was already known to be in Sachs' service, and he could not return from the Ramparts to discomfit the sorcerer this time!

The sorcerer let his breath out slowly, visualizing the grizzled whiskers and the long, inquisitive nose of his spy. As he heard the door below crash open, he willed his focus to narrow until there was only the image, and then—Mañero in movement as well as in feature—he scampered down the stairs.

"Search every room! I want every creature in the household brought here!" A deep voice vibrated through the walls.

Eric had come himself, then. Caolin snorted with amusement. The Regent had been one of his enemies long ago, but it was sheer misfortune that had enabled them to bring him down. Did the man think he was the sorcerer's equal now?

He slipped through an open door, merging with the group of chattering servants who had already been herded into the room. Fredegar Sachs stood expostulating indignantly, draped in a monumental, furred bedgown, while his mistress, who seemed to be naked beneath the coverlet someone had wrapped around her, huddled sniveling in a chair. The Guildmaster's porcine eyes roved anxiously over his hysterical household.

He's wondering which one of them is me, thought Caolin. *He's wondering if I'm going to give him away.*

But the sorcerer knew that he would only make himself more conspicuous if he tried to run.

He glimpsed Eric's tall figure in the doorway. Someone was chattering about an apartment on the top floor.

"—a person of note, sir, for the bed has a silken coverlet," said the guard. "And he's not been gone long either, for the wax on his candle is still warm!"

Caolin poked his head out to note the face of this informative guardsman and saw Eric's face darken.

"He's still in the house, then. No one has gone through the cordon outside. We'll start questioning the servants. Remember, he'll be wearing someone else's features, so have them identify each other. Single out anyone who doesn't fit. If that doesn't work, we'll take them to the palace and question them separately."

For Eric, this was positively inspired! But the Regent had no idea that by this time, shape-changing was the least of the sorcerer's powers. Caolin drew breath, pitched his voice carefully—

"My lord! My lord!" The cry seemed to come from the street. "Someone's climbing out a back window. He's armed, m'lord." There was a clatter of feet as guardsmen rushed toward the sound.

Caolin darted for the passage beneath the stairs. One of the maids cried out and pointed; the sorcerer shouted, and all of the lamps and most of the torches went out. The guard who had searched his rooms made a grab for him; Caolin stilled, trapping the man's startled gaze.

"Your throat is closing," he hissed. "You can't breathe!" The guardsman dropped his sword, tore at his tunic collar. "Your air is gone. Now die!" The man's eyes bulged; gurgling, he fell.

Caolin stepped back, wrapping darkness around himself, but one of the others had seen. A sword swung, the sorcerer felt a quick sting. Fury blasted through him; the fellow went flying, and others clasped their hands to their heads as the sorcerer sang out a sound whose overtones seared the ear.

Eric rushed toward him, roaring, but where the sorcerer had stood, there was only an open door.

Still shielded by shadows, Caolin darted through the kitchen and out the side door. Guards came running; he had time for a quick approximation of the face of the man he had slain.

"In there, quickly. The Regent needs you!" he gasped. "The sorcerer's getting away!" He stepped aside as they rushed in, smiled as oaths told him they had run into the men Eric had sent after him.

But the alley was still full of soldiers. He held himself to a walk as he started toward the main road.

"Wait! Where are you going? The orders—"

Caolin turned as an officer reached out to him, glimpsed beyond him a familiar bald pate—Ordrey—and another figure, overdressed in purple brocade. *The fool has served his purpose,* thought the sorcerer. *Let him serve me once more.* With sudden decision, Caolin pointed.

"I am sent to tell you that the sorcerer is out, and that he has taken the face of Prince Julian. And—oh, look, sir—who's that in the shadows? Oh, it's him, sir! Don't let him get away!" He dashed forward, and the guards leaped into motion behind him.

But Caolin had seen Ordrey melting away into the shadows. He stepped aside suddenly, and his hand closed on the plump shoulder.

"Be still, you fool!" he hissed. "It's me!"

The sorcerer's eyes were still on the hunt. For a moment longer, the young man who looked like Julian stood staring. Then he seemed to realize his danger, even if he did not understand it, and he ran.

The Regent's men gave chase. Heads were popping out of opening windows. Candles glimmered behind panes of leaded glass.

"Come," Caolin said hoarsely, drawing Ordrey after him down an alleyway.

"I won't ask where," said the little man conversationally. "After all these years, how could I doubt that you would have prepared a bolt hole somewhere?"

"The Puerta del Agua—" More shouting broke out behind them, and he moved faster.

But even Ordrey swallowed nervously when they paused beneath the lantern over the door of the inn and he saw that Caolin had assumed the features of Ercul Ashe.

TWELVE:
The Wind Lord's Throne

In the last light of sunset, they came to the Throne. Glimpsed beyond the curve of a barren slope, it was a knob of stone that glowed like hammered gold. Julian stood among the pine trees, letting its image fill his sight and his spirit. Now all doubts were gone. The very shape of that stone tower was a summons he could not ignore.

The tree trunk flexed beneath his hand as its branches whispered secrets to the wind. It was only a small wind, not the splendid storm that had taught him so much the day before. He had no words for the knowledge it had given him. The winds of this high country tingled with the presence of the Wind Crystal, and it was teaching him already.

Earth or sea may bear us, Julian thought then, *but we live and move within the element of Air. Earth supports us, and Water fills the depths, but who can map the winds? If I could master them, the winds would tell me the secrets of the world!*

But it was not enough simply to understand. He could not even communicate the things he knew now; to release the words that lay locked within him, he needed the Jewel.

"Julian—"

Abruptly he became aware of his body again. Rana was standing beside him. Her gaze moved from the tower to Julian's face.

"Unless you want to make a dry camp, we can't stay here. We passed a creek a mile ago. Silverhair has started back with the others already." For a moment she was silent. "Do you think the Jewel is up there?"

Julian nodded.

"We'll find it tomorrow then." She smiled, and the sun glow seemed to light her face from within.

Suddenly Julian wanted to reach out to her, but it was not his flesh that desired the contact. Somehow the turbulent emotions that had shaken him last year on the ocean had been transmuted into a passion of the spirit that neither of them feared. He let out his breath in a long, wondering sigh. Rana laid her hand on his. Her touch was firm, friendly, the clasp of a comrade, or of the sister he had never known—no, she was part of his soul.

"Yes, tomorrow." He fought for the right words. "Rana . . . thank you for coming after me."

"They think they find the Jewel tomorrow." In the stillness of midnight, the thought Mañero was sending to Caolin came clearly.

From time to time a burst of drunken singing drifted up from the courtyard below. The garrison of Blood Gard was celebrating its master's return. But to Caolin, it was only a discordant background whisper. The sorcerer sat unmoving, his whole awareness focused on the image that Mañero was sending him.

What an odd formation it was, this rock they called the Throne. Why had there been no record of it in the books he had stolen from the College of the Wise? The sorcerer had made it his business to learn the location of every place of power in Westria.

"*How long to reach the tower, and how long to climb it?*" he asked then.

"*Two hours maybe—an easy ride. But Throne's steep. Need ropes t' get up there, or wings!*"

That sounded promising. The Prince should be distracted for some hours before he actually touched the Jewel. If Alexander and his men came on them when Julian was still atop the tower . . . yes, there were interesting possibilities.

"*Why are you worrying? You're not the one who will have to make the climb!*"

Caolin suppressed a smile. "*Listen*—his thought grew more focused. "*Volunteer to put out the fire when you break camp, but leave it smoking.*"

"*What happen then?*"

"*What is that to you? When my men come, get away. They have orders to let you go.*"

"*Thank you, master.*"

In this kind of communication, it was hard to distinguish irony. Abruptly Caolin severed the contact and drew a few quick breaths in the pattern that would bring him back to normal consciousness.

His eyes opened on a confusion of light and shadow as a draft set the lamp flame flickering wildly over the black-painted walls of his temple. But all was secure. Ordrey sat on guard outside the door, and the endlessly repeated chorus of a bawdy song drifted up from below.

He took a deep breath and prepared to summon Alexander. Soon, very soon, it would be dawn.

There was music on the wind. . . .

Between one breath and the next, Silverhair found that he had passed from a dream of morning at the College of Bards, where the fragmentary harmonies of a dozen practicing students had combined into a single, strange music, to dawn beside a stream in the mountains, and a distant piping that came and went with the wind. He breathed in carefully, willing the pounding of his heart to ease. The others were still sleeping. Julian's arm was thrown protectively across Robert's chest. A flame of bright hair emerging from a tangle of blankets was all that could be seen of Rana, and he supposed that the other lump must be Mañero.

He sat up, shivering as the chilly air kissed bare skin. How could the others sleep through this music that set his spirit soaring? But perhaps it was meant for him alone. Swiftly he gathered up his gear. Even his pony seemed enchanted, for the beast submitted without protest as he slung the saddle on. Silverhair was already mounted when Julian sat up, rubbing sleep from his eyes.

"I hear something," the harper said in explanation. "It could be Piper. I have to go and see—"

"Up there?"

Silverhair nodded. Julian was frowning thoughtfully. Couldn't he hear?

"Go on, then. I'll bring the others. We'll follow your trail." Julian smiled, and Silverhair realized that he was letting him go first on purpose.

When I find Piper—if it is Piper—it will be hard enough to greet him without all of the others listening. But what can I say to him? Will he still be afraid? He lifted his head. The music sounded more strongly, calling him. *Piper must have forgiven me, or why am I the only one to hear this summoning?*

"Thank you. . . ." He headed the horse up the trail, feeling Julian's gaze upon him until he reached the trees.

When he came out onto the slope above them, a breath of wind was whispering among the big leaves of the mules' ears, the only things that seemed to grow in the stony scree. The first light flared from the snow-patched peaks; each dew-wet pebble glistened in its clarity. *A country of crystal*, thought Silverhair, *as it was in the days before the Ancient Times when the Maker carved out these mountains with an icy blade.*

The pony tossed its head and grunted, moving faster. Silverhair swung the harp case forward, fumbling at clasps. He told himself, *Piper will not fear me if I am holding Swangold.* But that was not the real reason. As his fingers closed on the use-smoothed wood, he realized that after all these years, his instinct was to meet any crisis with harp in hand.

His mount needed no direction. An embroidery of notes settled once more into the haunting melody that had awakened him. Silverhair plucked the dominant note and realized that the magic was already beginning, for the two tones were the same.

"My child, I am coming to you on the wings of music . . . listen to the love I am bringing you, son of my heart. Forgive me . . . can you forgive me?" sang the strings.

On the ridge, wind whipped at him, but now he could see the dip before the final slope up to the tower. There, just at the base of it, was a patch of color that moved. He saw the white blur of a a face lifting . . . then there was silence.

The sound of his own pulse roared in Silverhair's ears. He tethered his pony to a twisted pine in the lee of the ridge, and with Swangold still clasped in his arms, he trudged up the last hill.

He stopped beside a boulder, trying to catch his breath after the last steep climb. He had thought the boy might still fear him, but he was the one who was afraid. Then Piper lifted the flute to his lips and piped a phrase from Silverhair's own wandering song. The harper sat down abruptly on the boulder, knowing that the tears he was blinking away were not from the wind. Piper lowered the flute, and smiled.

"Did you know we would follow you?" Silverhair asked carefully. "Did you know that I would come?"

Piper nodded, and now it was the chorus of the song that he played.

He has grown! thought Silverhair, staring. But perhaps it was not size so much as a new definition in the bones of Piper's face that had changed him, or perhaps it was the alert intelligence in the boy's hazel eyes. Piper was too thin, stretched taut as a harp string by the stresses of the road. *Like me,* thought the harper. But he seemed well.

"I have not touched wine since the night you ran

away.'' Silverhair spoke suddenly. He had not realized how hard this would be to say. "I hated myself, not you. You don't have to do anything or be anything for me, Piper. I still . . . love you."

The last words were a whisper, but Piper heard them, for silent beneath the windsong, he had left his nest at the base of the tower, and his thin arms were holding Silverhair and the harp together in an awkward embrace. One hand came up to brush the man's tears away. Silverhair let go of his death grip on Swangold's sound box, reached out and put his arm around the boy. It was like holding a bird; he could feel Piper's heartbeat shaking the ribs beneath his hand.

For a moment all he knew was glory as the divine harmonies of the Wind Lord's music sounded in his soul. And then he became aware once more of his own body, and the boy beside him, and the great tower of stone from which, faint but pure, he heard the notes of Piper's song.

"Is *that* what you have been following?" He pointed upward, and Piper nodded eagerly. The boy pulled the flute from his belt and repeated the melody. Like an echo, the song resounded from the Throne. Piper touched the harp, and smiling, Silverhair settled it against his shoulder.

"You want me to play too? Very well. We'll play as we used to, and wake the music until the whole world can hear!"

He waited until the breeze brought the melody again, and then he and Piper began to play together, blending the music that came from without and the harmonies they heard within.

A hand touched his shoulder. Silverhair looked up and saw Julian, with the others behind him. He lifted his fingers from the harp strings, but whatever was making the music that rang from the mass of rock before them continued to sing. Julian's face was transfigured by wonder.

"Is that the Wind Crystal?"

Piper nodded, and Julian reached out to give his shoulder a quick squeeze.

"*I* couldn't find it, Piper, but I believed in you. You have succeeded beyond all our hopes."

"What took you so long?" asked Silverhair as the euphoria receded.

Julian grimaced. "That idiot Mañero left the fire smoking and we had to go back to douse it. There may be some disturbances when I take the Jewel, and the mountains are dry. I didn't want to take any chances with the wind."

Silverhair glanced past him and saw Mañero crouched well away from the others, as if a cross word would send him slinking away. The harper nodded. Then his gaze returned to the rock formation that loomed above them.

"When you take it . . ." he echoed. "That is the problem, isn't it? How are you going to get up there?"

"That's why I brought those ropes from the miners. Don't forget, I grew up climbing cliffs. I understand mountains."

"I hope so," answered Silverhair. "That tower must be two hundred feet of sheer stone."

From the top of the tower of Blood Gard, the walls fell sheer to the first outcroppings of the Red Mountain. To the platform at its summit, the Blood Lord had brought his tools of magic, while in the barracks below, his men huddled in silence, wondering what devilry their lord was planning now. Today the Ramparts were only a smudge of haze on the eastern horizon, but Caolin did not need to see them with his physical eyes. His attention was fixed on the cloudy crystal in his hand.

"*What do you see, Alexander—tell me!*"

"*A big upthrust of stone,*" came the answer. "*They're all at the bottom of it. No, someone's moving, starting up the side. Dark hair, must be Julian.*"

"*Good. Keep watch, and hold on to your crystal,*" the Blood Lord cut him off. "*When I call you again, be ready to tell me what you see.*"

Caolin stood up. The day was already hot; he could

see the pulse of heated air above the sun baked fields.
Hot air rising—yes, that's what he wanted now, to dis-
place enough hot air to draw the cold air eastward from
the sea. He set the cloudy crystal at the eastern edge of
his circle of crystals and began to pace around it, summoning the powers of the winds. The brazier in the center was already glowing; the air above it shimmered like
air above the Great Valley's plain.

> Wind creatures now I call, weightless, ye airy
> sprites,
> Winged ones who wait on high, Sylphs, now I
> summon ye!

The sorcerer cast a handful of incense upon the coals
and sat back on his heels as a puff of smoke burst skyward. The first name of power he called, and then the
second, casting charged incense from different pots upon
the coals, watching the shapes the smoke assumed as it
swirled upwar . Then he whispered the third name,
reaching for the core of his power, and exhaled all the
breath in his lungs in a long, slow stream across the
coals. Where it touched, a column of white steam arose
to silver the shadow.

The sorcerer took up his prayer fans—made from the
blunt, shadow-hued feathers of the great condor of
Awhai—and lifted them to the hovering cloud.

"Windherds, now hear me! I summon a great wind—
a west wind, a sea wind—to strike the eastern mountains!" Slowly he began to move widdershins around the
platform. "As the warm air rises, let cold rush in to
follow. Faster and faster, higher and higher!" He moved
ever more swiftly, the dark wings in his hands beating
the air. "Wind creatures, wind-keepers, let the great
winds grow!"

And the smoke cloud above him pulsed, swirled, grew
larger, lifted and thinned, stretching eastward like a banner of shadow as the wind began to blow.

* * *

Julian tightened his grip on the rock as wind gusted past. He glanced sideways, but the sky was still cloudless, and there were no trees near enough for him to judge from which direction the wind was blowing or how hard it came. When he had started the climb, the air had been still. Who would have thought the wind could rise so fast? He was only halfway. Could he finish the climb before it became too strong?

He moved one leg sideways, feeling for a foothold. It had been exciting to ride a spruce tree through such a storm, but it would be a rather different proposition to do it clinging to this wall of stone. A quick glance downward showed him Silverhair and the others watching him confidently from the edge of the rock and soil that lapped one side of the tower. Maybe he had boasted too loudly.

Wind whistled across the rock face, lifting the hair away from his brow. A seemingly endless succession of ranges curved away to every side. The route that had seemed easiest had brought him around to the back face of the tower. He was suspended in space, but at the moment, Julian was conscious chiefly of the drop below him, where the rock fell away another two hundred feet or so into a gorge. He tried to draw on earth power to help him hold on; the Throne was rooted in rock even if its head was in the sky, but all of the energy he could sense was rising. Why had he expected this to be easy?

Above him was a projection that looked strong enough to take his weight. He made a loop in his line and tossed it, hooking it over the stone on the second try, tugged gently, then harder, and used the rope to swing himself across and pull himself up to a new foothold. But the gusts were shaking him now; the wind was whispering. . . .

But that was ridiculous. He had only to keep his mind on finding hand- and footholds, one after another, until he reached his goal. This was no time for fancies.

"But you can't—it's impossible!" came the wind whisper.

"This tower belong to the Old Powers; no human can scale it."

"The Powers of the Air are against you!"

"You're going to fall!"

White-knuckled and sweating, Julian clung to the rock face, willing the voices to go away. Suddenly all he could think of was the gulf beneath him, the terror of falling, and the agony of his body smashed against the stones. Another foot, and another. . . . Sweat stung his eyes and he squeezed his lids shut as the wind flung dust into his face.

A glance downward showed him Robert watching intently, white with anxiety. Love had given Robert the insight to know that Julian was in trouble, but the sight of his cousin's wide eyes only reinforced Julian's fear. *Oh, my dear*—a breath of thought that was not terror whispered through his awareness—*this is why I didn't want you to follow me!*

"You're going to fall!" Evil voices yammered once more. The breath sobbed in his throat as he strained upward. The cliff felt smooth beneath his fingers; he slid helplessly. He had lost his link with the stone. Wind slammed him sideways, and he slipped, scraping his ribs.

I can't do it. No one could climb in this wind!

And as if his will had been all that held him, the rope slipped through sweat-slick palms, and Julian fell.

Piper knelt at the cliff edge, staring at the crumpled figure below. Here the slope that had enabled them to approach the tower had been carved away into a rocky canyon. Julian had come to rest partway down, his body lodged between a boulder and a twisted juniper tree.

"Is he dead?" Robert's voice cracked.

"He's fainted!" Silverhair spoke with the sharpness of desperation. "Get the other rope. If he doesn't rouse, one of us will have to go down after him."

Piper got to his feet, but Rana was already darting back around the base of the tower to get their packs. The witchwind whistled around the stones, distorting the harmonies that shimmered from the top of the tower. The boy eyed the rough wall that had defeated Julian. Strength had not been sufficient, but could those crevices give purchase to smaller fingers? He remembered how he had rescued Lis when they set their prayer sticks on the peak. Julian was not the only one who could climb!

"Julian! Julian!" Silverhair pitched his voice to penetrate the whistle of the wind. The Prince groaned, stirred, and looked up at them. "Julian, are you hurt?"

Rana scrambled down to them with the rope, and Robert loosed it over the side, bouncing as it slapped down the slope toward him.

"I . . . don't think so," came the answer finally. "Just got . . . the wind knocked out of me." There was a sound that might have been laughter.

Piper found it oddly painful to hear. *He praised me for finding the Crystal,* he told himself. *But he can't climb now. I could help him again. It would make Silverhair happy. . . .* He began to edge away.

Only now, when he was with his old companions again, was Piper realizing how much the Guardian's gift had changed him. During his journey northward, he had explored the alien territory of his mind, grateful for the silence. Just so a man who had been deaf might learn to hear again, or a man who had been healed of blindness learn to see.

None of them expected him to do anything. It was a moment for choosing, as it had been when he faced the Great Eagle on Cloud's Rest. But Piper understood what he was doing now.

I can do it, so I have to. I won't run away anymore. He began to untie his sandals.

The others were trying to swing the rope closer to Julian. Piper drifted back to the tower. A cheer from Robert told him that Julian had grasped the rope, but Piper was gazing upward, noting where the narrow ledge that had given the Prince a path ended. That was what had defeated him. It was no use trying the easy way, but he saw another. He slipped off his cloak, unclasped his belt, let go of everything that might impede him. The others were shouting encouragement to Julian as the Prince pulled himself upward. Piper smiled gently, got a good grip on the stone, and began to climb.

* * *

"Where's Piper?" Silverhair straightened, staring around. Julian was sitting up as Robert and Rana fussed over him, but where could the boy have gone?

"Look!" They turned at Rana's cry.

Julian had appeared small against that expanse of stone. Piper was a human mite inching upward. Then the wind gusted again. They saw the boy try to burrow into the stone.

No. . . . Fear constricted Silverhair's throat. *I can't lose him, not now!*

Julian swore. "It's not just the climb. There are voices in that wind that sap the will." He pushed himself to his feet and staggered forward, leaning into the wind.

"Piper, come back! It's all right. Piper, we'll wait and try again!"

The tiny figure shifted. They saw Piper's face white against the dull dark-red of the stone. Silverhair fought for breath, afraid as he had not been even when Julian began his climb. This child was so vulnerable. . . .

"I'll go after him." Julian's hand clasped his shoulder. "Don't worry, uncle. I'll bring him back to you!"

For the first time in his life, Silverhair's words were gone. The wind howled more furiously; he could no longer hear even the Wind Crystal's song. *Julian is right,* he realized then. *There's more than air in that wind!* He squinted westward. Could it be Caolin? How could the Blood Lord know where they were?

Julian took a deep breath and grim-faced, caught the flailing rope that he had set there the first time he tried the ascent and hauled himself upward.

"Stop him!" Robert flung himself after his lover, but the wind sent him sliding. Rana halted, her fist at her mouth, her face pale beneath the wild flames of her hair.

I can't stop him, thought Silverhair. *But maybe I can help.* He scrambled back to the base of the cliff and reached for his harp case. As gusting wind shook him, he crouched protectively.

"What are you doing?" screamed Robert. "Do you think this is a revel?"

"Wait!" Rana held him. "Have you forgotten who he is?"

Yes, who am I? wondered Silverhair as he pulled Swangold free. *A Master of the College of Bards . . . perhaps it is time to find out what that means!* Grimly he settled himself with his back to the boulder, facing into the screaming wind.

"*Maker of words and winds and wisdom—*" The words of the old hymn came to him. He remembered a sapphire lake set in silver snows, and how another sorcerous wind had blown. He lifted his hands to the whining strings and plucked a chord. For a moment it seemed to him that the pressure lessened, as if the wind had drawn breath to hear.

At Mount Mazama, Caolin had sung up a wind, but he was managing this storm from a distance. Was that a weakness? Silverhair struck another harmony, let awareness deepen, and sensed a gleeful, chaotic energy. He swayed to each gust, dug in his heels and braced himself more firmly. Wind splattered sand into his eyes, and he closed them.

Elementals, he thought then. *That's what we have to deal with here!* He tried to remember the lore he had learned from Siaran.

> *Ariel! Ariel! Windsinger, swiftly come flying!*
> *Ariel! Ariel! Highrider, hark to my crying!*
> *Now evil is near—oh, free us from fear—*
> *Come singing, all sorrow denying!*

His voice lifted in imperious demand, defying the despair that moaned in the wind.

> *Ariel! Ariel! Swift from the heights thou art winging!*
> *Ariel! Ariel! Sweet comes the sound of thy singing!*
> *Earth's song is thy breath—to deny thee is death—*
> *Life is the gift thou art bringing!*

Was there a difference? Silverhair's vision was filled with the gleam of bright eyes and a tumult of wings.

Ariel! Ariel! Now the wind's wildness is slowing.
Ariel! Ariel! Softly they spirit is showing
The folk of the air, how gently to bear
Thy blessings to earth, sweetly blowing. . . .

He curved his body protectively around the harp and drew out the sweet harmonies, softly . . . ever more softly, as if he were soothing a fretful child.

"Wind creatures, be still now—" he chanted softly. *"Be gone now, fly homeward, go back to the sea."*

And after a time it seemed to him that the chaos around him was easing, and above the sound of his harping, the Wind Crystal's melody chimed. Silverhair looked up and saw that Julian and Piper were near the top of the stone tower.

Higher, higher! his spirit cried. He settled Swangold more securely against his shoulder and began to strike a triumphant series of ascending harmonies.

Wind screamed in Caolin's ears. He threw up an arm to shield his eyes as ashes puffed out from the brazier. Then the blast had passed him. The ashes settled gently to earth again.

Coughing, the sorcerer lowered his hand. The winds that he had sent to strike the Ramparts were fluttering around him like frightened fowls. He began to summon his forces to redirect them, but even as he did so, the last flutter of breeze faded and the air settled to stillness. He reached for the cloudy crystal.

"Alexander!" Caolin projected all his will into the call. What was the fool doing?

"What took you so long?" came Alexander's sudden reply. *"The wind stopped, and it looks as if Julian is nearly at the top—"*

"What stopped it?"

"The wind?" Alexander's thought felt confused. *"Do you mean that someone could control—"* There was a moment's pause, and then, *"The harper is playing now, and music is answering from the top of the tower!"*

"Get him!" Caolin's thought overrode Alexander's objections. *"Seize the harper and stop his music. To save his uncle's life, Julian will give you the Jewel!"*

The Wind Crystal is close! thought Julian. Its music vibrated through the stone. He dared a quick glance upward. Piper had not moved, and Julian could see that the next handhold was beyond the boy's reach. He had climbed quickly, impelled at first by fear for the child and then finding his way made easy as the wind failed, but Piper was still ahead of him. He leaned against the rock and fumbled for the recovered rope draped across his shoulder.

"Piper, can you slip this loop across the jagged bit next to you?" Julian held one end and tossed the other upward.

Piper grabbed too late, and the rope fell, but he was still reaching—he nodded, and Julian threw once more. This time the rope flew straight to the boy's grasp. Piper gave him a quick grin, then strained to settle the stiff loop over the outcrop. Julian gave the rope an experimental tug, gradually transferred his weight, and when he knew the line was secure, leaned into it and began to climb. In a moment he was hanging beside the boy.

"Here—" He shifted to handholds and pushed the rope toward Piper. "You can get down this way." Piper shook his head and pointed upward. "What is it? Do you want a leg up?"

Piper nodded eagerly. Julian craned to look up and saw the edge of the rock face sharp against the sky; but the smooth expanse of stone beneath it was beyond the reach of even his long arms. Piper was right: together they might be able to do what neither could do alone. But it went hard to endanger the child.

A playful breeze blew the hair back from Julian's eyes, as if the wind were dancing to the harp music that pulsed

from below. The shimmer of sound that answered it from
the top of the tower flowed through him; for a moment
he understood the vibration without and within as part
of a single pattern, and his fear disappeared.

We all risk ourselves for each other, he thought then.
Below him he could see the gleam of Silverhair's bowed
head, and Robert and Rana, united in their anxiety. Their
hope uplifted him. *Piper has earned the right to dare
this deed for me.*

"Very well," he said aloud. "Step into my hand, and
I'll lift you." He reached out, grateful for the strength
of his shoulders, and grasped the boy's bare foot. "And
in the Wind Lord's name, hang on!"

Slowly, steadily, Julian thrust Piper upward, drawing
air in great tearing gasps. And at each breath, new energy pulsed through him. Lips curled back from his teeth
in a grin of triumph as he pushed Piper up and over the
edge.

"Is it there?"

Piper grinned down at him, reaching for the rope as
Julian threw it and tying it securely around a buttress of
stone. This time Julian's grip was sure. The great muscles of his arms drew him easily upward, and in another
moment he was sprawled atop the pinnacle.

Immensity swirled around him: a circle of snow-
splashed ranges and misty distances, expanses of sky that
curved away into eternity. Jagged edges of rock dug into
his knees, but he had no attention to spare for pain. The
tower seemed to sway beneath him, but it was the world's
flight through space that he was sensing, as he was hearing the world's spirit-song.

Piper tugged at Julian's arm, and abruptly his focus
drew inward. He blinked at the blaze and glitter of light
before him—no, it was a shimmer of sound. The air here
was untainted by mortality. Shuddering, he drew it in,
and with each intoxicating lungful, his spirit strained to
be free. He staggered, felt his hand guided forward. His
fingers touched something hard, closed instinctively
around smooth-planed stone.

"In the name of Air I bless you, son of the skies. . . ."

Awareness echoed with memory, sage scent and crystal singing and the bright flight of the spirit through the skies. Vertigo fought gravity. . . . He swayed, sang, flung his arms high in triumph. Bright laughter chimed around him; he saw the sparkle of eyes, felt the soft brush of wings. *Ariel,* sang the wind. *Ariel.* . . . Spirit leaped, body lunged to follow; thin fingers held him as he strained skyward.

Above Cloud's Rest, an exultant cry rent the air as the Great Eagle arrowed upward, and the clouds toward which he was soaring shaped suddenly into a pair of mighty wings.

In the mist-veiled secrecies of Awahna, the Lady of Westria smiled.

"He has found the Jewel," She said to the wind. "Will You help him find the words?"

"First, he must learn the music. But it is not over— our brother has been playing His games again. Watch what will happen now. . . ." The mists swirled as if a mighty form had passed through them, and every leaf in the Sacred Valley trembled. Then Wind Lord was gone, leaving behind Him an echo of silver bells.

From somewhere nearer the Throne there came an exultant howl.

Atop the Red Mountain, Caolin shuddered to the influx of sensations as Julian claimed the Crystal. Even though he had expected it, the blast of pure sound transfixed him.

"*Alexander! Now!*" He stood rigid, listening.

"*Julian, Julian.* . . ." At some level deeper than physical hearing, his spirit vibrated to the call. With unearthly clarity, he recognized Rana's clear voice, Robert's deeper cry, and Silverhair's trained tones.

"*Julian!*" The summons was closer. Consciousness contracted. He looked down and saw Piper's eyes widen in wonder.

I am Julian! For an instant he had known another name, but now it was gone as he returned to awareness of his bodily reality. And in that knowing, he realized that it was the boy whose spirit had just spoken to his. He gripped Piper's shoulder. The child's throat worked soundlessly.

"But I did hear you," Julian replied in the same way. *"As you hear me!"* He opened his hand, and radiance starred from within the Wind Crystal's perfect faceting. The silver wings of its setting glittered triumphantly in the light of the sun. At the edge of hearing, he heard it singing. Julian drew in a deep breath and pulled from beneath his tunic the chain on which he meant to hang it. He had done it! He—

"Julian!"

That was no voice he knew. The Prince looked down and saw light flicker on drawn swords. Armed men held Robert and Rana prisoner. Mañero was nowhere to be seen. But Silverhair . . . the harper was clasping Swangold to his breast, and the bright blade that lay against his throat held him still.

"Throw down the Jewel and I'll let him live!" The man who held the sword looked up, and Julian blinked in amazement as he recognized the Lord of Las Costas.

"Wind Lor—" Silverhair's protest was cut short. Even from this height, Julian could see the line of bright blood below his uncle's beard. But the harper did not fall.

Would Alexander really kill him? Julian had not known that the other man hated him so. He had to think! There must be a way! His fingers tightened once more around the stone.

He winced as the sharp point of the Crystal dug into his hand. *My only weapon is the Jewel!* he realized suddenly. But he had just found it. *Wind Lord, help me! Wind Lord. . . .* Abruptly he understood Silverhair's truncated cry. He projected awareness into the Jewel and felt a pulse of power against his palm.

"You must sing. . . ." The words were Silverhair's, but Julian knew that he was not hearing them with his physical ears.

"I don't know any words!"

"Use sound!" came the reply, and suddenly he was

hearing an echo of the music that had pulsed from the top of the tower.

"I am waiting!" came Alexander's shout from below. "Answer me!"

Julian laid the Wind Crystal against the hollow at the base of his throat. He took a great breath and let it out with a groan that deepened as he mastered his wonder. His voice strengthened, and the Crystal amplified it. Alexander's men stared around, trying to see from where the sound came.

The Prince drew breath again, let it out in a tone two steps higher, then three notes ascending, one down, a skip up a third; the whole was repeated again in the Jewel's own melody. Harshness eased as he heard the Wind Crystal transmitting the tones. He focused on purifying the sound he was creating, felt the vibrations pulse outward, faltered for a moment as they buzzed in his bones, then pulled in more air and sang. The air shook, and the earth; the blood throbbed in his veins; the light of heaven flickered; the whole world was quivering to a rhythm that quickened until the Las Costas men clapped their hands over their ears and cried out in fear.

Julian's hair stood up, and a steady tremor passed from his head to his heels, and then began again. He blinked, for the air was a shimmer of pulsing particles. Alexander moaned, but he did not lift the sword.

"Give me the Crystal!" he cried.

As if in answer, all of the stored power in the air released in a single flare of radiance. Julian gasped, momentarily blinded, and smelled the sudden sharpness of ozone. Alexander screamed, ripping loose the pouch that hung at his breast, and Silverhair rolled away. And then, from a clear sky, came the thunder. . . .

Thunder! Caolin shook to the awful intensity of *sound* as released energy exploded across the planes.

"No!" he shouted, and the men of the garrison started up in terror, reaching for their swords. A scream of denial followed; a block in the foundation of Blood Gard hummed and a thin crack rayed across the stone. There were more sounds after, wordless as the cries of a god in pain. The soldiers cowered, covering their ears.

After what seemed like a long time, there was silence.

The Blood Lord swallowed painfully. His ears rang, and his hand hurt as well. Carefully he opened it, and shattered pieces of crystal fell to the ground. Where the stone had lain, he saw the mark of the thunderbolt branded across the old scars on his palm.

Where he had gripped the Wind Crystal, Julian's hand bore the fading imprint of spread wings. He drew a shaky breath and gazed around. Suddenly the air was very still.

It's over, he thought dazedly. *I've won!*

In a few moments he would have to climb down from here. In a few days they would be back in Laurelynn. But he could not even try to imagine what awaited him there. For now, it was enough to savor the sweet air.

He stood atop the Wind Lord's Throne with the Wind Crystal clasped to his breast and saw the whole world spread out before him, and in that moment he knew that he was a king.

THIRTEEN: Sticks and Stones

The streets of Laurelynn were choked with people. It was market day, and folk swarmed toward the great square through streets clogged with hawkers whose sale songs rose and fell in unexpected harmonies. When Julian closed his eyes, he could hear other sounds: the brush of a broom sweeping stone, a muted clangor from a forge, pigeons cooing . . . even the soft lapping of water against the brickwork dikes that protected the city. The sounds of Laurelynn swirled around him, and with them the mixed smells of cooked food and wood smoke, horse sweat and dank river weed, all released by the heat of the day. Only when he opened his eyes did sight help him control the inrush of information.

If the Wind Crystal could do this when insulated by the silk in which he had wrapped it, what would it do when he touched it again? Only the knowledge that he had once feared the other two Jewels of Power as well kept him from casting the Wind Crystal into the river. Under stress, he had used the magic of the Jewel to save

Silverhair, but he knew that it would not be easy to master its powers.

As Julian and the others rode up the Southgate road, a woman in a sweet stall pointed at the dusty procession and laughed. The man beside her turned. The Prince saw his face darken. He whispered to the woman, her smile died, and she stepped into the booth behind him as if she were afraid.

It has nothing to do with us, Julian told himself. *He probably just doesn't want her to waste time by gawking.* He felt stifling air pulse from heated brickwork and sighed, wondering whether he was glad to be home. It had been a shock to descend from the clarity of the mountains into the heavy heat below. Even breathing was an effort here.

"It's the Prince . . ." came the whisper behind him. "Stanesvale's back. What's he been up to now?"

They knew who he was, then. Julian forced his fingers to unclench and reined his pony down the avenue that led toward the palace. He had forgotten what it was like to be encompassed by humanity. Someone sang softly.

> *Oh, who has seen the Prince of Stones,*
> *With oxen's shoulders? He can walk*
> *Just like a man, but is he one?*
> *He bows and grins, but cannot talk!*

Julian jerked around but met only blank incomprehension. He could not quite believe what he had heard. Robert kicked his horse up beside him, his face reddening.

"They're scum!" he exclaimed. "Don't listen, Julian."

"No . . ." he said thickly. His hand went to the Wind Crystal hidden at his breast, and he drew comfort from its hard angles. That lie would be put to rest soon enough, when he had mastered the Jewel.

"How dare he ride in here so boldly?" came a whisper, and then a flood of the unspoken thoughts that the Crystal forced Julian to hear.

"Drunkard." "Butcher." "Bastard."

Julian gasped as if he had taken a gut blow. Their taunts were destroying his victory. What had he done to them?

"Hey, Red, better watch yourself with that one! Remember what happened at Elk Creek!" came a jeer from one side. Someone tried to hush the speaker. Julian heard laughter. "That's true! Maybe she's already his whore!"

Fury spun Julian around, his hand on the hilt of his sword. Rana's face had gone white and her eyes were like stones, but she rode steadily onward. He groaned, feeling the shining thing that had grown between them these past weeks grimed and torn.

> The Prince of Stones enjoys a jape!
> He likes to see a maiden squirm!
> A cuff or two, a little rape. . . .

Robert's sword shattered sunlight as his mount leaped forward. A woman screamed. Folk scattered, and someone went down.

"Robert, no!" Julian's tone held the other man long enough for him to grab Robert's arm. An ugly murmur was swelling from the crowd.

"The pretty boy has a temper! My, my!" a woman jeered.

"At least the rock-basher's not choosy. A girl, a man, an oldster and a little boy! Which one of them's sharing yer bed t'night, eh?"

"Ride on, Julian!" cried Silverhair. "You can't do anything here!"

The harper slapped the rump of Julian's pony, sending it bucketing ahead, but the Prince could sense men's hatred pulsing after. He felt filthy, and furious. As the gates of the palace closed behind them, he stared back helplessly.

"It's not your fault, Julian," Silverhair said grimly. "I taught Caolin how to play this game a long time ago. I never dreamed that one day he would set the rumor-mill to grind *you*!"

* * *

"Liar! Everyone knows yer dice are loaded! Don't think yer goin' t' play off yer tricks on me!"

As Caolin turned the corner and swept through the cool darkness of the passageway, he heard the sound of a scuffle, a grunt as someone took a blow. He paused before the door to the garrison common room.

"You buggering mountain louse! What kind of stories have you been spreading? I've killed men for saying less than that about me!"

A scrape of metal tore across the answering laughter. A sword lifted into the light as the Blood Lord burst open the door.

"Be still!"

Steel cracked and clattered on stone. The swordsman stared stupidly at the broken blade, and the others stood frozen as the sorcerer glided into the room. Light from the open windows glinted from the metal studs on leather gambesons at each tremor that ran through the bodies of the men who wore them, and he could see beads of sweat forming on weather-bronzed brows.

"And *I* have killed men for even less reason," he crooned. "For no more than disobeying . . . my . . . rule."

Interesting, how fear could turn the face of even the heartiest of warriors gray. Caolin waited until the gasp of their breathing was the only sound in the room.

"You are *mine!*" he continued. "Quarrel if you will, but remember the punishment for stealing from *me!* Not death." He smiled thinly. "Death is a gift you will beg for if you disobey me. There are worse things than dying. If you are fond of stories, try telling each other about some of the other uses I might have for you."

Stop now, he thought, hearing a breath quickly caught, a stifled moan of fear, *or fright will kill them uselessly.*

"But if you can control your passions, then you may think about the rewards in store for those who serve me well." The Blood Lord pitched his voice to soothe and saw a little color return to blanched faces. "Lesser men will fear *you* when we march into Laurelynn. Save your swords for them, and feed upon their fear!''

"Lord Sangrado—''

The Blood Lord turned his head. Captain Esteban saluted, his glance flicking over the broken sword and the shaken guardsmen standing there. Someone moved in the shadows behind him, and Caolin recognized Ordrey.

"That man Mañero is waiting for you. He says you told him to report to you here.''

Caolin nodded. "I will see him. In the meantime, I suggest you find some occupation for these men. They are growing dangerously idle here.''

The sorcerer left silence behind him when he passed out of the common room, but Ordrey began talking as soon as they had mounted the stairs.

"Gave it to 'em proper, didn't you? Never thought I'd hear it. Why waste your time on those scumbags? A word to Esteban would do it. He's a cold fish, that man, but a good officer.''

The Blood Lord's footsteps rang sharply on the flagstones, but Ordrey kept up with him as they continued down the passageway.

"They can't fight for you if you scare them silly. Do better not to talk to 'em at all. *I* think—''

"Do you?'' Caolin turned suddenly, and Ordrey stopped short. "If you question my judgment, I wonder that you stay with me. Are you looking for a new master? Eric, perhaps, or Julian?''

A muscle in Ordrey's cheek was twitching, but he managed a weak smile. "I'm too old to change masters now, and you need someone who knows your ways. Better me than that fawning cur Mañero. I don't know why you trust him.''

Caolin stared at him and saw the smile fade. It was good to know that he could still make Ordrey afraid. Had he spoken too freely? But he had been long away from his fortress, and the men needed to be reminded whom they served.

And Ordrey did not know why it was so important for

him to speak with Mañero. The message he had sent to Alexander had come back wrapped around a broken crystal, and it would take more time than the sorcerer could spare to reach him on his home ground at Sanjos. But Mañero had been with him. Mañero would tell him what had really happened in those mountains.

He waited until Ordrey's high color had faded. Then he smiled forgivingly, and went into the room where Mañero waited for him.

"*Alexander* was there?" Eric's deep voice slid up a note as Silverhair nodded. "Did he know he was working for Caolin?"

"It didn't seem quite the moment to ask." The harper lifted his beard to show the pink scar. "But who else would have wanted the Jewel? How could he have found us without help from the sorcerer?" He reached for the earthenware pitcher, moist with evaporation, and refilled his mug with cool mint tea. All of the windows in the small Council chamber were open, but scarcely a breath of air relieved the heat of the day.

"Caolin knew I was about to claim the Crystal," said Julian. "He raised a witchwind to make me fall. I could not have reached the top of the Wind Lord's Throne if Silverhair had not soothed the elementals with his song."

Silverhair saw wonder in the Prince's dark gaze, and his throat tightened as he remembered that tumult of bright wings.

"And Alexander would have cut my throat if you had not called down the thunder with the Jewel," he said then. In memory, he could still feel the smart as he felt the prickle of perspiration beneath his cotton tunic now.

"His father must be turning in his grave!" Eric rested his face in his big hands. "Brian of Las Costas would rather have seen his son dead than the pawn of Caolin!"

"A pawn," said Julian gravely. "Yes, it might be so. Since I supported Robert when he refused to marry Carmelle, Alexander has been my enemy, but I don't think he would knowingly serve his father's foe. The Blood Lord has tricked him somehow."

"He's not the only one!" Silverhair said tartly. "Alexander can wait. In less than two weeks, the Council will be meeting. What we have to deal with now is those stories that Caolin has set seeping through Laurelynn."

"I know . . . I know." Eric's voice came muffled between his fingers. "It went hard enough last spring, when the boy was the hero of the sea war. How can the Council elect Julian when the whole city is crying for his blood outside the doors?" He lifted his head, and Silverhair saw with a pang the smudges of sleeplessness beneath his old friend's gray eyes.

He sighed. *Worry has worn hard on him. These past few years have not been gentle either to him or to me.*

"My lord, you must not wear yourself out for my sake." Julian echoed his thought, and Silverhair looked at him sharply. "You have done everything—"

Eric shook his head. "I bungled it. I knew where Caolin was skulking. I had the place surrounded, and still he got away! Sachs sang like a mockingbird when we questioned him, but that's little help. Caolin only used his house, he didn't confide his plans."

Julian leaned forward, one hand clasped around the silk bag that held the Jewel. "What about the stories?" he asked softly.

"I've a folder full of reports, if you really want to read them. Most of the tales are clearly fantasies—with no sense, no sources, nothing that one can get a grasp on, much less disprove!"

"But not all of them?" Julian's face was grim.

The Regent sighed. "There are some stories from up the valley that are pretty damaging, Julian. Drunken parties . . . fights. In Elk Creek, the rape of a young girl. It does no good to tell people that the Blood Lord is spreading rumors when there are folk who will swear they *saw* you do these things!"

"The Prince was in Laurelynn until the third week of July. That can be proven," said Silverhair. "And we all met up again in Stanesvale at the Feast of the First People. To get into trouble upriver and still meet us by then, he would have had to fly!''

"Even with the Wind Crystal, that's beyond me." Julian tried to smile. "But I think the question is not whether you could swear to my whereabouts, uncle, but whether anyone would believe you."

"It's Caolin's doing," spat Eric. "Though I'm damned if I know how! Maybe he was shape-shifting. *Someone* wearing your face committed these crimes."

"Does it matter how it was done?" asked Silverhair. "The Prince is being tried by rumor, not by a court of law." That was what was bothering him—and if this miasma of suspicion sickened his spirit, what must it be like for Julian? "All we can do is to distract the gossip-mongers with some new scandal. Then we can start spreading counter-rumors about the maligning of Julian."

The Prince raised an eyebrow. "In a week and a half?"

"Oh, I'll think of something." Silverhair smiled crookedly. "I know a lot of stories about Caolin. And I know a lot of bards."

"The College of Bards! *Master* Farin, I'd forgotten your friends." Eric grinned, and for a moment the harper saw the blithe boy he had known long ago. Then the Regent sobered. "But Julian will still have to speak in Council. He'll have only one chance to change the impression that he made last spring. Will your counter measures be enough to earn him a fair hearing?"

"No," Julian answered him, then turned to Silverhair. "I'll need the eloquence of Wind Lord himself to sway them. Six months ago you tried to teach me wordcraft and I couldn't learn from you. Now I have the Wind Crystal, but there's no time for a careful apprenticeship. Go to the Master of the Junipers, uncle, and ask him what to do. Ask him how to open me up to the element of Air by using the Jewel, through a ritual."

"Open you up?" exclaimed Silverhair. "Are you asking me to break your mind? In Wind Lord's name, do you have any idea what a sudden experience of the pure force of an element can do?''

"I know what I'm saying." Julian drew a careful breath, and deep in the young man's brown eyes Silver-hair saw his fear. "Don't you remember? In the end, I had to master both Earth and Water that way. And I have already channeled the thunder. Oh, yes, Master Harper, better than anyone. I know!"

Rana listened to the murmur of the city beyond the palace gates and thought about thunder.

"That's what we need now, Piper," she said to the boy beside her. "A great-grandmother of a thunderstorm to bring us some fresh air."

She put down the basket of clothing she was sorting and rubbed her arms to still their twitching. She had felt like this just before Julian had summoned that explosion of energy from the sky. Today, though, there was nothing but dust in the air, and no threat to call forth Julian's power. Except, of course, for a constant, suffocating awareness of the filthy thoughts of the people of Laurelynn.

"It's like being in a house with an untrained cat! You know when it has made a mess somewhere, but you can't find it. And you can't get away from that pervasive, disgusting *smell*!"

Piper wrinkled his nose, then sneezed. Rana eyed him curiously. Now that they were back in Laurelynn, she was beginning to appreciate how much the boy had changed. He was no longer dumb—he was *silent*. But that silence was like the stillness of the forest, all awhisper with the movement of invisible lives. Thought moved through his eyes like the wind in the trees.

Even if he can't talk, he has returned to us, she realized.

"I think this tunic might fit you," Rana said pulling out a bundle of sky-blue cloth. Piper had grown in body as well as in spirit. His wrists and ankles poked out from the clothes he had been wearing, and in any case, the garments were stained and torn. But there was plenty of outworn clothing in Lady Rosemary's stores.

Rana fingered the silver and blue embroidery that spiraled around the hem. "You'll look like a prince!" Piper laughed, and that too was something she had not heard from him before.

"What are we going to do, Piper?" She sank down on one end of the bench beneath the grape arbor and the boy drew his legs up across from her. Bees were humming companionably above them, and the dappling of light and shadow made new mysteries of his face.

"No, what am *I* going to do?" Rana sighed and closed her eyes. "You're doing all right. Now it's my turn!" After a space of silence, she heard the first tones of the flute, which began to gently release awarenesses that she had locked away.

Julian, atop the Throne, summoning the lightning. . . .

The power that had coursed through her during the storm. . . .

I did it too! she thought suddenly. A fragment of melody echoed in memory: the chant to the Lightning Lady that Silverhair had sung.

"Oya caro bel oka, a fu le le!" Oya likes a good hard lover. Even with her eyes closed, she blushed. It had been difficult to persuade the harper to translate that line for her. But surely Oya was above sweaty grapplings with men. Oya's lover was the storm wind *Julian's wind. And the lightning he summoned was me!*

Rana shivered, wondering if she dared to believe that. Was there a way for them to unite that would bypass all the things that made her afraid? Julian had avoided her since they returned to Laurelynn. She could read in his eyes a sick awareness of the lies they were telling about him, and her, and Robert.

Strangely, she found herself resenting the coarse jokes about the Prince and his lover even more than the ones folk made about her. Nothing that folk said was as bad as the nightmares she had lived with for over a year. *If I cannot cure the dreams, then perhaps, like Piper, I can*

*put them behind me and go on. Julian, Julian, let us seek
the skies together and be free!*

The flutesong soared suddenly. The bee-blessed bower
and the steaming city beyond fell away. Awareness of
Piper's presence vanished; even her body was gone as
essence arrowed upward. Only the music remained as
Rana flew free.

Piper continued to play. After a time he saw Rana's
frown ease, saw her face grow as still and empty as a
house whose owners have gone away.

Was I like that before the Eagle returned me to myself?
The flutesong wavered as longing for the old mindless-
ness shook him. Perhaps his silence gave an illusion of
serenity, but the peace he had found in the mountains
was beginning to fray.

Music is not enough for me, he told himself. *Not anymore. I'll practise my writing. I'll learn the signs they
use for trading with the tribes. It was easier when I only
existed, and did not know. . . .*

But most men seemed to live their lives that way. Because Piper could not speak, too often folk acted as if
he could not hear. They spoke without thinking in front
of him, a stream of consciousness put into words that
never dipped below the level of surface reality. But now
he was listening.

Maybe I'm not so crippled after all, he told himself.
*Maybe words couldn't reach them. But music gets past
the barriers.*

He took a deep breath, and the flute's sweet singing
soared like an escaping bird.

The music of Piper's flute floated upward through
darkness. Julian had heard it often during these days;
it was as if the boy were trying to use sweet sound
to transform the sullen murmur of the city that surrounded them. Listening, the Prince paced along the
walkway that edged the roof of the palace, letting the
cool breath that dusk had released along the river bless
his cheeks and brow.

The watchman's bell tolled through the town, calling the hour. Julian felt a tightening in his gut and steadied his breathing once more.

A footstep echoed the bell. The haze of dust that lay like a gray pall above the valley blotted out the stars, but a little light was filtering through the curtains of the room behind him. Julian recognized Robert's easy grace and felt a tremor in his belly once more. Robert had known that he wanted to be alone.

"Julian?" He could hear Robert swallow. "I wouldn't bother you now, but there's no more time. You've been so busy. . . ." There was accusation in his tone, and Julian bowed his head, accepting it.

"I thought that we could be together more freely in the mountains," Robert went on, "but there was no privacy. Then I told myself that we could be alone together back here in Laurelynn, but you never seem to have time. When I heard the songs that have been tormenting you, I wondered if perhaps you . . . believed them."

"No!" Julian reached out, grasped his lover's forearms and felt strong muscles flex beneath his hands. "Robert, it has nothing to do with you! This quest has been so strange. Sometimes I almost doubt that I have a body anymore." He stopped, wondering if that admission might hurt the other man even more.

He was glad that the Wind Crystal waited in the shrine far below. Robert's words were bad enough. He could not have borne to hear what his lover did not say aloud.

Robert's hands lifted at last, gripped his shoulders. Clasped so closely, Julian caught the other man's scent—a hint of sage sachet, and from his body a muskier odor that made his own maleness stir. Earth called him; he let awareness deepen, drew up strength from the soil. And through that contact, Julian understood part of what had been happening to him.

"It's not you, my more than brother—never you! To master Air, I must walk between the worlds of sense and spirit, and of the sexes too. When I join with you, Robert—'' he laughed raggedly as he felt the pulse of desire—''I'm too much a man!''

His lover's grip tightened painfully. ''I believe you. Your flesh is solid beneath my hands, but I feel you slipping away. Julian, don't do this ritual. You have the Wind Crystal already. Isn't that enough?''

''Don't you trust the Master of the Junipers to watch over me?'' Julian tried to laugh.

Robert turned, and the dim light showed the strong column of his throat, the perfect line of cheek and brow. Julian felt a pang of longing—for what? Robert's body was his whenever he desired. But that was not what he wanted. Abruptly he understood the desperation that emanated through Robert's hands.

''No, not when he is also watching over Westria,'' Robert said then. ''He will have mercy neither upon himself nor on you.''

''Perhaps, but do you think I grudge the price I pay. I *asked* for this.''

''But it will change you!'' Robert cried.

''Think, Robert,'' Julian said gently. ''Am I the boy who rode beside you on the border patrol? He would not have seen the god in you.''

Robert shook his head. ''Oh, Julian, I only wanted you to see me as a man!''

Julian worked his shoulders back and forth helplessly. ''Robert, can I put your need before Westria's? I must be *more* than a man. . . .'' He felt a sigh shake Robert's leanly muscled frame.

''You already are.'' His strong hands clasped Julian's head, his lips brushed the Prince's brow. ''They are waiting for you in the shrine,'' he said. ''It's time to go down.''

Julian nodded, and felt the shiver shake him again. To master each of the other elements, he had passed through death's transformation. How would Air destroy him? Despite everything he had said to Robert, he was afraid.

* * *

He looks frightened, thought Silverhair as Julian followed Robert into the shrine. *Perhaps we should have waited.* . . . The Master of the Junipers stood before the altar like an oaken image, leaning on his staff. The deep eyes were watchful, but if the old priest felt either uncertainty or compassion, he was not letting it appear. Julian himself had said it, there was no more time.

Silverhair lifted his hands from the strings and set his harp next to the altar as Piper ceased to play. *Wind Lord!* prayed the harper, *be with us this night, be with Julian!*

"Child of earth and ocean, why have you come here?" Suddenly the Master's staff barred Julian's way.

"That I may learn to speak the Word of Power," said Julian.

"What will you give?" came the implacable demand.

"The breath of my body and my eternal Name. . . ."

"Enter then," said the Master softly, "and let the Mystery begin!"

Julian knelt before the altar, where the Wind Crystal winked in the candlelight. Silverhair took a steadying breath, his nostrils flaring at the scents of damp earth and old incense, for the shrine was set deep in the foundations of the palace.

Swiftly the Master of the Junipers cast the circle. The harper felt a sense of pressure that built until his ears popped, then suddenly eased. He could no longer hear any sounds from outside.

The Master nodded to Silverhair, who turned to face eastward.

> *Grandfather Eagle, great spirit of inspiration,*
> *Fly from your eastern eyrie—*
> *Your grandchildren call you!*
> *Grant us clarity of purpose,*
> *Fan us with the wind of the spirit,*
> *And bear us clear vision!*
> *Welcome, Grandfather!*

"Welcome, Grandfather," echoed five voices as Piper picked up the footed pot in which sage was smouldering.

Silverhair took the prayer fan, and they moved sunwise around the circle, fanning the pungent smoke to purify each of the others.

There was passion in Robert's eyes as he gazed at Julian, and Silverhair understood why the Master had chosen him to invoke Fire. The reasoning behind choosing Rana for Water was clear also, and he smiled encouragingly. Then they came to Rosemary, with a scent of herbs about her even as a stroke of the fan set the sage smoke swirling, and he knew that the power of fertile earth was present too.

The heavy flow of the sea balanced the swiftness of the wind; the ceaseless transformations of fire were countered by earth's endurance. As Rosemary finished her invocation, Silverhair could feel the circle settle to a new stability. He let some of the tension in his shoulders ease. This careful structuring of forces was a far cry from his own ecstatic communions with the Spirit of Music. Even at the thought, he felt the tug of that divine intoxication. But he resisted it. Not yet—not now! He must not upset the Master's precise balancing of powers.

Julian was frowning a little, as if he were trying to hear something. Or perhaps he was trying *not* to hear, thought the harper, if some of the things they said about the Wind Crystal were true.

"It will be all right, Julian." He tried to send reassurance across the circle and was rewarded by a faint smile.

"Wind is the breath of Life . . ." said the Master. "The wind carries the Word that made the world. Breathe in . . . and out . . . in . . . and out. Let the body relax. Let the spirit still. Breathe in . . . and out. Feel air filling your lungs, feel energy entering, filling, flowing, glowing, growing." The harsh voice deepened. Silverhair felt himself sway to the rhythm and understood what the adept was doing even as the words entranced him.

A new scent brought him partially back to awareness. The Master was lighting a small pipe of clay and bone.

He offered it to earth and to heaven and to the powers of the directions, murmuring. The sharp reek of tobacco caught at the lungs. Silverhair took the pipe from the old man's hand and made his own prayers, took a deep breath of strong smoke and passed the vessel to Robert, feeling its power awaken new energy to tingle along his veins.

Words welled through him suddenly.

> *Wind Lord, wide-wing!*
> *Blest breath of life bring!*

Robert blew a swirl of smoke skyward.

> *Powers of life that reign Above,*
> *Obey the holy Word of love!*

Rana took up the pipe, and the thought—

> *The wind is a lover that kisses the sea,*
> *And lifts up her gift and bestows it to free—*

She paused, her eyes widening as she sought for an ending, and thrust the pipe at Rosemary.

> *The dry earth from death*—sang the older woman.

> *The gift of the breath*
> *Brings down the power of the Word in its hour!*

"So be it!" cried the Master of the Junipers.

> *Windmaster, wordbinder! Messenger, fate-finder!*
> *Wingfoot, beside us, be ready to guide us!*
> *By Thy sacred Name I call Thee. . . .*

He struck the bowl-bell in his hand suddenly, and as its echoes shimmered into silence, intoned a name that had been old when the Ancients came into this land. The candle flames flared, and the Crystal on the altar hummed.

"Hermes . . . hear us! Open the Way!"

Julian clapped his hands to his ears, whimpering.

The Master gestured to Silverhair, and the harper pulled Swangold into his arms. Unbidden, Piper lifted the flute, and together they chorded that tone into something that human ears could comprehend. Silverhair saw Julian let out his breath in a long sigh. The Master whispered something; Julian nodded and then lay down. The priest faced the altar and lifted his hands in a last invocation before taking the Wind Crystal and laying it upon the Prince's breast.

Sound! Sweet sound. Silverhair felt it ravishing him even as he fought to retain control. He cast a desperate glance at the Master and saw him nod, remembered him saying that when a ritual was properly constructed, it was safe to loose the spirit, for only those powers that had been invited would come through.

He struck the strings more strongly as music poured through him. Piper's flute lilted ecstatically in a series of ascending trills like the swift-darting flight of a lark. The harper's spirit followed, but he no longer knew what his fingers were doing. Harp and harper became one being; harp and flute one instrument; instruments and melody became Music. Silverhair felt the rush push him past the false bounds of being, till seeing and hearing and feeling were One. . . .

He's out! thought Rana, watching Silverhair's eyes roll back in his head. But the harper's fingers still flickered across the strings.

The Master bent over Julian. "Release . . . let the tension go, lad. Let the music lift you. Remember your breathing, that's right, and let the tension go."

Rana gulped dry air, felt the hair lift along her arms; a sharp tingling swept her. *How can he relax?* she wondered. *The air is alive with power!*

"What is your Name?" The Master knelt beside Julian, his hands cupped above the Wind Crystal, reflecting the power it radiated back into the man on whose breast it lay.

"Ju—Julian."

"No!" came the swift reply. "What is your true Name? Answer me!"

"Stone . . . Star . . ." he stammered.

"Those are old definitions. Who are you now?"

"I don't understand!" Julian's chest rose and fell. "What do you want of me?"

"Your identity," came the implacable answer.

Earthmaster . . . sea lord . . . man . . . warrior . . . lover . . . fool. Tongue-tied, mindless fool! All of the names that Julian had ever called himself were squeezed out by the adept's relentless compulsion. The Prince's deep voice grew rough; words became a painful babble. He was gasping, rolling his head back and forth against the stone floor.

Stop it! Rana's heart cried. *Why are you tormenting him this way?*

"Listen—" The old man's voice was abruptly gentle. "To give names to others, you must know your own, and if you cannot find that knowledge in the flesh, you must seek it elsewhere! You know how to do that, you have done it before."

Julian drew a ragged breath. "I can't! Not this way. My body holds me. I'm still bound!"

In the silence, Rana was once more aware of Silverhair's music. She blinked, saw the shimmer that followed each shift of the harper's hands, saw power pulse outward and felt pressure throb within. *This is the wind's way,* she understood then. *The winds rush over the earth as the waves wash through the sea, and the friction of their passage builds this power. The wind is free!*

Power built within her and brought her to her feet. A quick step took her to the altar, and she grasped the eagle-feather fan. The air around Julian sparked with undirected energy.

"There is pattern in this chaos, and its Name is Oya!" Had she spoken aloud?

The adept nodded. "Be still. Don't stir!" he whispered to the others.

Rana poised above Julian, quivering as she strove to clear the channels for that energy. The Master shuddered, let his breath out and relaxed.

"Child, what are you waiting for?" came a voice within. *"Set him free!"*

Rana reached out and drew the feather through the air above Julian's body. From crown to soles she stroked, once, twice, again . . . saw his twitchings become regular tremors that rolled from head to foot. In Julian's face she saw agony, she saw fear, but neither he nor she could afford mercy. A pulsing of energy ringed his body. Once more she caught it with the feather, fanned it down, down. . . .

He convulsed, lips curling back in a silent snarl of pain, and then went still.

A wrench like death.

Soul, severed from body, sucked swifter than thought through a tunnel of darkness. Reality rushed uncontrolled into madness; a mote of awareness adrift in the maelstrom swirled mindless. . . . Weightless, awhirl, falling upward forever; no substance to cling to but a fragment of knowledge. *I have done this before.* . . .

This is death, came the thought in an instant of clarity. Perceptions steadied. Julian looked down and saw a circle of people staring at a body that lay still upon the stone floor. His body. The realization shook him; he gasped convulsively, jerked downward, and saw that the form he wore now was connected to the body below by a shining silver cord. How very strange it looked from outside. He had never realized how blunt his nose was, how long the arms lying slack by his sides appeared. Piper and Silverhair were still playing, and now Julian could hear each separate vibration within the music.

"To float free of the flesh is the death of Air," came a thought close beside him. Julian turned and saw that the radiant form of the Master of the Junipers hovered above his own slumped body. *"You must not be afraid. . . ."*

"No," answered Julian. *"I remember now."* The Master had once before guided him out of his body—to seek Frederic's spirit—but that transition had not been so abrupt. And he had already been in the Underworld when he walked and talked with the adept in this way after his battle with the sorcerer at Spear Island. *"But why—"*

"Listen—"

In some way that had no reference to direction, Julian *turned*. Sound waves sent by flute and harp were caught up in a greater music. The Master had disappeared. He glimpsed a flurry of feathers, bright eyes, an oddly familiar grin. Wind whirled him helplessly.

"Silly boy—" Laughter chimed around him. *"Use your wings!"*

Of course! Here, he could fly! Julian flexed muscles whose use he had learned in a hundred dreams and soared after that winged brightness into an endless sky.

"This is the realm of the Air," said his guide. *"Here dwell all of the winds of the world!"*

Julian saw them sporting like children among the noble bastions of the clouds. In an instant, thought encompassed the game they were playing. *Tides and currents,* he thought. *The sky is like the sea.* He understood the rhythm of earth's respiration at last.

But that was only part of what he sought here.

"Word-shaper," he addressed his companion, *"tell me my true Name."*

"I am not the Word," came the answer. *"I am only an instrument. Listen to the voice that speaks through me as I will speak through you."*

Julian stilled; the skyscape boiled away below him. He felt the rush of a great wind that came from distances too vast for comprehension. In that wind he heard the primal vibration of Creation, as Pure Being declared its Name. . . .

And in that moment, Julian knew his own.

But he could not sustain that Presence for more than a moment. Gasping, he fell away to the level of images, where Wind Lord awaited him.

Images? No, *words*. . . . The doors of his spirit gaped open, and all the words in the world were fluttering through. Pure delight set him to laughing, for there was no other response to this explosion of sound and meaning. Wind Lord was laughing with him, and suddenly Julian remembered how Mañero had tried to tease him.

Is this what I was so afraid of? This joy?

Still exulting in that realization, he found himself once more in the shrine.

"Laugh!" his spirit cried to the others. *"Why don't you laugh and share my joy?"*

Rana was still standing above his body, the feather poised in her hand. Her head was thrown back, her eyes closed. Then she smiled.

"This is the way for us!" her response reached him. *"Now I too am free!"*

"Julian, I love you." Silverhair's thought came with perfect clarity.

This, then, was the Power of Air—this perfect communication, free from the distortions of preconception or personality. Here he knew and was known; here all was understood. Swiftly Julian directed his attention toward the others, with an exchange of gratitude for Rosemary, and for Robert, a giving of all of the things he had never known how to say.

He found Piper, and felt the child's wonder at the touch of his mind.

"Julian! Do you hear me? Julian!"

"I hear you, Piper. Don't you understand . . . you are one of the reasons I had to risk this. I know what it is to be bound. I will find a way to set you free!"

The boy's laughter amplified his own. A surge of delight sent Julian spiraling through ceiling and stonework, bursting into the shadowed sky above the sleeping world. The darkness was deeper around the Red Mountain, as if some congestion of the spirit did more than night to hide it from his view. But it was the city below that drew his attention.

"People of Laurelynn—" he sought them, his shelter-

ing wings spread wide. A susurrus of sound pulsed from the city, an unresolved music that throbbed to the slow rhythms of thoughts blurred by dream.

"Hear me, oh my people, and we will sing together! Laurelynn, listen, and open your spirits to the sweet song!"

FOURTEEN: Shaper of Words

Listen, a wind whispers now from the darkness.
Falsehoods it hisses, from whence, no one knows.
But a lie bears the scent of the man who has
made it—
'Tis from the Red Mountain that wicked wind
blows!

Silverhair drew a series of dissonant harmonies from
Swangold's strings with one hand, while with the other
he wiped sweat from his brow. There was shade beneath
the trellised vines in the Grape Garden's courtyard, but
no leaf stirred. It was close to the third week of September; haze held the heat of the sun within the Great Valley
like the lid of a cauldron, and the land and the men who
lived there steamed and sweltered, waiting for the equinoctial storms. The Master of the Junipers had once told
him that the period preceding an equinox was often difficult, but surely Westria had rarely experienced such
tension as it did now.

With his left hand, Silverhair touched a linking line

of melody from the harp strings, letting the murmur of speculation die away. His visit here had been planned to look like chance; his first songs were ballads of the road that lulled his audience into acceptance. But his listeners were sitting up now, frowning as they realized that this was no simple entertainment. And here and there he saw a look that told him someone had recognized the tune that he had written after the Battle of the Dragon Waste.

> *Oh, look to the spider who spins on the*
> *Mountain—*
> *Webs of deceitfulness, tissues of lies—*
> *Once more he seeks to enslave and ensnare us.*
> *Again we must armor our souls and be wise!*

"I know you now, Farin Silverhair!" called a man sitting at one of the far tables. "I remember how we drove the Blood Lord from Laurelynn after his treachery twenty years ago. But to prove him false won't prove the truth about Prince Julian."

Now even those who had been confused had figured out what was going on. A murmur ran through the garden like wind; then the place grew still as they waited for the harper to answer. He wiped his forehead again and drew breath.

"Then you will have to make up your own minds about me!" another voice cut in—a deep voice, with just the right tone in it to put a listener at ease.

Silverhair jerked around and saw Julian himself sitting there. He was wearing a sleeveless tunic and loose-gathered breeches like any other man of Laurelynn on a hot day, but suddenly he stood out from among the rest as if he had worn the royal mantle and crown.

"It's all right, uncle," came a silent whisper. *"It's up to me now."*

"I'm as confused as everyone else by the stories I've heard about me," the Prince said. "What did you want to know?"

The silence, which had been expectant, was now

stunned. Silverhair thought they could not have been more still if the Blood Lord himself had appeared before them spouting flames.

"In the meantime," Julian added plaintively, "I do hope that you folks haven't drunk up all of the beer!"

The server recollected himself and scurried toward the kitchen. People remembered to breathe. Someone shouted after the boy to bring out the barrel and he would pay for it—they all needed a drink in this sun.

But it was shock, not the sun, that had set this thirst upon them. Silverhair sipped at the cold tea in his mug and set it down again, hope singing in his heart. Perhaps the ritual with the Wind Crystal had worked. Perhaps Julian would know what to say. Of course these were the kind of simple folk whom Julian was used to, not the full Council of Westria. But if he could sway *them*. . . .

The Prince had leaned back against one of the posts of the trellis, every line of his body suggesting ease. But his eyes were watchful, narrowing as the man who had challenged Silverhair moved toward him.

"You've got courage anyway, coming here!"

"I have nothing to hide," answered Julian.

"Not even what you did at Elk Creek?"

"I was in Laurelynn at the time that is supposed to have happened, falling in love with my cousin!" The Prince grinned suddenly. "That story *is* true, and even with the aid of the Jewels, I can't be in two places at the same time."

"That's so. If he was in bed with pretty Robbie, 's not likely to go rapin' some girl," came a loud whisper from somewhere behind them, echoed by nervous laughter.

Julian pretended not to have heard it, but a slight loosening in his stance told Silverhair that he, too, had realized that the tension around them was beginning to ease. The servers came back with a trayful of mugs and the beer barrel, and the atmosphere relaxed still further. Silverhair slid Swangold back into her case, knowing that his part was finished now.

"But ye weren't in town later," said a woman, "when they say ye got drunk and set fire to Cerrito Blanco!"

"I was in the Ramparts—" Julian began.

"You lie! I was there!" came a new voice, shaking with anger. An old woman stumped forward, a worried young man following behind her. "I saw you!"

Now the Prince turned. "Did you, mother?" he asked very gently. "Was it truly me that you saw?"

There was a long silence, and Silverhair shivered a little, seeing the light of Wind Lord's divine laughter in Julian's eyes. The fight went out of the woman. Slowly she shook her head.

"He looked something like you—they said he was you. I don't know."

"Did he look, perhaps, like this man?" Robert spoke from the door.

He shoved a bulky, brown-haired fellow before him into the garden, and three of the Regent's guardsmen followed. Silverhair blinked, looked from Robert's captive to Julian and back again. For a moment the man's stance and his dark hair and straight brows had made him think that he was seeing double, as if Julian had mastered bilocation after all. But the Prince was staring as if his own ghost walked toward him. No, thought Silverhair as he looked from one to the other. There was a *shining* quality to Julian now, as if he had become just a little translucent to the light of the sun. They were not the same, not the same at all!

Robert's captive stood silent, gazing at the ground. The old woman darted toward him, stared up at his face for a moment, then flew at him suddenly with clawed nails.

"It's him!" she shrieked as her son dragged her away. "I marked him well by firelight. It's him, in the same purple shirt that he wore!" The crowd erupted in a babble of commentary.

"Who are you?" asked the Prince. When there was no answer, he grasped the captive by the beard, forced his head up and waited until the man had to meet his eyes. *"Who are you?"* he asked again, adding the compulsion of his mind.

"I—I'm Jul—Julian," the man mumbled.

"Are you then my mirror?" the Prince asked softly. "Think, man, remember. Was there a time when you had another name?"

"*He* told me I was Julian," came the stubborn response. "Where is he? *He'll* tell you who I am."

"The Blood Lord!" said someone from the crowd.

"Did you plan this?" Silverhair asked Robert. The young man shook his head, still watching the Prince and his double as if he could not believe his eyes.

"I got to thinking about Eric's story of their attempt to capture Caolin," Robert said. "Afterward, the Regent's guards realized that the man who told them the sorcerer had taken the shape of Julian was already lying dead inside the house at the time. I knew then that the person they talked to had to have been the Blood Lord, and the man they went chasing was someone who looked like Julian. It was no use searching for Caolin, because he could look like anyone, but this other man's face would stay the same. So I got Eric's permission to search again, and we found this fellow down by the Puerta del Agua Inn."

"Julian is right," said Silverhair softly. "He *is* a mirror, a distorted reflection with everything that we love in Julian reversed." All around him, people were coming to the same conclusion. "This news will be all over town by nightfall." He grinned suddenly. "And I know a hall full of bards who will make sure it loses nothing in the telling."

"But who *is* he?" Robert asked Julian, who had turned the captive over to the guards. "Can you find out his name?"

"In the same way that I learned my own," said the Prince, and in his voice Silverhair heard an echo of music. "But I think it may be better for folk to see him as he is now, believing himself to be me."

The vine leaves in the trellis trembled as a hint of coolness stirred the air. Silverhair took a deep breath, wishing he could read the wind. But even he could feel the first hint of change.

"Tomorrow, in the Council Hall," said Robert slowly.

"Yes," Julian nodded. "Tomorrow. . . ."

"That puppet prince of yours has disappeared from the inn," said Ordrey. "You should never have left him. Who knows what trouble he'll get into alone?"

Caolin clasped his traveling cloak and threw its folds back over his shoulder, keeping the back of his hand turned toward Ordrey to conceal the new scar across his palm.

"He has served his purpose. He doesn't matter now." The Blood Lord turned, took a folder of papers from his desk and slid them into his satchel. His other things had been packed already. The memory of his flight from Laurelynn still rankled, but the way had been prepared for his return. He could command men from every province now. This time he was going to the Council in his own person. Once he reached its sanctuary, they would have to hear him, and then all Westria would recognize his power.

"What if they capture him?" suggested Ordrey

Caolin smiled thinly. "They'll think he is Julian, or me."

Mañero gave a bark of laughter from his corner, and Ordrey glared at him.

"Oh, you know everything," he said peevishly. "And I'm only a donkey. But at least I understand that something can always go wrong!"

"Fredegar Sachs has been released for lack of evidence." The sorcerer let his voice deepen soothingly. "And I have secrets here—" he tapped the bag—"that will compel loyalty." He blew out the candle on the desk, blinking as his eyes adjusted to the thin dawn light filtering through the curtains.

Nothing will stop me, Caolin told himself. He had felt a tremor on the astral two nights earlier and had recognized the echo of the Wind Crystal's power. But always before, it had taken Julian time to master the Jewels. And time was the one thing the sorcerer had made sure the Prince would not have.

"Master, you use this—everyone be surprised!" Mañero held out a packet with something black inside. It looked like body hair, straight and short.

"More of Julian's hair?" He did not need that either, but the little man looked so hopeful. He dropped the packet into his pouch.

Ordrey was still shaking his head as the Blood Lord swept past him and descended the stairs. The guards who would accompany the sorcerer were already mounted. Horses stamped and sidled in the early morning chill, threw up their heads and snorted at the wind.

Caolin paused in the doorway, sniffing the air. A high haze of cloud was beginning to drift across the heavens, and last night had been cold with a near frost that the growing warmth of the sun could not entirely deny. Autumn was coming.

This is the hinge of the year, he thought. *Everything will be different now.*

Through the open window came a cool breeze from the river. *Just like last spring,* thought Julian as he pulled a long gown of azure linen over his head and shook himself so that its folds hung free. *No,* he corrected as he belted the garment and reached for the silk pouch that held the Wind Crystal. *I am different now.*

His hand went instinctively to the unaccustomed smoothness of his chin. He had shaved off his beard the night before, the better to distinguish himself from that poor fool who had been misrepresenting him. His throat felt naked, but perhaps that new sensitivity came from the Jewel.

He faced his image in the mirror, seeing his square jaw pale where the beard had hidden it, his heavy brows straight above troubled eyes. *Is this the face of a king?* Once he had thought his features without distinction, but in the past year or two, experience had fined away the last childish blurring. For the first time, Julian considered the face of the man he had become, accepting his physical form as he had accepted his name.

He could hear Robert's voice from the next room, and Silverhair's softer reply. *Not yet*, he thought, gazing at the shut door. *Leave me alone for just a little while.*

The Wind Crystal sang to him through the silk that cocooned it. Julian closed his fingers around it, delaying the moment when he would put it on. But not, this time, from fear. The Jewel meant too much to him now to be donned as a girl puts on her necklaces to go to a fair.

He tipped up the bag, let the winged Crystal and its silver chain run with a soft shiver of metal out onto his palm, and the music within him surged triumphantly. He took a deep, careful breath and felt awareness shift inward as he exhaled.

Maker of Winds, Shaper of Words, his spirit cried, and suddenly more words came gusting after.

> *Oh, Bird-winged Messenger, now bear*
> *Me where Thy own breath may inspire*
> *Desire. . . .*

Pure speech was uplifted by itself to itself in offering, with his spirit as the instrument, as if the Lord of Music should take up a harp for his own pleasure. For a moment Julian hovered on the brink of understanding a purpose deeper even than Westria's need, then the word wind carried him away.

> *Now let me apprehend*
> *(Oh, lend me understanding) Thy*
> *Most high Meaning, Lord, I pray.*

In the Council Hall, they would be gathering already. What could he say to them? How could he make them understand what this land truly was, and what it was meant to be?

> *I say a word, a world is made—*
> *I bade it be, in me, anew.*

Now truly may my making be
To Thee, reflection, and to men
Who listen, truth that they may take,
Oh, Maker of Winds, Shaper of Words.

Slowly he became aware of a sweet, humming silence. The Presence that had overshadowed him but a moment before had left him master of himself, but he could feel it waiting.

Julian kissed the Crystal, slid the chain over his head so that the Jewel rested upon his breast, and smoothed back his hair. The starburst of House Starbairn glittered from the blue cloak that was laid ready across the chair. He picked it up, thinking, *now I am truly the Stone and the Star.*

"Julian Starbairn of Misthall!"

The herald's cry set whispers rustling through the Council Hall like the wind that was rippling through the round leaves of the aspens outside. Rana saw Julian's shoulders straighten, drew herself up and caught Robert's eye so that they would all start together.

She wore a gown of midnight blue embroidered with tiny silver stars; silver combs set with crystal pulled back her hair. But Robert was in a short tunic the color of the pale morning sky. That had been Rosemary's idea . . . perhaps the colors would communicate to people something inexpressible in words. But as they began to move together, Rana wondered if anyone was going to even notice them.

Perhaps it was the way that the folds of Julian's cloak swung from his broad shoulders, or perhaps it was the unaccustomed purity of his face without a beard that drew the eye. No, those were only surface things. What was making her breath unsteady was the shimmer that she sensed, more than saw, around him.

The clarion pierced the babble with an imperious sweetness. Together, the three marched down the steps toward the first of the benches in the section allotted to the Royal Domain. Whatever else Julian might be, the Council itself had made him Lord of Misthall. For a moment Rana was so conscious of Julian's nearness that the faces around her were a blur. In a curious way, she was aware of Robert as well, with Julian the link between them.

Then her sight cleared, and she saw that the bench behind hers was already occupied. A swirl of vivid purple caught her eye and she recognized Silverhair, with Piper and his grandmother beside him. And Frederic was there too, standing next to the Master of the Junipers. *All of the Companions are once more united. Now we shall certainly see victory!*

There was no need for words, but Julian's joy was as clear as if he had shouted. Just below them were the empty thrones of the king and queen, and beyond them on the Council floor, the Regent's chair. Rana gazed around the hall, frowning as she recognized Carmelle behind her brother. The other girl was staring at them as if she could not quite believe what she saw. Rana caught Robert's eye, and his grin and her smile grew wider as Carmelle's face reddened unbecomingly.

The herald continued to announce the principal landholders, and then the Commanders of the Provinces, the speakers for the Seneschalate, the Free Cities, and the College of the Wise. Finally the Regent, crossing the floor with his usual heavy tread, cast an anxious look up at Julian and stopped before his chair.

"Are we met?" Her grass-green cloak swirling, Mistress Anne strode to the hearth at the center of the floor. Bells jangled sweetly as she brought her herald's staff down.

"Well, met," came the full-throated reply.

"Then in the names of Earth, Air, Fire, and Water and the Maker of All Things, let the Autumn Sessions of the Estates of Westria begin!"

With a rustle of clothing and a new surge of whispering, the assembled people of Westria sat down.

Tanemun the Seneschal bustled forward to light the Council fire, appearing even more worn and nondescript

than he had six months ago. Rana's nostrils flared as the
spicy scent of burning cedar drifted across the room. Her
gaze moved over the mass of faces, and she stiffened as
she saw someone else she recognized. As if to mock the
Regent, Fredegar Sachs had boldly resumed his place
among the representatives of the Guilds. She turned to
Julian, but Tanemun was already speaking.

"—and so we can delay no longer. Let us make a final
decision today regarding the fitness of Julian of the Stones
to rule Westria, or let us choose another sovereign."

It was beginning. A shiver pebbled her skin. *"Julian,
my love is with you,"* she said silently. And then he
looked at her, and she knew that somehow he had heard.

We have all the arguments, thought Silverhair, *but will
these people be able to hear them?* Philip of the Ramparts stood up, and the hall grew still.

"Lord Tanemun is right—this has gone on far too long.
I will speak first then, and voice my vote for the right of
Julian of the Stones. I am not supporting him because
he is kin to me, or because his father was our king.
Before I ever knew the boy as a cousin, I had him as
squire, and there are many among you who know how
closely one learns to judge character in that relationship.
He needed teaching, but I never had to tell him the same
thing twice. Invariably he put the good of his men above
his own. He has a gift for the right action in an emergency. During the past four years I have watched him
carefully, and it is my reasoned judgment that only Julian
has any chance of making this tattered country of ours
whole."

"Only Julian?"

Silverhair looked around and tensed as he saw Alexander of Las Costas rising, the goldwork on his black
tunic glittering balefully.

"What about the rest of us?" Alexander surveyed the
circle. "Are we nothing? Have we no skills, no wisdom?
Are we so unfit to govern ourselves?"

"It has seemed so, these twenty years past," said

someone from a back bench, and the tension eased a little as everyone laughed.

"Of course, when there was no clear authority," Alexander responded. "Why should I care for anything outside my own borders? That's what the Regent was for. But he could not hold us together—"

"Because I had not the right—" Eric began, but Alexander overrode him.

"I am talking about responsibility! I am talking about each province taking charge of its own affairs and its relationships, adult men and women dealing with solid realities in the clear light of day!"

"As you did in the Ramparts?" This time Eric's voice had a battlefield volume that no one could have overcome. "Was it adult and responsible to skulk after Prince Julian and try to steal one of the sacred Jewels?"

"I didn't—I wouldn't—" Alexander began.

"Silverhair, you tell them!" Eric roared.

The harper rose in his place, and the sound in the room told him that folk were looking at the Prince as well, and that they were realizing now that the crystal that blazed from Julian's breast was no mere ornament.

"I've a scar on my throat to show that he did!" Silverhair's voice rang across the babble. "Would you have killed me, Alexander? Would you have killed me to force Julian to give you the Jewel?"

"I wanted to stop him! I feared that if he had the Jewels, folk would be distracted from the real issues. The Jewels are only baubles, but people believe in them."

"You believed in the Wind Crystal, Alexander." Silverhair's voice had gone soft, but now the hall was so still that everyone heard. "You believed in it when Julian summoned the thunder to save me from your sword." The other man was silent. Silverhair went on. "—And how did you know where to find us? Who told you where Julian was going, and why?"

"You stand there preaching, harper, but all of your songs are of a time that's past!" Alexander found his voice again. "There's more support for my ideas than you might think. It was a man from the Seneschal's office who told me—"

"Who?" Tanemun asked sharply. "Show me the man who would so betray his loyalty."

"I don't see him among you, but his name was Ercul Ashe."

Eric went white. Silverhair felt his heart leap in his breast, and fought for control. Here and there folk were frowning, trying to remember where they had heard that name.

"What's the matter?" sneered Alexander. "Did you think that all of your servants are slaves?"

"Ercul Ashe died twenty years ago." Eric's harsh answer stilled the din. "Caolin used his face to sell the army of Westria to Elaya, and killed him when Ashe revealed his master's treachery." Now the high color was leaving Alexander's face. He shook his head, but Eric continued implacably. "You, who are so proud to be the son of Brian of Las Costas—do you finally understand that you have been serving your father's murderer?"

Alexander sat down suddenly. In the silence that followed, only Loysa Gilder moved.

"Twenty years ago Lord Caolin executed a faithless servant who did not understand what all of us can see now. He said that Westria could not prosper without him, and he was right. Raiders pass freely across our borders, and only Elaya's disarray keeps that ancient enemy from overrunning us. Do you think that this dissolute prince can save us? It seems to me that the past few months have demonstrated his true character only too well!"

"Or *someone's*—" Eric gestured, and guards escorted a shambling figure onto the floor. "Was it perhaps this man, manipulated by the Blood Lord, who committed the crimes that have made men fear?" He stood, tipped up the captive's chin and turned him so that all could see his face.

"You, lad. What's you name?"

"My name's Ju-Julian, *Prince* Julian." came the answer.

"And how do you know that? Who told you that was your name?"

From somewhere to Silverhair's right there came, very distinctly, the word *"Katiz."* He searched across the benches reserved for the Free Cities, blinked as his vision blurred, and tried again.

The captive's mouth had opened to answer the question, but it never closed. What vague intelligence he had shown, faded from his eyes. He stood swaying, smiling slackly at nothing, and no amount of questioning could make him speak again.

But everyone else was talking. Was this a trick that hadn't quite come off, and if so, who was behind it—the Regent, or the Prince? Or this mysterious Katiz?"

"Not Katiz," Julian said softly. "This is Caolin's work. The man's mind is bound."

Silverhair shook his head. They had been so sure that producing Julian's double would answer all arguments, and now. . . .

The herald was calling for silence with a jangling of bells. Once more Loysa Gilder got to her feet.

"It is foolish to attempt to dispose of one option without offering an alternative. Let us consider one. And to help us do so, I call to the debate a landholder whose voice for too long has been absent from this hall!"

Silverhair blinked again, for the place that he had been unable to bring into focus was moving. Like mist swirled away by the wind, it cleared, and he saw a figure garbed in silver-gray, but as it moved, crimson blazed from the lining of cloak and sleeves. He saw hair nearly as pale as his own, and then the man turned, and Silverhair felt the hand squeeze shut in his chest. *An illusion,* thought gibbered helplessly. *That is the face he wore twenty years ago.*

Vaguely he was aware that Frederic was supporting him, and was grateful, for he knew that the Master of the Junipers must have been as stunned as he. He struggled to breathe, felt a warmth flowing into him from Frederic's hands, and drew a harsh breath as the pain began to ease.

"Caolin," he whispered when he could speak. "It is Caolin!"

"Hold!" Caolin snapped sound across the hall like a whip, tangling the guards who had started toward him, silencing the roar of awe, of outrage, of simple confusion. He moved down the steps and on to the floor with a sense of homecoming that was almost physical. This *was* where he belonged, and it had been so very long!

"You will not touch me, for your own law protects me here. I admit to no crime, but even had I been properly tried and found guilty, having reached this floor, I would have the right to speak to you. If you lay violent hands upon me, you destroy the very law by which you live!" He turned with a swirl of crimson and silver, caught Tanemun's gaze and saw the man's face sour as if he swallowed bile.

"Is it not so?" he asked softly. "Seneschal of Westria, is it not so?" He smiled at Tanemun's reluctant nod.

"My lords, my ladies, representatives of the people of Westria. . . ." He let his voice out as a fisher casts his line, lightly, concealing the hook within the glittering fly. "Twenty years ago I was cast out of this assembly—yes, it is true—but that is an old sorrow, and I have not come here to reproach you. For twenty years I have watched Westria. For the last two I have lived in your very midst, and there is little that passes in this land unknown to me.

"Your Regent calls my fortress a canker, and seeks to prison me within it." Once more Caolin smiled. "You can see the limits of his power. But if he can do so little against me, do you not wonder that I have done so little against you? Do you think that I hate you? No—" he shook his head sorrowfully—"no ruler of Westria has loved this land as I have, none has known it so well."

"Julian knows," came a shout from the sector of the Royal Domain.

"He may know the *land*," Caolin echoed, "but this is an assembly of *men*. You are trying to decide how the people of Westria shall be governed. You are trying to decide between tradition and creativity, between inheritance and excellence, between hierarchy and equality. Are you children? Do you need a parent to watch over you, especially when that parent is himself a child?''

The Blood Lord watched the trouble in people's faces as his words reached them. He could feel the intoxication of his eloquence tingling through his veins. Let the boy keep his bauble; no magical toy could give him the sorcerer's mature and practised power.

''Would you watch over us, then?'' asked a man of the Ramparts.

''Do you have the right to question me?'' Caolin recognized him, and remembered on which report he had seen his name. ''You, who paid gold to the slavers of the Barren Lands to pass you by, and told them how to come upon your neighbor unawares?'' He waited for the shocked murmurs to still.

''Which man of you will condemn me? You—'' the sorcerer pointed at another—''a husband whose brutality has brought two wives to early graves? Or you—'' the long finger transfixed a woman—''whose daughter works as a whore in Laurelynn because you would not shelter her and her child?'' He shook his head. ''I know whose weights are false, I know whose deeds are forgeries, I know who lies with her neighbor's husband without the wife's consent or will.''

Now there was stillness. He could see them wondering whose sins would next be proclaimed. *Whisper your secrets to your friend or to the reeds around Laurelynn,* thought Caolin. *Both of them report to me!*

''But *I* do not condemn you,'' he said finally. ''Take responsibility for your own fates and let innate ability determine who shall rule you. You are men! People of Westria, why do you need a king?''

''The right to answer that question belongs to me.'' Julian was on his feet before he realized he had risen.

''Wind Lord,'' his spirit cried, *''Help me!''* And the answer came instantly. *''Child of starry heaven, allow the spirit to speak through you, and let the fearful mind be still.''*

Julian drew in cedar-scented air and started toward the Council floor, aware of the whispered comments that followed him and the multitude of thoughts unspoken.

"You speak to men—" he saw Caolin's eyes narrow in speculation—"but Westria is more than humankind. Because men forgot that they were part of the land, the world was torn by the Cataclysm. Is there a man or woman here without a name?" He allowed silence for a moment as he surveyed them.

"My name is Mastery . . . " came the voice that had tormented him six months ago. *"I am your master, Julian—why do you fight me?"*

Julian felt his throat tightening and forced his attention back to the crowd.

"There is no one here who has not sworn to the Covenant. That is no rule of royal making—it is the very foundation of Westria. As every holder among you keeps peace between his people and between them and the land, so the sovereign does for Westria. *That* is why you need a king!"

"A ruler maybe, but why must it be you?" came a shout from the Las Costas sector.

"It will not be you!" Caolin's voice spoke to his soul once more. *"You failed before—that bit of rock is not going to help you now!"*

Julian set his hand over the Wind Crystal. *"It's not true! I refuse to listen to you!"* He glared at Caolin, willing him to hear, and saw the sorcerer's disdainful smile.

"You cannot win."

"Ignore him," came the thought of the Master of the Junipers. *"Remember, his spirit is deaf to yours."* Julian closed his eyes and felt music swell within him. More words battered at his awareness, but the music overpowered them.

"Because I *am* the king. . . ." He did not think that he had spoken loudly, but he could feel the echo of his words throbbing through the hall. "I have won and mastered three of the Jewels of Power . . . no, not mastered, but been transformed by them. The fourth will come to

me; it is my destiny. I have been chosen by the land—
by the Lady of Westria—"

He felt a sharp pulse of astonishment from his friends,
for he had never spoken of this before, and saw on Caolin's face some emotion that passed before it could be
identified. He could not have found words for what had
happened between himself and the Lady even had he
wanted to tell them . . . but now all of the words that
had ever been locked within him were winging free.

"And as I have been chosen," Julian said then, "I
choose you. Break the king's staff and melt down the
royal crown. Select what leaders you will. It changes
nothing. At my knighting I pledged my life to this land,
and if you will not have me to reign here in Laurclynn,
I will set up my high seat in the wilderness. I do not
defy your laws, but a greater law than yours has already
bound me. I stand here to show you the way between the
worlds." The music was sounding, louder and louder.
He saw Silverhair's face rapt with listening, and on the
Blood Lord's face a deepening frown. Could not the others hear?

"Those are the words of an adept—" he picked the
astonished thought of the Mistress of the College from
the tumult. *"No,"* came the Master of the Junipers'
proud answer, *"they are the words of a king such as we
have never known."*

"Let Julian be our king!" Robert shouted, and there
was an immediate chorus of affirmation.

"Will you let the beasts rule you?" cried Caolin.

"Better the beasts than one who thinks he is more than
a man!" Frederic replied.

"The Blood Lord asks you to choose for yourselves."
Eric's deep voice joined his son's. "But we know his
ways of old. You have heard of how he spies on your
every movement—how long do you think he would leave
you alone?"

"I speak for the Ramparts. We will have Julian for
king!" cried Philip, rising.

"And I for the Corona!" echoed Sandremun.

"Lords, ladies, this is not the proper form . . ." babbled Tanemun, but no one heeded him.

"Seagate votes for Julian of the Stones!" Eric roared.

"Julian, Julian, Julian. . . ." The Council Hall rocked to the chanting of his name, and the Prince felt himself lifted by its power. Folk were standing in the Las Costas sector now, shouting. Julian saw Alexander's head bowed as he listened to his Councilors.

"Please," thought the Prince. *"I need your independence, and your pride!"*

As if he had heard, Alexander looked up. Julian held out his hand. Slowly the Lord of Las Costas stood. The Prince saw his mouth moving; the confirming shouts of his people amplified his words.

"Las Costas chooses Julian of the Stones."

Julian took a step back at the blast of emotion he felt from Caolin.

"You fools, you fools! *Still* you do not understand. *I* know what is best for everyone."

He believed that! Wonder held Julian's tongue as he perceived that the Blood Lord's words were quite sincere.

"You must obey, you *will* obey!" the sorcerer screamed. "Are you so impressed by this boy with his pretty stones? You have no understanding of real power!"

And that was true as well. The hair stood up on Julian's arms as force built in the chamber. Could not the others feel it? The Master of the Junipers was on his feet, with Frederic beside him. There was a stirring in the sector of the College of the Wise. *"Stop him,"* came the thought of the Mistress. *"I cannot,"* the Master replied.

"Fools indeed!" The trained voice of the Mistress of the College pierced the din. "Your choice has been made for you. Only a shaman king can stand against the Blood Lord's power. The College of the Wise chooses Julian!"

"You were wrong!" Loysa Gilder screamed at Sachs. "We're beaten. The Free Cities vote for the Jewel Lord, and I don't care what your pet sorcerer does to me!"

The chanting vibrated through the floorboards; even the smoke of the Council fire shimmered in rhythm. Julian's pulse pounded to the waves of sound that buffeted his eardrums; with it, his breathing rose and fell. Awareness expanded: he *was* the sound, he and the people in this hall were one voice, one being—he and the people and the city and all the land.

"Words, words! What good are your silly acclamations?" The sorcerer's voice slashed through the chanting, shattering unity. Julian's consciousness shrank back to individuality; the scars on his brow tingled as he recognized the power that had felled him on Spear Island.

"You have challenged me! You have raised the wind, and now you shall reap the whirlwind!"

FIFTEEN: The Whirlwind

The crowd's clamor clattered against the walls of the Council Hall in roulades of pure sound. The impact rocked Caolin; his outflung arm cleared a circle of stillness around him as people surged toward Julian. They lifted the Prince on their shoulders to bring him to the throne.

"Not yet!" Julian's shout pierced the hubbub. "Give me the authority of the king, but I'll not claim the honor of the throne until I have mastered all four of the Jewels."

That will be never, thought the Blood Lord furiously. *And while I hold the Red Mountain, your claim to rule Westria is a lie!*

"When you've mastered the Jewels and cleared the land of vermin, is that it, lad?" cried Eric as if he had read Caolin's mind. "Let's make a start now. Guards, seize the sorcerer!"

The people bayed like hounds as the Regent started for Caolin. But the sorcerer was no longer there. After a moment of shock that Eric could so forget the law, he passed through the crowd in a blur of shadow. Folk tripped over each other and knew that he had eluded them only when they heard his laugh.

The Blood Lord filled his lungs with air and let it out slowly in a long, controlled vibration that absorbed all other sounds. He drew breath before it faded, shaped mouth and throat more precisely and increased the volume, hearing the surrounding clamor diminish moment by moment as that note penetrated consciousness and commanded it.

Silverhair and the Master of the Junipers recognized it, but he had been too quick for them. This was the tone that paralysed the will. And Julian . . . he saw the boy's face whiten and knew that somehow he understood as well.

Now the sorcerer began his variations, letting the sound distort as it pulsed from his throat in uneven half-and quarter-tones. Those nearest were rubbing their arms where the hair was bristling, and covering their ears. Again and again he repeated the sequence that was the antithesis of melody. He looked around and saw a face he recognized.

"*Loysa Gilder, you have betrayed me! Your only reward will be torment now. . . .*" Caolin let the tone carry the rest of the message; her imagination would paint a more lurid picture than anything he could devise. There was a man in Tanemun's office who had been taking bribes; he projected his message and saw the fellow cry out and fight his way toward the door. Men and women were sinking to their knees, weeping.

Ordrey was near one of the doorways, gripping the false Julian's sleeve, and Mañero was behind them. "*Hold him!*" He turned as Eric pushed toward him.

"*Eric! Stupid, hulking old Eric . . . your time is past. You're beaten.*" Eric faltered, glaring around like a maddened bull. "*They're all mocking you, Eric. The young men look at you and laugh!*" The Regent's face flushed, and the sorcerer knew that he had hit the mark once more.

"*I know all your little evils, your petty fears,*" he exulted, *"and I will use them to destroy you!"* Why had he even troubled to try to play their game? He was not bound by human laws.

Caolin swayed, dizzied by triumph, and let his song of unmaking pulse out with full power. He saw Silverhair shaking and pitched his song more precisely to reach those sensitive ears.

"Farin Silverhair, you stopped me once, but your harp is not here now. You're powerless without it, harper, and when you plead to me for mercy, I will laugh!"

Beneath his feet, the flooring trembled. The air shivered as that uncanny pulsation distorted vision as well. *"Nothing . . . the world is nothing,"* sang the sorcerer. *"All that you think you know is illusion."* He showed them the empty place at the heart of things, where men fear to see. *"Come to me when hope is no more. Be swallowed by the darkness within and you will find me there."*

Some of the people had managed to stagger outside. Others lay senseless on the floor. And still Caolin sang. He sang the futility of all effort, the ultimate entropy. He sang, drunk on despair, until no one stirred in the hall.

"You need struggle no longer, for I know the way through the empty land. I will lead you. Come to me, come to me!"

Julian took a step forward. Around him, men were moving one shuffling step at a time as the sorcerer's will drew them on. When Katiz had sung that song, Julian had been paralyzed until Silverhair's harping transmuted it. He rooted his spirit in the strength of earth and clung, though the pull of the sorcerer's compulsion was pain.

Silverhair. . . . When he sought his uncle's mind, he sensed only agony. He thought, *he depended on a tool, and it has failed him*—but he had no time to consider the implications. While he was distracted, he had moved a foot closer. The cloud with which the Blood Lord had veiled himself was thinning, but the face that emerged from those shadows was not the same as the smooth mask the sorcerer had worn into the Council Hall. For the first time, Julian saw the flesh worn to the skull, the features distorted where old scars pulled slick skin awry, and eyes like doorways into the darkness of which he sang—the true face of Caolin.

The confidence borne by that revelation shocked Julian into another step forward. Everyone else still capable of movement was beyond memory. Except . . . he forced his head around and met the Master of the Junipers' burning gaze.

"You must stop him!" came the Master's command, and Julian realized that it was taking all of the adept's will to stay where he was. *"Use the Jewel!"*

Julian clutched the stone at his breast. *"I don't know how to use it to destroy!"*

"Sing the world back into being!"

The Prince felt a point of pain as the Wind Crystal jabbed his palm, and in that moment he remembered the Throne, and the Jewel song. He forced his breath to carry sound; it was more like a kitten's mew than music, but another sound followed it, and the Crystal's amplification transmuted them into a hesitant melody. He sought for the next note, and found strength coming into his voice at last.

"You poor princeling, will you contest with me?"

Julian's singing faltered. *"I will never serve you!"* his spirit cried, but Caolin did not hear. The Blood Lord had never been able to hear the speech of the spirit, even before he fell into evil long ago. But if Julian answered aloud, he would lose the tenuous protection of his own singing. For a moment his note caught the sorcerer's in an odd harmony, and he forced out more sound. But the Blood Lord overran him.

"Foolish, foolish child, don't you understand? The world was made by vibration, and it can be unmade in the same way. I can unmake you. . . ."

"Don't you listen to him! Find the harmony!" Suddenly Silverhair's mind was with him, feeding him knowledge of chords and intervals. Julian felt the floor shiver as dissonances clashed and crossed. The air was tingling, but the Prince had good lungs. With gathering

volume he began to weave the Blood Lord's singing into harmony.

As Julian's voice grew louder, the Blood Lord increased his own intensity. The panes in the tall upper windows in the Seagate and Domain sectors shattered. In a moment the rest of the windows had gone. The glass in the skylight split; Julian saw a man's cheek sliced open by a falling shard, and he dodged as the remainder of the pane crashed down.

The Council Hall quivered. The sorcerer shouted. With a crack like the world's ending, two of the great beams that joined in the center split, and the roof began to give away.

Braced rafters groaned as the complicated relationship of balanced stresses that upheld them was broken. The ceiling sagged. Could the others get out before the entire structure collapsed? His fingers tightened convulsively on the Wind Crystal. Pain lanced through him, becoming a great shout that denied everything in Caolin's song, and bearing all other sound away. His ears rang with silence.

"Run!" he shouted then. "The roof is falling!"

Julian's cry reached men's minds at a level beyond reason. As the sorcerer's spell had moved them, now the king's command set them scrambling toward the doors. His friends lagged behind the others and waited in the doorway, but Caolin was moving as well.

"Julian!" The sorcerer's call compelled attention. Julian blinked at the blur of gray and scarlet . . . and then focused on the glitter of a knife. Ordrey's fingers tangled in dark hair and jerked back the head of the nameless man with Julian's face so that the pale throat was exposed.

"My knife blade sears your neck, Julian. Do you feel it?" Caolin cried.

Involuntarily the Prince's hand went to his throat. His fingers felt smooth skin, but the skin itself smarted. He rubbed furiously, denying the illusion, and Caolin laughed.

"Like to like at last is drawn, separate parts now make one whole," chanted the sorcerer. A trickle of crimson twisted across his victim's skin, but the man did not move. The Blood Lord unfolded a small packet and pressed several dark hairs against the wound. "All that differenced fate is gone, bodies twinned will share one soul!"

Julian shuddered, scarcely aware that his neck had stopped hurting as he began to realize what was happening. The sorcerer's chanting rose in intensity.

"Song of power thou shalt sing never—thus the power of speech I sever!"

The knife flashed, and a red mouth opened suddenly beneath the jutting beard. Then everything turned crimson as lifeblood sprayed the sorcerer's pale robes.

Julian fought for breath. Mañero howled, crouching on his hands and knees beside Ordrey.

"Silence!" shouted the Blood Lord, and Mañero cowered against the wall, rubbing his throat and grimacing. The body of Julian's double sagged in Ordrey's arms.

"What powersong will you sing now? Voiceless forever, how can you use the Jewel?" The gibe seared Julian's soul. He swallowed painfully.

Caolin's cold gaze dismissed Julian. *"I see the rest of you, shivering by the door! Silverhair, Frederic, Rana, Robert. . . ."* His intonation of their names was an irresistible summoning. *"Come here!"*

Silverhair took a tottering step back into the hall. Somewhere above, another rafter sagged a foot farther and a cloud of dust puffed down. As Robert and Rana followed the harper forward, white-faced and staring, Caolin began to describe what he intended to do to them.

My lips may be bound, buy my body is still my own! Julian thrust himself between the sorcerer and his prey. *Wind Lord!* Could spirit speak where lips were dumb? Awareness rushed inward, and in that stillness, Julian formed once more the syllables of his own true name.

"Don't move!" snapped Caolin. "The Jewels were mine once, and will be again, starting with this one—" He stretched out his hand.

"You have no power over me," Julian said aloud.

For a moment surprise held him as still as it did the sorcerer. He swallowed, felt his vocal cords whole and unharmed. Then a subsonic vibration buzzed through his bones. Instinct too swift for thought sent him hurtling backward, thrusting his friends before him as the cross beams that arched from the eastern and western corners of the Council Hall crashed down.

Coughing, Caolin reeled away from the chaos of falling timbers. He shrieked in anguish for the victory that had been within his grasp, and another beam fell.

"Master, this way. There's a door here!" A desperate hand tugged at his sleeve.

Caolin felt his head clearing as he drew in cleaner air. A staircase twisted upward before him. He thrust the other man aside and began to climb.

"My lord, come back. It's not safe—you'll be trapped there!"

Old memories were surfacing now. The roof of the Council Hall might have fallen, but the parapet around it was supported by the pillars of the porch and walls. Internal and external staircases alternated at each angle, but that was not what drew him upward.

The parapet was open to the unfettered winds, and the force of hatred that shook him with every breath he took could be released only by the unleashing of elemental powers. Panting, he pulled himself out into the open air.

The hazy clouds he had seen in the dawning had thickened. They loomed above the familiar dark bulk of the Red Mountain in masses like moving towers. He sniffed warm wind heavy with moisture; then a cool breath from the east touched his cheek. Ordrey and Mañero crawled up after him and sat gasping.

Dust was still rising from the ruins of the roof. Splintered beams pointed downward. He glimpsed broken benches and a patch of floor.

Already I have destroyed his throne! thought Caolin. His gaze sought the cloud towers. *Soon he won't even have a capital!*

"Tell him he cannot go up there—" the Regent began.

"Father, you can't give him orders anymore," answered Frederic. "Have you forgotten that we just made him king?"

"While the Blood Lord threatens my city, I have no right to that name!" Julian started toward the southern stairs.

Silverhair had collapsed as they emerged from the ruined hall and still lay unconscious, with Piper hovering beside him. Frederic was supporting the Master. But Robert and Rana stood together, watching Julian.

"Then you can't forbid us to follow you," said Robert as he and Rana fell into step behind him. Julian expanded his awareness, found his balance between the male and female energies of the other two, and realized that he needed them.

"Come then." He could sense a weird stirring in the air above him. He had already delayed too long. With the man and the woman he loved most close behind him, he began to climb.

"Master, I think they're coming after you," said Ordrey.

The sorcerer nodded. Then he focused his forces, projected power out from his palms and turned slowly, establishing the protective field. He let out his breath in a long hum that set the air aquiver. Such a warding would deflect even arrows.

He took a deep breath. "Wind creatures now I call." He had lit no incense, but the dust of destruction drifted on the uneasy air. He had no feather fans, but his hands could shape the wind. And the greatest tool of magic, his mind, was always at his command.

> Stormfather, cloudkeeper,
> Cloudgatherer, rainreaper,
> Close, dense, dark, immense!
> Come to my summoning!

He called the storm clouds closer, coaxed the east wind to strengthen. For a year at the College of the Wise, the

logbooks of the weather watchers had been his study. He
knew that his victory was fated, for today the elements
had placed the tools he needed ready to his hand. Closer
came the clouds; he waited for the moment when moist
air would meet dry.

A flicker of movement drew his glance. "Caolin!"
Julian's call came distorted through the barrier. "The
building is surrounded. Will you surrender now?"

The sorcerer shifted his attention for a moment from
the sky. "Fool, do you think you can hurt me? Even now
you do not understand my power!"

Caolin stiffened as he saw the telltale blur of the squall
line below the black clouds. He drew charged air deep
into his lungs, opened his mouth, chanted.

> *Wicked winds across the earth go whirling,*
> *scouring all before you, swirling,*
> *funnel fast unfurling,*
> *horror hurling,*
> *twirl!*

Arms outstretched, the Blood Lord began to turn to
his left. A quick glimpse showed him Julian, still watching. No doubt the fool was wondering what he was up
to—soon he would see! Still spinning, he sang.

> *Disaster and despair come swiftly, breeding*
> *hunger, horrid, ever-feeding,*
> *o'er the land doom leading,*
> *swiftly speeding,*
> *greed!*

Blood stained robes flared outward. Widdershins
whirling, the sorcerer spun, glimpsing a dark pulsation
in the cloud that grew with every turn. He screeched
triumph as shadow shot a tentacle earthward, becoming
larger as it began to feed.

> *Darkness over all the earth swift-flowing,*
> *death the fields of men is mowing,*

> *winds of evil blowing,*
> *anguish knowing,*
> *grow!*

This was the servant who would destroy the city that had defied him. When Laurelynn lay in ruins, the rest of Westria would be easy prey. Now, to guide it—

> *Magic makes a monster maw of power,*
> *hatred hails the haunted hour—*
> *I call you to this tower,*
> *fatal flower,*
> *now!*

The sorcerer's shout jerked Julian around, staring at the dark lily whose stem skimmed the earth to the south of them. As he watched, it grew larger, denser, and he knew that it had begun to destroy.

"What is it?" whispered Rana from behind him.

"Tornado," Robert answered her. "They're uncommon, but I saw the one that passed through Rivered five years ago. It will pick up anything aboveground."

"It's like a waterspout."

"Yes, but this spout could suck up Laurelynn. Julian, we must warn the people!"

Julian eyed the evil creature that was twisting across the flat plain of the valley toward his city. It was coming so fast!

"You're right. Get down there, both of you, and—"

"Not without you!" said Rana. Julian looked from one set face to the other. There was no more time! Wind whipped his hair across his face and away again as he gripped the rail.

"Eric!" Upturned faces told him he had been heard. "Tornado's coming, sound the alarm! Get folk into cellars, ditches, anywhere that's underground." In a moment he heard horns blowing and the clangor of bells. But was that enough? He threw back his head and sucked air into his lungs.

"People of Westria, take cover! Get down!" The shout

came from both mind and body, and it resonated across the planes. It reached every conscious creature within ten miles of Laurelynn.

The Lady of Westria rose from Awahna, stretching out imploring hands. The Great Eagle burst screaming from His eyrie and hung in the eye of the wind.

"Fire-bringer!" came Her call. *"This is no time for your games. Stop this madman before he kills My city!"*

"Wait," came the thought of Wind Lord. *"This is the king's final testing in my realm. Let us see what he will do!"*

Julian staggered at the power that rushed through him with that cry. But forces far greater were focusing in the figure of the sorcerer. He began to edge around the parapet toward him.

Caolin had ceased his spinning. His loose sleeves flapped wildly as he drew the tornado toward him like a newly captured mustang that bucked and fought the rope that restrained it, but still obeyed.

He doesn't see me, thought Julian. Ordrey glared at him, but clearly feared to disturb his master with a warning. And Mañero only grinned.

If I could break Caolin's concentration, he would lose control of that thing. Julian took another step, then jerked back, his skin tingling painfully as he struck the sorcerer's warding. Once he had pierced such a shield in the spirit with the help of Lady Madrone. But this circle, being smaller, was stronger, and he could not push his physical body through.

He drew breath, seeking a tone to transform that energy, but all sound beyond the evil keening that grew ever louder as the tornado approached—was whirled away by the wind. Everywhere was noise and movement, as if the world were being reduced to its primal vibrations.

The sky was like a great bruise, poisoning the last of the light. As Julian stared, the funnel snaked toward a farmstead just across the river. The building exploded; for a moment a whirl of white splinters gleamed, then darkness devoured it. Caolin had released the emptiness within him, and now it was eating the world. The tornado's hoarse roaring deepened as it ground its latest meal to dust. Julian's ears rang with changing pressure.

Did the thing have a soul that he could speak to? Julian fell back, felt Rana and Robert supporting him. *Wind Lord, help me! Anyone—* Chaos howled around him; he tried to still his awareness long enough to set his spirit free.

Inside Caolin's circle, a long howl split the air. The sorcerer clung to his link with the tornado, but the sound rose and fell with a dissonance that did not belong to the storm. As his will wavered, the funnel spun in an aimless circle. The Blood Lord turned.

Mañero tipped his head back, his face contorted in fear—or some perverse ecstasy—and produced another burst of sound.

"Stop him!" snapped the sorcerer. Ordrey shook his head helplessly, and Mañero howled again. The Blood Lord gripped the little man's bony shoulder and shook him, saw amber eyes glinting with laughter, and thrust him away.

"Idiot, be silent, or I'll give you to the storm!" A sweep of his arm brought the funnel swirling toward them, sucking up water as it crossed the river, pulverizing a new pathway through the merchants' quarter of Laurelynn. Mañero yelped and rolled away from him, *through* the sorcerer's warding, and crashed into Julian, who reached out in an instinctive gesture of protection.

"Don't defend him!" cried Caolin. "He serves *me!* Who do you think set Alexander on your trail?"

Julian jerked away, staring, as Mañero found his feet again. The funnel gaped above them, and in that moment the sorcerer refocused his fury, and flung it straight at Mañero.

The little man spun with an odd shimmer, as if sparks of light were spitting from his turning form. In a moment he must fall—but the glow expanded—for an instant Mañero stilled. Caolin glimpsed his mocking grin. Then the

man shape disintegrated with a report like a monstrous
fart, and a choking stench that drove the sorcerer back
against the railing. The odor numbed all perception, but
the hungry maw above them sucked it upward until
Caolin at last smelled only charged air.

The sorcerer shook his head and saw against the form-
less whirl the shape that had been Mañero limned in lines
of light that reformed into another shape: furred, four-
legged, but still laughing as sharp ears pricked and it
waved a ragged-plumed tail.

"But I killed you!" cried Caolin.

"Silly man, you set me free!" came the cheerful answer.

> Deceivers' spells themselves deceive—
> What you have wrought, you shall receive!
> The trickster summons Me—thereafter
> He must pay my price in laughter!

Coyote threw back his head in a yip of pure delight.
"The hairs you use to bind the boy's tongue this time
come from my own tail!"

The sorcerer tried to speak, but his tongue would not
obey him.

"Why did you betray me?" cried Julian.

"So you have to use your power! Unless you learn
Sound at the Throne, could you sing against his power
song?" The Guardian began to laugh. "And it was
funny—you both chase each other in circles like cubs,
each one think he's My master, while I laugh at you!"

"You do this every time, don't you?" Julian asked
slowly. "Every time you are killed!"

"Can't you see the joke? *He* can't take a joke at all,
but don't *you* think it's funny?"

Glowing amber eyes moved from the sorcerer to the
Prince once more, and Caolin gulped air. Now the storm
he had conjured was within him. *"And did you do this,
wretched spirit, to see what it would teach me?"* He
reached for the churning energy above, at one with it as
he had not been even in his first summoning.

"Oh, dear, he's angry. You better do somethin' now, little king. I helped all I can!" Coyote laughed and with a final shimmer, disappeared.

Funny? Julian's city lay in ruins; that obscene storm was once more getting ready to gobble them, and this fire-thief, gift-giver, and legendary trickster—as well as one of the great Guardians of Westria—wanted him to *laugh*? A hundred tales that he'd heard from Silverhair and others rioted in Julian's memory. And there was little enough to encourage trust in any of them.

But at least Caolin's magic circle was broken now.

"Draw on my strength, Julian," came Robert's thought. *"And mine,"* Rana echoed him.

He could feel Robert's vigor like an open flame on his left and Rana's surging energy on his right. And he was balanced between them; he was the mist born where the sunlight struck the water, a mist that swirled upward, seeking the skies. This time he left his body easily. Without substance, he had nothing to fear from the storm.

Movement . . . light . . . sound . . . laughter. Around him, the elementals of the Air were playing.

"Ho! A human sprite! Sisters, do you see?"

"Do you think he'll play with us?"

Julian willed himself to turn, and human habits of perception interpreted what he saw as wings, as slender limbs, as bright eyes, appearing and disappearing from swirling masses of raw energy.

"Stormchildren," he called. *"what is the game?"*

"There!" they pointed. *"See there! The whirlwind brings us toys!"*

Julian looked, and saw from above the mad widdershins whirl of the beast that was eating his city. And even as he looked, a chicken was tossed upward, madly squawking, followed by a cartwheel, someone's flapping cloak, an unhinged door.

"Don't get too close," the sylphs cautioned. *"It will change you too!"*

Unwittingly he had drifted nearer. He gazed downward, wondering. Was this mindless hunger the maw of

Caolin's darkness? The sorcerer clearly thought so. Julian could sense the Blood Lord's lust for destruction even from here. But nothing in the whirlwind answered it. Even the sylphs' warning had held no terror. What had they said? *"It will change you—"* And that was what it was doing: exchanging down for up and in for out in ceaseless transformation.

But he did not want it to transform Laurelynn.

"How do I make it go away?" he asked.

"I told you—humans don't have any fun!"

"We don't know anyway!" An elfin face floated close to him. *"We only play!"*

Julian sped upward through boiling masses of cloud. *"Paralda!"* he called. *"Holy King. Come to me, hearken to me, help me now!"*

"Who calls?" sang the wind. *"Who summons the king?"* Cloud shaped swiftly into a royal amphitheater, luminous with filtered sunlight, and created a throne, and upon it a great sparkling figure mantled in shining wings.

"It is the King of Men who call upon you," answered Julian. *"to take your whirlwind away!"*

"A man invoked it—let a man disperse it, if he can." The King of the Powers of Air laughed, and all up and down the Great Valley, folk heard thunder.

"With your permission," said Julian, *"and if you will tell me how."*

"You know how. Upon your breast you bear the talisman!"

Julian looked down and saw that although the Wind Crystal remained with the body he had left far below, even in spirit he wore its simulacrum. *It is true then,* he realized. *Once I have found the Jewels and understood them, I will need them no longer, for they are part of me.* And knowing that, he knew what he must do.

Sylphs, shrieking like children on a slide, darted behind him in bursts of light as he sped downward. They squealed delightedly as the swirling gulf appeared below them, cocooning him in a shimmering cluster of cloud. Julian barely hesitated.

"Ho, transformer, it's time for your own transformation! Changer, let all be changed!" came his cry. And then they were into it, sucked down and up and in and out in dizzying succession.

When Julian was a child, he and his foster brothers had let the waterfall carry them into their secret pool. He had rolled down grassy slopes, pumped short legs to make a swing bear him skyward until he transcended gravity. And through all of those games, he had laughed, intoxicated by the dizzy speed. He laughed now, and from the Jewel at his breast exploded a pure pulse of joy.

"Caolin, can't you feel it?" Julian cried. *"This is the Power of the Wind Crystal! I give it to you!"* From far below, he heard Coyote's laughter, and his own rolled after it in thundering peals.

Dry electric air rushed inward. Charged ions shifted; the forces that had held the tornado together relaxed suddenly, and the moisture that had been trapped within it was released in a flood of rain.

Thunder clapped, sudden, deafening. Caolin reeled away from the railing, his hands to his ears. Julian lay slumped in the arms of his friends. His enemy's destruction had been within Caolin's grasp, but the thunder was mocking him. The ravenous shadow he had summoned was misting into brightness. The sorcerer raised a scarred fist to defy the heavens and saw, straight up within the thinning funnel, a blinding patch of blue sky.

"Caolin! Don't you understand? The joke is on both of us. Take the Crystal if you want it, and be free!"

A Word kept Robert and Rana without power of movement as the Blood Lord hurtled toward them. Caolin's hand was poised above Julian's body before he realized it. The boy was dead, or unconscious. *How had he heard him?* Laughter boomed and rippled across the heavens. Was he hearing it with his physical ears? *No one* could penetrate his shielding—*no one* had ever spoken to him mind to mind except when he controlled the linkage. *No one except Jehan. . . .*

Caolin shook his head, and the world came back into

focus, but he could still hear laughter. The pale, rain-wet face before him bore a faint smile, and in that smile, for the first time, he saw a reflection of Jehan.

The king's face had worn just such a smile when he lay dying. . . . *And it was my doing—mine! Oh, my dear lord, even now will you not let me go?*

From across the ruined roof came voices. Eric's head poked above the parapet. "There they are!" came a shout. "Take them!"

"Never!" Caolin looked back at Julian, who still wore that smile that profaned memory, and at the Wind Crystal that winked so mockingly from his breast.

"You have all the others, but Fire will be the answer to everything," hissed the sorcerer. "By the magic of fire, I destroyed your father; with fire and sword, I will destroy Westria!"

Sodden robes clung to his gaunt frame as he looked back at Julian. He shuddered at the hateful touch of the rain.

"By fire I will destroy you, who dare to claim *his* crown. I will break your spirit and your body, but you will never touch me, Julian . . . never . . . ever again."

Ordrey was pulling him away. Caolin went unresisting, stumbling down stairs he did not see. Nor did he hear the gulls that circled in a clamoring cloud as his servant led him through the debris-choked secret byways of Laurelynn, or the roaring of the wind-driven rain.

SIXTEEN: The Master Singers

The grasses on the hills above Misthall were ripe with summer's ending; golden curves wind-ruffled against the pale sky. When the wind shifted, it carried the fragrance of sun-cured hay. At one end of the garden the bards had built a stage, shaded with bunting as purple as the grapes in the arbor. Julian and Master Andreas had already taken their places on benches. Two of the junior students were hastily finishing the decorations, while in the space before the stage, an assortment of musicians simultaneously tried to tune.

Then all the bright scene was stilled by the clear call of a horn.

Silverhair settled Swangold against his breast, and the harp mistress bent to her own instrument, with a precise flick of her finger testing a last string. The morning sunlight glistened on a silver threading in her auburn hair, but time could not alter the perfect line of arm and shoulder as she drew the great harp into her embrace.

Light sparkled blindingly from silver and brass, glowed in the oiled wood of the instruments. A quiver of anticipation passed through the musicians; someone, tuned too tight by anticipation, plucked a string prematurely and earned a hiss of reproof from Master Ras. And then, from the road below, they heard voices sweet with distance, strengthening to a deeper beauty as the singers rounded the bend. Two by two, the surviving students of the College of Bards came marching around the gray bulk of Misthall, under the arch of the arbor and into the garden.

> *Strike the drum and sound the string;*
> *Lift up voice in praise to sing;*
> *Fill the air with merry noise;*
> *Pipe and horn gloriously ring;*
> *Bards of Westria, rejoice!*

As each instrument was named, it joined the music. The verse ended and the full consort repeated the melody, elaborating the harmonies as the singers filed past in a blur of purple gowns and climbed the steps to the platform.

"*As the pipe sweet air respires. . . .*" The last note was held, and a dozen wind instruments extended it in piercing beauty. "*As the sea sings on harpwire. . . .*" Silverhair and Siaran were ready, and a long glissando rolled through the waiting air. "*As the drum evokes earth's deep. . . .*" Grinning, the percussionists added their deep heartbeat. "*As the fiddle's bow strikes fire. . . .*" The string section shimmered into life, for once completely in tune.

"*Thus the Covenant we keep!*" Now they were all playing together in that surge of pure sound that had enraptured Silverhair the first time he had performed in consort. But this verse had new meaning for him now, for he had shared the search for three of those elements with Julian. Was this what it was all for? Was the battle between king and sorcerer only part of a greater quest for the meaning of the Covenant of Westria?

Lady, bless all that combines
To make music: bless our minds,
Bless our throats and tongues and hands;
Bless the reed and gut and hide,
Bless the wood and bones and bronze.

Instruments and voices together soared in invocation. And for that moment they were a single being, and as one they sensed the answer.

"Strike the drum and sound the string." Rejoicing, the chorus repeated the first verse of the anthem. Silverhair felt himself descending into his separate self again and sighed, regretting that lost unity. There was a little rustle as the singers settled to listen to the rest of the recital. Then Master Andreas introduced the first performers.

Julian, looking like Wind Lord himself in a white gown with a silver circlet gleaming from his brow, had been given a place of honor to one side of the stage. As usual, Rana and Robert sat to either side, the girl in hyacinth, the young man in a tunic the color of red wine. They had hardly left him since Eric had brought all three down from the collapsing roof of the Council Hall after Julian's duel with the sorcerer two days before.

No shame to them if the Blood Lord's magic struck them senseless, thought Silverhair, *considering what it did to me! I will never let Swangold out of my reach again! I defeated him three times, but Caolin is beyond me now.*

Then Piper played a solo that set the flute master to eyeing him like a falconer who has just found a wild tiercel perched in his mews. When he was finished, Cub, who had come over from Registhorpe to join his sister, started the wild clapping. Silverhair grinned.

"He has a place now at the college, if he wants it. They won't care whether or not he can sing!" whispered Siaran.

The harper nodded. But where would the bards teach him?

The sweetness of flutesong drifted into silence. Piper gave them his quick-flashing smile, then darted offstage.

"I see that not all the musicians in Westria come out of my school," said the Master of the College of Bards. "Now I want to call on someone whom I feel should be counted as one of us, though I would be hard put to identify his instrument. But he is our host today, and it is fitting that we honor him." He turned to Julian.

Master Andreas was in the Council Hall, Silverhair realized suddenly. *He knows what Julian did on that day.*

Julian's hand went to the Jewel at his breast. Light flickered between his fingers as he rose to his feet and bowed to the master.

"My lord, this is for you." Master Andreas held out a bundle that fell open in rich purple folds. It bore no device, but its meaning was clear. Julian stood for a moment, staring.

"I will accept this and wear it . . . as the mantle of a student in your school," his deep voice responded. With a sudden flare of violet, he draped it across his broad shoulders. But he did not look like a student, thought Silverhair. He looked like a king.

"I still need to learn the notes, but at least I have heard the music!" For a moment Julian's dark gaze touched his uncle, then continued. The little murmur of surprise that had swept the crowd stilled.

"I am your host, but to me that is a privilege. And it is only fitting that I should provide a setting for your festival, since the destruction of the hall where you had intended to hold it is partly my responsibility." He grinned suddenly, waiting for the ripple of laughter.

"That speech in the Council Hall was no fluke," whispered Siaran. "He's playing them like a harp."

"But there should have been no need!" Julian exclaimed. "You have been homeless for a year now—I meant to try to do something about that—but there have been distractions." Again the students laughed. Silverhair would not have thought a sea war and a half-ruined city amusing, but the boy's wry humor was hitting just the right note. Somewhere Julian had learned laughter.

"Yet you cannot wander forever. Therefore I give you my pledge—and now that pledge will have some meaning—to help you find a new location for the college, or to rebuild your old halls. In the meantime, all that I can offer you is what you see, and the acoustics seem to be adequate. Will you accept Misthall as your temporary home?"

"But it is yours—" Master Andreas began.

Julian shook his head and smiled. "It will be some time before I can tarry by any hearth, even my own."

A whisper of excited speculation stirred the students. Siaran was weeping openly, and Master Andreas stood shaking his head, searching for words.

Oh, Julian, thought Silverhair, *what a gift! You could have found no better reward for them, or for me.* This time there was nothing wrong with his breathing, but for a moment he felt a little detached from his body, as if by a mere act of will, he could float free.

"What, are you speechless?" Julian asked gently. "Well, perhaps it is only hunger. Come now, my master—it seems to me that the wind is bearing some very pleasant scents from beyond the arbor."

He is right. I rose too early to face breakfast, thought Silverhair wryly. *It must be emptiness I feel.*

Julian held out his hand. "Come with me, all of you, and let us keep the festival!"

Piper sat on a bench halfway up the hillside and gnawed on a drumstick. Below him, the garden was blooming with purple like an unseasonal field of lupines as the students sat down to devour the roast chicken and late corn, the ripe grapes and apples, the fluffy pastries and all of the other delicacies that the folk of the Domain had prepared for them. There was plenty for everyone. Even Cub wanted time to digest a bit before they went exploring. It had not been too difficult for Piper to evade the other boy for a little while.

He was happy, he told himself. Even without speech, he could learn all the music he desired at the College of Bards. He needed to do some thinking, that was all.

Piper finished the chicken and tossed the bone into a clump of coyote brush, then sat licking his fingers, watching the swallows dart back and forth to their mud nests beneath the eaves of Misthall. And suddenly he remembered the bright wings of the Wind Riders against the sunset, and his throat ached with unshed tears.

He thought, *I could have stayed with them too.*

But he had asked for the Wind Crystal instead . . . for Julian.

"Are you sorry?" The voice was in his mind, but it was not his own. Piper turned and glimpsed a flicker of purple, but he knew already that the face above it would be Julian's.

"You needed it." The boy shivered a little, remembering how badly the Prince had needed it at the end.

Julian turned, as if he could see through the sheltering bulk of hill behind them to the dark presence of the Blood Lord's mountain. Was Caolin there? Everyone said that he must be, for his body had not been found. Piper shivered again.

"Are you cold?" Julian asked. He dropped down beside the boy, draping the fine purple cloak around them both. Piper did not answer. It had been a wind of the spirit that had chilled him, and for that, Julian's presence, not his cloak, was the only protection. He fixed his eyes on the tawny tree-dappled slope before him, and the peaceful waters of the bay. Beyond them, the Lady Mountain was cloaked in purple too, and crowned with silver clouds.

Overhead, a red-tailed hawk balanced on the breeze. She slipped downward, once more she hovered, and then dropped a few feet, as if she were descending invisible stairs.

"I thanked everyone else, down there," said Julian presently—"except you. And I owe you the most of all."

"It made Silverhair happy. It was the only thing I could do," Piper's thought replied.

"You make it sound easy. But nobody else even thought to try. I was sitting on my behind in Laurelynn, moping, and it should have been my job!" Julian shook his head. "To do what you did, you had to make some hard choices. I know about choices. I think I know how to reward you . . . Piper, I'm going to treat you in the way that the Guardians have treated me."

Piper swallowed. Julian's gaze had gone dark and unfocused. *Is he seeing the sorcerer?* Piper wondered. *Does he want me to climb the Red Mountain and beard Caolin in his den?*

"I want you to do a harder thing, Piper," Julian answered softly. "I want you to remember what it is that binds you. I want you to look into your soul and tell me what you see."

"No." A sharply shaken head underlined that refusal.

Julian sighed. "I said that too. But nobody believed me. Maybe it was because I was saying 'no' with my lips but 'yes' in my heart. I won't force a choice upon you, Piper, but there's too much spirit in you to stay prisoned against your real will. And I can help you find out what that is. . . ."

Piper turned away, his knuckles digging into his eyes to hold back the tears.

"Little bird . . . little bird . . ." Julian held him close, rocking him as he would a small child. "It's hard—don't you think I know?"

The boy nodded, remembering Julian's agony when they laid the Wind Crystal on his breast in the ritual. His body had twitched with pain, but he had asked for more, because he needed that knowledge to defend them.

"Would it make Silverhair happy if I tried?"

You know it would," came the answer. "He loves you."

The hawk blurred through the air. There was a moment's tumult in the grass, and then the bird beat heavily upward, strong talons clutching her prey.

With a convulsive sob, Piper reached out and grasped the Wind Crystal.

Harpsong . . . a rush of air beneath spread wings. *Will you do it? . . .* Wind-whisper through dry grass, a girl's laughter . . . *I don't think I could bear to see those blackened timbers again. . . .*

Piper whimpered as the maelstrom of sound and sense swept over him. And then another will set its protection around him, and he heard only the sweet-chiming song of the Jewel.

"Not that way—why do you think the Master cast a circle around us before?"

This time his protection was Julian. Piper lay back on the soft grass with a shuddering sigh. The Prince unclasped the Crystal. Gently he laid it on the boy's thin chest, and the Song grew louder.

"You can close your eyes now," said the voice in his head.

Yes, that was easier. Now he could concentrate on the beautiful music and let it carry him to the skies.

"Piper, are you listening? Piper, I want you to remember your home. There was a lovely piece of tile set into the fireplace. Remember that tile, see the blue spiral of leaves and flowers. . . ."

Piper sees firelight on whitewashed walls, a reflected glow on the pretty tile set among the stones of the overmantle, beneath the pegs that hold his grandfather's sword. His mother gives it a swipe with her apron as she passes, to keep it shining. A thing from the Old Time, it is—a treasure from the ruined castle on the hill. Sometimes he puts himself to sleep by telling himself stories about the brightly clad men and pretty ladies who once lived there, and imagining the music to which they used to dance.

"That's right—let yourself relax and remember. You're in control of this, Piper. Nothing that you remember can hurt you anymore."

Piper twitches a little and slides deeper into memory. What does the voice mean? What could hurt him here? He's home. . . .

"Now I want you to move on to the time when things changed. Where are you, Piper? What are you doing when the strange men come from the sea?"

Suddenly it's noon, the air is heady with scent released by sun on the leaves. Piper has escaped his chores and is pattering along the trail through the pines. There's a nest of sea eagles on the cliff, and the young birds are just beginning to fly. If he's lucky, maybe he will see them.

He stops to catch his breath and hears voices. Who could be arriving today? Piper slips off the trail and sees them coming, a half dozen big men in salt-stained clothes. There's a glitter of gold about them, and the shine of steel. An occasional gutteral order sets them moving faster, but he doesn't understand the words.

Will his mother forgive him for running off if he brings the news? Still hesitating, Piper shadows the newcomers all the way back to the yard.

"Mother!" He makes up his mind at last and calls to her. Then he steps out from among the trees. "This is Hurst Holding. You come to trade?"

His mother appears in the doorway. He sees her hand go to her mouth; then she disappears. Suddenly the clamor of the bronze dinner bell splits the air. The strangers start forward, swearing. When they pull open the door, Piper's mother is waiting for them with a sword.

"Mother!" he shrieks, running across the yard. Steel flares, and someone cries out. Then the rest of them are surging forward. A hard arm imprisons him; he feels the sharp tickle of a knife at his throat and goes still. Now the men are laughing.

"Don't hurt him!" That's his mother's voice! The men haul her out into the light. There's a torrent of abuse from inside the house, and he knows they have his grandmother too. "Piper, don't move—" A blow stops his mother's words, but he stays still, at last obeying, for there's not another sound from her, not even when they tear at her clothes and push her down. He doesn't move until the third man sprawls atop her and finally she begins to scream.

"Quiet, ducky, or I kill you too!" The words are harshly accented, but this time he understands.

"Piper, what is it? What's happening? Tell me!"

"I can't! I can't! Nobody can hear!"

A fury of movement somehow frees him. Then he is

running, but even when he reaches the hilltop, he can still hear the screams. . . .

After a long time, Piper realized that strong arms were holding him. He shuddered and jerked away.

"The Song, Piper. Listen to the Song." The voice was strained, but Piper found himself relaxing. When he listened to the music, there was no other sound.

"It's over, Piper. It wasn't your fault. It's all over and done."

Piper shook his head, but the other would not let him be. *"I didn't warn them,"* he cried. *"I couldn't. Words don't mean anything!"*

"You made the wrong choice then. You made the right choices later on," the voice continued implacably. *"To do nothing can be as bad as to say nothing. Listen, Piper, words have power. I'll give you power over me."*

Piper's eyes opened. He saw the Prince still sitting beside him, his fingers just touching the Wind Crystal that lay on Piper's chest. Julian was right. The horror was in the past now. The dark eyes met his, and he heard Julian's voice, though his lips did not move.

"If you will promise to say it aloud, Piper, I will give you my Name. . . ."

I put my life in his hands when we climbed the Throne. Now he is giving me his, Piper thought. He nodded.

At first it seemed to him that the song of the Wind Crystal had grown louder. Then he realized that it was forming a word.

Piper sucked air into his lungs and let it out in a long sigh. Once more he tried, and with the third breath, came a sound. Stiff lips formed it, a tight throat reluctantly let the whisper past . . . "LIGHT-BEARER."

The Wind Crystal flared between them in radiance that transcended sight, with music that was more than sound, and both the brightness and the music were the sound of that Name. From end to end of Westria it rolled, and beyond the manifest world of Westria, from sphere to sphere.

Wind Lord heard it in the heavens, and an echo of merriment blazed from a chorus of clouds. In the fastnesses of Awahna, the Lady of Westria heard. "He is king, and soon I will claim him," She told the other Guardians. "There is only one more test for him, and he is almost ready to face it now." But the Great Eagle lifted silently from Clouds' Rest and began moving westward, sliding swiftly across the sky.

From somewhere down the hill came shouting.

"Great Guardians, Piper! I didn't think of the noise," gasped Julian. "In a minute the others will be all over us. Let's get out of here!"

Piper shot him a swift look and gave a chirrup of laughter.

"Can't run," he whispered hoarsely. "You said so."

"Oh, Piper!" Julian hid his face in his hands. "What have I done?"

"*You—*" he made himself voice the words—"trusted me."

Julian raised his head. Silverhair was scrambling up the hill, with Cub close behind. Piper lifted the Wind Crystal from his breast and pressed it into Julian's hand. Then he stood up, brushed himself off carefully, and waved to them.

Rana exchanged a worried glance with Robert as they followed Julian back down the hill. What had the Prince been doing with the Wind Crystal? There didn't seem to be any danger, but like some quake of the spirit, they had all felt the aftershock of power.

"Food left?" Piper trotted ahead of them, with Cub beside him. Silverhair stopped short in the trail, and Robert grabbed Rana's arm to keep her from running into him. They exchanged glances, then turned back to Julian.

"Piper, you can talk!" After a stunned moment, Cub said it for all of them.

"So that's what he was doing—" Rana began, but Julian had reached out to Silverhair, who was shaking his head and laughing.

"Talk? Of course he can talk!" Silverhair's cheeks were wet with tears. "Everyone can talk now, and sing.

Oh, Julian, are you going to solve all of our problems today?''

"Only the ones that are bothering the bards," Julian answered. He waited until the harper steadied, then let him go.

"Julian, do you know what you have done?" Silverhair asked. "I understand now how a father feels when his son surpasses him, and that's more than I ever dared desire.'' He smiled suddenly. "Piper—" the boy turned—"do you want to learn the words to my songs?''

"Yes.''

"And the harp? Will you let me teach you to play?''

Piper nodded, his eyes dancing.

"What happened? Did he fix your voice with magic?'' Cub's changing voice betrayed him and squeaked up the scale.

"Be quiet, brat, and maybe he'll fix yours too,'' hissed Rana.

"Tell you . . . later.'' Piper's speech held only a hint of hesitation. "Hungry now.'' He dashed down the trail, Cub at his heels.

"What *did* you do to him?'' Rana asked then. Julian turned to look back at her and she blinked, as if the sun had come out from behind a cloud. But the sky was clear.

"I found out what it was that he was afraid to say,'' he said finally. "And now I'm hungry too!'' He grinned, and she breathed a sigh of relief. They passed through the rose garden and rounded the corner of the hall. "I'd forgotten what this kind of work takes out of you! I think that one of the turkeys still had a drumstick—that would just about fill the gap right now.''

Somebody shrieked, and they all broke into a run toward the arbor. They saw the remains of the feast on the long table, but people were scattering. A moment of clear view showed Rana that the drumstick was indeed still attached to the turkey . . . but the bird itself was moving! She added her own squawk of outrage to the clamor as the creature disappeared behind the table, and another as it reappeared a few feet up the hill and she saw the tawny shape that was dragging it away.

"Mañero!'' Julian's shout echoed from hill to hill. For

a moment the coyote dropped his booty and grinned at them. Rana caught the glint of a very familiar pair of amber eyes. "I'm sorry! If I'd known you wanted to come, I would have invited you," the Prince broke off, red-faced and gasping.

"It's no use, Julian," said Robert. "He probably thinks it tastes better this way. Why should he change his manners just because now we know that he's a Guardian?" He sniffed, and Rana slid her arm through his with a sudden rush of affection.

"Well, I'm still hungry," muttered Julian. "And if that wretch has left us anything, I'm going to eat it! Uncle, come on."

Silverhair shook his head. "That's not what I need right now." A look passed between them.

"Play for us, then."

Silverhair pulled Swangold into his arms with a sigh of relief. He had not exaggerated his need. The harp should still be in tune—she must be, he could not wait even so long as it would take to adjust the strings.

He plucked a single note that throbbed and separated into overtones that vibrated ever more softly in the still air. It was pure sound . . . and true. The harper's trained ear knew that his instrument had not betrayed him. He relaxed, savoring the moment between sound and stillness. But it never quite ended. The air was in constant motion through the trees and across the grass. The faint whisper of invisible friction told where it passed, and the shimmer of sound as it touched the harp strings was only an echo of that deeper song.

Silverhair's fingers flickered in a swift arc across the strings, and single notes were lost in a more complex music. Music moved from his spirit through his fingers; hearing, the harper began to understand. Harmony was here past comprehension, relationships unguessed, yet in the song he heard them, felt the things that—all unknowing—he had desired, now placed within his hands.

He sighed, returning to awareness of the world, and

saw the others gathered near. How long had he been
playing? He smiled at Piper, and the boy reached for his
flute case. He drew the slim reed out, for a moment blew
and tested, and then suddenly its pure breath of sound
was added to the harper's music, lifting it with windsong
to another realm.

But Piper was not the only flutist. Others uncased instruments, began to join him, trill and twitter, notes
aflutter, swooping, soaring, swirling 'round the harp like
singing birds. Horns added deeper calls, as sweet as
swan-song; a trumpet challenged—it was the only one,
for charging fingers pattered out a drumbeat. Trees
swayed as earth itself joined in the song. Siaran's big
harp was in it too, low notes descending from Swangold's heights to ever deeper realms. *Now come the
strings!* he thought, and as that morning, strung bows set
fire to incandescent air. *This is the soul of Westria singing! Do you hear it, Julian, and understand?*

Julian shivered, drunk on the music. It was like that
of his visions, but he knew this was real. *And wasn't the
other?* an inner voice asked. *Are you still being foolish?
Wake up and listen, for this is the truth of the world!*

They were all of them playing; sound pulsed through
him. His very bones were buzzing, his vocal cords vibrating to every new tone. *Why am I envious?* he thought
of a sudden, *after what I did for Piper? If I dare use it,
I have an instrument too!*

He was smiling and shaking, the tremors ran through
him. In a moment his ties to his body could be unbound.
But that was not his purpose; it was this world he wanted,
the melody manifest, all hearing the sound. Like Piper,
he was resisting; he saw the boy watching, tipped back
his head, and let all the power that was in him flow out
with his breath in a long surge of pure song.

> *We are the makers of music, we are the children
> of song.
> We are the voice of creation, here we belong. . . .*

Words came to him suddenly, riding the wave of sound he had started, and then all of the others were singing as well.

"*I am the song the wind makes as it wakes in the dawning,*" sang one of the students.

"*I am the sound of the Eagle's swift wings as he flies,*" another answered.

"*I am the thunder of clouds when they think they are laughing.*"

"*I am the singing of sunlight that falls through the skies.*"

One by one, they built the song.

> "*We are the makers of music—we are the children of song.*
> *We are the voice of creation, here we belong. . . .*"

Once more the chorus resounded from hill to hill.

"*I am the song that is strong, yet fears not to be tender.*" Robert's voice lifted in a new sequence, and Julian's spirit soared.

"*I am the spirit that sings with both passion and power.*" This was Rana, and Julian had his balance again.

"*I am the singing of will from the word no more sundered!*" Piper's verse continued, and suddenly Julian was everything that had been sung.

"*I am the instrument, I am the played and the player!*" Silverhair's baritone throbbed like one of his harp strings.

At once wholly himself and the soul of the music, Julian sang.

> "*We are the makers of music, we are the children of song.*
> *We are the voice of creation, here we belong. . . .*"

Where did those words come from? Where did they go? None of the singers could have explained it, then or after. And when whatever it was that sang through them was finished, still they swayed together, bound by a softer music like the breathing of the wind.

The windsong lifted in a great swell of sound that rose and faded, shaded from one harmonic conclusion to another in subtle gradations so that the ear sensed its movement without ever knowing when or how it changed. Through the charged air it traveled in long vibrations. Unheard, but not unfelt, it passed throughout the length and breadth of Westria. And everywhere it traveled— even, for the space of a breath, on the Red Mountain— for that moment, there was harmony.

The music pulsed into the sky above Misthall, where the Great Eagle balanced on widespread wings. By the vibrations of that music, the Eagle was lifted. Behind the Lady Mountain, the sun was setting; its rays reached outward through banks of glowing cloud like pinions of light. As if the Wind Crystal itself had taken wing, every feather blazed with radiance. And as the last notes of music distilled into silence, the Eagle became a Bird of Light that expanded until it was one with the sky.

THE BEST IN FANTASY

THE TOR DOUBLES

Two complete short science fiction novels in one volume!

THE BEST IN SCIENCE FICTION

ELIZABETH PETERS

☐	50770-3	THE CAMELOT CAPER	$3.95
	50771-1		Canada $4.95
☐	50756-8	THE DEAD SEA CIPHER	$3.95
	50757-6		Canada $4.95
☐	50789-4	DEVIL-MAY-CARE	$4.50
	50790-8		Canada $5.50
☐	50791-6	DIE FOR LOVE	$3.95
	50792-4		Canada $4.95
☐	50002-4	JACKAL'S HEAD	$3.95
	50003-2		Canada $4.95
☐	50750-9	LEGEND IN GREEN VELVET	$3.95
	50751-X		Canada $4.95
☐	50764-9	LION IN THE VALLEY	$3.95
	50765-7		Canada $4.95
☐	50793-2	THE MUMMY CASE	$3.95
	50794-0		Canada $4.95
☐	50773-8	THE NIGHT OF FOUR HUNDRED RABBITS	$4.50
	50774-6		Canada $5.50
☐	50795-9	STREET OF THE FIVE MOONS	$3.95
	50796-7		Canada $4.95
☐	50754-1	SUMMER OF THE DRAGON	$3.95
	50755-X		Canada $4.95
☐	50758-4	TROJAN GOLD	$3.95
	50759-2		Canada $4.95

Buy them at your local bookstore or use this handy coupon:
Clip and mail this page with your order.

Publishers Book and Audio Mailing Service
P.O. Box 120159, Staten Island, NY 10312-0004

Please send me the book(s) I have checked above. I am enclosing $_____
(please add $1.25 for the first book, and $.25 for each additional book to
cover postage and handling. Send check or money order only—no CODs.)

Name _____

Address _____

City _____ State/Zip _____

Please allow six weeks for delivery. Prices subject to change without notice.